# THE BOY WITH THE SALTWATER SMILE

### The Hickory Heart Book 2

## LAUREN NICOLLE TAYLOR

OWL HOLLOW PRESS

Owl Hollow Press, LLC, Springville, UT 84663



The Boy with the Saltwater Smile




Library of Congress Cataloging-in-Publication Data
The Boy with the Saltwater Smile / L.N. Taylor. — First edition.

Summary:
When Ash, Lye, and Luna are joined in pursuit of a cataclysmic secret, they will risk their lives, their powers, and everything they have to save each other and the land they've come to call home.

Cover Illustration: Stephanie Brown, Offbeat Worlds
Typography: Les Solot
Map Illustration: Evin Kierans
Interior Illustrations: Lauren Nicolle Taylor

ISBN 978-1-958109-18-2 (paperback)
ISBN 978-1-958109-19-9 (e-book)

DARK WEST
SHEN MAINLAND
RIVER
RIVER
EMPEROR'S PALACE
CROW'S NEXT ISLAND
CHAR TERRITORIES
GLASS SHARD ISLAND
BLACK
SALT
CITY
MONASTERY
BIRD CAGE ISLAND
ABALONE ISLAND
COCKLE FAN ISLAND
COALSTONE VILLAGE
PEARL SHELL BEACH
N
W
E
S

# 1
## ASH KI

Ibrush my fingers over the rough tent canvas. Black, simple. *When nothing else is.* Dozens dot the green valley. A temporary village. Though this is the only one people fear entering.

*Breathe in. Lift your lips. Remember.*

She was rough in that Char way. Blunt and dangerous like a club. But beneath the hewn exterior, her fierceness and dedication pulsed purely Luna. A selfless inner surrounded by rings of hickory. *Now she is...* Raking a hand through my hair, I chew on my lip, chin dipped to the earth. My heart beats through layers of flesh and bone. Hers through thick, charred wood. She's still Luna. She's still those good things. They're just... hiding.

Heat pumps fluidly from the small gap in the fabric. Air throbs with pain and nostril-singeing smells. *Does she notice? Do her senses wince and flinch?*

A tusk rat darts between my legs, long teeth plowing a path through the earth. I shift. Try not to jump in fear. All Char eyes are on me now. They watch every step, every movement, collecting evidence against me.

My fingers tease the tent flap, running up and down. It shouldn't be this difficult to enter, but there's a wall of grief, a wave of blood to pass through. Luna hides behind it, summons it over and over.

My toes press into the dirt, creating pools of leftover rain.

I inhale deeply, put on a tattooed smile, and step inside.

"You're late." Luna's voice is skimmed of emotion like separating the okara from soymilk, leaving it flat. Her eyes roll over me as if I'm another prisoner, stopping curiously on my mouth for a moment. My smile tips like an ink bottle, spreading. Her cheeks color. But then it's gone, and I wonder if I imagined it.

The tent flap sways closed and we're surrounded by warm candle light. But there's nothing warm about the Atmosphere in this space. I shiver at the unclean knives piled on a stained barrel, the seagrass rope showing wear from many victims straining against it. Her eyes dart to mine. Once an amber swirl, they've crusted and crystallized.

"What have you done today?" I ask carefully.

She cleans a knife in her hand slowly, smears of red disappearing into the black cloth. She places it on a table with the other cleaned blades. "Questioned the higher commanders. Even the Mogui have ranks. I found out that—"

"Did you…" I interrupt. It used to bother her but now she merely breathes in and out with patience, waiting for me to speak. "Did you eat?"

She nods sharply, all angles and determination. "It does me no good to starve myself."

I step closer. The smell of old and new blood is unavoidable. Rust and salt. Luna holds her ground, her toes wiggling in her slippers. "Sometimes, when grieving, people find it hard to eat." I reach for her arm. This is the point where she usually pulls away, but she lets me touch her. And it might as well be a dagger to my heart for the way she stares at our skin connecting with such detached fascination. A hammering warning in my chest tells me to walk away. To cut my losses. But I watch the way her eyes crinkle even as they observe me like a specimen. A snake in a jar. And I can't leave her. I can't let go of that small splinter of hope telling me she's still in there. That she might need my help getting back.

I squeeze her arm gently. There's nothing soft about her skin. But then, there never was. She's strong. Hard muscle. Her lips part and she inhales fast, almost like a hiccup. Then she withdraws and pulls her sleeves over her skin, patting her chest. Her hickory heart.

"I do not grieve, Ash."

Her head inclines, long plaits swinging. They kiss the instruments of torture she barely needs. I *feel* her hand on another stone, ready to place it atop the wall that keeps me and others out.

She cracks her knuckles and stretches her fingers wide. "Luna," I start. *Please*, I want to say. *Please stop burying yourself.* But how do I make her open up to an enormous pain? How do I convince her it would be a good thing? Convince the town to be swallowed by the earthquake. My face falls, smile plunging to the dirt, lost among tiny pawprints. *I can't.*

Outside, her youngest brother, Ben Ni, lies with the others. Wrapped and ready for burial.

"Send in the next one," she murmurs. A voice simultaneously like the bringer of death and the sweetest song. My Luna. Mayhem and music.

Wick spiders march in a white line across the floor, wending around my feet and climbing up the empty chair. If there were a way for my heart to sink to my feet, I think I just felt it. I want to tell her how much I care for her, like that could bring her back from the darkness. But it won't. *I don't know what will.*

"I *wish* you could see what you've…" I give her ample time to cut me off because I don't know how to finish my sentence.

"Wishes are a waste." Luna believes these words to the moon.

I bow my head quickly and leave the tent, lifting my eyes to the blue, scarred sky as I exit. Wishing on every cloud, every hidden star, that she'll find her way back to me, to Lye, to her brothers who need her.

Wasting wish upon wish upon wish.

# 2

## LYE LI

The heart is a strange instrument. Necessary but flawed. I stare at the field of Char and Shen men, cradled in this nest of a crater with stone sides reaching to the sky like begging hands. Their beating hearts push blood out of open wounds, while river water rushes through the center of the battle-fresh plateau just as quickly. They huddle in groups, prisoner and soldier. Hate and pity. I shake my head. The heart is flawed. Just like the Keeper.

I sense a ripple trying to keep its widening circles closer. It doesn't want to reach the edge of the pond. *Ash.* He backs out of Luna's tent and those ripples cease. He's still and icing over. Hands rise to his face and fall back limply. I know there are words on those cracked lips. Loud, frustrated words. But his mouth sets to a thin line and he watches a line of insects file under the tent flaps. Luna's tiny, terrible army.

Torture is part of war, the part my little brother was never going to tolerate. My feet press into the mud. Thick sludge I can't feel anymore as my shoes are so crusted. I lift my foot, inspecting. There was a time when I would have screwed up my nose at such filth. But then, there was also a time when I willingly did the chancellor's bidding.

Ash counts faces, trying to choose Luna's next victim. I can take this burden for him. I step toward him and a hand catches my arm.

General Fah gets a turtle snap through his skin for his trouble and he sharply withdraws. I turn to a weary, burned to embers expression. "Keeper. I must speak with you."

I tilt my head. Not enticed by yet another man giving me orders. I put up my hand. "One moment, General." His frown could strip the green from trees. But he salutes, standing sturdily like an oak that knows its fate. *Am I beginning to think like a Char now?* I snort and General Fah's eyebrows rise.

Ash paces in front of bound Shen, hands fisted as I approach. "Brother." I place a hand on his shoulder, washing warm ocean waves over his cutting ice. Resisting, his ice crackles. "What is the matter?"

The opening to the "torture tent" parts. Amber eyes observe me. Ash points to the men, hand bouncing over their heads one by one. "I'm to send the next one in." He huffs. "Like cattle to the slaughter."

One of the Mogui draws in a sharp breath. They are used to administering torture, not receiving it. I cluck my tongue. I don't want to connect with his Shen eyes. They'll be eyes I glanced at in a long line. In a face I didn't bother to remember. But I changed this man's life. I led him right to this place and this penalty. Hooks hang from my ribs, each marking my responsibility. Luna may be the torturer, but I'm reason for it. At least in part. I touch my arm. The scars should bleed with fresh blood, but they don't. They've turned dark and ropey—not unlike my soul.

Ash's eyes run over my arm and lift to my face. "This is not a suitable task for you." His eyes are briny and deepest ocean blue, where very little lives and what does is horrifying. "Your heart doesn't deserve the heaviness that comes with bringing a man to his torturer."

Again, the Shen prisoner draws a fearful breath. I force myself to look. Disappointed that he's just an unremarkable face in a sea of others. I don't remember awakening his power. They're all holes punched through paper, beads slid to the other side of the abacus. And it shames me.

Ash stares at his feet. "Lye, I can't leave her." His slow, painful attempt at a smile is so characteristic of my brother. "I'm scared if I don't keep watch, if I don't monitor what she's doing, she'll disappear completely."

I frown. I don't want my brother to give up hope, but I know how hard it is to claw your way back from a dark place. And you have to *want* to do it. "If you keep watching her torture these Shen, she'll be lost to you anyway," I say, too bluntly.

Ash's body is cut by sun and by words and he shields himself from both with a grin. Just a tease in the corner of his mouth, a split of white teeth. "You should know by now how stubborn I can be."

My nose twists at his disheveled appearance and unpleasant odor. "You need to bathe. The only heart you'll win right now is that of a dung beetle." The word *heart* stings him in a thousand ways, but if I need to be harsh to get him away from here, so be it.

Ash lifts his dirty sleeve and sniffs it. "You can be quite callous," he remarks, no real hurt in his voice.

I walk quickly down the line and tap the head of a Fire Mogui. He coughs over dramatically, and I roll my eyes. "This one," I announce. When the Mogui pretends he can't get up, I sigh. "Oh, don't be so ridiculous!" So bloodthirsty in battle, the Mogui have proved to be quite spineless once captured. I suppose bloodthirsty does not equate to brave. A snake slithers fast and unnatural through the grass and under the tent wall. "If you answer her questions, no harm will come to you."

I march the man to the tent, and it folds aside briefly. Heat makes the air wobble before my eyes. A soft hiss sails over candlelight and I retreat. I can't go in there. She won't allow it. And I don't want it.

Ash is painted forlorn and fallen. Shoulders hunched and hard. An acorn rolled far from its tree. But I sense a waterfall of hope in him, a flush of mist that floats to the sky. He won't give up on her.

"This is not a suitable task for you," I repeat, more forcefully.

He shakes his head. "You're not in command, Lye. You can't give me orders."

My fingers dig into his subclavian vein just below his clavicle, sending flickers of fire bordering on burning. "Take a break!"

The general is still waiting for me, arms folded, tapping his foot impatiently. I solidify my insides, stand tall even as the warm wind, laced with moisture, threatens to blow me over.

"KEEPER," he growls, low and intolerant. "I do not appreciate waiting." He gestures around the camp, which currently looks more like a wrecked ship washed ashore, complete with scavenging sea-gulls and rotting smells. "We have much to do and to discuss. Come to my tent." He taps a finger sharply into his palm. Then opens his arms to guide, expecting me to fold into the cradle they offer. Instead, I sidestep. Leaves swish and the scent of wet star blossoms scatters through the stench of decay. Sweet and new. Washed of impurity. Ready to start over. Which is what I must do.

Gold light sifts through the air. A sense of spirit. I counsel with the dead, with the boy who saved me. I dream of what he would say if he were here, and it is "No."

Fah's walnut jaw creaks. Needing oil. "No," I murmur.

"Excuse me?" The general leans in, truly believing he heard me wrong.

I've spent too much time contained. With eyes to the sky, I inhale. There are stars to count and clouds to watch. Plans to make and battles to plot. "Walk with me. I don't want to be crammed into a stuffy tent, do you?"

A sharp exhale. Flaring nostrils. Like a bull who has reached the fence line. Fah's offered arm is rescinded, placed behind his back. "Very well." We are the battle drum and the baton. Though I do not know which is which. Only that we must march to the same beat.

The general and I stroll across the battlefield. Washed of blood, but the smell still clings to the earth. It's part of it now.

The squelch of feet suctioned by mud is all that can be heard for several long seconds.

"We need to send a small party to await the Carvresses arrival at the cove," I tell him, emulating his stride, hands in the small of my back, shoulders swinging like the land is mine. "Then I shall speak with the chancellor, see if there's any value in keeping him alive, though I doubt it very much." Flashes of black teeth and sharp nails drag across my vision. I blink. Try to stand strong.

The general purses his lips, walnut chin jutting. "I cannot risk sending good soldiers away from camp right now. Scouts have reported a flash of orange, a ghost of white. Which means there are likely still Shen hiding in the jungle."

We approach the galloping river and stand on the edge. The volume seeks to drown our voices, but I shout, "You fear losing more men. I understand. But..."

Fah's body tightens and he brushes his jaw, tracing the intricate cravings beneath his lower lip. "Fear is not my problem. I wonder if the Carvresses are coming. How can we know our message reached Setsu Yan?" He rolls his shoulders. They crackle like electricity, while some flickers through my fingers.

I shift my feet along the riverbank, tapping something man made: A broken arrow. Crouching down, I retrieve the splintered pieces. Probably fell from a Shen's sheath. I press the sharp tip into my skin. "I am absolutely certain Luna's message arrived at its destination. She is..." Bigger and brighter than all of us. *A new sun that could incinerate the earth.*

He finishes my sentence. "Powerful, yes. I don't doubt it. But it could have been too late. The Shen may have already attacked. What if we are all that's left of the Char?"

"You speak in a hopeless tone, General." His eyes widen at my brazenness. His Atmosphere shifts from trust to distrust and back again like a hoarder bear tasting a new berry, not sure whether it's toxic. "We need hope right now and we *need* action. The men cannot just sit here waiting. Send a small party. Give the Char something to think about other than the men they've lost and the families they left behind. Without something to fight for, we may as well give up." My eyes skid to the stack of carefully wrapped bodies and he follows my gaze. "And we really must bury the dead."

He's immovable. "That is not the Char way. They must be set to the sea. You do not understand our traditions, so I shall forgive your thoughtlessness. But just because you have knowledge of the Char from Luna Yan, and bring something to the table, don't think you're one of us. Don't think you can give the orders around here."

Around us, the crater of Crow's Nest Island rises like a screaming mouth to the sky. The only way out is over sheer cliffs or through a tight, winding labyrinth. I don't see how they'll move all these bodies to the sea. I grit my teeth. I'm a termite slowly working away at the base of a tree. It will take time for Fah to trust me. *If he ever does.* I have to keep scraping away. Tiny bites and gnawing. I laugh softly, hoping these are Char thoughts working their way into my mind.

I nod but stand my ground. "I respect your ways. Can you respect mine? If there are Shen soldiers hiding out there, they are a danger to the Carvresses. What good would it do to have them travel this far only to be killed when they land?"

The general smiles strangely, brass and dark wood. "I'd like to see them try." The hardness in his stance softens. "However… perhaps we shouldn't risk it." His legs relax as he begrudgingly concedes.

I lasso a rope over his words and pull them to my chest, trying not to bounce on the balls of my feet. I attempt to be stoic. Commanding. "A wise decision, General." And before he can say another word, I state, "I shall select the men this evening."

As I turn to camp, the general catches my arm again. I'm impressed at his lack of reaction to the thin threads of lightning I send through his fingers. "As to your other request—you may face the chancellor, Keeper." He accidentally twists his injured arm, wincing. I send healing wind to speed up the process. He winces in pain, but it will be better for him in the long run. "But let's not pretend this isn't for your own personal reasons. I don't claim to understand the complicated relationship you have with the Yan family…" His eyes pool deep with sadness. "But it strikes me as something akin to family, and what the chancellor did to young Ben Ni… well…"

*There is no fitting punishment. Nothing that could possibly make up for his crimes.*

My lip threatens to quiver. "Please, General. Call me Lye Li. I am the Keeper no longer."

His voice is knotted with knowing. "If only that were something you could simply decide for yourself."

We return to the camp in silence. Soldiers and commanders. Shoulders parted by an inch of difference. A very tenuous strand of respect stretching between us.

*If only. If only. If only.*

So many regrets and wishes in those words, living like parasites in my blood.

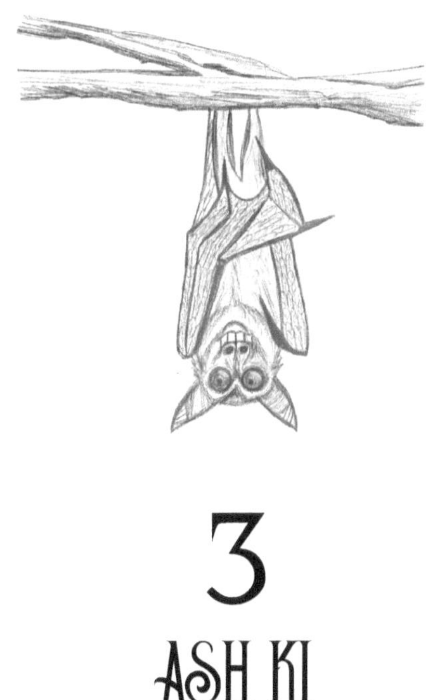

# 3

## ASH KI

I dread her and I long for her.

Freshly clean, water dripping down my neck, I stand at the tent entrance and wait for Luna to emerge. Less a butterfly and more a black-winged bat. Beautiful either way.

On the outskirts of camp, the fire burns high and pointless. The night is mild, but the Char like to gather around it. Knock knees and bash shoulders. Forming a circle that will break like poor quality thread when I approach its border.

Small hands grip the canvas. They shake. They're bluish in the moonlight. I know the feel of them pressed to my back in anguish and desire. It has left a dent to be repaired. But *these* hands withdraw. A deep breath in and out from a little, ironlike chest, and Luna steps into the world. Delicate and vicious. A rakka possum curls its tail around her ankle and she whispers something, shakes her hand, and it scampers past me into the broad-leafed trees that shine an oily green. Our eyes connect briefly, crystalized ginger to sea green, and she goes to touch her heart. Her hand slips before it connects but it's how I know she's still in there. That, and this nightly ritual.

She comes to my side and we walk to the fire.

She brushes stray hair behind her ear. Her chestnut mane is tightly braided and she winces as her fingers move in small circles over her scalp. "You smell better," she acknowledges.

I laugh awkwardly, not sure if I should make a joke. Knowing even if she laughs, it will be a hollow, lacking laugh. I suppress humor, press it between pages I will reread for clues later. "Did you learn anything new today?"

She shakes her head. "There's nothing new. Shen and Char are enemies. Shen wish to see us eradicated like vermin. They fear me and I disgust them." Her voice is wooden. She stops suddenly, ear pricked as bird or bat wings slap at palm leaves. "Antibat," she whispers, identifying the strange fruit bats of the island, named for their square teeth and feathered wings.

I risk a touch. Just a brush of my thumb against the back of her hand as it hangs at her side. "We're not all enemies. Lye and me, we're…" She gives me a few seconds before she sends bites up my arm. They're measured, though. She doesn't want to hurt, just warn.

"You and Lye are not Shen," she states, though she seems neither pleased nor displeased about it.

*Is this her way now?* I sigh and tug the breath back like clouds to a mountain. I refuse to believe it. "No, I suppose we're not anymore."

I want to ask her what we are. What am I to her now? But I'm terrified of the answer. Scared of the word *nothing*.

"Luna," I start. "When will you let me…"

She nods her head towards the fire. "They're waiting."

HER FACE lights lava orange and her cheeks flush pink. But it's just the heat of the flames. The body still reacts. The unwarmed eyes stay neutral, hard-set amber you could carve.

Char men are stripped to loose shirts, pants rolled up to their knees. They thump each other hard and shove bottles under noses. Taking large gulps.

I search for my sister and it doesn't take long to find her. I roll my eyes. She doesn't know how to even try and fit in. Change her shape, just a little. She stands on a levelled log, one foot pressed into the hollow behind her knee. Gray robes flapping in the warm breeze. Her hair waves in the hot air like new bean shoots. Men glance at her like she's a perched bird they're not sure of. If she wants them to trust her, she needs to come down to ground level every now and then.

Pain breaks her expression when she sees Luna. But she doesn't watch for long. Her eyes lift above the fire and men. I know this to be her planning face.

Luna's expression remains calm as she regards Lye, and I despise it. I want her to show anger. Bitterness. Anything resembling emotion. I see her hand fisted at her side and it gives me hope. I snort, smoke stinging my eyes as the wind changes direction. How pathetic that her anger gives me hope. The truth is, I would feel a change if there were one to feel. Luna and I have been connected since our powers combined. It's how I know every detail of the wall she lives behind, stone by stone. How I know the wall could become a fortress.

Luna breathes deeply, seeming to compose herself, and signals to her brothers, both staring flatly into the fire. She walks in even steps. Measured. Not too slow or fast.

The bottle is passed to the Yan brothers and Sun takes a swig while Joka pushes away and passes it down the line.

They make space for her on the log. Not for me. I sit heavily on the earth scattering the ants marching to the beat of Luna's broken heart.

"Little Luna!" Sun exclaims. Luna's eyebrows rise ever so slightly and then she settles into the seat between her brothers. "Tell me you made those Shen soldiers suffer!"

Tipping her chin to chest, she wears her shirt lower now, frog closure buttons resting open to her wooden sternum. This, she doesn't hide from. "I did what was asked of me, brother."

Sun swipes his mouth and rests his head on top of hers. She allows it. "You're a good soldier. I bet you enjoyed making them wince, just a little. If it were me I would…" He makes a fist, slamming it into his palm. She tilts her head, observing him.

"I did not enjoy it," she murmurs and Joka lifts his head a fraction, eyes tight.

Sun humphs loudly. "I'm sure you didn't exactly *not*, not enjoy it either, right, sister?"

She frowns. "It did not upset me to do it, no. But it brought me no enjoyment. There was this one uncooperative Air Shen…" Holding her palms to the sky, she takes two fingers, creeping them up her arm. "He cooperated after the pincer crickets."

My arms feel like young bamboo as I stretch away from her. *What's left of her.*

"Pincer crickets are harmless, sister." Sun waves dismissively, his words starting to run together as the wine catches up with him.

Her perfect, pink mouth forms horrible words. "One pincer cricket is harmless. But hundreds… Hundreds can very carefully and painfully separate your skin from your flesh."

Joka finally looks at me and our expressions match. Fear. Fear of what will happen to Luna when she finally gives into her feelings and has to face her actions. We know it will occur. Then the atrocities she's performed will claw at her, drag her down. She'll drown in an ocean of Shen screams.

"Little sister, please," Joka pleads. "Can we talk about something else?"

Sun jiggles his knee and the three Yan siblings wobble on the log seat. I catch their sideways glances to nothing. The ghost of their brother sits shoulder to shoulder with the living. Sun stands suddenly. "Let's talk about what we should do now. I'm tired of sitting in this sweat-filled bowl. I need to move." He cuts the air with practice punches.

Joka sighs. "We're waiting for the Carvresses."

Sun points at me, arm like a gang plank he'd happily shove me from. "And what about him? This trrraitor to the Shen," he slurs. "I don't like the way he looks at ourrr little Luna. Like she's a brrroken clock that needs fixing."

He sways a little, feet sliding forward. I stay where I am, ready to defend myself, but I'm not starting a fight. Luna exhales, long and loud, and her brothers quieten, watching her carefully. Her eyes find mine and they kill me for their lack of affection. "I am not unlike a broken clock, Sun." Her fingers trace the upper end of her wooden sternum. "Understand that Ash is only doing what he thinks is right. However misguided it may be."

Sun's pointing finger wavers. "It's clear he cares for you."

She nods. "Yes." The word floats in the air like dying smoke. I'm not stupid enough to think she'll say the same about me. Not the way she is now.

*Look at me,* I think. *Really look at me.* But her gaze is piercing. An arrow shot straight through. Sun doesn't realize how right he is. Luna *is* a broken clock content for time to stop, or maybe she wants to retreat to a world where time means nothing. Her wish will go ungranted. Ben Ni's death weights the tip of her second hand trying to move time forward. The moment it starts ticking again, she'll be flooded with hours to days to weeks of pain.

Lye's elegant voice cuts through the group like an axe, silencing the mumbling of Char men who are bored and restless. "The general and I have decided we can no longer wait for the Carvresses to come to us. We require two men to travel to the abandoned village and look for their arrival at the northern cove of the island." Sun's hand shoots up with many others. I sit on mine.

Lye selects Luna's oldest brother with a confirming nod from the general, who's hanging back like a fishing basket full of holes, and then her determined eyes find mine. She wishes me to go. Before she can point her dry and decided finger in my direction, I turn away from the fire and stalk into the jungle.

Wet leaves brush my face. As I move further into the forest, hopper mice bounce at my feet. Little white puffs sticking close to my shoes. I swing around at the sound of footsteps following mine. Luna is right behind me, Lye behind her. The two women I love are stationary like trees. Spaced well apart. Paleness against the dark.

Lye calls out. "You are the best man for the job. You'll be able to sense rogue Shen before they get too close. Ash," she pleads. "I need you to do this." Luna is closer to me, back to Lye, the long stem of a dragon flower brushing her waist. The sound of my sister's voice grinds her will, I can tell. It bites at her composure, and small sparks of emotion escape between the cracks. Lye knows it too, which is why she hovers, ghostlike, several paces behind.

I smirk. Which produces confusion. But I'm imagining the quickest way to snap Luna back to me would be to force her into a small space with Lye. The smirk dissolves like ice in hot water. Even though I want Luna back, I cannot put my sister in danger to do it.

I reach for Luna, *always*. She allows me to touch her for one painful moment. I grasp her arms and squeeze. "I don't think I should leave you. Aren't you worried you'll go too far? Disappear too deeply into this dark place"—I draw a circle in front of her heart—"you've created."

Sending ocean spray to her, I try to remind her of home. Her place, her peace, before all of this. She blinks, forehead sprinkled with moonlight, and I almost have her. But then she pulls away.

"It's not a dark place, Ash. It's a *nothing* place. And it's what must be." Birds begin to call for dawn even though the sun has barely set. The noise grows. She's trying to drown me out with her Blood power. "You should go on the mission." Her arms tense. "It's important the Carvresses make it to us safely."

I shake my head. *Nothing place*. "You speak nonsense, Luna." The bird calls lull briefly as she actually listens to my words. "It *is* a dark place. Your conscience is in there sleeping, and when it wakes, how many of your actions will you regret? How many bad things can you do before you can't come back?"

The bite of a shark starts to sting my hands. "Ash. Let go." I close my eyes, holding tight, the feeling of tearing teeth and bleeding flesh taking me over. *I can't let go.* My knees buckle and I lower to the ground. The shark releases its grip. Gills fluttering open, saltwater flooding its system.

"Ash. Let go." Lye's scarred hands take mine and pry them from Luna's. She is gone before I open my eyes.

"Why do I do this to myself?" I ask my sister as she helps me up.

"I think you know the answer to that," she replies with a strange smile.

"I just don't want her to ruin herself."

Lye runs a hand through her short hair. "I don't want that either, Ash, but you need to give her at least a little time. A little space."

"I'm not afraid of her," I whisper tersely.

Lye's face changes. Planed with experience I will never understand. "Perhaps you should be."

"She won't hurt me." Of this I am convinced.

Lye puts ups a single finger. The foliage blows open and closed, showing me pieces of the sky to hold onto. "She won't *kill* you. But she has already hurt you."

Stars burn—too far away to harm and too beautiful to look away from. I ignore her. "Will you watch out for her while I'm gone?"

Lye bows. "I always watch out for her, brother."

# 4
## ASH KI

A sharp dig to my stomach. I shoot up, icicles in my fingers, ready to slice through flesh like a knife. My cheek is poked with a stick. "Get up, Shen boy." Sun's deep and disrespectful voice fills the dark tent. He uses his balsawood foot to hitch my blanket and pull it from my body. My limbs pull into my chest instinctively.

"The sun's not even up yet," I groan, rolling my face into my mattress.

He chuckles, amused. "The Sun *is* up. He's up and he wants to get moving. And the Shen boy better follow orders or he's gonna get a lashing or two."

I curse, stumbling out of the tent with my pack, arrows clattering against each other while Sun taps his stick, impatiently boring a hole into the earth. Cursing again, I drop one and my bow slips over my head. I look like an ox ready to pull a plow.

"I thought Shen believed themselves above everyone. Your cursing could strip the lipstick from a concubine." His tone rises one note of impressed.

I'm glad he can't see the way my cheeks flush at his comment. Slinging my pack over my shoulder, I hop from foot to foot putting my shoes on. "After you," I grunt. The air is cool and damp, mist clinging to my skin.

Sun thwacks the back of my legs sharply. "We walk together. Side by side."

I don't know what to think. His words put me beneath him, but his actions treat me as an equal. I wish I'd sought Luna's advice before I left. But, I assure myself, even if she can't quite reach me, trapped beneath frozen waves, she wouldn't put me in danger. She must believe Sun can be trusted with me.

*I hope I'm not putting too much faith in the girl with the hickory heart.*

THE RUSTY smell of old blood clings to the edge of the water as we follow the river. The dead have been moved but they left something behind. Sun keeps his head up, eyes on our destination, while I can't help but stare at his foot. Balsa, being porous, should soak up mud, moisture, and other things, and I want to ask him how it feels. Does it get heavier? Or is it sealed in some way? Does he seal it? Oil it? The questions build inside my mouth, puffing out my cheeks like a pointy-eared chipmunk.

I slap at a bug buzzing near my ear and Sun glances to me from his stretched tree height. Searching for Luna in him, I find it in his high cheeks, dotted with tiny, dark freckles. "Ai ya, Shen boy! Will you be offering me brass soon?"

I cock my head, eyebrows knotted. Mud slurps at our feet, and we have to stomp to move fast. I imagine we look pretty strange from a distance. Knees up, robes crusted with dirt. "Brass?" I query and Sun snorts, looking down over his sloped nose.

"You Shen. A brass necklace or cuff. For courtship rites." He rolls his eyes when I still appear lost. "Ah! You were staring at me like I'm the last dumpling on the table." He waggles his eyebrows.

My jaw clenches at his suggestion and I tighten my robe, trying to put distance between us, but he easily catches me. The sound of squelching is followed by a hand on my shoulder, yanking me backward. "Hai! You could do worse!" Sun scoffs.

I concentrate hard on not drowning him in saltwater. "I was looking for Luna in you," I mutter, regretting my words the moment I say them. I sigh and follow with, "Clearly she got all the looks in the family."

Sun grins, self-assured. "Well, that's a lie," he says calmly, running a hand through his hair, scanning the tree line. I've been so focused on this awkward partnership, I forgot there could be Shen eyes watching us from the jungle. He nods, satisfied, and keeps walking. Sweeping his arm to my back to shove me along. "Though the best-looking Yan was…" His eyes rise to the sky, to the red-tipped gulls squawking overhead. Sun doesn't finish and he doesn't need to since I know he means Ben Ni. Inhaling slowly, I breath in compassion for a man who has just lost his brother and may also lose his sister.

My face falls. "I am sorry about your brother… and Luna."

Sun blinks, gazing at the sun. "Yes. Luna is fine."

I open my mouth to argue, but his finger goes to his lips in a considered, quiet movement. He stalks closer to the tree line, large body tense and ready. I reach out for other Shen, but I'm not as good at this as my sister. Things slip in and out of my senses. Narrowing my eyes, I search for Shen colors among the plants. Flashes of blue Water Shen robes in the undergrowth. Sun grasps the hilt of his knife tightly and crouches.

Scratching breaks the silence. Leaves tossed aside. Claws and feathers, not skin and cloth. A bright blue turkey pops up from the longer grass and blinks its yellow eyes. Sun lifts his hand, knife still at the ready, and I laugh. Loudly.

"It's just a turkey. Leave it be," I say, watching him creep closer, focused on the bird.

"It could also be dinner," he hisses as he crawls.

I think of Luna then, practical and practiced. Swinging fish over her shoulder. Impressing me without trying to. My eyes dance over the trees to the sheer rock of the crater. The feeling of combining powers surges to the front of my mind. The unbreakable connection we now share. I stare at that rock so hard it starts to wobble in my vision.

I sense a shift in the Atmosphere. Wind strengthening. Warm air suddenly turning cold.

It moves like a moth. White cloth flapping behind green. Sun's so intently focused on the turkey, he doesn't notice the Air Shen raise an arrow to his bow and he only moves when it whizzes past his ear. His hand flies to his face, coming back bloody. I'm quick to respond, notching an arrow and releasing it. Aiming for the Air Shen's chest, I hit my mark before he can release a second arrow. Red blooms like ink on a white page, and the Shen falls.

Jumping up, Sun runs to where the Shen fell. I follow, heart pumping wildly.

I skid to the body, to find open eyes that see nothing. The soldier's already dead, fanned out like a resting crane. Raking a hand over the Shen's face and closing his eyelids, Sun turns to me with a swirl of gratitude.

He crunches my hand into a fist. "You saved my life, Shen boy." He puts his hand over mine, squeezes it once, and pushes it away.

I purse my lips. "Do you think maybe you could start calling me Ash now?"

He snorts. "No. I don't." He stands, tapping his chin. "Besides, my guess is before the day is finished, I will have repaid my debt."

I tilt my chin to the sky and sigh. If he is going to be this difficult then so shall I.

As the sun glides over the crater, a yellowing lantern pulled along by a patient old man, I begin my assault. I release the stored questions in my chipmunk cheeks, asking everything I can think of to irritate, perplex, and infuriate Sun Yan. Each one pecking him like spat out pumpkin seeds. *Small on their own, but in great numbers...*

By the end of the day, we reach the edge of the evacuated village on the northern side of the crater. Sun stops suddenly, swinging around and bringing his face so close that drips of sweat roll from his nose to mine. I force a smile though my hands vibrate with the need to shove him away.

"No! My balsawood foot doesn't get soggy in water, Shen." His dark eyes dance with impending violence as he answers my latest question. He moves his lips very slowly. Pronouncing every word. "A word of advice. If you want to fit in with the Char you should learn to never tease, make light of, or ridicule a wooden part. It is..." His eyes roll to the side. "It's incredibly insulting."

My mouth quirks as I push a little harder. "You know your sister said something similar to me when we were sharing a room. It was very close quarters, you know. No privacy. No place to dress without being seen. We shared much during that—"

I almost hear his temper snap. The sound like dry bamboo broken over someone's knee. He grabs me by the collar and throws me to the ground. Haphazard structures rise behind us. The teetering bamboo homes of Crow's Nest Village. Each built atop another with ladders connecting them. He presses his balsawood foot to my throat.

"I know what you're trying to do, Shen."

From my upside down view, the village appears very unstable. If I took one plank from the base, the whole structure could tumble down like a child's model. I blink. Sun's furious face, framed by dying light, frowns upon me. He presses my neck harder and I gurgle.

I could grasp his leg and send a waterfall to pummel him. The sheer force of tons of water hitting at once would feel like a flattening boulder, but I hold off. I stare at Sun as he glares at me. My mouth twitches.

"I know what you're trying to do," he repeats.

Wet earth seeps through my clothes. "And what is that?" I smirk.

Then Sun laughs. It's a deep sound, like the rounding of a drumskin with the flat of a palm. His foot releases and I can breathe. He offers his hand and I grab it, pulling myself up.

He clicks his fingers. "I told you I would repay my debt by the end of the day." He laughs and punches my shoulder lightly. "I just saved your life."

"How so?" My head swivels, searching for a threat.

"By not killing you for your smart mouth." Sun's expression darkens when he warns, "But if you ever talk about my sister like that again, I will drop you off the cliffs like a rotten melon."

"I don't think Luna would appreciate that very much." I have too much hope in my voice. I'm not sure of *this* Luna.

He arches an eyebrow. "Perhaps." He checks doors as we climb further up the village. The bound bamboo structures make strange panpipe noises when the wind sails across the hollow tops.

I shrug. "At least the Luna I knew before would have a problem with you dropping me from a cliff. She is…" Detached, emotionless. "Different now."

Sun breathes in deeply and seems to have an internal conversation with himself. Silence stretches between us for a long moment. "You know you don't deserve her, right?"

I nod. I know. *I've always known.* This seems to please him, and he relaxes a little. A small chuckle from deep within his chest. "Good. Well, if you want my advice, you need to give her time and space to figure out *what* she is, *who* she is now. If you don't, you will certainly lose her." He makes noises of slight exertion as he throws himself upward. The people of Crow's Nest must be very fit to do this every day.

"You're only a couple of years older than me. What makes you think you're so wise, that you know what is best for her?" Luna is on the edge of shadow. If I don't pull her back, she'll tip into darkness.

"You know, it surprises me that you don't have any brothers. You certainly behave like you do." He pushes open a door to a small building and sniffs. "Like you're the little, annoying one."

I try not to let those words warm me. It's too soon. "I have a sister."

Sun snorts. "Not the same."

We step over the threshold to smells of burned wax and coal. I release a detail with my trust. "I had an older brother, though I don't remember him. He died when I was very young."

Sun's voice peels away a layer in the dark. "I am sorry. It's an awful thing, to bury a sibling."

I don't feel sorrow for this older brother I lost. Though I have vague memories of my mother's grief, the shape of my brother is unreal, simply shadows in the background of my life. My memories don't want to come clear. Besides, I can't really dwell on these thoughts right now. My lips curve upward.

Sun fumbles around for a match to light a candle. The glow reveals a home abandoned in a hurry. Clothes strewn on the floor. A pot of rice porridge on the hearth growing fluffy green clouds of mold.

We need to swallow our issues and focus on the task at hand: Bringing the Carvresses back safely. Only then can we plan our next move.

# 5
## LYE LI

I don't know how I should feel. He is my blood. My brother. Yet there's nothing but loathing between us. Blood dries. It cracks and turns to dust to be swept away by palace staff. It becomes part of the earth. And the earth beneath our feet is black and infertile. Nothing can grow from the blood lost between me and the chancellor.

I feel a deeper connection to the ghost of Ben Ni than I do to him.

"I sense you out there, Keeper." His voice is high and parched but proud. Still foolishly believing he can live through this. *Succeed.* "Lye Li… Sister?" he presses. "Come talk to your older brother. Come tell me what you must." The cobra luring in his prey.

I step inside, before anyone hears him call me sister.

Hushed warnings and shadowed fingers drum my back. My conscience, my ghost companion, stands in the doorway. I huff and walk through the boy like mist.

My arm flies to my nose. The stench of an unwashed man with festering skin wounds is beyond words. Storm clouds of wrath gather in my palms. He should cower. At the very least, he should look less satisfied, but his arrogance and ego are untouched. Bound and looking like a dirty rope himself, he stares with snake eyes. Calculating how best to manipulate me.

"I see you still cling to your proud ways," I manage, staring at the wounds inflicted by Luna's animals and insects. She has no need to make skin to skin contact with her victims like the rest of us, though I know she does. She can summon any creature she wishes to carry out her torture. The chancellor's arms are covered in red, raised bumps. Spider bites. His ankles are raw and bleeding. Not unlike Luna's power: raw and flowing too fast, like blood from a deep gash. I grimace, my hand hovering over my stomach as I think of Ben Ni. Pressing in and in. A wish lives in that touch. *It could have been me. Should* have been me and not him.

He straightens. "I see you are as weak as you always were." His eyes narrow and my body wants to shrink away. My knees shake and I lock them. I will not let him get to me.

Shakily, he pours liquid from a teapot. Rituals he can't let go, even in these circumstances. The black tea shows no steam. Cold and bitter charcoal. He takes a sip, purses his stained lips.

"Tell me, what is the next move for the emperor, given the failure of your mission?"

His jaw tenses ever so slightly at the word *failure* as he swallows the tea with an unpleasant expression. "Have you told our brother that I live?" He clucks his tongue. Doesn't wait for an answer. "So many lies, sister. I know it was part of the deal. That you would support my promotion to chancellor in exchange for me keeping the family secret." He strains his bound wrists, trying to find space where there's none. "But circumstances have changed."

I snort, storm clouds charging with electricity. "*You* wanted it kept secret because you were ashamed of what you were: A child conceived through violence. Even though our mother did everything she could to protect you, you blamed her. She never…" I bite down on my words. This does no good. He had love. He had family. But he was twisted from the moment he was born. Bitterness strangled him. Mother said he was born wrapped in the cord. Not around his neck as with some babies but around and around his little body like a net. It was a deathly omen. Like her own womb had tried to contain his malevolence.

Mother blamed herself for the anger living inside him. Swearing he was caged in it like a curse. Always, always she chanted that it wasn't his fault. But circumstance only takes you so far down the river of evil. At some point one either accepts the course of the current or fights it. I should know.

He rolls his eyes. "She was weak, like you." My nails dig into my palms, desperate to harm. My scars itch like insect bites. His head knocks toward them. "You punish yourself for what? You should be proud of all you have achieved. The Char you have killed should strengthen you."

"How can you have no shame for your crimes? The lives you've destroyed?" I step closer. He radiates calm seas seeking to swallow ships. A false lull. "Do you at least feel guilt for the waste of life? Thousands of Shen soldiers, all dead for nothing!"

He tries to shrug but can't because of his chains. There's something of Ash in his movements and I hate it. "I wouldn't say it was for nothing. The Char girl. The girl with the hickory heart. She is living proof a hybrid can be created. Had we not come to Crow's Nest, we wouldn't have this information."

Unable to control the waves of fire lashing through my body, I slap his filthy face, pulling my hand back fast. It produces a smile and my stomach twists with nausea. "Luna is special. And you will not get the opportunity to use her!"

"You are too confident." He seems so sure he will come through this. Like he knows something I do not. I reach for his Atmosphere, a clue to where his mind is going, but hit an ice wall.

"And you have no reason to be confident." It's infuriating but also a nail in his coffin. He will tell me nothing new.

"Perhaps it is a family trait," he baits me. "Does our little brother share this fortunate characteristic?" His glance betrays hunger for more words, desperation in the vile green of his eyes. But he will get nothing more from me.

A sick sneer crosses my lips before I can stop it. He cannot be turned. Cannot be useful.

The chancellor must die.

I turn and leave. Suddenly. He shouts after me, but the words fall on my back and to the ground like loose snowballs.

The general needs no convincing when I request execution.

The chancellor *will* die. Hopefully before Ash returns.

# 6

## ASH KI

The blunt house shudders and shakes and I worry someone has pulled out an important plank from the structure. Our roof is the ceiling of the home above us. The whole village feels on the verge of collapse. I kick back dusty covers and follow the banging and grunting. The house shudders again and I brace myself on the kitchen counter. Sesame crackers and pickled okra are neatly arranged on a plate, and I raise an eyebrow. Sun laid out breakfast for me. I shove the cracker in my mouth. It's chewy and sweet, the tiny roasted sesames wiggling between my teeth. Picking at them with a fingernail, I'm drawn to a rhythmic, emotive sound. I peer through the slightly ajar door to the outside.

Sun hits a post supporting the tiny veranda. He punches and pulls back. Punches and pulls back. Performing a drill. He uses his balsa foot with deadly precision. Kicking hard and accurate. Over and over. Hands splinter. Blood drips between his fingers. His face is intense and unchanging, engraved with pain. The post shows the damage—it's about to break in half.

Sun's grief is in every sharp crack and frayed fragment of timber. It pours from his back. It pulses through his fists and feet. It may destroy this house but at least it goes somewhere. My shoulders tense at the thought of Luna. Grief floating inside her chest like poisonous gas. She won't breathe it out, won't release it, and it could kill her.

I lean too heavily on the door and it creaks. Luna's brother continues to bounce from foot to foot. Taking smaller slaps at the post. "Hard to look away from such staggering prowess and power, right?" he says, wiping his nose on his shoulder. He swipes his eyes, and I pretend I didn't see the hanging tears.

"Shen don't need physical strength to fight well," I retort without much conviction.

He laughs, nodding in my direction. "Clearly! My father could snap you over his knee." He stops and wiggles the now flimsy post. Porch shingles clatter and clap. "We should leave." Sun's eyes track upward.

I duck instinctively, though that wouldn't save me. I swing up a ladder. "I'd like to meet him. Your father."

Sun thumps his chest and scoffs. "I would like you to him meet too." Optimism tests the air and is quickly squashed as the ladder wobbles beneath me and Sun laughs. "He would hate you."

I swallow. Not a good start. But I feel as if Sun and I are coming to a rough friendship. I glance down at his rigid expression and adjust my thoughts. *Or at least tolerating each other.*

We climb. Up the canyon wall and through the city built into the cliff. Ladders and platforms. Tied with vine and strengthened with bamboo. I don't know how they live like this. *How on earth do they feel secure?* The whole structure threatens to slide away if a single tie loosens. One crack in a ledge and we become a rockslide.

"Is this how you live? On, err, Coal Village?" I ask, panting from the climb, dizzy from the height.

Sun groans. "Coal*stone* Village. And no. We live by the sea. Or in the sea, really. We hug the mountain that pours into the water. We sit on the land or water, not in it."

I make the mistake of turning my head and instantly feel unsteady. My grip tightens on the rungs. "Does it ever get washed away?"

He clucks his tongue. "Hasn't done so in a while, no."

"Why not build further inland? Level the land and create something more solid." Gritting my teeth, I make myself keep climbing. My hands find a natural balcony and I pull up and over. The view is breathtaking, but I retreat until the reassurance of a wall is at my back.

Sun's head appears and he shakes it. "That's what you Shen don't understand. Nothing in this life is solid or permanent. The sea is our home. We respect that we are borrowing its space. We don't own it." He leans over the edge without fear, releasing a satisfied sigh.

"And if it all washes away?" I ask.

He smiles. "Then we start over."

*We start over.* I keep hold of those words for a later purpose.

To my left, the balcony fades into a blackness so complete it's opaque. "Which way now?" I ask, dreading the answer.

Sun points into that blackness. I pray there are no bats in this cave.

SUN'S WHISTLE is absorbed like a mouth swallowed it. I gulp and he elbows me with a short, tense smile. "Keep your head down."

"Why?" I squint, trying to catch some light. My fingers pulse with water. The cool, slow drip of moisture down cave walls, and something else, damp and unknown.

A hitch of a chuckle. "You'll find out."

Sun steps into the black-as-a-tarpit cave, leaving me standing in the light like a coward. I thump my chest and force myself to walk forward. Sun's footsteps on the spongy cave floor are barely audible. "Just tell me there are no bats in there," I shout, and my words return to me, mocking. *No bats in there! No bats in there!*

Impatiently, Sun growls. "There are no bats." *No bats! No bats!* I shudder as I follow.

The slope of the cave is steep. Uneven, carved steps lead us downward. I bow my head as instructed, tempted to press my hands to the ceiling but at the same time wary. The only sound is

Sun's steady breathing, which I try to emulate, and the very soft shush of the sea somewhere below us.

Down. Down. Down.

Sun is silent and I don't know whether it's because of the cave or something else.

"Is this the way you came in before..." I start. "Um. Before the battle?"

Sun doesn't respond. Small light spatters the black. He's a few feet ahead of me and is folded over like a broken wheat stalk. Curious, I watch his back, not paying attention to my feet and I slip. Straightening to regain my balance, my hand reaches for the wall. My head hits something hard as glass and noise grows from where I made contact. Glass against glass, a shattering noise, but shards don't rain down.

Sun's face, turned back to look at me, is aglow, purple and blue. He frowns, rolls his eyes and increases his pace, still hunched. Cave coral sparkles over our heads and stretches downwards. Long, crystal-like arms reach for me and I duck out of the way.

Sun curses and I curse him.

"Why didn't you say the cave was filled with coral?" I shout, shoving his bent form.

His shoulders, lit with purple light, rise and fall. "I didn't think you'd know what it was and I couldn't be bothered explaining it to you." He treats me like an idiot and now we're both in danger.

We bend in half, almost crawling. Cave coral grows at an alarming rate when it senses food. Glassy arms thin to a needle point, trying to pin its victim and suck away life. "Shen have caves," I mutter, wanting to frost his limbs. "We're not that different, Sun. We don't *live* that differently to Char."

Between smashing and a strange stretching sound like wood bending to the shape of a boat hull, Sun grumbles, "I thought all Shen lived in cleared townships. Huddled against nature."

"We do live in cleared townships, but we don't huddle away from nature. We know our environment," I retort.

I hear him mutter, "Only to exploit it." I can't wholly disagree so I don't respond.

A different kind of light, whitish yellow, beckons us. *Sunlight.* We trip and fall, rolling under the thickening coral trying its best to cage us in. It rattles like bottles clanging in a bin. Crowding the entrance.

This seems like an unfair way to go. Impaled by mindless, hungry coral. Trapped to rot in a cave. I grind my teeth, thinking of Luna and Lye. One would grieve me. The other would slide her grief into a queue of unfelt feelings.

Death will not be quick.

Sun and I exchange glances. "We have to charge through it. There's no space left," I manage as I jerk away from a sharp point. He nods and we dip our shoulders, using our bodies to crash through the thin sticks. Glass cracks and whines. Colored glass daggers fly outward from the impact. Sweat-soaked and out of breath, we fly onto the pebbly beach.

The minute the coral is touched by light it goes white and dies. I turn back to the entrance packed with thin, shattered ends of coral. The purple and blue glow begins to fade.

My scalp is wet with blood. Just scratches. My hands and arms are covered in them. Sun lays on his side, pebbles clicking beneath his rolling body, clutching a cut in his side. A sharp piece of coral punctures his robes. I curse and crawl toward him, knees sinking into sharp rubble. I'm not sure how I feel about him, but Luna cannot lose another brother. That would create a hole so deep no one could pull her out.

He wraps his hand around it, ready to pull.

"Just wait a minute! Let me help you," I urge.

He grimaces, shaking his head vehemently. "I don't want a Shen touching my skin."

I grin. "You Yans always say that… to begin with."

Sun's cheeks flush red with anger and I realize what I've inferred. I smirk, letting him sit with that image for a moment. The blood drips slow. I don't think it's a life-threatening wound. All the same, I could numb the area and pull it out in a more controlled way than he could. I don't say any of this because I know he won't listen. I just press my palm to his temple to calm him and use my other hand to ice the area around the wound.

The dull thud of wood banging against wood lifts our eyes to the sea. Sun sounds shocked as he mutters, "What the…" and I take advantage, sliding the coral from his side while his attention is elsewhere. Blood pools sluggishly from the wound and I double up his sash, applying pressure.

"Sit up and keep pressing on the wound," I order. He doesn't look too pleased about taking orders from me, but something else plays across his face. Amusement perhaps, though I don't know what he's got to be amused about.

The wooden knocking comes from a beautifully carved drag-ons-head boat jostling between simple canoes. The Char ships are anchored in the distance.

I scan the beach for the Carvresses, although I don't even know what one looks like. I picture a tree-like creature, with branches for arms, leaves for hair. But I see nothing like that or anything else. I flap a hand at the suspiciously quiet Sun. "Wait here."

He shuffles on the pebbles but doesn't stand. He looks trapped between several emotions. Maybe being saved a second time by a Shen has taken its toll, because I see shame. I huff and leave him, feet slipping over marble-like stones to the jungle, searching for something I don't understand. Something mysterious and desper-ately sought by my emperor.

Halfway down the small stretch of beach I realize I should confirm what a Carvress looks like. I turn to Sun, who is watching me intently. Opening my mouth to yell, I am suddenly rendered silent by a sharp shove to the ground and a knife against my throat.

# 7
## LYE LI

Should I not feel darker, heavier, like lead weights my shoulders, at the thought of my brother's execution? I scratch at the fresher, scabbier marks on my arms and flick bits into the dirt. *He* won't get a mark. He doesn't deserve one.

The feeling is the opposite. The moment the general agreed to the chancellor's execution, as long as Char traditions were respected, I felt like my toes barely scraped the earth as I floated skyward. I tilt my head to the yolky sun, rising steadily, happily in the sky. Yes. I should feel heavier. But I simply don't. There's nothing in my heart for the chancellor. Nothing left.

I glance at the tent that shudders and shivers pain like a living thing. It screams with torture both external and internal. It reminds me there are other burdens I bear. I breathe in deeply and approach Luna's tent, though cave would be a more accurate description. At least I can give her this peace. Deliver the news that the man who murdered her brother will be punished.

I press my feet into soldiers' leftover footprints. They sit neatly inside. I am steeled by my new purpose. Char men lift their eyes to me briefly but quickly look away. I wish there were a way to prove my loyalty. I wish I could scrub away my Shen parts. But the Atmosphere surrounding me is birds hopping toward an open palm full of rice. Distrust and a need to believe, all tied in a messy knot. Luna could have been a bridge. But she's fighting her own demons. Or has given into them.

The tent flap parts and her tiny pale hand is followed by an even paler face.

Inside, I sigh. Inside, I exclaim, *Oh Luna!* But I bite down on pity. Her caramel eyes are soured and ringed with purple. She blinks like the light hurts her, gaze falling to the ground, to her dirty feet splattered with the blood, sweat, and tears of grown men.

Setting my shoulders, I address her as she starts to disappear back into the dark. "Luna." She turns slowly. Each movement measured and considered, expression neutral. She bows.

"Yes, Lye." Flat voice, matte eyes. Not calm—more like something that has boiled over and solidified, leaving a bleak, dry stain.

I search for sparks of anger or blame. But the fire has been smothered. Perhaps it smolders under the surface. I beckon her into the light. "I wanted to tell you the chancellor will be executed very soon."

She nods slowly. Every movement thought out before it's completed. A puppeteer of her own body. "I suppose that is fair." She stretches her fingers, knuckles cracking. "I was not able to get any useful information from him." She glances up. Blood power swirls around her. "And I tried. Exhaustively." The disgruntled sigh of a hard worker.

Swallowing, I reach out to touch her hand. It shrinks inside her coat. "I know you did. You've done good work. But you can stop now. The general and I…"

Luna's hands clench and I hear the flap of dozens of wings as moon-sun birds line up along the spine of her tent. Hopping up and down and nattering like gossiping women. "Stop?" I sense a faster beat. Not from her. From the Char men around her. They wrap hands around weapons, muscles tense. I sigh, deep and dark. Understanding, all too well, this kind of regard. Luna and I belong to a very lonely club. Power is an isolating thing. They respect but also fear her. The birds' chatter rises in volume and suddenly ceases like fingers clasped their beaks closed.

"I can't stop. Not yet. There are still Mogui to be questioned."

My chin falls. I feel her need to sink below the waves of her work. To lose herself to the task at hand. I know it well and I also know it has no good end.

"There are only base level soldiers left. They won't know anything useful." I keep to the facts. Appealing to her on an emotional level won't work right now.

Luna breathes in and the birds rise to the air in a white cloud. As she breathes out, they settle back on the tent canopy. My eyes follow this, and I try not to look as alarmed as I feel. "Very well." She nods, eyes closing for a long moment. There's a fight in her. A suppression of emotion that goes on and on. But her hickory heart wins. Her eyes open and stare blankly. "What should I do then?"

*Grieve. You should grieve.*

"You can sort and clean weapons with the others," I say, pointing to a pile of blood- and mud-streaked swords. The tangled mess of arrows to be salvaged. Char waste nothing.

Frowning at the task, her heart beats steady and strong. Her fingers are splintered with memories of harm. I do not envy the ache she will have when her deeds begin to haunt her.

She walks at a pace you could set a metronome to toward the pile of Shen weapons. The moon-sun birds scratch their claws on the thick canvas roof, blinking black eyes at their master. Awaiting instruction.

# 8
## ASH KI

A stray wisp of silken black hair brushes my nose. Escaped from the tight bun of a middle-aged woman with a stern, disastrous expression. Her dark eyes take one piercing look and instantly despise me. "Who are you?" she demands, tone conflictingly filled with warm music and rising bread dough as she presses the flat of the blade down on my neck. "You better tell me fast before I slit your throat."

A voice like a flute. "Goodness! He is young." Wood skittles over stones. I seek the source, but the woman above me holds my head still. Air barely whistles past my voice box as I try to speak. My hands are pinned to my sides, but I get a finger to the woman's hip. I focus on raging water. Something to knock her over. Nothing happens. I blink and she smiles. Feathery strands of white shimmer on top of her head.

I try to speak again, and she eases off just slightly. "My name is Ash Ki Koh. I am a…"

She stares at my tattoo. "I know what you are, Water Shen. Now tell me, what are you doing here and what have you done to my son?"

Son. Pieces fall into place. Sewn fragments that make sense now the quilt is laid out before me. This is Luna's mother. I take in her dark eyes and black-as-a-moonless-night hair. Searching for the patchwork scrap belonging to Luna. And when she purses her small but full lips and blows air out in a frustrated yet restrained way, I find it. It helps me and harms me to meet the woman who raised her.

I keep my body still as I wait for Sun's game to end.

A bellowing laugh makes me grimace. "Mama, wait!" Sun's voice is warm with an edge of panic. "Don't kill him just yet."

Her face tilts to Sun as he slowly eases from the ground and limps our way.

Shadows suddenly crowd me, and I gasp as nine pairs of wooden feet meet my eyes, connected to long, slender wooden legs. From there it just gets more unbelievable. These women, these Carvresses, are not just sorcerers of wood magic. They are themselves carved of wood. From their perfect toes to their incredible heads of wooden hair. My mouth drops open like a drawbridge no one is manning.

"When can I kill him then?" Luna's mother asks, relaxing enough that I can shuffle out of reach. She sheaths her knife and folds her hands neatly in her lap. This older, darker-skinned version of Luna causes a jumble in my mind. This woman has a flesh heart. She knew Luna before—before everything. I don't know whether I envy or pity her. My eyes drop to the ground when I think about how much she doesn't know about her own daughter.

Sun's still chuckling, and I growl, "Thanks for your help."

He shrugs. "It was too amusing to stop." His mother, *Luna's* mother, looks disappointed at the prospect of not slitting my throat. Sun crouches, taking her hands in his. "You can't kill him. I'm sorry, Mama. He's actually quite useful." Eyes connect with mine and slide away. It's probably the biggest compliment I'm ever going to get from him, and I grin.

She huffs. "Why does he smile like that? Shen don't smile." She stands, straightening her skirt.

Sun rolls his eyes. "This one is always smiling, whether it's called for or not."

*A smile hides a hundred lies and a thousand truths.*
*It is a shield and a door.*
*It is my first defense. My last effort.*

My teeth show while my heart pounds absently. I'm missing Luna and feeling guilty. Wanting to know this woman feels like a clue to Luna's past, even if it's a part of her that doesn't exist anymore.

The Carvresses huddle in a bizarre wooden line. Tree ring eyes take in everything with an innate wise-ness and experience. Their bodies emit a low and calming hum whenever they touch each other. Sun bows low and I copy him, trying not to get caught staring in awe. They're the strangest, most beautiful creatures I've ever seen.

"Where's Papa?" Sun asks, apprehensive.

She smiles a loving smile. "You know your papa."

That doesn't seem to be an answer, but Sun understands and laughs gently. "That I do. That I do."

I'm still hunched on the ground, waiting for a knife to puncture my lungs, unable to stop staring at the Carvresses with wonder and fascination. Sun offers his hand to me and his mother watches this curiously. "Mama, this is Ash. He's, er, he's…"

I bow. "I'm a friend." Shifting to stand, I find Luna again in her wary but wanting to trust glance. "An ally."

She steps forward, palms pressed together. "Ki Anah." Then she turns to Sun. "Where are your brothers?"

Sun's demeanor changes like a card slapped face down on the table, shoulders tucked and eyes sinking. I quirk an eyebrow. *Shouldn't he tell her about Ben Ni?* But it's not my place, so I keep my mouth shut. Perhaps there's a Char way to do this I'm not aware of.

This is where a smile covers words not ready to be spoken. I splash a crooked one over my face and it causes her to frown, immune.

"They're back at camp. General Fah sent us to retrieve you."

"He sent both of you?" Ki Anah exclaims. "As comrades?"

Sun scrambles to his mother's side, towering over her but seeming younger. Perhaps it's a universal thing that happens between child and parent. A kind of regression. It makes me grin to see Sun dancing about his mother, awaiting her command. Until Ki Anah glowers with an intensity that would strip the hide from a cow's back.

"Sometimes a smile is hiding something," she says, pointing a hard finger at my chest. *How right she is.* But I do my best to look innocent.

I genuinely chuckle then, realizing that for once, I am innocent.

Sun slaps the top of my head and mutters, "Are you trying to get yourself stabbed?"

The Carvresses shuffle in a mass, slipping on the round pebbles. One breaks from the group, swiping dried saltwater from her cheeks and rubbing her hands together. "How intriguing that the general would make a Shen and Char work together!"

The Yans stare at her. Catching each word like it's precious. I try to borrow that reverence, but I'm on the outer edge of this connection. They react to her almost like she's their mother.

"To make that decision, he must have had good reason. Good reason indeed." Her eyes are glossy, honey timber, *mesmerizing*, and I find myself wafting on her words, swaying with her movements.

Ki Anah and Sun bow in agreement and step aside as she skitters to me, making sounds like children's games and bottled laughter. I freeze.

She cups her oddly warm wooden fingers under my chin and lifts my face. I want to pull away, scared of what she will see, feeling bare and open. *A book with not enough words.* She blinks her wooden shutter eyelids. Her hard, carved lips that look soft whisper, "Secrets. Smiles. Love." She taps my chest and a warmth spreads through my chest like a fever. "Too much love."

I laugh nervously, my mask slipping. "Is there such a thing as too much love?"

She withdraws. Straightens like a snapping cane. "Sometimes... yes." And I believe her completely even though I'm not sure what she means. "Orphans carry a lot of unused love around, like stones in their pockets." I bite my lip. Fingers clenching into fists. "It's important to empty them before you jump in. Otherwise, you'll sink."

The sea wind whips cool air around us, refreshing and salty. "Jump in?" I'm leaning into her like a starved beggar.

She shakes her head and I expect splinters to fall from her hair, but it moves fluidly. The breeze disturbs it and that disturbs me. "Yes." She says nothing more. Leaving me confused and the butt of Sun's next joke, I'm sure.

As we wind our way to the cave entrance, coral crunches down like gnashing, hungry teeth. Sun whines, "It will take so long to go around."

The Carvresses glance at each other and shrug. One enters the cave, standing tall.

"Wait," I shout, hand outstretched. "It's dangerous."

Coral surges to her shoulder but snaps as soon as it connects with her "skin."

The honey-eyed Carvress lays a hand on my shoulder. It's peculiar to have a Char casually touch me because there's no part of her I can reach with my element. "You'll find there is little in this world that can harm us, child."

I shudder. I'm sure the chancellor and emperor could find a way.

With nine wooden warriors smashing the coral ahead to protect us, we ascend.

Heartbreak waiting for us in the center of the crater.

# 9

## LYE LI

They look like dolls. Powerful, fierce, enchanted dolls. And I long to speak with one of them. Long to have their eyes fall upon me and judge me. But just like dolls to a greedy child, the general scooped them into his arms and put them away. Kept them safely away—from me.

Two Char men guard the tent entrance. Arms crossed loosely over their chests, eyes on the moon folded over like a paper plate. I could easily disarm them and force my way in. Rising from my seat, steam builds pressure in my fingertips.

Ash catches my arm and I sting him. Just the graze of a shadow ray's wing. He sharply withdraws and sighs. My brother has returned with new knowledge and experience of which I am jealous. He also returned too quickly. I tuck the secret I'm keeping behind my back and list ways in which Ash and the chancellor are not alike. They are countless because although they share blood, they are not truly family.

Ash breaks my thoughts. "If you want the general and Carvresses to include you, then you need to respect their traditions.

You must wait for an invitation." I behold an exhausted but warmer face. It did him good to get away for a while.

"You know if we were at the palace, I'd be in that meeting." I point at the tent. "Why do Joka and Sun get to be in there? Shen would never allow fledgling soldiers to participate in such important conversations."

His lips hitch upward. A sympathetic smile like the snagged end of a skirt caught in a door. "Firstly, I don't think you should start any sentence with 'if we were at the palace'. You left that life, remember? And secondly, they are in there because they received an invitation from the Carvresses. Yes, they are new soldiers, but the Yans are a special family." His eyes flit to the side. "The Carvresses trust them."

"All very easy for you to say since you've already met them." I huff, taking a step toward the tent, though I don't intend to follow through.

His eyes are gilded, white light on water. "Yes, I did" is all he says.

I tap my foot, desperate for details. "And? What was it like? What are they like?"

His head sways, entranced. "Honestly, I don't really know how to explain it... I think you have to meet one yourself. Form your own opinion."

I frown but accept, switching subjects. "So, you met Luna's mother?" I ask, awkwardly elbowing him in the side, careful not to hurt him this time. His smile spreads thin as desert sand through the street. "It went that well, did it?"

His eyes drift to the former torture tent and the white birds huddling on top like a breathing snow blanket. "How is she?" he asks, a tease of torment in his voice. Pain and longing.

"She was ordered to stop her interrogations," I answer, creeping backward to perch on the edge of a crate. Ash collapses next to me, tipping it. We stare at the general's busy tent. Crammed full of Char tradition—Char past and Char future. It all lies with them, protected only by flimsy walls and exhausted soldiers. The sounds that pierce those walls are foreign and beautiful. Music but not.

More like a warm breath. A loving heartbeat. My hands knot and Ash risks patting them.

"They'll let you in. One thing I've learned about the Char is they're fierce and guarded but willing to listen. They will hear you out." His face falls to footprints in the mud. A new terrain. "How'd she take the order to stop working? I bet she wasn't too pleased about it."

I smack him with my words, leaving the ghost of handprint. "She was neither pleased nor displeased." My sigh digs deep into the earth, rolling through tunnels made by one-eyed moles. "I am sorry, brother."

To himself he whispers, "I wonder if I'll sink…" as he pats his pockets. Then he raises his head and smiles an impossible smile dragged from a reserve the rest of us don't have. "Her mother might be able to shake some sense into her. She certainly had an interesting effect on Sun."

A triangle of light appears, and Char enter the night. Shadows move like flesh and bone when the owners are wood and brass. Ash jumps from his seat, disappearing between tents before I can say another word.

Joka, Sun, and an older woman who must be their mother take determined steps to Luna's tent, following a well-trodden path but to a different kind of torture. Their voices are dark and murmured. The mother's face, whitened by moonlight, does not appear grieved. They must not have told her of Ben Ni. I search for his ghost, long for its wispy hand on my shoulder, but he's nowhere. I let out a loud sigh. He *is* nowhere. What I feel and see of Ben Ni is not real. It is comfort sculpted from guilt. I smooth my robe over my legs. It is comfort, nonetheless.

As they pass me, the brothers bow. Joka stops abruptly, glancing at me with an expression like the twist of a wanton wrapper. He starts walking away, mutters something quietly to himself and spins around, marching back to stand before me. Sun and their mother reluctantly return.

"Lye Li Koh," he says respectfully, bowing again. "This is our mother Ki Anah Yan."

Bowing, I make poor attempts to brush dirt from my clothes. She smiles briefly but retreats. "It is an honor to meet the mother of such wonderful children. My debt to the Yans is deep and wide-ranging. I owe my…" Joka gives a slight shake of his head behind his mother, a plea in his eyes, and I close my mouth. Fingers scraping over acres of mud, I fumble for my waist cord, pulling it tight. "Forgive me. I will let you get on with your evening."

Ki Anah lifts her porcelain chin, eyes narrowed. There is shrewdness in her regard. Joka presses his hands into her back, ushering her along the beaten path of so many soldiers. Making her walk the trail too many mothers of war have before her. "We're taking Mama to see the youngest now." A purposeful omittance of names.

At the mention of her younger children, her face changes to eager, expectant, and brimming with love. My heart breaks for her. Selfishly, I think of how much she will hate me after this. Though it is only fair.

Pressing my palms together, I bow again.

The word Keeper is uttered in a fearful and awestruck tone as they leave. Ki Anah exclaims, "Apa ini? Why has she no hair?" and my hand flies to my head self-consciously.

*Oh Luna. I do not envy what you are about to face.*

I search for my brother between canvas walls, but he's nowhere to be seen.

Pressing my lips together, I exit the camp. This was never going to be an easy journey, a simple change. Doesn't mean it won't be worthwhile. A flush of heat warms the back of my neck. I have a vision of the boy who had big plans for the world and who believed it could be better. *For you, my friend, I shall make it so.*

THE RUSH of water beckons like a siren song. I taste the slight salt of a stream fed by spring and sea. Animals shuffle around me, some large and hungry. But their connection to Luna and hers to them is strong. Her control is wide reaching in this place. It's alarming and reassuring. Power and safety.

Robes lifted, I wade into the fast-running water, washing my dirty feet, cooling my skin. I plunge my hands down, scattering marron and fish. River weeds wrap around my wrists like ropes, and I'm yanked back to the palace for the flash of a second. My arms straining against bindings. The chancellor sneering. Trying to *turn* me. Change me.

It was effective. I grew powerful. Each gain of strength adding height to my pedestal. Until I was so high, I couldn't see the people below. Couldn't hear their screams or understand the lost looks in their eyes. Now I must descend. I must change… again. I cannot return to the girl before the Keeper crown was laid so heavily on her head. That girl with unmarked skin and an unmarked conscience doesn't exist. I'm stepping into a different life. Though I hold no illusions it will be less gruesome and violent than the previous one.

I turn my arms this way and that, the moonlight catching the water and giving what's left of my skin a glow, highlighting the scars.

A knock of wood on stone. I swing around, robes dunking and becoming instantly heavy. "I'd float like a raft. But you, young Keeper, you'd sink like a stone, so heavy is your heart." The river tugs at my clothes like hungry children. Trying to drag me under and away. I dig my feet in and fight the current, frightened to move. A Carvress has sought me and I don't wish to scare her away, though her voice and manner imply she is not easily startled.

Gliding down the curved bank like a ribbon dancer, she touches the beach. Swift and effortless. The emperor loved silk acrobats. The twist and twirl of yards of colored silk that never touched the ground. It required such control. The Carvress moves with similar grace. Each step, each movement, perfect from beginning to end.

She stares at my soggy robes, face moving up and down several times, and I begin to feel uncomfortable and a little cold. "My name is Lye Li Koh," I say too proudly, hugging myself. "I am the Keeper no longer."

Moonlight bounces off the water, painting her smooth face silver. Her wooden eyes crinkle impossibly at the corners. Kindness and fury smashing together. "Whether you acknowledge it or not, you will always be the Keeper. Always, until you die." Her gaze slides to my scars. Her words pin my heart like a casualty scroll to the back of my chest.

I push through the water and onto the beach while she watches, statue still. "Do you have a name?" I ask.

The Carvress nods. "Our people simply call me the Carvress of Sand Otter Island. But that is not my name." Her eyes lift to the stars, blinking quickly like she's holding communion. "My name is in the old language." She lowers her head, a strong, chiseled expression. "And I don't share it easily."

"Oh." I stand beside her awkwardly, dwarfed by her height and radiating power. I can't sense her Atmosphere. She's an unknown planet. Her orbit, her gravity is alien. She doesn't live by the same rules as the rest of us. I go to pull my sleeves over my arms and stop myself. "Did you seek me, Carvress?" I ask, eyes on the river moving like rippling rolls of fine fabric under this light. It looks solid, like you could walk on it.

I want to ask her what she's made of but that seems rude. A Char would just know these things like how to talk to a Carvress. The wooden woman's voice is charcoal dark, her skin bleached light. "I sensed that you wished to speak to me." She swivels slightly, looking down on me but not in a condescending way. We are the two halves of the Char-Shen equation, though I'm not sure even the greatest mathematical brain could balance us.

I sway with the breeze, my hip accidentally grazing the Carvress's hand. It's as hard as marble. "I don't want to be shut out of the planning." A rustle under leaves. A need pushing its way up and out into the open. "I… I want to become a Char. Have a wooden part. Is it allowed?" My voice is high and intense but I don't care. This feels right. My friend, my spirit, tilts his head to the side, smiles. "Is it even possible?" Holding my arm out, I imagine it wooden, strong. Planed and clear of scars. "I need to start over. Can I start over?" *Can I start over?*

The Carvress laughs like sandpaper brushed along the most delicate fibers. "That is a lot of questions." She pinches my elbow gently. "Are you sure you want to know the answers?"

Eagerly, I nod. "I need to know if there's a place for me here." *Make it so. Make it so. Make it so.*

She smiles, showing pale wooden teeth, perfectly carved. "If you want to be Char, it can be done." She bends like a crane dipping its beak to the riverbed and selects a round stone, casting it across the water so it hops along the surface.

Hope jumps just like the stone. "I can start over?" I run my palms over my bumpy skin. Be new. Not like I was before, but not clawed and marked as I am now. My mind races futureward, reaching for the thin clouds that mar the sky. "This could be knotted oak or ringed bamboo?" The excitement in my voice is too much and I tell myself to calm down.

Her head swings side to side, foreboding, plaits thwacking her shoulders like drumsticks. "You cannot *start over*. You will not be reborn or renewed. That is not how it works, Keeper Lye Li." She takes my scarred arm and taps her fingers over the lines. She counts them in her head. *So many. So many.* The tally of my sins. "These are part of you. If you choose to become a Char—and it does call for you, I hear it—these," she lifts my arm under my nose, "will come with you."

She releases my arm and it falls limply to my side, brushed by rough Keeper robes. I pick up a large, rough-cornered stone, toss it into the water. It sinks with one sorrowful plop. The river will batter it over and over until it's polished smooth. I have certainly been battered, but I am far from polished. *Why can't that be me?*

I sigh, limbs hanging from my shoulders by tough threads of disappointment.

"I'm sorry to have disappointed you," the Carvress of Sand Otter Island says, though she doesn't sound sorry at all. Another stone pings across the river to land on the opposite bank. She gives a satisfied humph. "But you made those marks for a reason. They're a reminder of your responsibility, no? Your part in all of this?" She sweeps an elegant arc through the humid air.

I can't speak, just nod.

She grabs my wrist, squeezing it hard, passion to her voice. "We all have our part. It cannot be erased. You should not want it to be erased."

I wish it wasn't so, but she is right.

A cloud of moon-sun birds puff across the sky, blocking the sliced moon as they change their color. They shriek and bash against each other, disoriented. I squint at the flashes of white changing to black puncturing the night.

The Carvress observes the flock, mouth grim.

"We shall accept your scars, Keeper Lye Li Koh." All my names sitting together in unease. *Can I add Char to the front?* "You must do the same."

She taps my fist and my palm opens to the pour of loose stones. She selects one and holds it up for me to take. "I'm trying," I whisper as I take it. She coasts up the riverbank and onto the silent battlefield.

"It's all about the shape of the stone. Smooth and flat like a disc of dumpling dough," she throws to me warmly in her wood shavings voice. "Practice."

The birds swirl and separate, fighting for a direction. *Accept.* The word feels like a weapon in my hand. One I must turn on myself.

# 10
## ASH KI

It is wrong to spy.

My leg slips on the branch and leaves flutter to the ground. I grip it tighter, holding my breath as Joka, Sun, and Ki Anah enter Luna's tent. Ki Anah taps her chest lightly and the brothers crowd around, pushing her inside.

Loud voices. "Luna!"

"Little Luna."

On the roof of the tent, moon-sun birds stretch their wings and peck each other, irritated. Their white feathers turn dark when the tent flap flies open and light pours onto the grass. Ki Anah tugs Luna's arm while the brothers provide a moving barricade, forcing her out.

"Luna, come out of there. It smells like hundred-year-old duck egg. I can't stand it!" Her hand is dramatically over her nose as she pulls a listless Luna toward the trees.

My heart aches. My heart wants to take her place. Because I know this will be awful. This will be devastating.

All I can do is watch.

They move slowly. Breath hitching. Eyes catching each other, daring someone to speak. Sun opens his mouth and closes it. A swinging door to the truth. Joka runs a hand through his hair and stares through the thick trunks. I sense their desperate, throat-drying fear of this conversation. I feel it too. Selfishly, I want Luna to feel it. I want to witness some kind of change in her. But I also don't want her to suffer. My expression rearranges several times. Smiles are experimented with and discarded. My limbs shake with the unfairness of what's to come.

Ki Anah releases Luna and inhales slowly, her regard coasting from child to child. "Though your *friend* Ash explained it, I don't understand why you are here. The last we heard, you were cast out of the army." She puts her hands on her hips. "Explain, daughter, why are you here and what is wrong with you?"

Joka steps forward, hand out. "Mama," he starts.

I can't see her lips tremble, but they couldn't be doing anything else. "I… I want to see Ben Ni. Where is he working? You said he was here… He *is* here, isn't he?" Ki Anah's gaze shifts, counting her children and missing one.

"Mama, I'm sorry. Ben Ni, he is... here… but…" Luna bows very low.

Ki Anah's body tenses. "Sorry for what? I don't understand," she says again though I think she does understand. She just doesn't want to. There's a heavy question weighting her lips with words she doesn't want to utter. She trembles. Shakes her head. "Where is my…"

She stomps her foot and looks at the sky. Arms straight and straining. Comets plummeting.

*Luna—Be brave. Be strong. Be there. Allow grief in.*

Luna swallows and I notice a tremor as she reaches for her mother's shoulder. Her eyes are round, roughened with pain, and I lean forward in my perch. "Mama, Ben Ni is…"

The boys sniff. Ki Anah's cheeks redden and she nurses her pain. Holds it close, not ready to let it go until the words are finally spoken. "Tell me. Luna, please, where is my beautiful son? Where is Ben Ni?" She looks through the trees like he might appear, like the branches will rustle and he'll stride out to meet them. And I find myself wishing the same.

Behind me the moon-sun birds grow restless, half-black and half-white. Luna cups her mother's face in her small, pale hands and whispers something I can't quite hear. Ki Anah collapses with a broken cry like her ribs have shattered inwards and are piercing her lungs.

"No!" is all she says as her family huddles around her like a shield. "No. No. No," as she drags clumps of dirt into her hands and squelches mud between her fingers.

Luna holds her mother longer than her brothers. They sit in the mud while Joka and Sun guard. I hear weeping and hope some of the tears are Luna's but it's hard to tell. Luna strokes her mother's hair, staining Ki Anah's skin tamarind brown.

Sun crouches down. "He was a hero, Mama. He fought bravely, saving many Char lives." Their collective pain billows outward like scalding steam. I feel it. I hold it. I try to find Luna in it.

She sniffs and heaves. "He was my baby."

Luna pats her mother's back rhythmically, a solitary timer. "He was... he was the best of us."

The boys hang their heads as Ki Anah unfolds from the forest floor and rises. She reaches for her sons, grasping their heads in her hands and bringing them down to press her lips to their foreheads. It is a sweet, painful moment to watch.

Luna remains on the ground, staring at her handprints. "I couldn't save him," she whispers to the dirt.

Ki Anah grips her daughter's shoulder. "Get up, daughter," she orders sternly, putting on her mother coat and fastening it tightly at her waist. The Yan siblings stand in line as she points at them. "Ben Ni was many things—dreamy, intelligent, and so, so kind. And I love him. I will always love him." Her voice cracks on the word *always*. "I will miss him. But he was not the best of you. There is no best or better." Her words soften and she pounds her chest. "Please. You must take me to see him."

Luna turns away. I want to hear her cry. I want to know that this broke her open. A horrible but necessary wish.

Sun and Joka volunteer to take her when Luna can barely shake her head no.

She raises her hand. "Please, give me a moment."

"Of course, Little Luna." They bow and head toward the makeshift morgue. Hemming their mother in and, I suspect, holding her up.

A rakka possum curls its long furry tail over my ear and I slap it away. It crawls over my shoulder and scurries to Luna's feet. It rubs its head against her shins, and she kicks at it. "Shoo," she mumbles with small emotion. "I don't want you. Go away." It continues to curl around her legs like a cat, a scattered rumbling like the last rice in the cannister coming from its soft chest. She looks to the sky and screams, "I don't want this!" Like she can banish the grief from her body.

The moon-sun birds lift suddenly from the tent. Flapping anxious and confused. Changing colors as they collide. Light to dark. Dark to light. The squawking and scratching pulls men from their beds. Char soldiers watch the cosmos with wide, sleepy eyes. While I watch Luna. Her heart and mind fighting. Her bewilderment and irritation clear. She steps backward until she hits a tree, sliding down into the mud.

Moon-sun birds swirl overhead, hitting branches and falling, getting back up and starting again. The poor creatures are slaves to Luna's storm of confusion. She takes a deep breath, holds it, and I feel her closing over like cooling lava. "You can come down now, Ash." My feet hit the ground as she's talking. I reach for her desperately like I can somehow stop what's about to happen. Jam the door before it slams.

She allows me to touch her arm. It's warm and soft and heart shattering. "I feel you, you know," Luna murmurs. "Ever since we joined our powers, I feel you more strongly than any other creature."

I slide down beside her. "You think me a creature?"

She half laughs. "No, not really. If anyone's a creature it's me." Turning to me, her face splits with immense pain and the need to run from it. "Right?"

I tilt my head and smile. "Never." She watches my mouth like the upward movement of my lips is completely foreign. I risk touching her face, my hand tingling with agony at the feel of her skin. Not because she's hurting me but because I'm terrified this is all I'll get. "I feel you too, Luna. Losing Ben Ni was…" She straightens and stands suddenly. Ripping my heart with the quick sweep of her hand. But not my hope. I saw the emotion in her. I *felt* it. She can't hide it from me.

The moon-sun birds come together, coordinate, and fly over the crater edge. "They were annoying me," she says bluntly. "Time to fly home."

Our eyes meet. Hers blinking away potential tears. Mine trying to capture her and keep her close. She's a frozen waterfall that won't be fulfilled until it thaws. Luna knows it. She just can't accept it.

"I need to find Mama." Luna forces her voice flat like she's smoothing the bubbles from a rice paper roll. Then she pushes. Stamps down to crush herself. "The body will upset her." Her eyes tighten and she wipes her palms on her tunic.

*I feel you, Luna. And if you feel me, you know I see a person who cannot do this forever.*

THE FINGER of blame for why Luna continues to hide from her grief moves in a circle, trying to find a target. I walk, scraping the side of the camp. The finger lands on two souls, walking back to their tent, shoulders slumped. Sadness easy to identify. *In them.* So why have they allowed their sister to deny her feelings for so long?

Thumping the earth behind them, I don't get a single word out before they spin around, Sun with his knife, Joka tense with his arms crossed over his face.

Gruffly, Sun whispers, aware of sleeping soldiers, "What do you want, Ash?" The knife drops slowly. His eyes lower, gaze burrowing holes through the dirt at his feet.

Joka's intelligent face tilts as he observes me. I know I look like a desperate urchin. My fists clenched, chest swelling. I feel like I'm running out of time but no one else is aware of the countdown. The clock is dragging closer to the point of no return for Luna and no one cares. "He needs to know why." Luna's more refined brother strokes his chin, fingers slipping absentmindedly to his bamboo neck.

I don't wish to break in front of them so I take calming breaths as I look from one to the other. Sun's expression is forced stony as he asks, "Why what?"

Joka sighs loudly, like he thinks his brother is as dense as a rubber tree plant. "He needs to know why we haven't done anything to stop Luna."

Sun shifts awkwardly. "Oh, that."

I attempt to smile and can't—there are none that work in this circumstance. "I don't understand how you can let her go on like this. Why you don't help her." Anger bubbles inside me. Steam popping mud on the earths thin crust. "Doesn't it bother you to see her so... so cold? So disconnected?"

Sun frowns, anger riling in him also. "Of course it does!" He thumps his chest. "Every time she sweeps her fingers dismissing her animals or speaks in that flat tone, it's like she's slicing at my heart." He breathes faster. "It hurts in a way that steals my breath from my lungs. We've already lost a brother. You think we want to lose our sister also?"

His grief is a whipping tornado threatening to collect me and send me shooting into the sky only to come crashing back to earth. "No. But that's what I'm struggling to understand. We could lose her if we don't do something."

"We are doing what we're supposed to do. What *we* decided was best. We're her brothers, her family, and we know her much better than you." Sun towers over me, though his intimidation is lacking. I hold my ground.

Joka grabs his brother's arm. "Calm yourself, Sun. He cares for her. You know this. I think it's reasonable he should question our plan." The smell of cooked fish coated in fire ash permeates the tents. The last catch before the ceremony.

"So you have a plan?" I jump at it too eagerly.

Joka nods. "I hate to see her like this, we both do. Losing Ben Ni was hard enough, but the idea that we could lose Luna, it is…" He stares at the sky, voice cracking as he finishes. "It is too much to bear."

I turn slightly, knowing she's close by. "Then come with me. We could confront her together, force her to open her heart to her grief…"

Sun claps a heavy hand on my shoulder and pulls me to face him. "There is no forcing Luna to do anything. I told you she needs time."

"Our plan is to give it to her. To wait and be patient, no matter how hard it is for us. You are not Char so you don't understand the physical and mental stress her heart has put her under. She never had a chance to adapt to it properly and she didn't have the support she was supposed to have." Joka bleeds sorrow. "That I do regret."

"But what if she's too far gone? What if you give her so much time that she forgets who she is?" I challenge, unconvinced.

Joka looks upon me kindly. "She can never be gone. She will never forget. She is still Luna in there. She's just mending herself the best way she can. In small pieces that the rest of us can't see. But I know she will come back to us." He smiles. "Ash, you lack faith."

I want to believe him. They seem so sure. Perhaps this is a Char thing I can't quite grasp. But she's Shen now too. I huff. "Perhaps I do lack faith, but have you ever stopped to think maybe you have too much?"

Sun laughs, though it's short and hard. "There is no such thing."

# 11

## LYE LI

Ash has not returned to our tent. I flick back my light bed coverings and sit up. The words of the Carvress of Sand Otter Island have anchored in my head, preventing sleep. Acceptance is a hard fish to catch. Every time you think you've got it hooked, it dives down and takes more line with it. It's a push and pull that I'm unsure ever ends.

My brother's Atmosphere when he left was strange. Optimistic *and* anticipating disaster. Perhaps that is how we all feel right now, stuck in this muddy hole. I sweep wispy hairs from my forehead and shuffle to the edge of the cot, searching for my slippers. I shove them on and break into the cool night air. My eyes immediately go to Luna's tent, now hard to place amongst the others as the moon-sun birds have flown away. I breathe in long and hold it. It's a relief they're gone. What may take their place though is unknown. Animals seem to compliment her mood.

I wind between tents, tripping over ropes, in search of my brother. Reaching for a sense of Water. I grasp at the tail of a current. A stream coming to a dried end. I charge between two snugly pitched tents.

My legs snag on a tangle of ropes and I fall in the mud, emitting a very inelegant humph, my foot still caught in the ties. I pull on them hard, not realizing I've tugged the supporting pole out in my haste. One side of the tent begins to collapse, and panic comes from inside as the occupant's bedroom falls on top of them.

A man growls and groans. Another snores. "Sun! Wake up!" I roll my eyes from my tangled position. Caught like a crab in a net. Of course, it had to be the Yans' tent.

I struggle. Making it worse. "Hey!" Joka's fine voice peels around the corner followed by his disapproving, lantern-lit face. "What do you think you're doing?"

When he sees me, his expression flips to embarrassment. "Keeper." He bows. "I'm sorry, I didn't know it was you."

I force a smile. "Why would you?"

His smile is slim but genuine. "True." He places the paper lantern on the ground. The golden, tea stained picture on the side shows a jolly Char man standing in a boat with a long oar plunged in curling waves. I wish to read the characters written on the side, but Joka blocks my vision, giving me a quizzical look as he crouches to help me. I'm a rabbit in a trap and his hands are too close. I jerk away when his fingers brush my bare ankle. He looks up. Shadowed. "Sorry. I didn't mean to be untoward. It's the last thing I'd want to do, I mean, you being the Keeper…"

He's as flustered and uncomfortable as me and it brings a true smile, a quiet studying smile, to my lips. "Don't apologize. I'm the one who knocked down your tent." I gesture to the concave canvas. "Well, your half of it anyway."

Joka snorts loudly. "Can you believe my brother? It didn't even wake him." He shakes his head, pulling up a tent peg and finally releasing me.

We stand, and our sudden closeness feels very awkward, so we move to open ground. "Ash could sleep through anything too. I thought it was something all men could do."

Joka laughs, high and wheezy. "Not all men. Maybe just the ones who don't overthink. While I lie awake a long time before falling asleep, going through lists of possible outcomes for the next day. Thinking over the things that happened and deciding whether I should have done them differently. I also compile miles of other useless thoughts that stack up in here." He taps his head.

I giggle, covering my mouth. Not wanting it to escape. I understand exactly what he's talking about. "It must be nice not to be an overthinker." We're face to face in a small clearing and I'm aware of listening ears on the other side of these tents.

Joka transfers weight from foot to foot. "Perhaps, but then I've always thought thinking things through can be as valuable as quick action." I nod in agreement. He looks left to right and stoops down. "May I ask, Keeper Lye Li, what are you doing over here? Isn't your tent next to General Fah's?"

Squelch. Shift. Squelch. Shift. I'm copying his movements without meaning to. "I'm looking for Ash. He hasn't returned to our tent."

Joka taps his chin and his face falls. "Tonight has been a hard night for the Yan family. I'm guessing it has been difficult for your brother also."

My eyes drop too. "I'm so sorry for Ben Ni, Joka, he is… I mean, he was…" I can't finish. "How is your mother?" I ask, my mouth jumping ahead of my brain for a moment, because his words will be like a dagger to my stomach.

He motions for us to walk. "She is a Yan and she's handling it as best she can. She'll stay strong and be calm for the rest of us."

"You know she tried to kill my brother," I say, trying to sound light, force dancing feathers into my voice.

I expect him to joke, or laugh, but instead he disapproves. "She only has her own experience and that of her husband to guide her. It makes her mind less open to the possibility a Shen could be an ally. It's a shame really, because if she'd stopped and thought about it even for a moment, she would have realized he was not the enemy."

My fingers electrify. Clouds on notice for spring rain. "I appreciate your open mindedness. I wish everyone else could see my brother and me that way."

He runs a hand down that remarkable bamboo throat. "Char require action. They need physical proof; as in your loyalty as a true and solid thing. If you can show this, they will respect you eventually. Just don't give up."

We wander to the edge of the camp, where the trees meet the clearing. Palms slap each other angrily in the wind. Joka cracks his neck, matching the crackle of crowded trees. I halt and turn to him. "I wasn't planning to give up. And how are the rest of you?" I ask, though I know how Luna is.

He gives a sad smile. "It is… hard to accept. Though we must. For Luna, more so. She takes everything and holds it in her heart, even the hickory one, unwilling to release it yet. But I know she will come back to us. I know she would bleed dry for her family. And Sun, well, he is grieved, and he'll throw some punches before he's done grieving, but I think he will get to that place of acceptance quicker than the rest of us." He sits down with a huff.

"The benefit of not being an overthinker perhaps," I suggest.

He shrugs his narrow shoulders. "Perhaps… Everything is unknown. There's so much yet to plan. It feels like grief may have to wait."

He glances upward at the navy, silk curtain sky, moth eaten by stars. I follow his gaze, addressing air instead of each other makes this conversation easier. "Grief doesn't wait for anyone," I whisper to the white lights. They scream bright and truthful. They see everything, including things we don't want them to see.

Joka clasps his hands, a mustering of sorts going on beneath the surface. "Lye, I think you're terribly brave switching sides like you have. The men will see that. I promise."

Color rises in my cheeks. I don't feel brave. Most of the time I feel like a fish flopping on land. Pulling useless, useless air into my lungs. "I just need to get the general to respect my opinion more. Then I could really help your cause."

Joka purses his lips and thinks for a moment. "Fah is a good man but a traditional one. If you can find a way to communicate your ideas without damaging his male ego then I suggest you try it." He turns to me then, dark eyes flooded with sincerity. "You're not in this for the glory," he states, like he knows me and my heart's intention. And though it sparks a little irritation that he should be so presumptuous, he's right. I nod.

"I have no interest in accolades or credit. I just want to set things right."

"Tell him so. Tell him he will get all the credit if your plans go well, and if they fail, you'll assume the blame. He can't argue with that." Joka taps his chin twice. "I know he won't."

He stands, twists his torso, stretching. "I best fix my tent before the night is over." Our heads swivel in the direction of a dawn sun approaching and the noise of breaking branches. A huffing, puffing Ash is headed our way.

"Thank you for your counsel, Joka." I bow.

"My pleasure, Lye Li."

As my brother crashes toward me, I start to panic. I allowed myself to forget. My feet tip lightly toward the general's tent, hiding from Ash's view. In all the excitement of Carvresses and the pain of Luna's mother arriving, the chancellor has been allowed to live. Like a snake, he's managed to press to the side while other events took place, buying hours of time. Perhaps days. I should have pushed harder. I should have insisted they execute him the moment my brother left camp.

Every time I face Ash, lies dig deeper. Rotting roots spread. He will figure it out… and soon.

# 12

## ASH KI

I spent the night tracing the crater edge. Running my hands over jagged rock, feeling it grate the skin of my palms. The coldness and roughness just about right for how Luna is to me now.

Blinking my tired eyes, I drag my heavy feet to camp. Char black gathers around the general's tent. A small but formidable woman in their center. I tilt my head and speed up. She's not as Luna described. I expected Ki Anah Yan to be a soft woman who used knives to chop vegetables, not to press to my throat. Touching the scratch running across my jugular, I shake my head. Yan women are always a surprise. That much is sure.

The sun just breaks free of its yolky home and spreads blood crimson over the sky. It warms and warns.

I hover at the edge of the circle of Char men who are chanting low. Fists pumping in a suppressed kind of way. I find my sister at the front next to the general, looking horrified. Her pallor like an unwashed sheet. I push through the men, but someone catches my arm and pulls. Fluffy duck down moves through me. Luna. Her honey eyes are softer by the slightest degree and when she whispers my name, I grab the sound. Clutching it in my hand, feeling it dig into my skin.

"Ash. It's all right. Lye is in no danger." But my sister looks like someone just slapped her and the chanting, though quiet, is dark as death. "This is our way."

The general waves and the men part. I wait for an announcement. For Lye to be struck or bound or something, because the air is tensioned like the quiet before a mobbing. But the Char leave her behind. Her expression is still like she's about to be hung, but she's left by the tent alone while soldiers turn their backs to her. Ki Anah marches proudly through the middle, head down, hands clasped. Once she has passed, men close around her protectively and follow.

"What's happening?" I ask, receiving multiple disapproving stares. Luna sifts through the crowd to fall in with her mother. They're heading to the chancellor's tent.

Lye is sinking to the ground, torn by something I don't know about. But I decide to trail the procession, pushing to the front, eyes questioning. Joka takes pity on me and whispers, "Mama wishes to face her son's murderer. It's Char tradition to allow this before execution."

I didn't realize his execution had been ordered, but I'm glad for it.

Solemnly, men pull aside the tent flaps and Ki Anah stomps inside. They fall shut and she's alone with *him*. I turn to her children. "Is this safe? Should she be left alone with that monster?"

Sun snorts. "Mama can handle herself."

Luna's eyes show amber chips of worry. It's fleetingly promising to see the change in her stony exterior. But as soon as our eyes connect, I witness a winding back. A hardening. "We're here should she need us." Her fingers flick outward. Animals probably pause in their daily scratch, ears cocked, ready to act.

The Char are statues. Hands clasped in front while the low chanting continues. I don't understand the purpose of this. The black-toothed bureaucrat will only spit poison and hate at her. I want to charge in and cut him open before he can speak a word. But Char tradition must be respected. I bow my head and wait.

Joka mutters to his brother. "What do you think, Sun?"

Sun spits and sniffs, swiping at his nose aggressively. "Not a chance."

A stricken Lye leans against canvas that can almost support her slight weight. Almost. She stumbles and ends up on the ground. She pulls at her short tufts of hair, wishing for the long curtain she used to hide behind. I squint at her dramatics. "So… this has nothing to do with my sister?"

Joka gives me a curious look. "No. Not at all. Although…"

I step closer. "Although what?"

He bends back, making space for me like a sail billowing in a sharp wind because I'm invading his space. My distress building and falling outward making me forget my place I feel Luna's mood jump. Her powers snapping their teeth but being restrained. For now.

"Lye was against waiting a second longer. She was trying to convince the general it was best to execute the chancellor immediately and seemed incensed at this tradition."

My mouth sets grim and hard. *Why would Lye care when it was done?* When she's worked so hard for acceptance, it makes no sense for her to fight against Char tradition.

My fingers grow cool. Sheet ice cracking over a pond. Thin and treacherous. Razorblade sharp.

WE HEAR nothing. There's a Char with wooden ears in the crowd of soldiers and I search his face for signs. His eyebrows rise in surprise while his eyes are hollows of sadness. Once he notices me staring, they fall to a neutral position.

It's a long time before Ki Anah emerges. She lingers in the entrance for many seconds. Grains of sand that seem to slide down the neck of the hourglass at half rate. She composes herself, forcing her words, her body to be straight and tall. The men are waiting for something. I hold my breath, wondering what is next.

The chanting ceases and it's silent except for the rush of the river and the stray squawk of birds. Luna's eyes turn skyward, and the birds dive out of sight as if they've been scolded.

Slowly, Ki Anah untucks her shirt, revealing the curve of a wooden hip. She reaches into her pocket and withdraws a piece of charcoal, scratching a black mark against the cherrywood.

Luna's trying to paint satisfied across her face when really it reads half empty. Joka and Sun are pleased. The other men salute and disperse. I look to Luna and she explains, "Mama isn't going to show the chancellor mercy."

I cross my arms. Now that I understand the purpose of Ki Anah's visit I am relieved at the outcome. "As well she shouldn't."

Ki Anah, quietly trapped in her grief, is too proud to cry and too hurt to speak. She grasps each one of her children by the face and brings their foreheads down to her lips. Except Luna, who she bends down to meet. Their eyes connect and Ki Anah's sadness seems to double. I shift awkwardly, stuck in this family moment when I should have left with the others.

I'm about to leave when the small woman with wooden hips grabs my face. I freeze, wondering if she will kiss me too. She tilts my head back and forth, rubs her thumbs under my eyes, and stares hard. She clucks her tongue and frowns, then says something that shakes the earth beneath my feet. Cracks growing. Water rising. Everything changes and all for the worse. She taps my forehead sharply with her finger, branding me. Marking me rotten by association.

"You and *that man* are kin."

Kin.

*Kin?*

*It's not poss...* I can't even finish the words in my own head.

Lye approaches me with an apology in hand. She looks like she just set the devil free. She did. She has. She lied to me. My mind folds back time. For how long? Lies are everywhere. Scattered on the floor. Floating past us as we played in the marsh. They coat every grain of rice she served me. They nestle inside every scar.

I step away from the Yans, from what a family should be, and march right to my sister.

My lying sister.

# 13
## LYE LI

My worst fear, once a trapped bird, desperate to fly, wings shredded, feathers long and greasy and hungry for air. An ugly, ugly bird. Made uglier by me. Is finally free.

I bite down on every element and force myself to be a powerless, dead thing in his grasp as he half drags me to a tent. I know he would never hurt me. So I must do my best not to hurt him. At least not more than I already have.

He points to a stool. "Lye, sit."

I sit.

He paces, hands tugging at his hair. Big dark breaths of black polluted water pulling in and pushing out of his Atmosphere. His anger fills the space; an uncontrollable flood, wiping out everything in its path. Breaking thirty-foot trees in half like matchsticks. And I'm drowning in it. I deserve to drown in it. I kick my legs at half strength.

"Ash," I whisper. "Ash," I plead. "Brother." The word stops him dead. Pools of water turn to quicksand at his feet. He'll sink with me if I don't find a way through.

"Tell me he's some distant relative. Tell me he's not who I think he is." *Desperately.* Desperately, he clings to these phantom buoys. When he knows.

He knows. He knows. He knows.

*Hide me from this shame. Help me say what I need to say.* I search for Ben Ni in the corners, but he won't help me here. Feeling deserted, I am stranded on an island inhabited only by lies. My tongue dry, I whisper the truth. "He is who you think he is."

"The brother we lost? The chancellor is that brother. Our brother?" He wants it to be false, *needs* it to be, but I don't have another lie left. My head falls. He shakes his head. "But he died." His voice shrinks to a tattoo dot, still leaving a mark.

I still see love for me in his eyes. That's Ash—a heart so big it will probably kill him. "He was a royal seed child."

Ash's face turns as gray as his namesake. Feet churning the dirt in their agitation. "But our mother never said anything. She never said eldest brother was only a half-brother."

I rise, wanting to approach him, but he puts a palm up to stop me.

"The emperor swanned in on horseback and picked the youngest and prettiest to come to his bed." My stomach turns as I picture our mother, eyes cast low, barely able to breathe in her tight silk bindings. Trying so hard not to be noticed. No one *wants* to be chosen. "Mother was 'chosen'." Ash winces. "But you know it was no honor to be forced to lay with the emperor. It was her shame and his folly." I remember when the old emperor died. How mother lit only one incense stick for him when everyone else in our village wasted ten.

His mouth twists at the thought and he gestures between us. "But we're not…"

"No. We are children of her marriage." It is minor consolation.

He sighs small relief, but his Atmosphere continues to swell close to breaking. It's a lot of information for him to take in. "That's why Father left." This is not a question. It's a realization. One of many to come as my web starts to buckle and snap. I nod.

I stare up at my stormfront of a brother, eyes dancing on waves of very new feelings. One of which is distrust toward me and it breaks my waterlogged heart. "Ash. There's so much to tell you, but we don't have time for it all now. One thing we surely both believe is the chancellor must be executed. He's too dangerous to live. He's a twisted, evil man." The tide retreats. Ash is listening but not trusting.

He throws his hands in the air, casting dark clouds around the room. "I don't know what I believe. You've been lying to me my whole life. I don't know how I'm supposed to come to terms with that, Lye." Ash's shoulders slump, eyes softening to gray-green.

His words erode me, eat at my conscience. He's right. Lying this long became second nature and I'd forgotten the truth. Mother asked me to protect Ash when he was younger, but I could have told him when he was grown.

"I'm sorry. I didn't want you to suffer. I didn't want you to be hurt when you realized your brother was a monster." *And I didn't want him to hurt you.*

"What I don't understand is how I forgot him. We are not so far apart in age that you would remember him and I would not…"

This is where the awful heart of our deception breaks open like a meat flower. Coaxing the tiny petal bird to its stamen, snapping shut over feathers and fear. "You did remember him. You would ask where he was all the time. You l-loved him," I stammer. "Though I don't know why. He showed you very little affection. Shaking you from his leg like a starved, stray pup."

Ash holds his head, hands full of golden-brown hair. He pulls like he's trying to tear memories from his brain. "I don't know what you're talking about. I don't remember him at all." He breathes anger like air, flame-like in its intensity. His Water element creates steam in him that scalds just as painfully as a fire. "Lye." He looks up, stares with vast ocean eyes. "What did you do to me?" Ribs part with ice. He's trying to calm himself but it's not working very well. His Element is overtaking.

My mouth quivers. These lies seemed so small compared to the others. I did it to protect him. I had to. "Remember, I was young too, Ash. The dutiful daughter, I did what mother asked me to do. To protect you." Words tumble like stones, hitting the ground hard. They don't make for a believable sculpture.

"*Sister*." The word sounds like a plea. "The truth. What did you do to me?"

There are things a Shen can do. Bad things. Manipulative things. And the Keeper can do more than most. My neck can barely support my head. "I used my powers to make you forget him."

His jaw tenses. "That's impossible! You don't have that kind of control."

"You're right, I cannot use my blood powers to influence men. No one can. But a child's heart and mind are more… malleable." I don't want to say this, and I don't like when he looks at me like that. Horrified. Unrecognizing. He waits, eyes almost shut, like he's not sure he wants to hear it either. "Every time you asked after our brother, I used my powers to distract and suppress. You'd start talking about him and I would make you smile. I would lift your lips against your will and force a false happiness into your Atmosphere, encouraging you to put all your effort into laughter and smiling and in trying to make others do the same. After a while, that effort forced the memories of our brother out of your mind. They just fell away."

He runs his fingers over his lips like they burn to touch.

I creep slowly toward my brother. He pulses waves of hope and devastation, crashing over each other with no break in between. I reach for him as he whispers something I can't quite hear.

"What did you say?" I ask, placing a hand on his shoulder.

He swings around, a fury I've never seen raging like burning oil on water. "You stole from me. You changed me. All for protection? How could you do it, Lye?" He drags in a heated breath. "And what's worse is you meant to kill him before I could learn the truth. Not because you wanted to protect *me*." His fist pumps the air. "You did that to protect yourself."

I open my mouth to defend the indefensible, but it's filled with water. It beats down on me over and over and over. Waves crashing upon my head and pounding my body into the sand. Turning and twirling until I don't know which way is up. My breath bubbles and my lungs burn. I gasp for air but there is none. Just saltwater and my own shame.

THE AIR tastes like acid clouds. I draw it in, grateful for anything resembling oxygen. Ash leans over me, concerned but distant. A small ocean between us. "Will she be all right?" Joka's voice seems far away even though he's just in the tent doorway. It's a rescue rope and I grab it, pulling myself to shore. He must have come when he heard Ash shouting.

"She'll be fine." His voice is still laced with anger but it's cooling.

I sit up. "What happened?" I ask, elbows digging into the dirt of the floor. The canvas flap folds over and it's darker again.

Ash offers his hand and then stops himself. Holding back. "My anger overpowered you." He's surprised, as am I. "I'm sorry, sister. I didn't mean to hurt you."

I wave his apology away. "It's no less than I deserve."

He kneels beside me. "You didn't deserve that." He floats closer, bobbing just out of reach, but I know he'll get to a place of forgiveness, one day. "I could have killed you." His smile. I ache for his smile. Even if I had a hand in shaping it, that smile was always a natural part of his personality. I need to assure him it's still his, but I don't know how.

I cross my legs and frown. "I did mean to kill him before you found out. But only because I was absolutely sure it would do you no good to know."

He purses his lips, eyes flicking to the door. To the unmixing world of Char and Shen on the other side of the canvas. "You don't get to decide what is good or not good for me, Lye. And just because…" he starts, eyes lifting to a faraway thought I fear has something to do with salvation.

"Just because what?" I ask, stepping toward a heart that's drifting away from me with the tide.

He runs a hand over his jaw, looks to the side and his mouth quirks a fraction like a foot lifting from a prickle in the dirt. "Never mind."

He leaves before I can make it worse. Before I run desperately into the sea, splashing and clawing at the water with useless arms. There is no salvation. There is only darkness trying to slither around justice like a worm.

It's from my position on the dirt floor that the general finds me. He claps his heels together and announces the chancellor will be executed after the burial ceremony.

# 14

## ASH KI

The chancellor must attend the burial ceremony from the riverbank. A post has been driven down in the harder earth and he'll be shackled and made to watch the Char soldiers put to rest. Then he will have his throat cut.

My brother.

The words are nonsense and yet they pull all these pieces together I didn't know were missing. It explains my father's disappearance. This slow and deliberate fading that happened from the time I was around three. He was there, right by me and then he was a step further back, then two steps further back. Slowly, he put distance between us until we didn't even notice he was no longer in the room. He just evaporated like steam from a kettle.

It also explains the rise of the chancellor from palace servant to advisor, his royal blood and his blood connection to the Keeper elevated him. I feel like a fool.

I curse and spit on the ground. Lye is right about one thing—my brother's done a great deal of wrong. I didn't need to spend much time with him to understand there's something black and twisted in his chest.

I stare at the humble post that will soon be sprayed with my brother's blood. *Is he beyond help? Can that black, twisted thing be scraped clean and straightened?* I don't know.

Luna helps her brothers move the dead to the edge of the river. Expressionless, sweat sticking her hair to her forehead. Her eyes hard in the center but warming at the edges. I believe someone can do horrible things and come back from darkness. My hopeful heart needs this to be true.

Char grasp the black-clad bodies by head and ankles and stack them like logs. But I've learned there's more to them than rough and unrefined edges. They have deep traditions and reasons behind their actions. Like leaving the villages the Shen burned to the ground untouched. It wasn't cowardice or spooky superstition as my Shen teachers taught. Once burned, a Char is indistinguishable from the wood the village is made from. They cannot rebuild lest they build over a Char's body. They let the sea claim the village so the Char spirit can rest without disturbance.

I wipe my hands on my trousers and wish I had some eucalyptus oil for my nose. The dead have waited too long to be buried. As I'm about to walk over to help them, General Fah's voice grabs me and turns me around. He looks uncomfortable, standing at attention in full uniform. I raise an eyebrow. My opinion of him teeters on thin rock battered by waves. It could easily tip into the water and be swept away.

He clears his throat and says, "Ash Ki Koh." He bows and I return the gesture.

"General."

His sword bangs at his side. "I was wondering what Shen do with their dead? Are there specific rituals that must be recognized in order for your warriors to be at peace?"

My chin tucks in, shocked, and my lips curl into an awkward smile. A question resides in the corners of that smile: Is it my own or are my sister's fingers pinching the edges of my lips? The general is taken aback by my grin but holds his ground. "I am surprised you care to put Shen soldiers to rest."

Now he raises his eyebrows. I try to wipe the smile from my face but it's edging into something different, a higher respect. For him and the Char people. My lungs fill with guilty air. I know the Shen would never even ask this question, let alone try to respect the Char traditions, and it brings me shame.

"Char honor their enemies. We all fought hard and bloody. But the battle is over. Shen dead deserve peace as much as the Char."

I stare at him for a long time, trying to figure out the man who pushed Luna to break me out of prison. To the man who takes counsel from the Keeper and now asks me for the burial rites of Shen soldiers. He has grown and changed a great deal in the time I've known him. It impresses me, as not many have such capacity. It also gives me faith.

The general's expression becomes impatient and he coughs, startling me. "For a Shen to be at peace, they must return to their element," I answer.

Luna places a body on the pile and looks up with a strange expression. I try to hold her eyes and am surprised when she doesn't look away. The general follows my gaze and groans quietly. "What does that entail exactly?"

Her steps are evenly spaced. The sun reddening the top of her light brown hair. "Fire and Air Shen are cremated." I gesture with my hands. Eyes fixed on Luna. "That may sound strange, but Fire Shen return to flame while Air Shen return to the sky in smoke. Water Shen are put to water same as the Char. Earth Shen are buried."

Luna slips in beside the general, folding her hands behind her back, watching me with that strange push and pull. Detached and tied to me. Always fighting. "And what of Blood Shen? What must be done for them to achieve peace?" Luna asks. A question with multiple meanings.

I await a reaction as I answer, "They are left." She blinks and whatever I thought I saw freezes over. But I *feel* small fear. Like she doesn't really want clarification but must know.

"Left?" they both query.

My eyes fall to my feet. "To the animals."

"Oh," Luna whispers. "I suppose that makes sense. It is good news actually. I could have a water burial and also be left to the animals." I hate the way her voice sounds as she talks through her own death like she's talking about the shape of the moon. The color of the sky. "The fish and crabs would soon take care of me."

The general nods sharply. "Thank you for your assistance. I'll make sure Shen traditions are followed."

I clasp my hands together and bow low. "You impress me, General," I confess. "The Char impress me. It means a great deal that you would respect our dead in this way."

He rolls his eyes and frowns. "We may be different, Shen and Char. But in death, we're all just souls torn from flesh and bone, searching for a final resting place."

Gruesome but accurate.

He marches away a little taller. His behavior is encouraging for what I have planned.

Luna lifts her arm to touch me in a disjointed, puppet-like way. "Today we will both bury our brothers." She pats my arm awkwardly and I stare down at her efforts, not knowing whether I should be happy or sad at the strained place we find ourselves in. But then she whispers, "I feel you, Ash. And I am sorry."

I quirk my lip. Tears on my tongue. "Thank you, Char Luna Yan." I feel like the man who's studied a rare bird from afar for years and finally, one lands on his arm. I will do just about anything not to scare it away.

Bowing quickly, she re-joins her family, leaving a trail of the lightest snow in her wake. She helps her mother tighten her bun, hairpins between her pearly teeth. The forest is quiet. As if every species from bird to beetle has been warned that today is a solemn day. They probably *were* warned.

# 15
## LYE LI

*You're there. Sandwiched between other brave men. Entombed in darkness. Waiting to go home. Once it is done. Will you leave me, Ben Ni?*

Shoulders rounded. Eyes down. Power controlled.

Bodies stacked like egg rolls ready for frying. I wince, disgusted at the places my brain takes me.

I clear my throat. "General, may I speak with you?" Nodding his walnut jaw, he brushes dirt from his shoulders, the gold trim on his uniform grimy and tarnished. "You've been so generous allowing me to contribute to the Char cause. I want to do more," I start. The pretense of meek and mild is hard to maintain. His eyebrows stay in their neutral position. "I mean, what I want to say is, I'd like to further prove my loyalty to the men."

His jaw works slowly, the curled carvings reminding me of pipe smoke. A thought long held on his tongue is finally released. "You know, I was thinking the same thing, Keeper. Having you as an ally presents all manner of new possibilities, and perhaps we haven't been utilizing your strengths in the best way."

I frown, wondering what he means by "best way." The Carvresses sit calmly by the bodies like sentinels at the river edge, solemn expressions on wooden faces. One Carvress, who appears senior, keeps her palm pressed against a wrapped body. The Carvress next to her has her hand on the senior one, and so on down the line, so they're all connected like a chain. Soldiers bow low as they pass.

I spit out the dark request I've been hoarding. "Let me execute the chancellor." Fah's frown deepens. Thick bark swathing his thoughts. "He is a powerful water Shen. I don't want a Char soldier to risk harm by performing the task. Allow me to face the danger alone."

He strokes his chin. "You may perform the execution. But let's not pretend you're doing *me* a favor, Keeper."

I bow, clasp my hands in front of me. "If it would help…" I remember Joka's advice. "You can say I resisted, and you ordered me to perform the execution. It will show the men who's truly in charge."

A tight smile. Followed by another deep frown that frightens me, lines of determination furrowing his brow. "That seems appropriate. If you truly wish to prove yourself, I have thought of another far more impactful way." He points to a soldier. "Not there. You must leave space between the bodies so they will burn." I'd prefer to slink away now. I got my wish and I don't want to hear his. I sidestep, but he catches me in his gaze.

In his eyes I see good purpose mixed with misguided ideas followed by a genuine want to do the right thing. *Whatever that may be.* I salute. "Anything, General."

"Luna Yan is…" he starts, and I shake my head vehemently, instantly understanding his intent. *Not anything.* He wishes me to make more Lunas, more Char-Shen hybrids. Why is it men look straight past the cost to the perceived benefit?

"You don't understand what you ask." How could I have switched sides only to end up in the same place with the same terrible problem?

"But she is a Char with Shen powers. More like her could help us win this war."

*No. No. No.* I plead with him without speaking and his hard jaw seems to impossibly soften. He begins to back pedal. "I would never force you against your will, Lye." He uses my name carefully, like he's reading it off an invaluable scroll. "I'm not him." His eyes land on the chancellor briefly and with disgust. "I simply ask that you think about it." When I open my mouth to say, *There is nothing to think about,* he places a hand in my face. "Really think about it... please."

I nod slowly, giving him hope I shouldn't, because it is the worst idea. I will never do it. Not even if he did try to force me.

BLACK CHAR and blue Water Shen are heaped together. Red of Fire and white of Air dot the riverbank, surrounded by firewood. Earth brown fades into black volcanic soil as Char soldiers cut and shape graves. As the sun goes down, the crater will burn. As the sun goes down, Char and Shen will reach their resting places at the same time. A tragically historical moment. One I wish *he* would not live to see.

The chancellor's skinny body kneels proudly by the river. A dirty blue smear on the grass wearing a look of scorn. He watches Char dig graves for the Earth Shen, and I hear his disdainful snort. He would never waste time burying Char and would leave them where they died. With every extra minute we let him live, he proves himself less worthy of life.

The air has cooled. A dusty mist settling over the treetops like a mosquito net. The trees move in the breeze and the mist veil rises and settles. A delicate dance between the elements.

I stand beside General Fah. His black uniform tucked tightly around a thinning form. Food is rationed as they feed Shen prisoners as well as themselves. A leather handled knife sits warmly in my hands. It speaks to me, whispering doubt in my ear. *You died so I would not do what I am about to do. Can I oppose what you fought for? Died for?*

My airy companion, Ben Ni sets his jaw, giving me nothing. He was a beautiful, forgiving soul, but also naïve. His experience of family was so different to my own. I look to the sky and check myself, staring down at the water to where his body and so many others will be committed. He says he forgives me.

A bite in my heart. A small press and hiccup. I wish. I wish. I wish.

I wish the bridge between dream and reality could be crossed.

Char begin to drop bodies in the water. They shout, loud and blunt. Almost a bark, though so full of pain and heartbreak it could also be a howl. One harsh, throat-scraping shout per body. The number of wrapped-in-black soldiers is high. Their voices will grow hoarse by the end of this day.

Ash stands closer to the Yan family and other soldiers who have accepted him into their ranks. Sun turns toward my brother and gives him a nod of camaraderie, and the reason for the sudden change in the Char's attitude to him becomes clear.

My brother uses people to put distance between us. I think he'd like to put an entire ocean. His confusion and feelings of betrayal are unbroken waves. Cresting and dying. Cresting and dying. He wants to trust me but he thinks he would be a fool to believe me now. *He may be right.*

A splash and then a cry. A splash and then a cry. Each one a scratch against my ribs. A mark I yearn to cut into my skin.

It's done carefully. Lovingly. Each dead soldier given the same amount of time and consideration. A silent procession. Living Char position themselves along the beach, keeping the bobbing bodies from coming aground. And as they pass, the men signal their safety with the Call.

I squint down the line of the river cutting through the crater. Listening to music flowing from it like a giant flute. It is the saddest song.

The Calls combine and the crater vibrates with a honey buzz. A magical, unearthly harmony guiding them home.

Legs aching from standing so long, my mouth turns dry at the sight of the last body: Ben Ni. I place the knife at the general's feet and approach the Yan family. Ki Anah swaying like an unbreakable but frighteningly delicate twig. The brothers and Luna ready to catch her if she falls. Something tells me, she won't though.

I pass kneeling, bound Mogui with heads bowed. They slip glances at the Char. Most hateful. Few fascinated. Some even grateful. But all are captivated. It's impossible not to be.

The Mogui shake their heads like the music both hurts and enthralls them. Their prejudice catching and beginning to peel from their skin like aged paint. It will cling and not fall away easily. But the respect the Char have given their fallen comrades has crackled their exterior. There is hope in that.

Living Water Shen are positioned by the river.

Fire and Air Shen have been permitted to kneel beside the great pyres, ready for lighting. I look to the graves, regret working its way down my throat. All the Earth Shen are dead. *All. Of. Them.*

The river warbles a calming song. It runs soft hands over our fretting hearts and tells us to let go. The Char are waiting. Ash moves closer to the Yan family, his chest filled with sorrow. Face a mask of tranquility.

Luna's hand is tightly wrapped around one of the ropes binding Ben Ni's body.

Her brothers have a hand on their sister's shoulders, but they will not pull her back. I am surprised by Luna's behavior. Hope wiggles between the cracks of my pragmatism. *Has she opened herself to grief?* My brother and I find her face at the same time and have a similar reaction: disappointment.

The crowd of men shift uncomfortably. Eyes moving to the many Shen still left to put to rest.

"Mama, you need to let go. You must let Ben Ni be at peace." Luna stares at the sky. Birds appear from unknown corners and sweep into a rough circle. Flying around and around like they're caught in a tornado.

Ki Anah kneels by Ben Ni, both hands gripped tightly around the body and Luna's hand over her mother's, trying to pry her away. The mother sobs, her small body shaking like an egg about to be cracked open by a baby bird. "What if he can't find his way home?" she moans, her voice filled with pins and pricks. The pain spreads like giant wings, shadowing everyone, unable to be contained.

I find Ash's eyes and he nods, allowing me in. Carefully, I approach the broken mother and place a hand on the back of her neck. I send the gentle warmth of the sun on a broad leaf and then the calming still of the surface of an unbroken pond. The nuzzle of a cub to its mother's breast. She takes a big breath in, like she could inhale all the air in the crater and sighs.

Her suffering is enormous, and I can't hold it much longer. My arms weaken.

Joka kneels beside her. "He knows how to get home, Mama."

Sun wraps his large arms around the three of them. "We showed him the way."

Ki Anah grips her cherrywood hip tightly shaking her head with denial. "But he has no wooden part." She pounds the timber hard. "He died before he could join the Char fully." She taps the black wrappings like she could wake him. At only fifteen, Ben Ni was too young to receive his wooden part. It makes his bravery in joining the fight all the more impressive. "How can we let him go into the next world without protection?" Her voice is raw, like the words hurt as they travel up her throat. They hurt me like I've swallowed a thousand splinters. "How?"

The senior Carvress stands and swishes to the Yan family, kneeling down to touch the wrapped body. "With or without a wooden limb, your son is Char. Wholly. He sacrificed his life to save another." I swallow those splinters and hope to the stars they don't puncture my organs. "There is nothing more Char than that." She puts her wooden palm over the top of Ki Anah's. "Let him join his ancestors. In the afterlife, he will choose his wooden part."

Ki Anah nods. Eyes round like a child heeding their mother. "He always wanted shoulders." Luna makes a dry, brittle noise like she's full of sawdust while the Carvress smiles with sap sweetness and gently removes the grieving mother's hand from the body. Ki Anah finally releases Ben Ni and he falls into the water.

Tears flow from every eye except Luna's. She coughs and covers her mouth, clamming up. Ash swipes at his eyes and stares at the ground, hiding. Folding my hands inside my robe guiltily, I cannot judge because I haven't let him go either. I still need him.

Blue follows black as Water Shen are carefully placed in the water after Ben Ni.

Luna gives me one look. Remorse and blame. Though it's unclear where it's aimed. She mouths *thank you* and returns to her family. Ash hovers on the outer edge, wanting to be closer. Not knowing how.

The chancellor's pickled laugh is followed by a splutter as the pyres are lit and heavy smoke fills the air.

Flames burn high and crimson. The ash is gray and thick, mixing with the mist and making it hard to see. I narrow my eyes, trying to spot the black smear of a man. My head is filled with beautiful music and delicious vengeance.

I storm toward the general who hands me the knife. His dark eyes are saddened beyond words while his look shows strength, a readiness for the next fight.

I'm ready too. The knife feels good in my hand, like a perfectly fitted puzzle piece.

My gray robes swish through the smoke until I am almost camouflaged. The ashy clouds grow thicker and thicker, my eyes stinging.

The chancellor cackles. Chokes. But commits to his evil sounds. I follow them, knife horizontal and prepared.

Char stand out in the smoke. So do Water and Fire Shen. I am part death ashes, part death bringer. I spot his dark head. His blue robes. I raise the knife thinking only of blood, blood, blood.

He will die in seconds.

My wrist is caught by a strong, disarming hand.

My younger brother's hand.

I shock him with lightning. Stab him with beestings, but he holds on. He reads of a stubborn iceberg, moving slowly but forcefully.

Then we hear a break in the music, a cut in the Call, and dying screams where there should be silence. The clash and clamor of men brawling when swords should be hanging at sides.

Ash releases me, our motives twisting together momentarily, and we run into the fight.

# 16
## ASH KI

Luna joins us and it's almost like we're *us* again. Lye, Ash, and Luna. A time when everything was easier. It's laughable. Those times were incredibly difficult. But then the gravelly sound of a lava lion crushing dirt under its heavy paws brings me back to the present, to the girl with the hickory heart and blood powers that are dangerous and omnipotent.

The lion swoops in beside her as we tear toward the opposite end of the crater, swallowed by black robes as Char surge after us. Luna calls to her brothers through the blinding smoke. The lava lion roars and veers. Metal shrieks against metal or flesh in blood-ied thumps, men grunting. Cloth swirling and flapping. But our bearings are mangled, and we bang into each other instead of find-ing the source.

The brothers appear, their heels nipped by the lion. Luna praises the creature just as Sun stammers, "The Carvresses!"

Luna shouts up to her brother. "I lost them in the smoke."

An arrow whistles through the air. Men flinch but it's impossible to avoid what you can't see, and a Char to our right falls, blood pouring from his neck. Joka kneels to help him. And the group slows its pace. The lava lion snarls and creeps forward. Molten eyes glowing through the haze. Its tail whips me persistently, thwacking my knees with its strange stony fur. Luna pats my shoulder. "Take it."

I can barely see her. "Take what?" I ask.

"Its tail," she replies like it's obvious. "It wants you to hold onto its tail."

Reluctantly, I grasp the lava lion's tail, the texture like mossy rock. It growls softly and guides us.

The living Air Shen have escaped. All that remains are flames climbing the tower of bodies and a spray of freshly killed Char laid out like the spokes of a wheel around it. Under cover of smoke, the Air Shen made a break for it.

We hunt for a flash of dirty white robes in the dense air. But for those few lonely arrows, there's no sound and no way to track them since their point of origin is unclear. The Call has ceased. If they're out there, they're well hidden.

The lion roars and I imagine the sound splitting the fog and surging to the sky. A flap of white near the forest line catches my eye. I point, cutting through smoke that is half composed of Shen bones and flesh. "Over there."

Luna nods, flicking her hand. The lion bounds toward the injured Shen crawling for the trees. His scream is brief followed by the smashing of rocky teeth as the lion crunches down on his neck.

Lye crouches by a still breathing Char, though it's a dry, wheezing sound. "What happened here?" she asks.

He whispers one word before losing consciousness. "Boats."

Sun motions for us to follow him.

We sprint for the sea.

Branches scratch our faces and mud splatters our clothes as we chase the sun across the crater. We climb the ladders without thought. They rattle like loose skeletons as we throw ourselves higher. We slide through the cave. Ducking and smashing coral.

We know we're too late, but we run right into the sea anyway. Saltwater lapping at our knees. The orange fire of sunset echoing the burn of our muscles.

White Shen huddle inside a Char boat, sailing for the mainland with a secret that will earn them garlands of star blossoms and stacks of gold coins. When they tell the emperor all the Carvresses are on Crow's Nest Island, ripe for the picking, they'll be celebrated as heroes.

Sun curses and throws handfuls of stones into the water.

Luna swipes her hand, relieving the lava lion of its post. It curls slowly up the sheer cliff, melting into the dark gray rock.

She chastises her brother. "It does no good to have a tantrum about it, older brother. We knew the Shen would come eventually. Once they realized there were no Carvresses on the other islands, they were always going to sail here." She blows a hair from her forehead and puts her hands on her hips. "This just speeds up the inevitable."

I shake my head with frustration. "It more than speeds it up. It brings it right to our doorstep."

Luna gazes after the boat as it shrinks, a healthy breeze helping it along. Sun flaps his arms about. "Can't you summon a whale to flip the boat, sister? Or a shark to bite a hole in the hull?"

I smile. It's a hopeless, what will we do now kind of smile. Luna watches it with curiosity until Sun smacks the back of my head.

She closes her eyes, nostrils flaring. "There are none nearby."

Sun clasps his hands behind his head and curses some more. "Well, this is a real bucket of fish heads!"

"Fish heads? Are all Char phrases nautical?" He lunges at me and I duck, tripping us both into the water.

Luna's mouth quivers with pent up laughter. Almost lifts to a smile. But the force of what comes next pulls her mood to serious. Pulls all of us to serious. "The Carvresses cannot be found." Her eyes scan the coast for hidden Shen. "At all costs, they must be kept safe."

The boat of Air Shen slips over the rise of a wave and disappears. Headed home. Home. A strange feeling sweeps over me. An aching. A refuge. "I think I know the perfect place."

# 17
## ASH KI

My brother lives. Through all the chaos, he slipped through the noose, eel-like. Thoughts of an execution have been put to the side, though I doubt for long. There has always been darkness in Lye's eyes, but what I see now is a cold need for revenge. Her hand scrunches the dull gray cloth at her side, aching for a knife. But I can't believe anyone is beyond saving. *I won't.* He's half my blood. Half Koh. Good may be buried and compassion may be difficult to unearth, but no one is born bad, despite what Lye says. Men are shaped into evil. Raised into it by circumstance.

Surely anyone can fight their way to the surface given the right motivation. *Anyone.*

We return to camp on the heels of panic and the dark of night. Stress biting at our flying feet. When we tell the general of the Air Shen escape, taking with them the precious information of the Carvresses location, he calls an immediate meeting in his tent. Lye bouncing on the balls of her feet at the invitation.

The general strides to his dresser and lights a stick of cherry incense, staring at the blood red curls of smoke. His face crinkles with middle-aged softness and concern. Angular shoulders straighten as he places sharp arms behind his back, listening to people talk over one another, scrambling to make sense of what just happened. And trying to come up with a plan of what they must do next. Fah is imposing even as he observes. I wait for his walnut jaw to snap and call order to the chaos.

The Carvresses cluster to one side of the tent, heedful, a peaceful strength about them. When one speaks, the whole tent goes quiet aside from the chewing of last rations. We're surviving on fruit, fish, and mealy flour that is playing havoc on the soldier's digestive systems.

The Coalstone Carvress stands, perfect mouth pursed and ready. I tilt my head, wondering if I'll ever stop being awed by them. Wooden lips should clack and clonk when they collide, but they appear soft, voices warm and ferocious. "Today has been a terrible, terrible day. But we are Char. We're accustomed to terrible days. It is not difficult to build atop of tragedy. It's not difficult because it is necessary. We must..." She looks to her fellow Carvresses, who bob their heads. "We must leave this place, and soon."

Joka steps into the center, lanky body moving nervously like a puppet resisting its strings. He looks to the general for permission to speak. Fah nods. The younger man is here at the Carvresses insistence, so the older can't really argue. "But where will you go?" His eyes glaze as he retreats to images in his head, stroking that strange neck of his. "I can't think of a nearby island that would be safe. The uninhabited ones are too small to hide on, or too dangerous. The Shen would find you like *that*." He claps his hands together loudly and then shrinks from his own racket, embarrassed.

Lye emits a giggle, reminding me of her presence. My anger for her a complicated, folded thing I must keep in my pocket for now. Joka's dark eyes trail her, as many Char men do, most likely fearful of her power and reputation.

Luna's hand presses heated fingers into my back. *Steady heart,* I warn. I want to lean into her touch like a horse nuzzling its mate, but I bite my lip and focus. "I know a place." All eyes, wooden and otherwise, on me. "I propose a small group accompany the Carvresses to the mainland." Someone laughs. The Carvresses lean in to listen and blink shutters over stunning timber eyes. "The high marshlands are very isolated from the palace. Remote. Only one emperor ever visited and that was thirty odd years ago. It's my home so I know it well. There's a secret hiding place there. And with Luna protecting us, we would be extra safe."

Char shake their heads. The Carvresses' expressions vary from acceptance to distrust. Feeling like I'm losing my audience, I add, "She'd also have a way to send word to the Char army once the Carvresses are hidden."

Sun's hand shoots up, straight as a wasted arrow. "I volunteer to protect the Carvresses, General."

The Coalstone Carvress speaks in her dulcet voice. "We will go, but Ki Anah Yan must escort us. We trust her." They all nod and again I expect a knocking sound where there's none.

The general stomps his foot sharply, though the impact is lessened by the damp earth. Everyone's attention turns slowly to him. "Before you all start volunteering and planning your journey, I think you've forgotten who is in command." His eyes glow with irritation. The expression is one I'm well acquainted with from our torture sessions. "I have not given permission for this foolhardy mission." He shakes his hard jaw and groans. "Ah, I wish the elder of Crow's Nest were here. This doesn't feel right."

Lye bows low, creeping up to him, and I don't like the way she folds under his shadow like a baby bat. "With respect, General, I don't think it is up to you." She gestures toward the Carvresses. "It would be wise to listen to their preference about their own wellbeing." Her voice is soft and coercive, and I wonder what game she's playing. It goads me to see the Keeper scraping the floor with her nose.

Fah clears his throat, tapping his jaw. He's cornered and I push him further, his shoulders scraping the walls.

"The chancellor will come with us as a hostage and bartering chip. He could prove useful to trade if we run into outlying troops." Fah's eyebrows rise. "Not that I'm anticipating running into anyone. Like I said, the high marshlands are rarely visited by any royal servant. But an insurance policy is always wise."

The ebony Carvress nods and opens her palm to me. "The boy speaks wisdom. Dangerous wisdom but... We agree with his plan."

Fah considers it just as Lye's expression could melt the wax from a table. She is seething. I know her teeth grind together while she tries to stay calm.

"The chancellor must die," she murmurs.

The general addresses her like no one else is in the room. "The more you say that, the less I believe your intentions are honorable and your judgement clear. The Shen boy has a point. He may be more valuable to us alive. And you are right about one thing—the Carvresses must have final say." He bows low to the Carvresses. "Forgive me for forgetting my place."

The Coalstone Carvress waves her hand like she's sanding a wall. "These are unprecedented times, General. We're all breaking somewhat from what it has always been." I swear she glances toward Luna and me.

Lye's hands form stones while her countenance gathers electricity. Lightning and thunderclaps build in her fingers. "I may have a personal investment in seeing the man who killed my friend and so many others brought to justice. But then, shouldn't the rest of you?" She appeals to the Char, but they are hushed. Luna would have been her only ally in this. If she were the old Luna. Surprisingly, this is going my way, but it doesn't feel good.

The general takes a deep breath, his walnut jaw tensing and then relaxing. "A mainland safe haven will work."

The Carvresses nod along with the general.

Lye seems to lengthen. Stretching up on her toes like she's a rubber band about to snap. "I agree a mainland hideout makes sense given the entire Shen army is currently sailing around or occupying Char territory. But keeping the chancellor alive only draws what Shen are still left to the Carvresses."

The general leans away, nostrils flaring like Lye's intensity is giving off a bad smell. "At least this way, they have some way of bargaining for safety." He turns to me, Luna at my back, and gives a sharp salute. "Permission granted."

"You're making a dangerous mistake," Lye mutters, though to whom, I'm not sure. She leaves the tent, an angry wisp.

I have won my case. But it feels somewhat hollow, like the crumbling nook of a long-abandoned den. There are too many unknowns. Too many questions left to answer.

It is decided. And it's for the best. Lye will stay with the general to escort the Shen captives to their prison. The Yans complete our small traveling party. I need distance from Lye. My anger for her still beats every other heartbeat. She will be safe with the Char. As safe as anyone can be right now.

Joka puts his hand up, seemingly shoved by an unseen force, just as we are about to exit the tent. "With your blessing, General, I would like to journey to Black Sail City with Lye, I mean, the Keeper, rather than travel with my family."

Fah nods, and the Yans bow to Joka with total acceptance. Luna's mouth remains flat when I wish even a hint of disappointment would split it.

SHE CATCHES my arm and pulls me between two tents. The moon has shrunk to a sliver, but I know it's her without being able to see much. She is part of me as I am of her.

She whispers a handful of words, fingers digging into my flesh, sending fresh dirt up my veins. Like a grave. "Please, be careful, brother. He is not like Luna." *No one is.* My sister sighs, cold and empty. "Some people cannot be saved."

# 18
## LYE LI

A figure sways by the riverbank. A dancing shadow, a breezy hum. She is angles and grace and should creak like an over-stocked boat, but her wooden joints only make the slightest noise to hint at their composition.

Tonight, I see the gaps between the stars rather than the light.

I approach, stepping over Shen prisoners who grunt and growl at my knees. They're more tightly restrained, ready to be loaded onto our ships. *Our ships.* I shouldn't call them that. I don't have ownership over Char things. I am Shen, though my attachment to that identity feels like one loose thread hanging on a nail. The other strands have been cut: Loyalty to the emperor, homesickness, belief in the Shen cause. I am stripped to nothing but scars and a need to belong. Clenching my fist, I wish for my thimble, craving just a small prick of pain.

Sweeping up a small twig, I strip the bark with chewed-down fingernails and snap off the end, leaving a sharp point.

Pressing it to my wrist, I squeeze a carved line in between other scars.... *It hurts*. It will hurt more in a moment but then, *his face, his face, his face*. It pushes into what little space is left in my brain. His eyes like a bowl of golden syrup. Warm. Sweet. Ben Ni shakes his head sorrowfully, tapping his chest and offering his heart in place of mine.

His heart makes a better offering. Full, strong, and undamaged compared to my blackened muscle. *Be worthy,* Luna said.

*I'm trying.*

*But is it enough?*

Frustrated, I cast the stick into the water. It barely makes a sound and is sucked past me with speed. The water hastening it out to sea.

I swallow. By now the dead have met the ocean and are floating toward the horizon. The sun waiting with a welcoming smile.

The figure crouches down, head in hands, rocking back and forth. I step gingerly to her side. Lifting my hand slowly, I place it on her back like it's a dying hearth that could still burn me. Restraining my elements, though they rush to help.

"I'm so sorry, Ki Anah," I whisper. She smells like a mother. Cooking oil, soap, and an un-pinnable sweetness. "Ben Ni was a wonderful, compassionate boy."

She sniffs, back tightening under my palm. "You knew my son?" Silk sleeve presses to her nose.

"I didn't know him well. But every one of my experiences with him was a good one. He was kind to me, helped me." *He saved me.* "I was with him in his last moments."

Ki Anah dabs her eyes and squats on the wet grass, hips cracking as she settles. She pats the space next to her. "I don't think I can hear an account. Not yet." She focuses on the silvery water. Ribbons of light glimmer in the river as star-eater eels flash their stomachs to the surface. Hungry for something they will never reach.

"You're not what I expected. Luna described you… differently." I stumble over my words.

"She thinks me old and traditional." Luna's mother stretches her arms in front, balancing on her haunches. "Like a used wok. Stained with flavor and darkened with food that will never scrub off." She snorts. "And she would be right in some ways. I've seen every swirl of egg. I've burned shallots in the pan and had to scrape it all out and start again." Her tiny laugh is pressed in brass. Rare.

Guarded. "But Luna is not a mother. She doesn't understand what a parent must do to keep her children safe. To make sure they are happy." I sense a biting down as she churns with regret. "And even then, you won't always succeed. Sometimes you lose." She turns to me, curious. "What you have done to Luna by awakening a Shen element in her—it is remarkable." She spins her hands in circles. "I always knew she was meant for something bigger. That she would fly up past the Coalstones and reach the moon."

"You did?"

She licks her lips and sighs, lifting her palms and pressing against an imaginary barrier. "Yes, always. That's why I tried to stop her."

Confused, I lean closer. "I don't understand."

"Children never understand." She clucks her tongue. "I knew there would be a cost. A great cost. I've watched my husband's soul shrink. Every battle, every life he took, cost him a small piece of his heart."

Understanding grows. "And now Luna has paid dearly."

Ki Anah flings a small, brass-plated laugh my way and pats my hand. It feels motherly. And something for which I'm unprepared. I burn her fingers with a flame surging for oxygen. She withdraws sharply and shakes her fingers. "Until she releases her grief, she will never stop paying." *Pause. Count the stars. Hope.* "But I know my daughter. She cannot do what she is doing forever. No." She speaks to the sky. "It will push her over the edge, and she will fall."

"Ash will catch her."

Ki Anah's mouth puckers at the thought of this and rearranges. She's trying to come to terms with this thought. But this is a lot for a traditional Char woman to accept. "And who will catch you, Keeper Lye?"

"I'm used to falling without a net."

She hums curly notes of a Char song. "Maybe the general?"

"He doesn't trust me. He definitely doesn't listen to me. I desperately want to help the Char, but they will always look at me like a foreigner. A potential threat." I throw my arms in the air. Feeling guilty for burdening her with my troubles.

Ki Anah stands. "I must check on my daughter." She bends back and the clicking of her hips is not just a nice sound, it's a sound I long for. For my own body to crick and crack. I glance down at my arm, running my fingers up and down the ridged skin. "A Char arm would suit you well, Lye Li." She taps her chin and looks around the surrounding trees, pointing straight as an arrow. "Sycamore. Strong. A symbol of protection."

"Sycamore?"

"Yes. If you want our acceptance, you need to show that you're truly one of us."

THE SAND Otter Carvress hacks at a sycamore tree. The trunk is a pleasing mottled patchwork of different colored bark. The inside reveals a rippling reddish pink like the underside of a poorly healed scar. Bright red sap bleeds from its wounds. I grimace at the same time as the Carvress smiles. It's flesh-like and ugly. The Carvress tsks and runs her hands along the length. "I don't like to be rushed. Usually, I would dry the wood in my workshop. If only the Carvress of Crow's Nest would have permitted me to use her space. Ah! Such a stubborn woman."

My eyes land on different timbers laying around the camp. Pine crates and oak barrels. Stronger, less conspicuous colors. I'm about to suggest an alternative when she shushes me. A gleaned wooden finger presses to my lips. "This one; it calls you." She presses her ear to the hunk of wood. "Yes! I hear it."

She shoves it at me. I listen carefully, hearing a pulsing music. A shortened scream. A sort of staccato. It doesn't sound nice. It doesn't even sound tuneful, but it's the only timber that made any type of noise when I touched it. "It's very red," I manage, unused to being the receiver of power since I am usually the giver. I feel restless and useless in this capacity.

I wish Ash were here, but apparently this is something I must do alone. My eyes lift to an allaying sky. A sheer curtain about to be pulled back on a window. He'd probably refuse to be with me in this moment anyway.

With the hunk of wood under her arm, she clutches my wrist and drags me away from camp.

With every hurried step, I remind myself I want this. *I do. I do. I do.*

The sun is starting to warm the ocean, though it won't light the crater for another hour. The forest, skirting the cliffs, breathes and catches coolness in preparation for heat.

The Carvress yanks me through the trees, speeding up like the sun is part of her. "Time," she whispers to her wooden chest. "I could have used more time."

I grow more fearful the further from camp we get.

Reaching the crater wall, we scrape along narrow ledges, pebbles tumbling from our feet and warning us how dangerous a fall would be. We find a hollow that blasts us with cold sea air, and the Carvress of Sand Otter Island seems satisfied.

She tosses me inside the open-ended cave, my knees grazing the rock, and I wonder if this is all an elaborate way to assassinate me. She laughs. A sawdust pouring onto a table kind of sound, soft and flaky. Above, a gray morning will be struck aflame. Below, the sea curls and curves around a small inlet. The wind whips around my ears like a nasty slap, and I put my hands to my cold cheeks.

The Carvress stands over me wielding the bloodied branch of sycamore like a club. She lifts it and I close my eyes.

I wait for a blunt blow. Wind whistles and gulls squawk. The Carvress's quiet voice cuts through the noise. "I am not going to gift you a limb when you seem so ready to die." I open my eyes, shuffle back onto my heels. Her eyes are sad. Pitying. It pierces me like a dart to the neck.

I know what I look like to her. I know I lean toward a ghost life sometimes. But I'm trying to grab hold of a purpose. I want this Char gift to anchor me to a new life. I grit my teeth. Stare back defiant and attempt to convince her of something I'm not sure of myself. "I'm not ready to die, Carvress. I'm willing to fight to the death, but that's not the same thing."

She takes my words and weighs them. The sap-covered hunk is wet and slimy in the growing light. "You want to mean the words you speak but..." She tilts her head. "Perhaps this will give you the strength you need to truly believe them." The sun points its spokes at us, ticking down the minutes. "We don't have much time. I warn you that without my tools, you get no brass joints. Just the forearm." She chops her arm with the edge of her hand, marking from wrist to elbow. "From here to here."

I nod. "Will it hurt?"

She rolls her eyes, dismayed. "Why do they all ask this question?" She addresses the heavens. "Of course it will hurt!"

Light breaks over the water and the Carvress orders me to close my eyes. She sings in an ancient language, though I understand some of the words. I've read the old language words for "sacrifice" and "offering" in ancient Shen scrolls. I catch the word "gift" and then, disturbingly, "death." And then I feel the pain she so lightly mentioned.

My skin feels burned layer by layer and my muscle feels pulled from my bones thread by thread. Then the two bones in my forearm are broken, neatly and excruciatingly at both ends. I cry out and am told sternly to shut my mouth unless I want my arm going in upside down. The Carvress sings throughout the brutish process and I dare not open my eyes. I don't want to see my skin peeled like a banana, blood and nerves in a tangled mess. I feel raw, exposed. I bite down on my lip so hard it bleeds.

After minutes or hours, an endless vacuum of time, my fingers start to numb. And I begin to panic. The elemental sense in them fades first, then the physical touch, until I cannot feel them at all. I want to peel back my eyelids but fear keeps them closed. *Has my hand been removed?* I attempt to make a fist. I don't know if I did. My throat dries to salt lines and drought cracks.

The Carvress makes a strange grunt, like this strains her. My elemental powers are smashing and competing. Caught in a storm. They buzz in one of my hands. Five fingers aching for release.

Five fingers.

Not ten.

The Carvress declares, "Ai ya! Well that is unexpected."

My eyes snap open. The sunrise casts weak spots of pink and yellow over the water. I stare at my arm. Deep, dark red with marks like burned, black ink tattoos running neatly up to my elbow. *My old scars made permanent.* I clench my fists. Pain singes at the joins between my real skin and the wood. Only one hand responds. My other hand hangs limply from my new sycamore arm. I feel no elemental power in my fingers, no lightning, no fire, nothing. Barely looking alive, it has a corpse-ish tinge. I try to wiggle these fingers, and they respond slowly. Sluggishly.

"What's wrong with my hand?" I ask, voice high. Acid creeping up my throat.

The Carvress shrugs. "I'm not sure. I suppose this could be the cost of a Shen becoming a Char." A cost. *Always a cost.*

"Will it return to normal?" I try to push myself to standing. Unable to use my limbs the way I want like a new bird refusing to open its wings.

The Carvress smiles. Beautiful. Benevolent. But unable to answer. "Perhaps. Perhaps not."

But I need my hand. I don't know how to fight without both my hands.

I lift the arm. It's lead heavy. It's so very obvious.

"Will it die?" My fingers flop around like a bunch of old carrots.

I use the wall to pull myself up. The Carvress looks incensed and impressive, towering over me. The sun bounces off her polished cheeks, her golden throat. "You need to stop asking me silly questions. I have performed the ceremony as you requested. You must now learn to live with your choice, however it may have turned out. What is done cannot be undone." She folds her arms over her wooden breast, her glare diamond hard.

To the Carvress, arm hanging heavily at my side, I whisper, "You could have just said, *I don't know.*"

# 19
## ASH KI

Her face is as gray as so many dead soldiers. Distraught. Pain billowing from her in clouds as she stumbles from the jungle. Without thinking I run to her side, bare feet digging into the mud. Cool morning air scraping at my cheeks and at lips I don't quite know are mine anymore. I catch her as she falls.

"Brother. I've made a terrible mistake," Lye mumbles before her eyes flutter closed.

I inspect her for injury. She's not bleeding, but she holds one arm tightly against her stomach. And her hand lacks color. Lifting her sleeves, I gasp loudly when I see the purplish tinge of an unfamiliar timber running from wrist to elbow, tattooed with hundreds of black marks.

*Oh Lye, what have you done?*

Scooping up my waifish sister, I carry her to our tent.

To wake her gently, I sprinkle snowflakes over her skin. Pinpricks of cold that land on her cheeks and melt. Sleeping like this, vulnerable and human, I can almost forgive her. *Almost.* I smile without teeth, so confused by what I've learned. Disconnected from my emotions because I'm unsure of what is real and what was put there by a meddling sister. I want to ask, but at the same time, I don't. My smile is part of me now. No matter how it came to be there. It's how people know me. How I know myself. I touch my lips. Like a scrambled egg, the yolk cannot be separated from the white.

She blinks awake, eyes like mine but holding far more secrets. Relieved to see me, she tries to hold my hand but her movements are clumsy and heavy. Her fingers behave like rain-soaked leaves unable to get to the sun. Every time they try, the weight of water pushes them down. She blows air through her lips slowly.

"Take my hand," she begs, staring down at the red-purple timber replacing her forearm.

I touch the wood. It's smooth and perfectly formed. The black marks make it look like a rolled-up accounting scroll from the treasury. Men hunched over long reams of paper, making quick ink strokes as they count the emperor's fortune. Although the color is blunt and ugly, reminding me of decomposing remains on the battlefield.

"Did you mean to do this, sister?" I ask.

She shuffles up to a sitting position, shakily taking the red bean tea I offer in her left hand. Her dominant hand, the right, flutters like a moth with torn wings. "I meant to prove myself. I didn't know this would be the consequence." She swishes the prized red beans in the bottom of her cup.

Lifting the arm delicately, turning it around. A thing of beauty and ugliness. "You mean the color?" I smirk. "It's not the prettiest timber I've seen but you'll get used to it." I eye it inquisitively. Despite not being ready for such a change, a small desire creeps in.

She shakes her head. "No. The sycamore *called* me. Its ugliness suits me just fine. Brother, take my *hand*," she urges. I gently take up her fingers. They're cool to touch. Weak to squeeze. "Don't move." I keep still, trusting her, even after everything she's done.

"What is this ab—"

But then she closes her eyes and whispers, "Forest fire." I brace, ready to extinguish, but I feel nothing. *Nothing.*

My eyes widen and she confirms my suspicions. "My hand is…" She sniffs, seeming smaller, younger than I've ever seen her.

"It's completely powerless. Useless!" she moans, flinging stray red beans onto her bedspread.

In that moment, I understand that for all her complaining about being the Keeper, it's still a big part of who she is. Taking away some of her power makes her feel less whole. And a whole lot more like the rest of us. I try to stifle my chuckle and fail.

"It may not work the way it used to. You may not be able to flash fry men with a touch of that hand, but it's not useless. A hand is not useless."

She flaps it about. "What if it dies?" I swallow. I'm angry with her but I don't want her to suffer.

"It won't die," I manage unconvincingly.

Slurping her tea and pushing it to me for a refill, she frowns. I pick the beans from her bedspread and pop them in the cup. I'm not wasting them.

"You realize what this means though?" She pulls the covers up over her legs and shivers. I raise an eyebrow, waiting. "Shen cannot be changed to Char without consequence. It makes elemental Shen weaker. If the emperor is to have his hybrid warrior, he must turn Char. But Char loyalty is as ingrained as the lines running through their wooden limbs. It would be impossible to turn an adult Char against their people. Perhaps, if he still has the children, they could be brainwashed into allegiance." She purses her lips, contemplating.

I am stuck on the word *children? What children?*

"What do you mean 'if he still has the children'? What children?" I poke at the beans in the bottom of my cup. The skin bursts, bean paste exploding out the sides.

Lye's eyes dart to the side, and she lifts her weighty arm into her lap with a thud. "There were whispers of Char children being held beneath the palace and I even heard a scream once." She cannot meet my gaze. "I do not know how many they experimented on. I don't even know if they're still alive."

"Ma ya!" *My god!* "Next you'll tell me he's got a fire breathing dragon down there too."

She frowns. "This is no time for jokes, Ash."

I prickle. Never knowing what is me and what she made in me. "Well... *I* am a consequence of your power too, remember?" She bites her tongue, tears welling.

Shrugging hard, I try to shed my anger but it hangs from my shoulders like a hook-clawed sloth, not ready to let go. Soon I'll be leaving, and even though we have much to resolve, she is my sister and I love her.

She winces as she twists her arm. "Do you think I made a mistake?" she asks, eyes wide, fuzzy hair sticking up at all angles.

It is so very conspicuous, and I suppress a twist of my lips. "I think you made a decision and now you must learn to live with it."

"And the children?"

It is horrible. Detestable. It is also completely out of our reach right now. It doesn't mean I won't carry this news like a brick in my pack. "Do you have any proof?" She shakes her head, trying to squash a red bean between two gray fingers. "I think we have joined the right side of this war now. If there are Char children being held in the palace, at least with us fighting against the emperor, they have a chance."

She runs her hand down the length of her new arm, sighing quietly. "When did you get so wise?"

I stand from the edge of her bed. "We take turns."

Seeming to lock herself, she clicks her bones into place and forces herself upward. She holds her arm to the morning light streaming through the gap. "It is rather beautiful."

I don't know about that, but for better or worse, it's part of her.

"You best come show the others, Char Keeper Lye Li Koh," I say, shaking my head at the long list of titles.

As I step into the sun, she tugs me back, using her new arm so I can't sting her with ice. "I still think our *brother*," the word is bitter on her tongue, "must die. Ash, please reconsider this plan."

I hold her sycamore arm with both hands and force it from me. "I am your brother. I love you and will always look out for you. But I have not forgiven you for lying to me nor do I trust your judgement right now. My plan is a good one. The general and the Carvresses agree." I level my eyes at her. Sea green against sea green. Waves that hold a ship but can also sink it. "Lye. Let it go and support me."

She takes a deep breath and holds it. Giving the smallest of bows. "Very well, brother. You support me and I shall do the same for you. I wish you a safe journey." She taps the marks on her arms like they spell words I can't see. "I wish so many things for you. I wish…" She doesn't finish.

Hot yellow light bathes us as the Char Yans and other soldiers beckon us outside. It's time to prepare. Time to separate. Time to leave the island.

THE CHAR ships are as heavy as they were before battle, only now half the weight is Mogui Shen prisoners. They nestle in colorful lines, heads down and hands to themselves. They're destined for Bird Cage Island, a sandbox with rib-like rock formations that scrape the sky. Char don't usually keep this many prisoners, so the island will be crowded and difficult to manage. But surprisingly, Lye bargained for leniency and an opportunity to carve out a new life for these men. I hope it's possible for the Mogui, so twisted with hate and bloodlust. The Char are more gracious than we deserve, and I hope they don't end up paying for their generosity in blood.

I wave to my sister as she stands like a figurehead at the helm of one the prisoner boats. Red arm gleaming like a skinned pig, hand paler than the rest of her. I grimace. It will take me a while to get used to it. Earlier, we said a brief goodbye. Our small family is used to being separated, but we're also very used to finding our way back to each other. Like the spotted ice birds of the north, we have a built-in compass guiding us to each other. We exchange faith like trading coins for cloth, sure we'll see each other again.

Lye left me a parting gift of two directives:

*If it comes down to a choice, fight for Luna. Always choose her.*

And, *when he betrays you, do not hesitate. Slit his throat before he can utter one more poisonous word.*

She said *when* not *if.*

The words imprint on the inside of my skull, and I tighten my grip on the chancellor's thin arm. He displays his bound hands. "You needn't squeeze so tight. I'm not going anywhere." His green eyes brightened as we traveled to the beach, reflecting the leaves and taking in the details of the island.

I shove him. "Get in the boat," I demand, not wanting to look in those eyes for too long. They seem like receptacles, gathering knowledge, capturing intentions.

The Yan family boat sinks low in the water, and Ki Anah huffs as she climbs inside. "Ai ya! We are too many. Too many. Too heavy." She pushes on the floor of the boat just to make it worse and water spills inside. Luna growls at her. Her teeth, though square, seem to have a fanged edge.

"Mama, stop! You're so... Ugh! We'll just have to take two boats." Luna lets her emotion out in little bursts. But nothing important. Just snips and snaps.

They bickered all the way here. It was amusing to start with but now it's grating on my already frayed nerves. "This thing." Ki Anah waves her hands in Luna's direction. "Maybe this *Blood* thing makes you disrespectful."

Sun rolls his eyes. "Mama forgets what she was like before," he says to me when the two women aren't watching. His large shoulders block the light from my eyes.

"What was she like?" I ask, a little too interested.

Ki Anah answers for him. "She was worse!" Sun chuckles.

Fish jump out of the water in a frenzy. Biting at the air like they think they're about to be fed. Luna's eyes darken and everybody is quiet. "Whatever I *was* is irrelevant. I am this"—she gestures at her small, strong body—"now."

The Coalstone Carvress pats Luna on the shoulder when everyone else is scared to touch her. Everyone except me. "You are Char Luna. Daughter of Setsu and Ki Anah Yan." I sense Luna's conflict again and again. Her reach for peace and the way it slips away from her just like the fish coming closer to the floating boat. A pendulum swinging. Never resting.

Ki Anah sits, making room for her daughter. "Setsu." She sighs and then she stares at Luna. "You haven't asked once about your father. Where he is, what he's doing. If he is safe."

Luna pushes out the boat carrying Sun, her mother, and five Carvresses with annoyed effort. "I do not worry about papa. He's a Char warrior. He'll be fine. Besides"—she flattens her palms to the ocean surface—"he knows the life, the risks." Coldness sweeps over all of us and Ki Anah's expression changes from one of irritation to sadness and disappointment. Her game is clear to me, though maybe not to the others.

The silver fish gape and gulp the air. Dying. Trapdoor mouths clap the water, jelly eyes stare stupidly at their master. Then Luna flicks her fingers and they disappear.

I know what Ki Anah is trying to do. But niggling Luna into emotion isn't the way to get through to her. This I know from experience. Sun jams a paddle into the water, so the boat spins around in circles as they wait for us to board our old boat and lead the way.

With his hands wrapped with cloth to prevent any skin to skin contact, the chancellor silently watches the Carvresses. Like he's slowly dissecting them and sorting through what he might use and what he might discard. I tip my head, searching for myself in him. His eyes are a tracing of mine and Lye's. Thinner. Fainter. My mouth twists into an uneasy smile at the idea of trying to find these similarities. Most people would distance themselves from such a monster. And here I am trying to find common ground.

His eyes bend a beam of pale light my way and he sneers. "What do you search for, brother Koh?" The word pulls my shoulders to my ears and my hand to the knife in my waistband.

I lean in as we rise and fall with the waves. "Do not call me that, Chancellor. We may be related but we are far from being brothers." His eyes roll at my words and land back on the Carvresses, who for their part, stare right back, a peculiar disconnect in their expressions like they're dissecting him also.

Luna narrows her eyes. "I suggest you keep your gaze on the horizon, Chancellor. Our Carvresses are not statues to be stared at, and I know a bird or two who would happily peck your sickly green eyes out if I so wish."

I shiver from the cold and the callousness of her words.

He lowers his gaze to his swathed hands, and they shake. He fears her. And my mind starts to wander into her tent, where men screamed, and my Luna carried out her torture. My limbs crack and lock. I wish things were different. But in this case, Luna is right—this wish is a waste.

Under my regard, Luna switches to regret for just a moment before a mask of detachment covers it, quickly like a hood pulled down as a soldier charges into battle.

This is going to be difficult.

Sun shouts over the waves as we sail past them, aiming his words at the Carvresses. "You keep an eye on Shen Ash. He has a thing for Char girls."

If it weren't so cold my cheeks would be as red as Lye's new arm.

A smaller, darker Carvress, seemingly carved from ebony, laughs, and the sound sprinkles the sea foam like lotus petals thrown at a funeral.

# 20
## LYE LI

I thought being on a large ship would be less rocky, but my stomach still roils at every lurch. Seasickness is the predominant cause, but my worry chases after Ash, alone with the chancellor. My older brother will try to manipulate my younger brother, even try to turn Ash against me. And I want to believe Ash is strong enough to resist influence. *I should believe it.* But his heart is too forgiving.

I grip the edge with one hand as we row against the current. My sycamore arm rests on the gunwale, kissed by salt spray. The fact that I feel the cold of the water on the timber makes me grin. It's enchanting, fascinating, and I enjoy learning more.

Wiggling my weak fingers tentatively, they respond, but in a distant way. I pray it will get better. They flop with the movement of the ship and my heart squeezes in my chest. I need to accept that they may not improve.

The wind is not in our favor and great oars jut from the hull like the legs of a giant water bug, though the ship does not skate across the surface. It fights with the sea, arguing its direction. Forcing the water to take its weight.

Char men hum as they row. It makes light of our current situation: We are not traveling well. At the helm, the general looks dissatisfied. I stumble toward him, arms flailing and searching for things to hold onto. Acid burns my throat and I talk to my stomach, warning its contents to stay down. He sees me coming and raises one eyebrow. He makes a point of standing solidly by the wheel, hands behind his back, keeping his balance with ease.

"General Fah," I manage as I throw myself at the wheel, gripping the sun-spoked center. "We're not moving very well."

He sighs witheringly. "No, we are not. Too many men are injured to row effectively." The ship bounces, and he takes the wheel in a very controlled way, though I know he has lost balance.

Letting go, my hands scrunch unevenly at my sides. *I'm going to fall over.* He points to a barrel bolted down behind me and I grab it gratefully. "How can I help?" I ask.

He assesses my thin arms. Good for swift, graceful movements. For sending a flood of lava through a Char's body before he can blink. Not particularly useful for rowing. "I don't think you can help, even with your new arm." His eyes shoot downward quickly and back up to meet my gaze.

Joka stumbles down from the upper deck, an interesting shade of green. He covers his mouth with one hand and grasps the steep railing with the other. When he reaches us, he bows sharp and panicky as it throws off his already unequal balance. I smile, hand to my stomach as a nausea drenched moth tries to flutter across it. His even voice is split apart. A seasick Char is an odd phenomenon.

"General, we're not making very much progress. Perhaps we should wait until the injured men are better recovered? As it is, there are some rowing with one arm."

Fah rejects his suggestion. "We have already waited too long. Black Sail City needs us. Your father needs us. Go below deck and rouse some of the injured men who can still hold an oar even if it's with their feet. They will just have to saw through the pain."

I tip my head. "Saw through?"

Joka's pale green face almost matches his bamboo neck. "It's a Char term. It means they just need to endure. Push through." He tries to make a pushing motion with his hands and begins to wobble.

Tall, thin Joka waits for me to show I understand while General Fah stares, long and impatient as lightning trying to find the earth. The general suddenly lunges like he might shove the young Char. Joka startles, bows and tumbles to the hatch.

"Wait!" I shout. Joka looks pained at the thought of standing still in front of the general. I address the proud man with the walnut jaw. "What if I could get the Shen to assist?"

The general's jaw widens and tightens into a sarcastic smile. "If you could do that, then you will have proved far more useful than I thought you would be." He eyes my sycamore arm. The black marks are filling with a white salt crust. My first instinct is to hide it behind my back, but I will not be ashamed of my choice. "You may have a hard time convincing them, especially now."

My fingers dance with the wind, light and brittle like herbs drying in the window. "Let me try."

He nods.

Joka waits by the hatch. He opens his arm to allow me to pass through first like I'm a lady. It makes me snort in a very unladylike fashion because I've never been treated as such. Being Keeper is a sexless, thankless calling. My womanliness was shaved from my head and hidden beneath thick, shapeless gray robes.

I descend into the belly of the ship, Joka close behind. Rung by rung, I compose what I must say to the Shen. My arm hits each one with a thud as I attempt to keep my balance. My feet hug the hard timber, my lip pulled into my teeth. When I pause, Joka steps on my weak fingers when I try, and fail, to hold the rung. I barely feel it but have a dirty mark across my skin as proof.

"Oh, I'm so s-sorry, Lye," he stutters, staring down, just a silhouette.

I shrug. "I didn't feel it." I shake my arm and continue down.

We hit the oar level. Porthole-shaped light paints the dark room with polka dots. Wooden limbs shine. Sweat beads. Saltwater tarnishes. There are many empty benches and the rowers space themselves evenly throughout the level. Up front a man chants their strokes. There's a constant Call sounding from one of the men as his larch hand grips a larch oar. It's a bizarre symphony of men grunting and humming accompanied by the most striking bell-like buzz. I tap the small stick of sycamore tucked into the band of my robe. The Carvress of Sand Otter Island shoved it into my good hand before she left with Ash and Luna. I haven't had the courage to touch it to my arm yet.

As we walk between benches, Char eyes burn me. I keep my arm folded over my chest, making sure it is seen. However, I'm not going to flap it around like a flag. I'm sure that's not the Char way. It's definitely not *my* way.

They give me quick bows followed by suspicious glances. I've stepped into their circle, but I'm still on the edge. It will take time for them to allow me near the center if they ever do. I sigh quietly. Wondering whether this was worth it.

But then a Char *touches* me. Touches my sycamore arm without fear. Without aggression. He's just trying to get my attention. It breaks me into polished little pieces because no one touches me this way. Not even Ash.

"Keeper Lye," he says, staring up. The boat sways and we move as if in a slow, unchoreographed dance. "Or is it Char Lye...?" The Char next to him, whose wooden knee glints under a disc of sunlight, snorts. "How are you adapting to the change?"

My fingers lift like a reluctant music student too lazy to press on the keys. My hand is the price. But *that* look, the look of an equal, of common ground to stand on, no matter how small, is the reward.

I turn it this way and that and smile softly. "Well..." I wait for him to offer a name.

He grins. "Captain Chuk-Lu."

"Captain Chuk-Lu," I repeat and commit to memory as the first Char to treat me like I am one of them. "Do you think your comrades would object to assistance from the Shen below?" My gaze drops between my feet. Light moves in a sickening way as we roll over waves.

"I think we don't have the luxury of objection. We are rowing in one place right now." He looks at the others. Some shake their heads, but none speak their concerns.

Joka is knocked closer, his bare elbow grazing my shoulder. It sparks. Tiny embers float through his veins. Small spot fires. He shudders and pulls away, a sharp breath pulling his ribs in and his body a good foot away from mine. It makes more sense this way. It's what I'm used to.

He cracks his bamboo neck. "Chuk is right. We cannot afford to be picky." He points to one side of the boat. "Could everyone move to one side and make room for the Shen?"

No one moves. Chuk-Lu slaps another soldier on the back and they both chuckle, exchanging a knowing look, then he snaps his head toward the rest of the men. "Joka Yan is the brother of Ben Ni Yan." Men whisper in hushed appreciation. "He has also been endorsed by the Carvresses. He may not have rank, but he deserves respect. And since I am one of the only surviving captains, well, you need to do as I order you anyway. Now move!"

The ship presses its ear to the water as men quickly switch. The stroke caller swallows his words and I swallow my fear. I still have to convince the Mogui Shen to help.

MOST SHEN soldiers start out as farmers. Or were born to farmers. We come from fields that stretch on forever like blankets laid end to end. Everything cut into straight orderly shapes and colored with gold, green, and brown. We know how to grow food. We know how to endure when crops don't yield. We are survivors.

All Shen are loyal to the emperor. Maybe because when those crops don't yield, he has suspended trade and opened the palace store to his people. But mostly because they just are unquestionably loyal like the principle of seed to flower to fruit.

I know I can't appeal to the traitor in them so I must appeal to the survivor.

The prisoners are kept on the lowest level, where water sloshes at their ankles and the only light is from fast melting candles. Hot wax slides down the sides of crates, turning cold and hard when it hits the water.

We climb down, saluting guards at the base of the ladder. Joka is more careful to not touch me. When we land in the water, I grimace at the cold and the smell, resisting the urge to hitch my robes and hold my nose.

Some Shen look up. Others continue to stare at their laps.

I clear my throat.

"We're not traveling well," I whisper, suddenly shy of their hateful glares.

A Fire Shen with a bun the size of an onion neatly combed atop his bao-shaped head, spits into the water. It floats like a shucked oyster on the inky surface, making me want to hitch my clothes even more. I climb a stack of crates, watching his stained and ragged red robes slosh about in the water.

"Why are you here, traitor?" he mutters, showing broken teeth likely shattered by a Char's wooden fist. "You come to gloat?"

I shake my head. "I've come to ask for your help." Some laugh. Most just ignore me. "We need strong men to help us row past the breakers, or we'll be stuck here indefinitely."

"You must be joking!" The Fire Shen stands and leans toward me intimidatingly. I hold my ground.

"Those that help will be granted leniency." Joka's neck cracks loudly as his head snaps around. It's a promise I can only keep if I work my way into a stronger position of power. "Most of you have families on the mainland." Some men lift their heads. "If you show you can be gracious… Show you can be trusted…" *It will look good for all of us.* "The general may grant favor."

The sneering Fire Shen slaps at the water, sending it spraying across my chest. "We are Mogui. Mogui are not gracious, they are killers. Our training was for one purpose only: To destroy the Char. How can you ask us to help them?"

I try not to look at what has sullied my clothing and stare straight ahead. "You *were* Mogui. Continue down this path and you shall die Mogui. You were not born this way, you were born to farmers and peasants, Shen with simple, good lives. Would you really rather die than try for an opportunity to return home?" The Fire Shen turns away and I realize some of these men will never be reachable.

Joka opens his mouth to speak but can't form words, stunned. A Water Shen holds up his tied wrists. "You give your word we will be allowed to return home?" He looks at me with a confused expression. Even as they think me a traitor, I am the Keeper. This still holds weight. It makes them lean toward a trust they probably shouldn't. But I created them. Like the Char are to a Carvress, so is the Keeper to an elemental Shen.

I nod. *Lies. Lies. Lies.* Pouring from my lips. "I promise."

Joka shakes his head.

*Shame. Shame. Shame.* Crowns my head thorny and cruel. I am more like my older brother than I thought.

Enough Shen agree to row.

Char guards reluctantly untie the Shen from the walls and posts and link them together in a chain gang, escorting them to the upper level.

As they file upward, Joka finds my eyes. Questions float like flotsam in his. He reaches for my arm, lets his palm settle on the sycamore for a moment. "What are you doing, Lye?" he whispers.

*I don't know. My compass spins out of control. Ash, the magnet that balanced it is missing. Travelling across the sea, homeward.*

"Proving my loyalty," I murmur. Though to whom, I'm not sure. I thought becoming a Char would keep me on the right side of the line. But a line drawn in sand is so easily washed away, redrawn, and washed away again. I swallow, making a cross over my heart. If I don't find a way to help these Shen get back to their families, perhaps the line does not exist for me anymore.

Joka is motionless, sloshing black water covering his feet, which he lifts every now and then, though there's nowhere safe to place them.

I open my arm and urge him to go first.

Taking a small dagger from my belt, I splay my weak fingers, ready to make a new mark for my deception. I probably won't even feel it so I breathe in and aim the tip at my smallest knuckle.

A strong, slender hand grasps the blade handle. A painful thing to do as I send scratching claws at him. I force my powers down.

"I ask you again, Lye Li; what are you doing?" Joka's voice is calmly concerned. It's a new, not entirely unwelcome, sound.

His smooth face is lit by waning candlelight. The Shen who are unwilling to help stare hatefully at their feet, Mogui until the end. "I am… it's a…" It's penance. Punishment. A reminder of one more awful thing I have done.

He evaluates me with intelligent, dark brown eyes. "It's a *what*?"

The way he stares pulls the truth from my throat like I'm choking on it. "It's what I do to remind myself of all the bad things I've done. It's like a running tally." I hold up my arm to show him the marks. He pushes it down gently.

"You want to scar yourself because you lied to those men?" I nod, eyes down, robes falling into the dirty water. He sighs. "Give me the knife." Hands out like a shifu asking for the contraband in your pocket.

I ache to cut. "But I deserve it."

"Only if you have no intention of following through," he murmurs. "How about instead of wasting your energy on pointless pain, you try your hardest to fulfil your promise?"

The boat lurches forward, and I fall palms first into the water as Joka thuds against the ladder. We're finally moving, accompanied by the choral collision of Shen soldiers chanting alongside Char hums. It fights in disharmony but somehow still sounds quite beautiful.

Joka hooks his arm under mine, pulling me up. "Marking your skin is not penance. This is not a real punishment since it's superficial. It's what you do when you're too lazy to face the real work of making up for what you have done." My mouth opens in shock at his bluntness.

Shaking his head, he mumbles something I only catch the end of. "—work to do, Lye."

He climbs the ladder quickly. Me, slipping and falling behind.

When I reach the top, he's there waiting with a stern yet encouraging face.

The boat rushes forward, lifting high over the waves and crashing down hard.

We run to the edge and expel our stomach contents at the same time. He smiles at me green-faced, and I'm sure my pallor matches his. He makes me feel like I need to try harder. Do more.

"What did you say to me down there?" I ask, scared of the answer but needing to know. Desperately needing a friend on this ship.

He grips the edge, eyes on the horizon. That nauseous puff to his breathing. "I said, we've got some work to do, Lye."

We. *We.*

The word grows wings. It flaps and flutters inside the cage of my body. Tearing its delicate feathers on the bars of my conscience.

# 21
## ASH KI

A strong wind hits the sails like a punch and the boat leaps forward. Behind us, Char ships make slow progress southeast. I sigh in a half-drowned kind of way, thinking of my sister and how we left things—an open wound, an exposed nerve.

Luna clicks her head and the movement asks me a silent question. I point the way the wind is blowing. "Just keep heading in a northeasterly direction and we should hit land by nightfall."

The boat is unbalanced. The chancellor on one side and four Carvresses on the other. It means we keep having to correct our course. Luna sees the issue too.

"Carvresses." She bows to the ebony one and one the color of the faintest blush. Luna gestures to where the chancellor sits. "Can you please move to the other side of the boat so our weight is more evenly distributed?" They nod and shift. They're not scared of him.

He, on the other hand, presses to the edge of the small boat like a discarded shadow. Disgusted and cowardly. I cock my head, wondering if this was how I seemed when I first arrived at the Char monastery. My lip curls. *Perhaps.*

Luna casts a disinterested glance his way. Speaking out across the waves as she steadies the rudder. "He's not much like you, Ash." She squints at the water, salt crusting her dark lashes.

"You don't think so?" The boat squirms under the force of the wind and she struggles to hold on. I place my hand next to hers, our fingers brushing. The curl of a possum's tail, warm and tentative, fills me. "I guess we only share a mother." The two of us stare at the back of the chancellor's long, thin head.

"You are much more handsome."

I wish I could be happy at her words, but the way she says it is completely observational. The possums tail retracts, and claws come out. I move my hand so there's a breath of salt air between us. I smile. A falsely proud smile. A cover.

"Well, it would be unlikely that perfection could be produced twice, would it not?"

She snorts with slight lightness and then it's swept underneath or inside something that must be close to bursting by now. Since all these feelings don't just disappear, I know she's storing them like a ring-tailed squirrel stores seed. Its double-plumed tail made for carrying food to its overflowing tree hollow. But like any space, it can only hold so much. I'm just wondering when and how it's going to come tumbling out.

Luna sighs, permitting herself a brief regression. "I hope Joka is doing all right." We look behind, to Ki Anah, Sun, and the other Carvresses sailing on our heels. "I hope he didn't break away from us because of me."

We hold the rudder tightly and when she turns to check on her family, her ear rests on my shoulder, my clothing a barrier to her blood power. For a brief second, it's just Luna. What she will allow, anyway. "I don't think so. Joka strikes me as a very pragmatic man. I think he went where he thought he would be most useful."

She lifts her head. Stares back out to sea. Wind tunnels between us, cold and powerful. "Yes, that sounds like him. Sun straight into danger. Joka using his head and Ben…"

Walls rise. Barricades made of feathers and bones are thrown up fast and rough. I speak for her. "And Ben Ni…?"

Her eyes are a frozen sun bursting with the need to make warmth. There's a *plea* in them. *Please don't mention his name. It's too much. Too hard.*

To our left, large, long-necked creatures spring from the water, braying huskily. The group startles, and one of the Carvresses exclaims, "Giraffe seals!" and touches her heart. "I have never seen one out in deep water before. They usually hug the coast."

While we lean over the edge to watch their acrobatics, the chancellor leans away, cringing. His blue silk filthy at the sleeves. His skin scabby and healing. One of the Carvresses climbs over his lap to get a better look and I think he might cry out in panic. She steps on his thighs, and he clenches his black teeth.

His washed-away eyes are on Luna. "She calls creatures with such ease." His voice calculates and measures.

She shakes her head. "I didn't…"

He scoffs. "Don't pretend. I of all people know what you're capable of, torturer." The giraffe seals stop propelling themselves into the air and lay on their backs, bobbing with the waves. Just their long neck and heads sitting proud above the water. Behind us, Sun leans over the bow, his face alight.

I hunt for feeling in my brother's eyes and find it. He's frightened of her, but also captivated. At least there's something we have in common. "She only did what she was ordered to do," I defend.

She ignores us both. Eyes on the horizon.

He gazes at his scabby fingers. "Well, she did it excellently." He shakes his head slowly. "Torture is a regrettable but necessary tool of war." I clutch the word *regrettable*. Give it more weight than I should.

The ebony Carvress turns to face the chancellor. "Ah, so is death!" Her small mouth runs flat as a frozen pond.

Luna pokes our baskets of fruit with her foot. "We should eat." Her eyes lift to the sun, dangling in the middle of the sky like an unripe melon.

Fruit is passed out and the chancellor picks through the basket with tied hands, moving things aside to find something specific. His eyes sweeten when he finds a leather peach at the bottom. He licks his lips and bites into the chewy, dimpled skin. I find my heart turning in my chest like it's recognized a long-lost friend. Leather peach is my favorite, but most people dislike them because of the chewy, bitter skin.

I smile, awkwardly staring, and he snarls at me. "Must you stare? It is demeaning enough eating with one's hands bound without an audience."

I look away, confused by my need to find a connection.

Luna elbows me carefully. "I feel you, Ash. And your thoughts are dangerous."

Sweet, sour, and salt fills the air as I try to decide if she's right. Whether she's even qualified to comment.

THE PALE pink Carvress, whom Luna tells me is from Pearl Shell Beach, jitters next to the chancellor. Her legs bang against the wooden bench, adding percussion to our journey.

I nudge Luna. "What's wrong with that one?" I ask, pointing at her back. The two Carvresses are distinct opposites of one another, dark versus light. Short versus tall. But they share dark eyes, almost black, with a peanut oil shine to them. It looks particularly strange in the pale one's face.

The two on the other side are more typical, if that can be said of a Carvress. Tall, slender, and swirling with golden timber. Their arms and legs spotted with galaxies of knotholes and grains, sap lines and rings. Luna's hair flaps forward with the wind like a flag as she whispers tersely, "Don't point. Which *one* do you mean?"

I gesture more subtly. "The pinkish one seems nervous. Jittery, sitting next to my... the chancellor. Perhaps she should switch places."

Luna frowns, mouth pouting as she observes the small Carvress. "I'm not sure what's wrong with her. I do know she's the youngest sister. Pearl Shell is also the most remote of our islands. Maybe she's just uncomfortable being around so many people." She shrugs. "Or being so close to a Shen."

Sisters. "They're sisters?" Luna tips her chin, touching the very top of her wooden sternum. "Why would she care if she's close to a Shen? He can't hurt her."

Luna opens like a small window, just a crack to let in some fresh air. "He cannot harm her. Does not mean he cannot *hurt* her."

Her hair whips forward and suddenly falls flat to her shoulders. The boat slides like it's been pushed over ice, the sails sag, and we are stationary.

Sun's loud cursing burns my ears.

The wind has died like a ghost that's decided to pass over to Hexie, the place where elements reach equilibrium.

The Carvresses touch each other's knees and blink their amazing eyes. Communicating without speaking.

I shield my eyes, searching for land and see nothing.

Sun and Ki Anah paddle closer until their boat bumps ours. "Well, this is just fantastic!" he grumbles. Ki Anah places a calming hand on his shoulder, and he sits down.

Luna and I exchange looks and lean over the edge, just as Sun mutters, "Better get used to their weird, silent exchanges, Mama. They do it all the time." He huffs, readying an oar. But there's no way we're strong enough to row against this current. Already our boats turn like a compass arrow, floating off course. We will still hit the mainland, but the last thing we want is to land by the palace.

Luna plunges her hand into the water, closing her eyes and making figure eights with her palms.

Ki Anah leans over the back of her boat watching. "What is she doing?" she asks, eyes wide and curious with just a splash of intimidation.

The chancellor answers, "Ignorant woman! She's calling animals to her, so she can use them to pull us the rest of the way." His words are met with animosity from all sides.

Ki Anah's mouth snaps shut as she burns holes in his face with her glare. She aims her questions at me. "What does Sun mean? How can Luna talk to you without words?"

My hands spin in anxious circles as I try to explain how we combined our powers and it left us linked. Kind of in each other's heads. Ki Anah takes this in with a disapproving look but she doesn't speak her displeasure. Her face scrunches as she struggles against wonder. A look I've seen in Luna before.

The chancellor listens shrewdly as the boat rises over small swells and carries us east.

Luna flicks her hand and water speckles my cheeks. "There's nothing close. Not even a school of fish."

Sun takes up an oar. "Then we row."

I shake my head. "We can try but we have only two oars per boat. The current is too strong and we're too heavy."

The Coalstone Carvress speaks. "What do you suggest, young Shen?"

My eyes scan the water, hoping something will come. All eyes are on Luna and me, and I smile awkwardly under the continued scrutiny. "I don't know."

The chancellor twists his rope like body, eyes landing on me. "You and the Char girl combined powers? Impressive." His stained gums give his lips an exaggerated appearance. He grins, teeth shining like lava rocks. "We could do the same to influence the current."

Luna warns me, as do all the concerned expressions in both boats. "He cannot be trusted."

My heart leans away as my body moves closer. I know he can't be trusted. But I don't see another way. If the current pulls us to the palace, we're as good as dead. I inch closer to the chancellor. "How can I be sure you won't push us further off course?"

His pointed chin sways from side, eyes bright and yet still foggy. "You can't." He holds out his wrists and I wiggle my blade underneath the ties. "Maybe I'll get you close to the south-western coast where the beaches stretch flat and pristine, leading inland like a welcoming concubine." The women cringe as he runs his tongue over his teeth. "Or maybe I'll land you right at the base of the palace mountain—a gift for the emperor. Take your chances, brother. You'll just have to see if you can overpower me."

I cut his bindings and take his hand.

And as our skin connects, his darkness eclipses the sun.

# 22
## LYE LIE

I like the sound of Char and Shen soldiers rowing together, clashing and struggling to find the right beat. Not quite harmony, but a sort of symbiotic relationship. It pushes and pulls like a tug-of-war game. Rubbing my palm over my sycamore arm, the back and forth feels like the competition inside myself.

The general frowns over the water. One hand on the wheel, the other rubbing his jaw. With his legs locked on the deck in a wide stance and his muscles flexed, he tries to make steering look effortless. He doesn't realize I am more than he thinks. I'm not a princess-like character but someone who threw the punches and took fists to the face. I recognize a false show of strength when I see it. Stumbling toward him to tell him just that, the boat lurches again and I clutch my stomach. My right hand reaches for the mast, slipping and failing to grasp. With a huff, I swing around to use my stronger hand.

Joka sits before me with his back against the mast and eyes closed. The sun heats his neck, making it pop like water-trapped wood on a fire. He glances up and yawns wide.

I frown at his manners. *Perhaps there is a little bit of princess in me after all.*

"Why do you look like you're about to do something unwise?" he asks, voice sleep-full. Rising slowly.

I purse my lips, still hanging onto the rope as we pitch over the waves. "I was not… I was just going to tell the general he needn't put on a show of strength for me. It's a waste of his energy."

Joka chuckles. A little high. A little awkward. "I assumed correctly."

"Why are you sleeping here?" I ask, leaning closer and ignoring his comment.

"Unlike some people, I've been rowing for three hard hours. We're taking it in short shifts." His dark eyes challenge me.

I pull my bad hand inside my robe. "I can't… my hand is…"

He nods. "I know. But you could do something other than looking green and thinking of ways to sabotage yourself." He taps his green neck for emphasis, and I have the insane desire to run a finger from under his chin to that defined notch between his collarbones. He squirms a little under my gaze.

My eyes go to the general again. "I need to speak with him about the Shen. They deserve leniency given their willingness to help."

Joka shakes his head as he rises. "If you ask now, he will say no. For the time being, you need to show you're loyal to the Char."

"But I talked the men into helping. Surely that…"

Joka stretches his long arms and almost falls when we crash over the swell. "No. You need to *show* him. Char are impressed by actions, not words." He flicks an impatient hand at me like I'm an annoying bug. "Go make yourself useful."

I pout, fold my arms over my chest and thump my ribs too hard with my heavy arm. I'm about to say, *But I'm the Keeper.* My mouth dries instantly, words roughening my tongue like I've swallowed desert sand. I'm not the Keeper. I'm not Char either. If I want to cross over that line, Joka is right.

My ghost companion, always hovering in the corner of my eye, slips into the shadows. Flesh and blood taking over my counsel for the time being. A different brother. A different perspective.

I stumble toward the hatch, try not to tumble down headfirst, and make my way to the kitchen.

I WONDER if it's universal. The calming nature of preparing tea. I pour the rose-colored water into cups. Half full, so I don't scald any more soldiers, and cram them onto a tray. The cherry-heart scent floats up my nose and brings me small peace. Grinding them was less calming and more cathartic as I used my wooden arm to smash the seeds open to reveal the heart. Cherry-heart has the energizing, purifying effect of pump blood faster and cleaner.

Balancing the tray on my arm, I grip the silver edge with my good fingers. I'm getting better at this, wearing less spills and managing to serve more tea as I practice. My eyes shoot to the pink stains on my robe. *At least it makes it look less dull.*

Carefully stepping onto the rowing level, I move between benches offering resting men beverages and food I've stuffed in my pockets. It's a small thing, but Char eyes are grateful. Shen are incredulous. The Keeper doesn't stoop to serving food like a common servant. I've awakened the elements of almost all these soldiers, but their faces are not familiar. They're just beads on a long string.

Yet they take what is offered. They bow, though not as low as they once did. Their Atmosphere is of distrust slowly unwinding. A snake wound around its eggs, protecting and not wanting to crush them.

Worrying my lip between my teeth, I return the empty tray to the kitchen. I have made a promise I don't know how to keep. Distracting myself by bashing open more seeds, I watch the small red hearts roll around on the counter. My eyes close for a moment, thinking of Ash, Luna, and the chancellor. They have the wind. Soon they'll reach the mainland. I bash the wood top loudly. *I wish I'd killed him. I wish it more than anything.*

The rhythm of oar strokes suddenly stops, and seeds roll off the bench and onto the floor, scattering like marbles.

The chanting has ceased.

The boat streams ahead.

I guess they *had* the wind. It has changed direction like a youth's heart, and now we're that much closer to the prisoner drop-off point.

Clambering up the ladder, I plant my hands on the wet deck, sensing only slight dampness in my limp hand. It's still dull. Ignoring the senseless limb, I push forward to speak to the general.

He seems pleased at the wind change. It rakes through his dark hair like a lover's gentle fingers. The sails are open, billowing like brave, proud clouds. Steeling myself, I attempt to walk in a controlled manner, stomach still bouncing around inside my body.

"General Fah." I address him sternly. "I wish to speak to you about the Shen prisoners."

His eyes rest on the mound of land, rising up like a head breaking the waves for a breath of air. "What about them?" he asks, disinterested. "Although soon, we won't need to consider them at all." He points. "Look to Bird Cage Island."

I narrow my eyes as the name becomes clearer with our approach. Long, curved rock formations jut from the water, wobbling like a mirage in the hot sun. "Yes, but the men who helped row. I promised them they could go home."

His fingers wrap tightly around the wheel, his Atmosphere closing in like fog to a mountaintop. "No, Keeper Lye." He over pronounces every word, making sure I understand. "*You* told the Shen a *lie* so the Char could reach Black Sail Island faster. You misled the enemy to get a result."

There is truth to what he says, which is why I don't argue. "Is there any way?"

He shakes his head once.

I mark the crime on the lengthening scroll, written in blood and feather bone charcoal. It will be a long-term promise. The Shen will not see it that way though, and I must accept their hate at my deception.

I shall welcome it and wear it like a medallion over my heart.

# 23
## ASH KI

The boat wiggles like a lizard shedding its skin. The chancellor's black-speckled fingernails dig into my skin as we join powers. Cold, black water pours through my body. Oil dancing over its surface with a mirror shine. I try to push back against him. My own water, sapphire blue and warm, bounces against his.

Scenes flash in my mind. Each one dragging a claw across my skin. The chancellor's memories. *A stretching, screaming newborn child, wrapped in netted umbilical cord. A mother looking away. Our mother. Her eyes are conflicted as she beholds the child. They cut at the baby with rice scythes, freeing him from a cage of twisted cord. He cries and she covers her ears, shaking her head. My father stands in the corner. The couple's eyes connect. Such sadness. Such shame. But also love. It hovers like a dark cloud. It clings to the walls. Parts of it follow the baby as it's taken outside. My father whispers, "Malu." Shame.*

The boat ticks left and right. Luna touches my hand and I swim for her. Her sudden concern niggles and I wish to wrap both hands around it, but the chancellor pulls me down and inside another vision.

*Lye lying in the dirt, her small body curled around a cane ball, long hair trampled and crusted with mud. A thin boy with mold green eyes who must be the chancellor kicks her side and snatches the ball. She whimpers, doesn't try to get up. Seeing her submissive is like a cut through dark tent walls. The boy sneers and tosses the ball up and down, taunting. A baby cries and the boy's head twists up, eyes wide with fear. Our mother steps foot outside our hut and shakes her hand at him. She doesn't seem angry exactly, more disappointed and worn, like this is one of many times. She kneels to the shaking Lye and scoops her up while a baby, which must be me, screams loudly in the background. The nasty boy with watery eyes runs away, clutching the ball. Our mother watches him go. She looks tired. She starts toward him and then changes her mind. Resignation obvious.*

The boat coasts forward but off course. I can feel it. He's trying to force us closer the palace. I struggle against him, but he comes at me harder. In these visions, people reach for him with care, and he bites them with little or no regret. A dark, twisted thing growing around his heart like the cord around his baby body. Each memory gets darker and more solid, pounding down like blocks of ice. *Torture.* Men and women and children. Suffering children with round, terrified eyes. Hands clasped and pleading. Finding no mercy. No feeling at all.

I fight. I swim. It does no good in this darkness. A hand tries to pull us apart. But we're cemented together. This feels nothing like when Luna and I combined powers. And maybe it's different with different people, but I can't find equilibrium.

I try to find weakness. Threading around all the atrocity, the greed, and wind back to that thin boy, standing over Lye clutching the ball. While his chest heaves, I can feel that he's close to tears. Flickers of pure jealousy and flashes of fear for his mother's judgment. And it makes him vulnerable.

I concentrate on my own memory. *Lye and I playing out the front of the hut while mother swept the floors with a barley broom. The dry swish, swish on the stones as we climbed the woodpile. The ground is the sea, full of monsters. We hop from a log to a pile of leaves, staying off the ground to avoid monsters dragging us to the bottom of the ocean. We giggle and squeal, trying to throw each other off balance. Our mother pauses in the doorway, watchful. I focus on her expression, and I show it to the chancellor. Untainted motherly love. She rushes to me as I start to topple, hands outstretched to catch me.*

His feelings of rejection rise like the tide.

I tumble through the air, hitting water hard.

The chancellors grip releases and I am free.

His eyes are rings of irritation. Displeased. Not hurt, just annoyed. And I understand him better now. He's someone who chooses the dark path over and over. Like being born this way suits him. I shiver and glance behind us. The sun has dropped, dangling over the water.

I turn to Luna. "How long have we been like this?" I ask, scared of the answer.

The chancellor cackles, slapping his knee.

"Four hours," she replies, glaring at the chancellor, who grins like a feral cat.

I search for clues as to how far off course he has pushed us but it's hard to tell. I snatch up his shirt in my fist and rattle him violently until his black pearl teeth glint. "How far off course are we?" *How close to the palace?*

He shrugs. Icicles stab at my fingers and I release him, throwing the bony menace into the benches. "I guess we'll soon find out." His eyes flick to the water as we plow through it. "The current is set now." He heaves himself onto one of the benches looking very pleased with himself, like he's already won.

"You didn't overpower me for long." I grip the side of the boat, trying to stop myself from striking him.

"We shall see, brother."

The Coalstone Carvress wobbles over to the chancellor. She pulls back her arm and punches him with her solid wooden fist. The sound is bone crunchingly satisfying. He falls back, unconscious. "I would have done that earlier, but Char Luna said it could hurt you while you were connected to that... man." She ties his hands tightly.

Sun lets out a Char chant, "*Gwai na yeng deh deh!*" Pumping his fist in the air with approval. They float in the same tunnel of water, about thirty feet behind us. Sun and another Carvress at the oars.

"What does that mean?" I ask Luna not familiar with all the words, though I catch 'devil'.

"It means the devil drowns in his own evil." I raise an eyebrow. "To put it simply, you get what you deserve."

The thin man draped over the benches looks like a lost scrap of fabric. I like him better this way, though his mouth is still a puckered, bitter frown. He lets out a weird, frightened shriek in his sleep, his body jerking. I jump back.

Then Luna makes a sound I haven't heard in a long time. Sunshine caught in a prism. Deep and dry and full of promise—she laughs. It's so good, it was almost worth the horrifying visions.

LUNA'S HAND swirls in the water as the ebony Carvress and I use oars to move us further along. We can't fight the current since we'd end up rowing for days, running out of food and water. Our best course of action is to reach the mainland and see how far off course the chancellor has pushed us.

"We don't want to have come this far just to deliver the Carvresses right to the Shen emperor's door," Sun shouts between the boats. "Are you sure?"

I flap my hands and shout back. "I am sure!"

They trust me because they have little choice. And Luna said I could be trusted.

The chancellor didn't completely overshoot our direction. I just don't know how far down the beach we'll land from our intended destination and how much closer to the palace. He flutters in his unconscious state like a cut weed. After that joining, I see shreds of hope in his love for our mother like the spaces between thickly planted water reeds, colorless, thin, yet there's still a possibility for light to shine through. It all depends on how quickly the reeds grow.

Luna continues to gaze at the water as I watch her. I was worried we might lose our connection, but I don't have harmony with him. Only with Luna. I don't *feel* him, for which I'm extraordinarily grateful. Staring too long, I am entranced by the graceful eights she creates, and the Coalstone Carvress taps the back of my head. "Concentrate!"

The colors of sunset race us to the mainland. Rippling spills of orange and pink approach like rivers of lava ready to devour our little boats. Soon we will lose the light. I sigh. *I'd rather hit land before that happens.*

Luna flicks her hands of water, small droplets kissing my cheeks. "There's barely anything with a heartbeat in this ocean. Where are all the living things?" she asks.

I pull my oar trying to match the Carvress's impressive strength. "The sea ceased providing bountiful catches some time ago," I answer without turning.

She breathes out loudly. Exasperatedly. "Why?"

I feel a little defensive when I say, "We caught a lot of fish. And those we didn't eat are in netted farms close to the eastern shore."

"You mean you over-fished," she mutters to the back of my head with tight disapproval. "If you don't leave some to reproduce then…"

The sun is folding in for the day. Light becomes murky. Pinks and oranges die to a hazy gray. "I understand how it works, Luna." I roll my eyes though she can't see me. "Look, I'm from inland. This is not my fault."

She huffs. "I'll be interested to see how Shen farm the land also."

The way she says "Shen" is exclusive, aimed solely at the chancellor. It leaves me floating like the fog gathering in front of the boat. Not Shen but not Char either.

She's frustrated. Itching to get a hold of some living creature to control. She splashes at the water angrily. "There's nothing! It feels manmade, like an empty dam."

Light disappears fast and fog presses down. I grimace. "Can we just focus on getting to land and worry about our unsustainable fishing practices later?"

Something catches in her throat and she makes an odd raw sound, her throat sanded. "You don't understand." I turn to face her. "I can't… I feel so… Useless." She throws her hands in the air dramatically.

*Welcome to my world, Luna Yan.*

I like that she feels something, even if it's negative. "You want to be useful? Why don't you hold onto the rudder and steer us out of this current." Land approaches and we're swallowed by an almost opaque cloud. She twists the rudder and we slow, using our oars to get us to shore.

I can barely see two feet in front of my face, but I hear the crash of waves on sand. The boats beach suddenly. Nose diving into the sand and sending us flying forward. I reach down, finding the ground easily.

The chancellor snorts and opens his eyes briefly. I knock my head toward him. "What do we do with him?"

Before I say anything more, Sun appears through the fog beside our boat. He grabs the Chancellor's covered hands, yanking him from the boat and plopping him unceremoniously into the saltwater. He scrambles and splutters. Splashing in two-foot-deep water like he thinks he will drown. I start to laugh but stop. I was not much better than him the first time I tried to swim. My cheeks heat like a glowing ember as I remember wood on flesh. Brass cool against my skin. The way her eyes lifted to the sky as she gasped. *Thinking about that night is not a good idea.*

Ki Anah is suddenly beside me, stomping to land, and my cheeks cool to ice. *Definitely not a good idea.*

Leaving the chancellor where he is, we pull the boats up the beach. There's no hiding them in this bare, foreboding place. I listen for noises of sea birds squawking, a seal bark, as I know Luna must be doing the same. It is silent save the rhythmic bash of waves.

The fog is thick, and we walk in a straight line from the shoreline, keeping close, until Sun swears and Ki Anah slaps him.

Fog does not stick to this rock. The Carvresses stop their chatter and we all stare up, up, up, into cliffs that reach to the sky. I swipe at the wet rock carpeted in green slippery moss. The chancellor emerges from the water and tries to slip eastward, drenched silk robes thwacking at his sides. Sun catches him easily, kicking him to the ground with his balsawood foot, while Ki Anah opts to tie his hands behind his back.

The chancellor spits sand. "I guess I was wrong about you. You have more power than I gave you credit for, brother Koh." I return to the cliffs. "We've landed between the palace and the river mouth. Although a little closer to the palace, I'd wager." His voice is triumphant. I swig my water and shove it at his lips. He gulps it like a baby, water dribbling down his chin.

If we don't get off this beach before the fog lifts, we could be spotted, and arrows will skewer our chests. I don't know how many guards remain to patrol this coast, but I can't risk it.

I put my foot into a notch in the rock and try to climb. I get about six feet up before I run out of places to hold. The cliff face is impossibly smooth and there are no labyrinths to navigate like on Crow's Nest Island. These rocks are impenetrable. My mind drifts to that night, when I first confessed to Lye a love she and I knew was destined to hurt me. Looking at Luna now, there is no question in my mind or heart that it is still worth every ounce of pain.

Sun throws the chancellor at the wall and attempts to climb too, getting slightly higher but not by much. He jumps down, landing gracefully like a troupe acrobat.

The chancellor crows. "They are unclimbable. You may as well just wait for your capture in the morning." He eyes Luna in a greedy, skin-prickling way that makes me want to wring his thin body like a wet rope. "Then we can begin our work, Char-Shen hybrid. Taking you apart piece by piece and discovering what makes you function."

Sun kicks him forcefully in the chest and some of the water he swallowed comes back out.

Luna is contemplative. Eyes gently closed like she's dreaming, arms out at one hundred and eighty degrees. She is silent and concentrated and then—she is golden.

# 24
## LYE LI

I wipe my cheek where the Shen spat on me as he was escorted from our ship. The saliva absorbs into the sleeve of the filthy robe I've been wearing for so many weeks. In this we are all the same, caked with mud and blood, craving baths and beds. My hair prickles over a thinly covered head. We may have to wait a little longer for those simple pleasures.

The Shen prisoners were right to curse me as we left them on Bird Cage Island. Their insults carried on the wind as they were taken by Char villagers and what soldiers we could spare to the safe and inescapable pits. The strictest instructions were issued to treat these Shen with humility. I saw more than one Char roll their eyes, as if they were insulted that they would do anything else. Their system is simple: A prisoner starts at the bottom of the carved stone pit. With good behavior they can work up the levels until they reach ground level. I like the idea they can work toward freedom. Shen are not so forgiving. They imprison to punish, not rehabilitate.

Bowing my head, I feel torn in too many directions when my focus needs to be on the challenge ahead. Some promises must wait, and war is not fair. I've picked my side and I must dedicate myself to it.

Wind fills our sails. Giving us this one blessing as we weave between Char islands. Bumps of green, sitting proudly out of the water like totems. There's a measure of defiance in the island dwellings, though I'd never say it. The Char pride themselves on living with the sea and land, not in it. I frown, wondering what Luna and the others will think of the Shen mainland. The ocean ravaged. The land sown and reaped a thousand seasons over.

Have they seen one of the great filter boats scraping the seabed, sieving out any leftover shellfish that have managed to hide? There's a rose-colored shame rising in my cheeks at the way the Shen have treated our earth.

The general claps toward me, clutching black cloth. He shoves it at me brusquely. When I don't take it, the lump falls to the ground. We stare down at the clothing on the deck between us. "It's a Char uniform," he states, sweeping a hand down and draping it over my sycamore arm. I can feel the roughness of fabric and I marvel at the fact that I can *feel* it. My wooden arm has sense as if it were skin. I run my fingers over the uniform, wishing I could accept it. But I can't. Not yet.

I push it back into his hands. "I cannot wear this, General Fah."

A tense fury scurries up his body. Defensive. "I don't understand. This is a great honor. And I thought it's what you wanted." He shakes the uniform at me angrily. "Why would you refuse? Is the Keeper too good for…"

I stop him before he says something he'll regret. "General, may I speak with you in private? I have a very good reason to refuse and I shall explain it to you."

Intrigued but still angered, the general escorts me to his cabin.

THE SUN has sunk below the horizon twice and now we float into the harbor of Black Sail City two days later. My heart darkens several shades, blanketed in shadow at the sight. The city burns. From here it looks like red-hot threads strung across blackened buildings. Another battle making a mess. But instead of a plateau, this battle is fought over a terrain of tiered levels. Buildings built into the mountainside, narrow serpentine alleys and a jungle trying to reach over from the other side of the mountain like a giant hand to claim all of it.

Our anchors drop heavily, and we search for Char, listen for them. The Shen army hold the western shoreline where ships would usually dock to unload and trade. A cleverly designed multi-level port. A ground level and tunnels below used to directly unload ship contents. The Shen flag flaps against the smoke at one such tunnel. A colorful circle of the elements with a five-point star in the center. Funny to think that I am that star. The Char appear to hold the furthermost "sail" of the three stone monoliths that give the island its name. I've never seen the enormous black rocks from this perspective, and they are as Luna described, defiant and imposing. The Char flag, black with a gold sun in its center, is tacked to the rock, stamped with the Carvress mark. Colored and black staked claims cover the island. Flags marking Shen or Char captured territory. But mostly, the view is of thick gray smoke. Homes are on fire, and a growing red scar of flames crawls up the mountain toward the monastery, which lies beyond the sails.

Char soldiers scramble around me, fitting their weapons and tightening their belts. There's no time for orders or *order*. Men jump over the side and into row boats, moving as fast as they can east of the city to where a black Char flag flaps limply through dense smoke. The general gives me a nod and follows his men.

I grip the railing, willing myself to do what is needed. Telling my heart it's the right thing. It gives the Char a chance at least.

The last rowboat is about to leave. I fling myself over the edge and land between Char men with strong, willful hearts and wooden limbs ready to fight.

As soon as the boat touches the water, arrows pierce the surface ahead. They're out of range, but not for long. Men row fast, taking a wide arc toward the mass of Char black on land. They see us coming and wave frantically. Trying to provide cover fire as we row, defenseless, through the water. Waves rock the boat. I see Joka climbing onto land and running inland with the others. I didn't get to say goodbye. There was no time. My eyes sting from tears and bitter smoke. Another friend, gone before I could ruin it. It is for the best. He won't understand what I have done.

A wave picks us up like a great hand, delivering us to the Shen. The rowers desperately try to pull back but it's too late. A flock of arrows cruise like soundless birds right for us. They hit the boat, tearing men apart beside me. I hold my arm to my chest, hoping it will act as a shield. The man beside me coughs blood and tips into the water. Just like that. Another life taken.

"We must get out of range!" I shout, ordering the men to row back out to sea. "Put all your strength into rowing." I stand at the front of the boat as it drags away from the shore. My arm up. My chin proud. The sea assists, digging its undiscerning fingers into the hull and yanking us back out of range. The boat bucks over a wave. My leg slips forward. A hand wraps around my calf to steady me and I react without thought, shocking it with quick lightning. The kind that blackens the top of a palm tree but does not destroy it. "I'm sorry," I murmur. The hand releases and I plunge into the water.

I dive down, lungs bursting, and swim underneath boats, popping up to draw in breath. The hulls knock my head, before I dive under again. Swimming west toward the Shen stronghold, hiding from the Char, I search for Shen colors. They call me closer. To a home I once had and must now live in again.

The water weights my clothes, and my breath comes fast and spluttering. I grasp the moorings of small transport canoes and tug myself to shore.

Arrows and fire. Men shouting while they search.

Flopping onto land with a loud, water-full slap, I drag in a long breath.

I scan the docks. Every door hangs open, broken on its hinges. Groups of Shen fly from building to building. And there are bodies. *Everywhere.*

A Water Shen gurgles by a cage, fingers curled around the wooden bars while a chicken clucks mindlessly within, pecking at her dying fingers.

I try to shut my mind to the suffering since I have a job to do. But I quickly touch my hands to the Shen's ankle. Freezing her body and brain. Numbing her until her blood drains away.

Hand still gripping the cold, dead flesh, I survey what's left of an open-air market: squashed vegetables strewn over the street; upturned carts; wandering farm animals, unaffected by the noise and violence. I release the woman, hearing her last breath as I creep low toward the open door of a shopfront.

Swords clash nearby, too many elements being thrown to clearly read an Atmosphere. An arrow whizzes past me and lands inside a glass box full of red fish. They surge around it like a cloud of blood. A Shen voice shouts, "Fall back!"

Fire orange uniforms stream down the steep slope backward. My eyes follow them. Leaning out from my hiding position.

They shoot as they trip and tumble. When they think they've got enough distance, they turn and sprint. Hopefully, they'll lead me to the Shen stronghold.

Keeping low, I track them, sticking to the edge of the street, ducking into doorways and behind crates and carts.

The Shen flag flies stoutly over an underpass by the edge of the water. The Fire Shen disappear down a dark hole.

I crouch, wondering how I can get close. The shoreline provides more cover. I wait for a rise in noise and run for a pile of fishing nets, throwing myself behind it just as a goat trots past me, bleating loudly, its split-black eyes terrified. It screams like a woman who's seen a ghost.

*I know you think this is a huge risk. But then we could say the same for what you did, Ben Ni.* His hands join behind his back and he nods in agreement.

Men gather near the entrance to the stronghold, searching for the source of screaming.

I raise my dagger to silence it for good, but it looks at me with such dumb horror, I can't do it. It continues to bleat with its tongue poking out, long and thin. I press my back to the pile of nets and decide to crawl. The next lot of cover is only a few feet away. The goat curdles blood with its screeching, and I curse under my breath, my palms sliding on the cold cobblestones. Knees grinding.

I wish it would fall into the water. I wish all manner of awful, awful fates upon the poor creature.

I don't think about what's behind me. Only what's in front.

Sudden pain sears through my side and I flip onto my back. My fingers find an arrow, the head half-buried, hot blood pooling around the wound.

Shen Blue flaps over my strangely angled body. I pull my sycamore arm deep inside my robe. Push words from a mouth that only wants to scream in agony. "I am Shen Keeper Lye Li Koh. Keeper Lye Li," I sputter. The point of a sword hovers near my throat.

"I know who you are," the Shen man growls. "You're a traitor."

I blink. Try to stem the blood. "I am the Keeper. I serve the Shen Emperor and no other. I am no traitor. Take me to your captain."

He's a fuzzy cloud of doubting eyebrows and curling lips. "I should kill you first. It would make me a hero to bring your body to my captain."

"If you kill me, you will never find the Carvresses," I whisper, feeling woozy. I use my last strength to tell him that I have come so far, across oceans and through jungles, past an army of Char and a boat full of Shen prisoners, to say. "I know where they hide."

I fight against my consciousness as it slips like seaweed through a drowning girl's hair. Because he will touch me with the tip of his blade, but he will not help me walk. No one touches the Keeper outside of awakenings. It is forbidden. I scrape myself together like I'm gathering twigs for a fire. The lack of human touch was just another way to isolate me from the world. Though perhaps it was better that way since I only hurt those I love. *Ash, I hope one day you can forgive me.* My sycamore arm feels like a dead lump under my clothes and I clutch it close to my side.

The sun is blocked by ash swirling through the air. I grit my teeth and refuse to look away as ash flakes land on my eyelashes. I am the Keeper and he will abide me. "Do you think your captain would be pleased to know you passed up a chance to find the Carvresses for your own personal glory?" I summon bloodless energy. "With my dying breath I shall scream your crimes."

Padded feet. The comforting shush of Shen language. The man turns to see comrades rushing toward us and he sheaths his sword, bowing. I grip my side tightly and summon the strong legs of an eggshell horse, its thin but impossibly strong skin covering muscles that only know to run.

I focus on shuffling forward as Shen crowd me, creating a forcefield. Not a single soul touches me but surround me in a tight circle. I try to shut out the words, but some curses pierce my concentration. The word Keeper is spat. The word traitor linked closely to it.

The tunnel sweeps over my head like a dead rainbow as I clop, clop forward at the point of ten swords, straight into the base of operation.

To complete my mission. I have much to prove.

If my brother could only see me now.

# 25
## ASH KI

Complaints start as small murmurs. Then slaps on the skin. Then cursing. The Carvresses are still, swaying from side to side whilst gazing up at the impossible cliffs. Those of us made of flesh are less than calm. Actually, we're starting to panic.

Luna moves her arms in small circles like a wind-up toy. Eyes still closed, parting the cloud of golden flakes surrounding her. The Carvresses watch with shining wooden eyes, the light reflecting off their polished skin and making them even more beautiful.

But no one looks as beautiful and frightening as Luna.

The golden specks buzz and burn our skin. Ki Anah makes a small sound of pain and Luna's eyes shoot open. Her fingers twitch and Ki Anah's face relaxes as much as it can considering we're encircled by a thick cloud of fireflies. They peel from the cliff, black to suddenly alight, streaming towards us to create a whirling hurricane of light and buzzing. The chancellor grimaces, his face splotched red. Bites rise on his skin. Luna won't protect him from the insects.

The rest of us are no longer being bitten. We are people-sized cutouts in this wall of living light.

The buzzing reaches a crescendo. Luna scrunches her fists, evening her breath. Her heart beating steady, no doubt, but her face shows extreme exertion. Ki Anah and I share the same look of concern. It is wiped from our faces as the fireflies surge outward and then cling to our skin.

The beauty of this moment is beyond anything. More than dream. More than magic. Luna called the stars. She called them to her, and they obliged.

The Carvresses lift from the sand, arms straight, feet pointed. Floating like paper spirit lanterns into the atmosphere, they take this in stride. Ki Anah, Sun, and I are less composed, and we take off like baby birds shoved from the nest too early. Sun curses, hands and arms moving jerkily as the bugs lift him up. I try to lock my limbs to make it easier, but the fluttering of thousands of wings against my skin makes it difficult to be still.

Luna is by my side. With her eyes closed again, she summons unearthly, earthly power. *She didn't summon the stars. She is one.*

As she uses all her strength to lift us to the mesa above, the black rock reflects our passage. Thousands of candles held to night-time windows.

We are covered well. Just part of the firefly cloud. No scout would spot us. They wouldn't believe their eyes if they did.

I turn my thoughts away from how far away the beach is. I try to block out the chancellor's squirming, panting, and whining.

I see only Luna and am awed by her magnificence. Her fierceness.

Her lips curl into a small smile as she directs the bugs. Her mouth opens into a laugh when I say, "This tickles."

Ki Anah looks less impressed and more disturbed. Sun looks like he's about vomit.

We fly over the edge of the cliff, and I ready myself for a fall and brace myself to run for cover, but we're carried further inland. Fir leaves brush our faces as we're dropped gently between large pine trees. Well, almost all of us are dropped gently.

The chancellor breaks branches, landing with a thump as he's released from several yards above. He curls into a ball, itching and scratching his legs. The rest of us are deposited carefully, the fireflies darting out from under our feet just before we would crush them into the ground.

Luna lands last, opens her mouth to speak but instead crumbles. From golden light to the sudden depths of darkness. My heart seizes, and I drop down to catch her before she lands on top of the chancellor. Her small mouth parted and exhaling toasted breath. A heart working hard to keep in time.

I stroke her cheek, tucking strands of hair behind her tiny ear. My shaking hand comes back wet with blood. Blood! This feat has harmed her. It hurts me more than chains tightening around my wrists as my head was plunged into water over and over. More than the worst torture. Because she is breaking apart and letting it happen.

I hold my hand up to the moonlight to show the others and Ki Anah falls to her knees beside her daughter.

The Coalstone Carvress shakes her head. "A flesh body can only take so much." The moon catches her carved cheeks, making her look cut from stone. "These dual powers are taking their toll."

Ki Anah hums softly. "She will be fine. She will be fine."

Sun and I exchange a serious look of worry.

I lift Luna, so light in my arms I wonder if she truly is made of starlight, and we walk through the woods. Searching for a safe place to rest when we know there is none.

# 26

## LYE LI

The damp, salt-streaked tunnel is decorated with color. Shen flags and weapons tied with element cloth. My hand seeks the wall for support, and soldiers part as I find it. The tunnel wall is cold and slimy, much like my bloodied side.

My lids are heavy, pulled down by my own muddy conscience. Right and wrong battle around me but can't find a way in. Perhaps, after so much time spent with the chancellor, I've lost the ability to know the difference.

Shen still keep a distant circle around me, and it makes me want to laugh. Bitterly. Hysterically. "I am not a bomb that will explode," I snap, sweeping my arm around and enjoying the way they bend away from me.

A Fire Shen with a dull spark in his eyes mutters to the black stone floor, "The Keeper shall only be touched for awakening." His face is scarred, and I sense the dying fire of too much death in his Atmosphere. Gray ash turning to white. It reminds me there's suffering on both sides of this war.

As we descend, the air cools. I clutch the wall, stumbling forward, wishing someone would help me but knowing distance is for the best. My sycamore arm feels heavier and my weak fingers seem numb.

Taking a breath, I choke on it, the arrowhead still partially wedged between my ribs. I want to reach for it and pull it out like a giant splinter.

My eyes search the space and find what I need—a cot about ten yards from the water's edge. I need to lie down before I fall down. The distance between me and comfort is only about ten feet, but it feels like miles. I release the wall and propel myself forward, collapsing with a horrible moan. Fresh blood spurts from the wound and into the blue silk bedclothes, turning them purple.

"Now you've done it," one of the soldiers says. "She's bleeding all over the captain's bed."

"I must see the captain," I order breathlessly. "Find him. Bring him to me." I flick my good hand around with a well-practiced royal air before my eyes close and the eggshell horse gallops away from me, its matte-beige skin cracked, as it should be.

"SHE'S DEFINITELY the Keeper. I would never forget that face." A sharp poke at my side and pain screams like someone opened a metal fan inside my chest. Cutting, cutting, cutting. I gasp and slap at what touches me. "But she seems smaller. Less than…" The man's voice thins. "Just less." Another poke with something sharp, metallic.

I wince and open my eyes. "Are you the captain?" I manage, barely able to speak. My mouth is dry and salted. A thousand regrets have roughened my tongue. An Air Shen stands over me, metal chopsticks gripped tightly in his hand. His hair is a soft, cloudlike white, tied at the back. I don't recognize him, but that's not unusual.

A woman works beside me, face grim. Padding my fingers around my body, I find silk and lamb's wool. I allow my head to relax in the luxury of it after so many nights spent sleeping on hardpacked dirt. The woman grasps the broken end of the arrow, wiggling it gently though she may as well be spinning me around by it. The pain is excruciating.

She holds a smooth black cup to my lips. "Drink," she orders. Everything is done cautiously and without skin contact. I am glad for it as it makes it easier to hide my arm.

I gulp the medicine eagerly. The liquid warms my throat and spreads over my belly. Comforting like milk and numbing like alcohol, though it is neither. I have missed the refined ways of the Shen. They have ways to treat wounds the Char have never heard of.

The medicine gives me the ability to focus on the man behind her who is assessing me like a dowry cow that's all ribs and hide. Underwhelmed. "I have information," I whisper. "I know where the Carvresses hide. You will not find them here nor on any of the inhabited Char islands."

The captain frowns, swishing his pristine white robe. His proud chin tips up as the ceiling shakes from an explosion. My eyes show fear at the noise, and he laughs. "Do not worry, Keeper. That's just the rumble of defeat. We have torn Black Sail City to its foundations and now know the Carvresses are not here. Instead they're conveniently gathered on Crow's Nest island. If we can just make sure we won't be followed by troublesome Char, then we can complete our mission."

I shuffle up to sitting as the woman twists the arrow in my side, slowly drawing it out. "You will not find the Carvresses on Crow's Nest island. The Char have hidden them."

He rolls his eyes at me halfway, but when I glare, he stops. I am the Keeper and from birth he has been taught to revere me. Those feelings don't just disappear. He clears his throat, bowing slightly. "I must trust my information, Keeper. My soldiers escaped from Crow's Nest Island and saw the Carvresses, all nine of them, with their own eyes."

I shake my head slowly. "Yes, and the Char witnessed those Air Shen escape. Did you think they would just leave the Carvresses there for you to collect? Destroying Black Sail City, though pleasing, is a waste of resources when you should be pursuing the Carvresses. It's what the emperor desires most."

The woman hands me a wooden cylinder. "Hold," she orders. As I grasp it, I force my face expressionless as she yanks the last of the arrow from my side. The captain watches, a slight eyebrow raise implying he's impressed.

"We're following the chancellor's orders to leave nothing behind." He stomps his foot. Caught in the cycle of order and attack, loyalty and fear.

I'm given bandages and awkwardly wrap myself. When I'm done, the woman presses a bottle into my palm. "Drink three times a day." I nod. She clasps her hands and bows low. At least to her the Keeper still means something.

Once she has left, I tell the captain, "So you also know the chancellor has been captured?"

The open-ended tunnel echoes with the sound of waves lapping and smells of salt-washed algae. The loading dock for the lower levels of large ships still has discarded crates and barrels which are being used as tables and chairs, places to store weapons.

The captain nods his head. "Yes, we know of his capture and your defection. You're a traitor and you deserted the Shen. How can we trust any information you give?"

Biting my lip, I look down, trying to look regretful. It's not difficult. There is so much I regret. "Do you have any siblings, Captain…?" I await his name.

"Captain Kinanh." He salutes me. It's a reflex, but also a good sign. "I have three sisters and one brother. We're all Air Shen." His hair slips from its binding, a wide stroke of white crossing his face.

"I left to protect my brother. Misguidedly, he decided to break me out of the emperor's palace. And once he stepped over the threshold, his fate was sealed." My chin dips, remembering the tug of Ash's hand and the minute he was fated to die if I didn't go with him. "I knew he would be executed just for entering the palace."

The captain's attitude stalls as he listens. Leaning in, his ears and mind suddenly open. "Are you telling me you had no choice?" He wants to believe me, his Atmosphere folding like a sapling in a strong wind.

I betray. I bend. I try not to break. "I didn't want to leave. I know my duty is to the emperor. But in that moment, I stopped being the Keeper and was simply Lye Li, sister. You can understand, can you not?" He nods along without knowing he does it. "And by the time I had realized my mistake, it was too late. So, I turned my attention to the Char army. Watched and waited. Learned their plans. I knew if I was to earn back the trust of the emperor, I would need to prove myself and hand him what he desires most."

Several orange-dressed Shen stream like eager flames toward the captain. Quick bows and whispered information I can't quite catch. The captain's attitude snaps back like the crack of whip as he points at me. "Your tale is interesting, I'll give you that. If there were a way to confirm, to prove you are still loyal to the emperor, then perhaps I could trust your information."

Pain creeps over my side as the medicine begins to wear off. I grimace, uncapping the bottle and taking a small sip.

I know I need to rest. But there's little time. There's never any time to heal.

Power crackles between my fingers. Allowing it to take over, I close my eyes and let it wash away my conscience. Let it grant me permission to utter these words. "I will take you to them myself. If I have misled you, if my information is false, you may take my life. Is that assurance enough?"

*Ash, forgive me. For this and so many other crimes. Just know, I tried to do the right thing.*

"I shall consider your offer." The captain nods and turns, running up and out of the underpass.

My head relaxes into the pillow while Shen guard my body, the color of violence and power. *My* colors. Orange, blue, white, and brown. The only red is blooming from my bandaged side.

# 27
## ASH KI

I gently scratch at the crackled blood by her ear, sweeping it from her skin. I take the night watch because I will not sleep. Not while she lies in my arms, weakened and overrun.

The chancellor, my brother, snores while tied to a tree, pointed chin digging into his chest. I watch him breathe in and out once and return my attention to Luna. The more I know of him, the more Lye's impressions ring true. If he can be saved it is by the narrowest of margins.

The air is cool and pine scented. Luna shivers and I hold her closer. Sun tried to take her from me, but I wouldn't release her. I *felt* the way power hugged her bones and then exploded from her fingers, leaving her almost empty. Acting as her pillar, her skeleton, while she rests, I will hold her up.

Ki Anah sits sentinel over us, pretending to sleep but one eye squints my way every now and then.

"You needn't worry, Ki Anah," I whisper through the shaded, moonlit forest. Scattering shapes on the floor bristle with every familiar breeze. This is my place. My home. I can't exactly say it feels good to be back. Only that I know it well and there's small comfort in that.

She folds her arms over her chest, trying to find the stars hidden between the pine needle fingers of the branches above us. "She is my daughter. I will never stop worrying."

"What I mean is—"

She sighs. "I know you care for her, Ash Ki. I know." The knowing sounds lost, an air of hopelessness to it.

Heat on my cheeks like sunburn, and I'm glad for the cover of dark. *Care* is a small word. Only one of many I would use to describe how I feel about the girl in my arms. I let a true smile stretch my lips apart.

Luna doesn't look peaceful, but I'm not sure she ever let a calm look pass her brow. Even unconscious she looks determined.

I trace her eyebrows, her round cheeks. Count the constellations of freckles along her jawline. Touch the silk of her light brown hair. I think she will wake. I expect it. But she continues to breathe unevenly. Holding oxygen, then sharp breaths like she's running from something. Small ribs contract. A battle rages inside that no one else can fight.

She's out of balance. I felt it hit her the moment her feet touched the ground. She let Blood power consume her.

SNAKE FANGS, rich in venom, puncture my veins, sinking deep, deep, deep into my flesh. Smooth as a fresh blade, they bite again and again. My eyes flutter open. I don't want to drop Luna, but it's a struggle to keep hold of her while she attacks me in her sleep.

I do the only thing I can think of on short notice: pour ice cold water over her. It startles the snakes and jolts her awake. Her knees fly to her chest, her hands go to her ears, and her lips part to scream. Sun kneels down, covering her mouth.

"Little Luna," he whispers. "You're baik." *You're okay.*

Hugging her tightly, I stand. Her eyes firefly bright but far away.

She strains to find herself in all the Blood. I offer a rope. "Luna, look at me." I press my forehead to hers, aware of all the eyes on us, wooden and not. "I feel you. Can you feel me?"

Gripping my upper arm, her fingers press into the muscle and smooth skin. Goosebumps rise as she runs her hand further up my shoulder. Her eyes brush over my face as she presses her lips together, concentrating. Pink rises in her cheeks, and I *feel...* I feel desire from her. My body freezes as she whispers, "I feel you, Ash." Head tilting almost coyly.

Swimming upward in fresh stream water, she focuses her eyes on mine and *I* focus on staying calm and strong when my legs want to buckle from the intensity of having her in my arms. Our new connection burns between us in a way I still don't really understand. But then she blinks like a shop blind closing for the night. Her eyes cool and she's disconnected again. She taps my chest and squirms from my arms. As her feet touch the earth, she draws in a deep breath.

"What happened?" she asks no one in particular.

The chancellor answers from the ground, feet scratching fervently at his ankles. "You had me bitten by a thousand bugs is what happened! You out-of-control, half-witted Char menace!"

Her fingers scrunch as she takes a threatening step. But her body wavers.

The Coalstone Carvress places a hand on her shoulder. "You need to rest those Shen powers, Char Luna, until balance is restored."

She stares up, dwarfed by the carved woman. "What do you mean, *rest?*"

The Carvress's splinter eyelashes flutter, gaze sympathetic. "I mean, you must stop using your Blood influence. For a time."

Luna steps back, shaking her head. "For how long?"

Sun grumbles. "Luna, you'll be fine without them. You don't need them to survive."

She gazes at her hands, suddenly very still. Very unsure. "Why must I do as you tell me, Carvress? You're no expert on Shen-Char hybrids." She lashes out in desperation.

Ki Anah grabs Luna's arm, shaking her daughter like a wet towel. "Daughter, do not speak to the Carvress this way! You are being disrespectful." Regret fills Ki Anah's face as she narrows her eyes at her daughter. "I didn't raise you to behave so poorly. Is this the Shen in you?"

Luna's arms tense and shoot to the earth in anger. "You don't what you're talking about, Mama. You're being…" She pauses, then snatches her insult from the air. "You're being a snap-toothed octopus!"

Sun gasps, and I cover my mouth though it doesn't mask the giggle. Disapproving Char growl at me. The chancellor catches my attention, the shadows under his eyes like soft pastels. "I don't understand it either," he says to me without his usual bitterness, just a curious expression, and I'm reminded he's only twenty-nine.

For whatever reason, the Char find her comment abhorrent. "Luna, you need to apologize to Mama, right now!" Sun warns while Ki Anah just gapes at her daughter like she's alien.

Everyone exchanges looks of concern though when Luna wobbles, her temper dying. The Carvresses move toward her, calm and caring but simultaneously frightening. Luna swallows loudly as they engulf her, creating a wooden cage.

I turn to Sun. "What are they doing?" He shrugs while Ki Anah's hand goes to her mouth.

The Coalstone Carvress talks low. "Just breathe, Char Luna. If you don't do as we suggest, the consequences could be dire."

Luna's voice is small and high. "How dire?" Bargaining with broken bones and crushed feathers in her pockets.

The Carvress with skin the color of a nervous concubine's cheeks speaks in a nervous voice. "You could die."

They separate, revealing Luna sitting on the ground, staring at her hands. When she sees us, her eyebrows drop like brackets that encompass her eyes and she taps her heart.

She stands and addresses me. "Ash. Where do we go from here?"

Wary glances. Except the chancellor, who simply scratches the bites on his arms and legs. Her eyes are halfway warm, like honey sitting on a cold shelf.

This copse of fir trees is narrow and long and will provide enough cover for today. "We need to head northwest. Once we meet the river it will be easier to navigate."

The chancellor snorts. "Interesting plan, brother."

The ebony Carvress kicks him and yanks him upward. "No one cares for your thoughts."

As we set off in a strange-looking line, I pull Sun aside. He scrapes his arm on the rough bark, getting sappy and grazed. "Tell me, what's so bad about being called an octopus?"

Irritation turns to sadness as Sun answers, "The snap-toothed octopus is renowned for being the worst mother in the ocean. If she doesn't eat her young, she often uses them as bait for larger prey." He wipes the sap from his arm and walks briskly to catch his mother, throwing an arm over her shoulder.

The chancellor watches this exchange with a melancholy expression, but it soon clicks into anger as he snarls and spits on the ground. Does he grieve for our mother? Miss her or wish things had been different between them? Despite my better judgment, I wonder.

# 28
## LYE LI

Do they search for me? Does Joka know what I have done? Would he understand? These are questions I shouldn't ask because I have to follow this path to the end. It was always the plan. It grew like a pressure system, clamoring at the inside of my skull. It had to happen just as lightning must find the earth. The heavens reaching down and reminding us of their presence.

*You didn't have to do it*, Ben Ni says, golden eyes too wise for someone so young. *You chose to.* "You are right," I whisper. And I shall own my choice.

Shen talk to me if I ask them something but do not offer conversation. So I listen, catching parts of plans, pieces of battle news, keeping them in my pocket to assemble later. The Char are outnumbered but have survived by fighting in small but deadly groups around the city. They know the city well and use it to their advantage. The Shen are preparing to launch one final attack to take down as many Char as possible before leaving for Crow's Nest Island. Then onto Sand Otter Island, destroying as much as they can on the way. They shall sail from Char island to Char island, spreading death like a plague. They will leave behind a trail of burning villages and thick black smoke composed of wooden homes and Char bodies. Swallowing a lump, I don't let myself panic and know I can do something to stop the bloodshed.

The captain does not return for two nights which gave me time to heal. Now he marches toward me, eyes dark. His once pristine white robe is smeared with charcoal and blood like a butcher's apron with a hand gripped around a dirty, short sword like he's still in combat. He stops abruptly at his bed, which I have claimed. My legs dangle over the edge and my wound pulses.

He spurts words like a nicked artery. "We cannot leave Black Sail until we've completed our mission. All Char warriors must be eliminated. Every single one. We can't risk them following us and hindering our search. We may be superior warriors, but they can still slow us down."

My hands grip the side of the bed unevenly, weak fingers always slipping. "Why would you risk Shen lives when the Carvresses can be easily taken? And all of this"—I sweep my flesh arm around the space as the wounded are carried in and the dead dumped into the ocean—"could be stopped."

He casts a doubting eye my way. The Keeper doesn't care for casualty. "We are not taking *heavy* losses." I wish to dig under the topsoil of our culture to discover why we view life as disposable and people as assets. *What twisted the Shen this way?*

I press my face into a serene, indifferent shape. A mask that doesn't fit any longer. "My duty is to the emperor, and I believe he would feel our soldiers are more useful alive right now." It seems obvious but I keep talking. "I don't know what kind of protection the Char army may have in place for the hidden Carvresses. There could be hundreds of warriors in wait. Booby traps. You know it takes many soldiers to bring even one down." I cross my arms awkwardly. "If lives are to be spent, they would be better spent obtaining the Carvresses." He absorbs my words. The Keeper influence holding him. "And that is the whole point of this war, is it not?" I narrow my gaze, produce an Atmosphere of towering trees and deep canyons. Deep, tall, intimidating.

"Yes. Yes of course it is." The captain's eyebrows fall. "And you are sure you can take us to them?" Eager like snapping turtles waiting for food.

As sure as my brother when he chose their hiding place. I bow my head. "I am sure."

I sense his belief in me. My loyalty to the Shen proved by my willingness to die if I betray them.

He taps his chin in long strokes. "It will take time to call the soldiers in…" He mentally composes a plan, running a battle-dirty hand through his white hair. I have won him over. It's a small victory that will grow bigger. "But!" His eyes light up, still holding onto the corner of distrust. "You must give me the information of their whereabouts now." It's what I expected and I'm ready to tell him.

My hands scrunch into fists. Real fear creeps slow cold fingers up my back. My betrayal runs as deep as an underground stream. Soundless. Lightless. Smoothing the canals. Greasing the way forward. I open my mouth to disclose the Carvresses location.

The sound of dozens of thundering feet rushing through both ends of the tunnel crushes any thought of further conversation. Swords are ripped from their idle resting places. Shen ready their elements: fire brews, hurricanes swirl, mud boils, and waves crash.

I grasp the bed and pull up, ready to fight. The captain swings around, meeting the sword of a fierce Char whose whole chest is wrapped in timber boards like a wine barrel. The Char's growl builds to a feral roar as he clashes with Captain Kinanh. I search for a weapon as Char and Shen fill the underpass.

My feet clang over a pile of knives. I hold one up in front of me as the fighting spills down to the water end of the tunnel. My hand sags with its weight but I must keep my good hand free for elements. I don't recognize these Char. They're older with mismatched uniforms and makeshift armor. Captain Kinanh is impressive and swift, putting down men as soon as they approach. He uses a mixed approach, as many do, a hand shooting in to incapacitate, then the crude sword to finish the job. The barrel-chested Char falls to the stones. His body has been inflated with hurricane winds and now his blood flows toward me through the cobblestone cracks like fast growing tree roots.

Panic and nausea run from my toes to my mouth. Kinanh's eyes are on me alone. He defends me.

*Guilt. Guilt. Guilt.*

I step to the edge of the water to do what must be done.

Char perish around me. Shen fall in heaps of colored cloth. But there are more Shen than Char still standing. They will win this fight.

There are Char men and women battling. All ages. Because these are not warriors. They're villagers. An old woman charges me, skirts parachuting out behind her, two wooden hands scratching and slapping. She shrieks, eyes wide and fearful even as she ferociously defends her home.

She ducks under swords and slaps out at legs. With her focus on me as she fights her way closer, the knife I weakly grasp shakes. My sycamore arm protests and vibrates beneath my robe. Char and Shen are never in harmony, always at war. It splits me down the middle.

The old woman slows as she approaches, tilting her head and searching my face for an element tattoo. She's unsure. Maybe I can explain. "I am…" I begin. I need to tell her the truth. I need to explain.

Captain Kinanh shouts to me. "Keeper!" My eyes swing to him, and the woman registers my identity. From villager to general, all Char know the Keeper, know her threat. I go to lift my sleeve, to show her who I truly am. But the captain shouts again, "Protect the Keeper!" Pointing at me.

That title brands me enemy and she lunges.

She thumps at me with wooden hands, punching my face. When her flesh accidentally connects with my skin I bite down on my powers, defending not harming. I know the captain is trying to reach me. I know he watches. And he will kill every Char here, even if they surrender.

If I reveal my true allegiance that will be the end of everything.

The woman lands a devastating blow to my arrow wound. I stumble back. The pain is like hot irons jabbed between my ribs that burn and burn and burn. There is no question. *It is right. It is right. It is right.* I summon my last strength and scream, "Captain! Glass Shard Island! They're on Glass. Shard. Island." The woman slashes at my flesh arm with a kitchen knife.

The last thing I see is my blood spraying across her ragged tunic before I plunge into the dark salt water.

# 29
## ASH KI

Wooden hands touch wooden tree trunks. I tilt my head, fascinated. I'm starting to get used to the replacement of wood for flesh, though there's still so much about the Char I don't understand. I'm the lamb being raised by a family of wild dogs. Wanting to fit in but knowing I stand out. Precarious in the knowledge that under any other circumstance, I would be lunch. My lips rise briefly, caught by a flash of sunlight.

A Carvress of yellowish honey timber runs her hand over the trunks of one the trees, scowling as her eyes turn upward. The trunk is scarred with round spots from cut branches for about twelve feet before they start and spin out.

"Why are all the trees like this?" she asks, tapping the trunk rhythmically and creating a mealtime bell sound with her Call. *Ding. Ding. Ding.* I guess the Sand Otter Carvress is made from pine. "Why have the branches been lopped to a certain height?"

I glance up. The heavenly ringing is distracting, but in a welcome kind of way. "The emperor likes them neat and uniform. It also prevents people from scraping their heads on low branches, I guess." I'm not eager to stop and talk. We need to move faster.

The Char gawk like I'm saying something ludicrous. "You're telling me the emperor ordered the trees cut this way?" Sun's voice is high and surprised. I gesture for them to keep moving but they ignore me.

The Sand Otter Carvress snorts and mutters something quiet and disparaging under her breath. When she leans her cheek against the trunk it's like she's leaning on the shoulder of a dear friend, and the bell sound grows to beautiful song. My hand reaches to pull her away from it, but I stop myself.

"Yes. He likes the natural world a particular way." The Char still stare like I'm an imbecile. "Um, Carvress." I bow. "You best stop touching the trees. Your, er, music is getting rather loud. And we need to hurry." My head swivels. "We don't know who's on the other side of these trees."

Ki Anah gestures to the canopy. "There is nothing natural about this." But she does at least speed up, as does Luna, knees plowing through dried bracken.

The chancellor whines as he's poked in the back by Sun's fighting pole. "That sound is unnatural! If my hands weren't bound, I'd cover my ears. Order *is* beauty. You Char are just too primitive to appreciate it." Sun whacks his ear, sharp and fast.

We ignore the complaints after that. He chirps and flutters like a snubbed male pepper bird, its long pink feathers flapping to get attention. My mind turns to children tugging on their mother's skirts, red cheeked and uncomprehending of adult things. Perhaps he's just immature.

Luna stretches her fingers but stops suddenly, forcing herself not to use Blood powers. Instead, she aims her thoughts at me. "Ash. I *feel* you and you give him too much credit." Her disconnected nature makes her share things she shouldn't. I frown, trying to indicate that what she just said was private. She doesn't get it.

We slow our pace again as the Carvresses turn away from us. Whispering to each other. Arms gesturing in irritation. I turn to Luna, who shrugs, and my annoyance grows. *We don't have time for this.*

The Sand Otter Carvress touches the tree again, hand stroking the trunk while she speaks loudly, "The trees don't like this treatment. It harms them."

I roll my eyes. We're never going to get anywhere if they stop at every broken branch and every trimmed tree like it's a wounded relative. I groan loudly.

The Yan family step back from me. Chins dipped. Eyes on the ground.

The Coalstone Carvress clears her throat and breaks the circle. "Sisters, we must keep moving."

The Carvresses turn their eyes on me, blinking ethereal in the morning light. I move through the group respectfully but purposefully, trying not to touch them. "You need to follow me!" I order. "I am your guide. I know how this world operates."

The chancellor scratches his ear with his shoulder. "You best listen to him." My eyes crinkle at his support, but then he laughs and adds, "With any luck he'll lead you right into Shen capture!"

Low murmurs and dissatisfied breath huffed through wooden lips follow the observation. But for now, they walk behind me, padding over pine needles and knocking limbs in a percussive way, like we're in a spring procession. Though what we're celebrating, I couldn't say.

LUNA RUSHES around the group of Carvresses to my side, two mangoes in her hands. It's good to see the break from Blood has improved her energy. She offers one to me before pulling at the purple skin, licking her lips. Her eyes almost dance as she bites into it but her feelings still hover to the sides. Even enjoyment of simple things is muted.

I peel the mango more carefully. Flicking the skin into the brush. "Are you feeling better?" I ask. A question so loaded it's overflowing.

She nods. "My strength is returning."

The mango is sweet and sour. A good balance.

The Carvresses natter at each other and I cast them a warning glance. It does little to nothing. We are sheltered and soundproofed by the trees for now, but that won't last. I gaze at my purple-stained fingers. "Do they need to eat?" Realizing I've never seen them eat or even drink water.

Luna smiles and *oh my heart*. I want to press that smile into my skin so that it leaves a permanent dent. But I sense the effort it takes. How guilt flashes over her face as she lets it die. "They do eat. But not like we do. Don't worry." *A ridiculous request.* "They'll tell us when they're hungry."

Something hits my head. A small pinecone. A glaring Sun is the culprit. He makes weird gestures with his hands. Palms together and apart. Together and apart. His mouth curls into a growl. Luna's shoulder brushes mine. A calm feeling tickles me like a moth closing its wings. I chuckle, understanding Sun's gesture. He doesn't want me so close to Luna. Just to irritate him, I sling my arm over her shoulder.

She keeps walking but her whole body turns stony. The moth's wings open to reveal a crying widow butterfly with stunning silver eyes and stingers in its feet. I hold position for a few seconds and release. Sun's disgruntled groan is reward enough.

"Sorry," Luna mutters. "I shouldn't have."

"No, you shouldn't have. You're supposed to be resting." Her eyes are a glaze of confusion. Delight crossed with regret. "And are you really sorry?" I ask, eyebrows raised. She runs her hands over the smooth cut circles in the trunks where branches used to be and where the tree wanted to grow. "It seems like it gave you pleasure to hurt me."

Her chin falls and she slows her pace, muttering as she slips between the others and to the back. "It did. That is what I am sorry for."

I shake my head as she disconnects from me. This seems impossible. Every time I think I'm getting through, another wall surges up in its place.

# 30

## LYE LI

Don't breathe. Just swim. Don't think about the river of Char blood running to the sea. I can't blame the Char peasants who attacked me. *They didn't know. They didn't understand.*

I hope it was enough and pray the captain believed my lie. If I can give Ash and Luna even a few more days by confusing the Shen and throwing them off course, it will be worth my life. I would have given it willingly once we reached Glass Shard Island and they discovered my deception. But fate has changed my story. *My ending.*

My lungs bursting for air reminds me I'm not dead yet. I can still fight. I *will.*

The water is black as oil and I am blind. Kicking my legs, I can't quite tell which way is up. Ignoring the taste of blood rippling through sea and attracting creatures to its scent, I fight hard. For my brother, for the Char, but also for myself.

I search for a direction and swim towards fading orange pools of firelight above me. My head bursts through the surface and I drag in a long breath, finding myself between large imperial Shen ships. The auburn light is a faraway fire burning on Black Sail

City. My heavy robe pulls me down and I shrug it off. The material bubbles up, lying over the surface of the water for a brief moment before it sinks. I bet it will lie on the sandy floor of the ocean to be picked apart by star crabs, slowly coated with sand until it becomes part of the sea.

My body starts to follow my robe, liquid lead replacing the marrow of my bones.

*Keep fighting.* His arms hook under mine, lifting me. *Don't give up.* How I wish you were really here with me, Ben Ni. But you're not. I am alone with only Shen shouting to keep me company. I'm too close to them.

I paddle sluggishly to open water, needing to swim eastward toward the general and Joka. *I need to...*

It's harder and harder to continue, exhaustion taking over my tired and wounded body. My sycamore arm floats independently, but it's not large enough to support my weight. I grasp a Shen anchor rope, the roughness biting into my fingers. Nothing on my body wants to work, especially not together. The slash on my arm from the Char woman has a brined appearance where the edges of the skin are white and dead, the inside of the cut a light purple. It doesn't bleed but I'm not sure that's a good thing.

Saltwater laps at my chin. My feet kick. My heart strains.

Water reaches my nose. Salt stings my nostrils.

I don't want to die here. Drowned between Shen ships. I don't want to die as the Keeper.

My eyes flit left and right frantically, water seeping into my eyes.

My head sinks below the level of the water. Darkness pushes long curled claws into me, trying to sink their hooks in. The shadow of death coaxing me down.

One last surge of energy. A last look at the stars.

I paddle hard to break the surface and my head butts something solid. Something buoyant.

It rolls to the side, and I realize grimly it's the Char man with the barrel chest. His whole body floats, of course. The black sash hanging from his waist is a lifeline.

Pulling the man to me, I wrap the sash around my body and tie us together. Cold water saws at my bones but the warm flesh of another Char who shall save my life presses to my cheek. I lay my ear to his stomach and feel no pulse.

Something electric spins from my throat. A careful cry. I want to scream bloody and raw but instead I weep soft tears over this unknown Char's belly.

My heart beats out a slow and broken rhythm. It speaks the words I cannot say for fear of being discovered.

*I am sorry.*

*Thank you.*

THE WORLD has dusk in its eyes. Sounds of battle drift in and out like the tide and the city burns in patches. Orange flowers decorating the side of the mountain like a wedding garland. I blink, slower each time. I wouldn't have thought it possible to fall asleep in water, but fatigue is winning. My grip on the barrel-chested Char is slipping. I hang like a child in a sling to his side. The sash keeps me lolling in place, rocking gently. The sea enticing us away from the island.

It's been hours. *I think.* My lower half is numb. When I kick it's as if I'm splashing through thick rice syrup. I can't find the energy to kick very often.

The bandages at my side are loosening as they soak through with saltwater. I shudder, lip quivering from cold. Something soft bumps my shoulder and I swallow my scream. Paddling in a circle, I hit soft, cold things everywhere I turn. Bodies pool together like lotuses on a pond. Only this is the farthest thing from beauty and sweet scent.

Saltwater enters my mouth as I pant, paddle and spin. There's nowhere to go. The bodies draw to me like magnets or like ghosts to remind me of all I have done.

My hasty fingers try to unknot the sash and disconnect me from the Char body so I can get away. *I need to get away from all this death.* I don't want to touch another bloated body. *This is. This is. This is.* The worst punishment imaginable.

Panic and numbness render my fingers useless. I flail and buck. Straining at my waist to get out of the bindings. *I need to get out of here.* I pull and pull and something gives. Not all the way but enough for me fly backward. My head knocks against something hard. Pain cracks through my skull and my vision blurs.

Whiteness on the water. A chant low and tuned with a slap of wood. "*Parut merah, merah. Parut merah, merah.*"

Red, red scar. Red, red scar.

# 31
## ASH KI

The heat is a dry, crackling thing, wafting in a haze around those of us who still have flesh. The Carvresses show no real signs of fatigue other than their slowed pace. Their faces remain pristine and clean, no hair plastered to their foreheads with sweat.

I narrow my eyes to look for flaws, shaking my head with a smirk when I see none. I wipe my forehead.

"What are you smiling about?" Sun asks with a suspicious look.

He offers me a drink from his waterskin, even as he seems to be plotting my death. I knock my head at the Carvresses. "They don't even sweat. They're a little too perfect, don't you think?"

It's the wrong thing to say and Sun stiffens. "At least they don't order the world around them to be perfect," he scoffs.

Thinning trees surround us, more stumps and discarded branches breaking up the forest. Red dirt scatters across the pine needles like ground paprika. We're coming to the end of this narrow line of cover. Soon the Char will see the vastness of the Shen mainland. Something swells in my chest. An *almost* pride.

Dirt thickens and pines disappear. The lands rolls out before us red as rust and yellow as fool's gold. A patchwork of red and yellow, sliced into neat crop squares of high fields of wheat and low mounds of just planted seeds.

The Char point at the land and the long steel structures that carry water to the crops then gasp at the scale. The flatness.

The Carvresses remain unimpressed. Nine women cross their arms over their chests and frown.

"*Apa ini?*" What is this? the Ebony Carvress cries. "Where are all the trees?"

The Coalstone Carvress flashes her teeth in a strange growl. "They are gone, sister. They are all gone."

I turn to them, confused. "I've never known there to be trees in the lowlands."

They shake their heads in sorrow. One of them whispers, voice filled with deep shame, "No, I suppose you are far too young to remember."

Ki Anah exclaims, "It is so, so different." Interrupting my thoughts.

The chancellor kicks the earth, sending dust into our eyes. "Superior," he hisses. "The word you're searching for is superior."

He breaks from the group suddenly. Running awkwardly, he tears at his hand wrappings with tar black teeth. He enters a field of wheat, just his dark head visible. Luna huffs and chases him, fingers out, calling to creatures nearby.

I roll my eyes, wondering why he would bother to run. He can't get away from us that easily. Sun laughs as he watches the chancellor's head zigzagging through the field in directionless panic.

Luna slows as she enters the field, arms outstretched.

Ki Anah puts a hand on my shoulder. "Should we help her?" she asks, fingers digging gently into my skin. "Is she able?" she directs to a Carvress who nods.

"She is able," the Carvress utters as she observes my brother's comical performance.

I shake my head. "Then she doesn't need our help." *Not for this any way.*

Luna stands several yards from the bobbing dark head. He turns in circles, seemingly lost. I scan for farmers and listen for the sound of plows scraping through dirt or the whistle of a master to his beast of burden. We are safe, for now.

The chancellor stops suddenly, head vanishing beneath the golden waves of stalks. Something nudges my foot, and I jump as a snake slithers past me and into the field.

Seconds later, a strangled scream bursts forth, and I head toward where I saw him disappear. Luna's body is completely enveloped by the crops, too short for her head to show.

I crush wheat under my feet, hoping she hasn't killed him yet. It's a small, guilty hope. My feelings for him are very conflicted. The wind rustles loudly through the field, not quite smothering a compressed gurgle.

The chancellor lies flat on his back, hands scrunched. Black violets, which sometimes grow at the base of the wheat, are crushed under his body, making him look like he fell on his own shadow. I smirk. His skin is stained inky from the dangerous flowers. I step back, not wanting them to touch even my shoes.

His face is turning blue, the whites of his eyes cracked with blood lines. A yellow grass snake is wrapped comfortably around his neck curling tighter and tighter.

Luna emerges from between stalks like a perilous prophet. Fists squeezing knuckle white. The chancellor squirms. The snake hisses.

*Perhaps I should let him die. He's probably more trouble than he's worth.* But then the image of my mother, face split between love and shame, enters my mind and I can't quite let go. If she loved him, there must be something left to save.

"Luna!" I exclaim. "Release him!"

Her eyes fly open with a mixture of pain and pleasure crossing her features. I hold her eyes, try to level her out. The snake relaxes but rests in a lazy line across his throat, ready to constrict.

He reaches his bound hands up to it, having pulled off the coverings with his teeth, and tries to use Shen power to kill it. His eyes crinkle and his mouth purses so hard with exertion it could crush a walnut. Black teeth gnash in frustration as he can't even call a single drop of water.

I laugh. "Ha! You've done it now, haven't you? All your squirming has crushed the black violets beneath you, and it has seeped into your skin."

Luna's eyebrows rise. The snake rolls onto its belly, showing its checkerboard scales. "What are you talking about?" she asks, stepping back from my brother suddenly like he's catching.

The chancellor sneers, his voice squeaky under the weight of the snake. "You are so new, Shen-Char." He shows his hand, wet with charcoal-colored streaks.

Luna turns to me with questioning expression. "Black violets can suspend a Shen's powers for a time." She takes a further step back from the chancellor. "Now, if he'd eaten it, he would be *impotent* for more than a day." The chancellor's grimaces at the suggestion.

"Wa!" Sun exclaims, appearing between the stalks. "How is it we never knew this?"

I shrug. "You never had a Shen on your side before. Besides, it only grows here in the lowlands. It wouldn't survive on your drenched-with-moisture islands."

"Are you going to help me, brother? Or am I to lie here until one of *our* farmers finds me?" He positions his words in order to reach common ground with me by calling me brother and referring to the farmers as our friends. I will not bend to his wishes.

Luna nods slowly and flicks her hand. The snake wiggles into the field. She reacts to its departure with a kind of unfulfilled sadness.

I risk grasping the chancellor's ankles, waiting for a sting of ice, but there's nothing but bony joints. His powers are truly suspended. I yank him from the bed of violets and crushed stalks of wheat, careful not to let the black stuff touch my skin. My foot rolls over something long and thin but hard. Jumping, I think I've stepped on one of Luna's snakes. But when I look down, I'm very pleased.

I grasp the rubber pipe, pulling it a foot from the ground. "Thank you, chancellor. Your escape attempt, though pathetic, has helped us greatly." I wink at him, to which he scowls. My smile ice bright.

I wave the others over, the Carvresses and Sun's heads sitting proud of the field just their chins grazing the tops of the stalks, Ki Anah slipping below, though I know her expression would be of a mother's deep unease.

The chancellor remains on the ground, elbows propping him up. "What is so helpful about finding a pipe?"

I shake my head in mock dismay. "So out of touch with your people!" The others look as clueless as the chancellor. I grin, placing it back down and patting it like a good pet. "It's irrigation." Still no recognition. "It brings water up from the river." My voice rises at the end. "If we follow these pipes, they will lead us right to it!"

Sun slaps the back of my head and though it stings it's encouraging the way he'll touch me without fear. *Even if it's to harm me.* "So much excitement over a hose. You farm boys need to get out more."

I let it roll off. I *am* excited.

# 32
## LYE LI

My fingers pulse from lack of circulation since my sycamore arm is pinned beneath a large, soft weight. My weaker hand searches for clues of where I am and finds a carved wooden edge, tracing shapes of stars and moons resting on waves. A small triangle of light sparks to my left and I twist toward it. I'm crushed beneath something that has a rotten meat smell. Wet hair that's not my own drops over my mouth and I gag.

I am being squashed by human bodies. Char bodies. The triangle of light is the sun. The overpowering smell is the result of the mass of bodies sitting in the heat.

"*Parut merah, merah. Parut merah, merah,*" a Char man chants, oars swishing through the water. "I hear you. The ghost ship captain always hears you. I hear your spirit and I will bring you to your family."

I spit the hair from my mouth and as calmly as I can, say clearly, but not too loudly, "Excuse me, Captain?" I kick my legs, soft, fetid flesh weighing me down, barely shifting. "Can you hear *me?*"

The singing stops. The movement of paddles stops too. "Eh?"

"Captain?"

I lift my sycamore arm, concentrating on it alone. Feeling the strength of it round and define. I push harder and the bodies shift.

"Ai ya!" The paddle comes down on top of the man above me. Sadly, he cannot react. "Ghost!" *Thwack!* "Ghost!"

My muffled voice sounds lost, listless. "I'm no ghost. I promise. Please..."

The body is heaved away from me, and I squint. The white light of the sun bouncing off the sea is blinding. The white timber of the carved boat intensifies the light. "Ah, ghost!" The paddle swings at my head, and I block it with my sycamore arm. They clap together pleasantly, and I gaze at the arm with a growing connection and a new respect.

Dropping his oar, the man scurries backward. "Captain..." I plead softly to this squat Char with a wooden... I tilt my head, surprised. He has a wooden nose, which given his occupation, seems rather counterproductive. As if sensing my scrutiny, he wipes it with the back of his hand and pinches it between his thumb and forefinger. Then he breathes in, carved nostrils flaring. *Extraordinary!*

"Please, I am not a..." *Ghost.* I was, but I'm trying to stand firmer on the land of the living. I'm trying not to waver and slip to the underworld.

He calms and pulls the oar into his lap. "You're not a ghost, yes, of course I see that now. I'm sorry, your living scent was masked by all these." He gestures at the gruesome pile. "My name is Hok." He thumps his chest in true Char fashion.

Char men, arrows still protruding from their backs in a shameful monument to Shen tactics, are piled three men high. Water seeps over the edge of the boat when we roll over a rise. My eyes close to the death. "I am sorry," I whisper.

The Ghost boat captain laughs. A crackling sound like dry leaves thrown in a fire. Brief but full of heat and life. "Don't be sorry, child. You didn't do this." He grabs an arrow and wiggles it. The lifeless body shakes and I have to look away. "Cowardly Shen soldiers did this."

He thinks I'm Char. An impossible smile pokes through my lips like the sun through a curtained window, shaded but very present.

In the light of day, I see my wounds are clean and white with salt. I concentrate on healing blood, and my arm pinkens. The captain tugs a cloth out from beneath his seat and dips it in sea water. He speaks as he wraps it tightly around my arm. "It is rare that I actually get to help a living Char." His gray eyes rest between dawn and full morning. They look upon me with kindness. "Very rare these days."

I check my arrow wound; it feels dry and crusted. Sore but not unmanageable. I am proud of my new scars earned in battle and not carved by a guilty conscience.

Hok pats the space beside him and offers me an oar. The invitation spreads an unfamiliar warmth through my chest. His Atmosphere reads of fish who trust the current, birds, and the wind. *Pure acceptance.*

"Help me bring these men home," Hok says. And with pain I'm happy to endure, we row to the eastern shore.

# 33
## ASH KI

Too many members of this group are used to being in charge, not the one who follows. A Carvress pops her head up curiously, graying face floating tall above high wheat and barley. I flash a smile, entertaining myself with a guessing game; her graying timber suggests she's made of cedar.

"Please, Abalone Island Carvress, you must stay low. I don't want you to be spotted," I plead, my smile shifting to terse as I try to stay calm. But this is the fourth time I've asked her. She rolls her eyes but ducks her head down. For now.

She mutters while elbowing the Coalstone Carvress, "I'm not afraid of Shen. They can't hurt me."

The Coalstone Carvress huffs and chastises her sister. "No, but they can hurt the others. Stop thinking only of yourself. We need to stay hidden for the good of the group."

The Abalone Island Carvress shrugs her sharply, carved shoulders. "*Hmph!* Always the righteous sister."

They rattle each other in a friendly way but I predict it deteriorating. They remind me of Lye and I when we're trying to decide on a course of action. Each always thinking they know what's best, especially the older one.

Another pokes her head up. "Please!" I whisper with more force. "Stay hidden!" My teeth grind. I don't have a smile for this.

Winding through fields, we follow the pipes over a low stone wall and into yet another field. Not too far away we hear the threatening *thwick* of a scythe cutting stalks. Harvesting the older, drier crops to take to the distribution market.

Sun's ears prick. "What's that noise?" He crouches, pole gripped tightly.

"They're harvesting," I answer with fondness, though my fields were rice.

The chancellor opens his mouth for the first time in a while. "Yes, brother, I remember it well. Cutting, drying, and packing. Our poor mule had to bear so much weight. Visiting the distribution markets was always such a fun experience as a child." Hearing the word "fun" come from his mouth makes the entire group stop and gape. The chancellor draws rough circles in the air with his tied wrists. "Ducking and weaving between the various produce carts. Excited about what food we could bring home. Climbing the high bales."

He has affection for his old life. I step warily closer.

Sun kicks the pipe with his foot. "Distribution markets?"

Lips lifting, I explain, "Farmers bring their produce to the markets to be shared with others in their district. The emperor takes half for the palace and to sell to foreign traders and the rest is divided equally amongst the villagers."

Sun snorts. "That doesn't seem very fair."

"We never went hungry," the chancellor and I say at the same time. I shrink from the simultaneous statement. The chancellor offers me a guarded smile like he's nervous. I want to stop and scrutinize his expression, but we need to keep walking. I'd rather reach the river before nightfall.

Two Carvresses nudge each other and whisper. I speed up to intervene, knocking Ki Anah's shoulder as I pass. She grabs my arm and pulls me close. "Let them bicker a little. It's normal, no?"

I raise an eyebrow. "Is it?"

"Do you not argue with your sibling?" She casts a sideways glance at Luna and Sun marching beside each other. One stooped, the other with her eyes on the ground. Sun yanks her plait, and she narrows her eyes. He seems disappointed by her lack of reaction. "Before Luna changed"—she taps her chest—"those two would argue all the time. Especially if it had anything to do with Ben Ni." Sadness sweeps over her features like an eagle dive. She presses her lips together and continues. "Sun thought Luna coddled him. Luna thought Sun pushed him to grow up too fast." She sighs. "Ah, in a way they were both right, but Ben Ni was who he was. Neither could change that."

"I'm sorry," I start but don't know how to finish. Sorry is such an inadequate word. Perhaps because it's overused.

She waves me off. "My point is, it's natural for siblings to fight."

I watch them coasting through the field. "Natural but likely to get us caught if they can't fight quietly."

Ki Anah agrees, I can tell, but she won't speak against them. Her hands knot in front, gaze downcast.

The Abalone Island Carvress's head pops up again and I groan loudly. The Coalstone Carvress shoots me a fierce look of protection but I hold my ground. Pushing the long grass aside I march to the front of the group and put my hand out. "Everyone stop."

Rustling stalks like a whispering wind ensemble. They stop and stare. I swallow and try to look like I know what I'm talking about. "You need to stop doing as you please and listen to me. I know this land better than you. I know the *people* much better than you. Stay low and shut your mouths. If we're caught, it will not take long for word to travel back to the palace. Shen farmers have horses and they're loyal. Even if they can't hurt you themselves, they will send for people who can."

The Carvresses blink. One steps forward. The pale pink colored one. "We have done as you asked so far. How dare you speak to us as if we are children." Her hands shake nervously. I run a hand through my hair, losing my nerve.

The chancellor strides toward them. They don't move. "The boy speaks the truth. Shen districts are connected like a spiderweb. Every strand leads back to the palace. You would be wise to listen to him."

The sound of every Chars' neck snapping back with surprise overlays the dry kiss of wheat on wooden limbs. All are shocked to hear him support me. For my part, I don't know what to think. My rounded eyes fall upon his for a moment, confused by his open expression, like a desert plain waiting for rain. Looking away, I don't want to hook too much hope to the exchange, but my stupid heart is already warming at the edges.

I tap my chest, nod and Luna whispers in my ear, "That's my move." And a shiver starts where her lips breathed warm air over my neck, all the way down my arm.

THERE'S A hollowness to the Yans' movements like their bones are as thin and delicate as the wheat straws they brush with absent fingers. The wheat is dry and almost ready for harvest but it's not dead. The Yans are similarly hovering between two worlds, wishing for Ben Ni to fill the space they leave for him everywhere they travel. Though I'm not sure Luna acknowledges his absence so clearly, only that there's an emptiness that no animal or no torture can fill.

I wish I could tell her this is not the way. I wish I believed she would listen.

Luna breaks the stalks as she passes them, seeming to enjoy the crack and crunch. Ki Anah takes Luna's hand to still it and squeals, withdrawing fast. Nursing her hand, she glares at her daughter. "Ai ya! Little Luna. What did you do to me?"

Sun looms behind them but doesn't say anything, yet.

Luna searches sky and sighs, ignoring her mother's shriek. "There are not many birds."

The Coalstone Carvress sighs too, her sawdust breath falling on my neck. "That's because there are no trees." Her voice is listless, the strength I'd heard before somewhat sapped. She drags her wooden feet through the dark red earth. The others mutter in agreement.

Ki Anah's voice grows like squid ivy in irritation. "Luna, daughter, I asked you a question. What did you do to me?" She flicks her hand, trying to shake out whatever Luna put there.

Luna doesn't look at her mother when she says with disinterest, "Oh. Sometimes when I don't know it's coming, a touch makes me react. What you're feeling is fire ant bites." She touches her chest briefly and bashes at the wheat next to her. "The pain will wear off soon."

Ki Anah's face scrunches with discomfort. "You hurt me." And it hurts me to hear the anguish in her voice and I wish it would penetrate Luna. But Ki Anah's trying to get through to someone hiding behind layers of wood and feathers and fur. It's useless.

The chancellor approaches. "I could help," he offers.

This causes everyone to slow their pace. Ki Anah jerks away from him and Sun keeps a tight hold on his waistband. The chancellor's eyes fall. Disappointed? *Impossible.*

Sun yanks him backward as the chancellor leans forward, eyes open and watery. "Don't you dare touch her," Sun warns.

The thin, silk-clothed man angles his head my way. "What about you, brother? You could numb her pain, could you not?" The chancellor cares not for Char suffering. He should be reveling in her agony, not trying to help her. Confusion swirls like a whirlpool, spinning the wrong way.

I nod, finding Luna's cracked gold eyes for a warm split of a second. It sends fire and flames between us. I *feel* her remembering the night I cooled her wounds after she was lashed. The fire is flattened as quickly as it rose, cold water splashed from above because Ben Ni was by her side during that lashing. His suffering forced her to realize her heart needed to open but his death made it shut and lock. My chin falls.

Tentatively, I reach for Ki Anah but she pulls away. "No, I'll be fine. Luna said it will wear off." She places her hand inside the folds of her coat and stares determinedly ahead. "How far to the river?"

The sun stretches away, pulling the light with it like a golden blanket. The pink, pale Carvress wavers, clutching at the wheat for support and stumbling when it offers none. One of her sisters grabs her before she falls. Each one looks a little splintered. The shine of their wooden limbs is dulled, the heat of the sun seeming to have leached the natural oil from their bodies.

I tap the hose near my feet. "Sun, can you see the river?"

Sun pops his head above the stalks and squints, mouth pulling down. He shrinks, cracking his neck. "All I see is a field. And then another field after that, and another, and another, and…"

I roll my eyes. "Okay. We get it."

Luna holds up her water skin. Its flattened, floppy state is concerning.

The air is cooling as it does on the plains. Hot days, cold nights. I bend down to squeeze the hose. It's cool to touch and feels like it has water in it. Sun reads the situation upside down and hitches his knife under it, slicing it open before I can say the word, "No!"

Water streams from the hose, pooling under our feet. The earth becoming soft and squishy like red bean paste. "You idiot!"

"What?" Sun asks, water dripping down his shirt.

"You've just sent several farmers our way to check on why their water just dried up."

He grins sheepishly, while holding the bleeding hose to his water skin. "Let them come."

I'd hoped we could sleep. Now we'll have to travel through the night.

# 34
## LYE LI

Rolls of black body-wrapping cloth flap from the dock, streaming out like squid ink and landing gracefully in the sea. Men curse and scramble to wind it in as the breeze plays with their tempers. My eyes close for a long minute because I saw these images days earlier and I feel the crawl of guilt up my throat to be seeing them again so soon.

Ben Ni. What would you say if you saw Black Sail City like this? I imagine his warm eyes falling on the scene. I invent words and feelings to the ghost hanging to my left. *Disappointed but ready to do what was asked of me. I would find the man in charge and offer my help.* I shake my head. I never knew Ben Ni. The personality that counsels me is fiction. He speaks in Ben Ni's voice, but this ghost is a collection of the souls I have harmed.

The Ghost boat moors, the stacked bodies given brief life by the bounce of the lip against the dock.

Hok hops onto land, offering his hand. I grasp it weakly, fingers failing. He eyes me curiously and slides his grip up to my sycamore arm. He yanks me onto the dock and turns away, speaking to a Char who nods seriously while encircling a bollard with rope. "Eleven men and four women," Hok says, head bowed low. "*Parut merah, merah.*"

"*Parut merah, merah,*" the man replies gruffly.

They will bind them and place them back in the water. A tear pricks my eye and pain stabs at my side. I grasp my wound as heat spreads. Doubling over, my grimace is of pain both physical and emotional. The men lean down, focused on me. "She needs to be with the other women." The Char knocks his head to the mountain. "In hiding."

"No," I protest, pushing all my strength into straightening myself. "I need to see General Fah. I am his close advisor."

The men snort.

Black-clad warriors run in and out through a makeshift fence of tangled wire, barrels, carts, and whatever could be pulled into a line. They're ragged, red, and angry.

Ben Ni pushes me in the back. *Stand straight, show them who you are.*

"Or Joka Yan. Is he here?" I ask, my eyes swinging around, searching for the young man with a bamboo neck and intelligent eyes that drill straight to the heart.

A deep, rumbling voice fills the air like a pot belly stove warms a room. "Did you say Joka Yan?"

Hok and the soldier step back from me, eyes bright with admiration. They bow to the owner of the voice and I spin with cranelike grace to face him. I'm met with an immense Char man. His dark eyes run over me with suspicion, but he takes a confident step closer. I begin to wither in his presence. He seems bigger than this small world would allow for, and I blink up at him feeling like a little girl.

*Speak.* "I did, yes. Joka is a dear friend of mine. We met during"—lies fold over me like sheet corners—"training."

His mustache moves as he talks, heavy brow creasing with doubt. "I did not know there were other women accepted into training. Only my daughter."

Salt shivers rush over my body. And I feel Ben Ni nod beside me. He is the father. "Setsu," I whisper. Hushed guilt piles over more guilt at the sight of this strong, solid man I could destroy with a few simple words. I shove them under my tongue.

His eyebrows rise. "Do I know you?" His fingers, thick as piano keys, brush his ill-fitting vest marred with rubble.

I shake my head. "No." But I know so much about you, Setsu Yan. My fate and yours are terribly intertwined and I hope you will forgive me. "We have never met, but I know of you, from Joka and Luna."

Face brightening, sunshine gracing his cheeks, his demeanor changes and then opens. "You know my Luna, Joka?" Words rush out like water over a burst dam. "How are they? *Where* are they? Did my sons fight bravely in the battle? Of course they did. The message said Luna was safe and on Crow's Nest, though I don't know how that came about. Did Ki Anah make it safely to the island? What of the Carvresses?" He reaches out to touch my arm and I recoil.

"I, um…" I answer the one question I know will distract him from the others. "Joka is here on Black Sail." I cough, pain shooting like spurs up my side.

"My son is here?" Excitement paints his features all pink and hopeful. It is a marvel to be so intimidating and yet so loving. "If my son is here, then we must find him." He touches me then and I feel like I'm resting in the warmest, safest place. My powers recede. I let him support my weight and then guide me to a collection of huts where Char men stride in and out with purpose.

"Thank you, Hok," I manage to shout as we pass through the barrier. He nods and returns to his grim task.

My ghost companion smiles proudly at my side. *This love,* he says, *is what we fight for. What we die for.*

I AM TREATED swiftly while Setsu talks. His large hands are surprisingly delicate and nimble as he adds antiseptic and rewraps my wounds. "There are pockets of Char fighting all over the island. I've been up the mountain, only just came down this morning. I was told Fah had arrived, but we must have just missed each other." He gestures around. "As you can tell, we are lacking resources and organization." He smiles broadly. "I am so glad to hear my son is here. Tell me…" He waits for my name.

I blurt it out before I realize it's a very Shen sounding name. "Lye Li."

Setsu's face is a mask, and I can't tell if he thinks it strange or not. "Lye Li," he repeats. Commits to memory. One that may become traumatic. "How do you know Joka?"

I feed him truth in small pieces. Enough to placate the hunger, not enough to implicate me. "We fought together. He's a brave soldier."

Setsu tilts his head, leaning back from his work and sighs. "Are you sure it's *my* Joka? It's a popular Char name, particularly on my island." He purses his lips like this annoys him. "We named him after my uncle, a famous warrior who defended our island during the battle of Suicide Cliff." His eyes drift distant. "We had first claim, him being my uncle, but that didn't stop Ten Thi from naming his son Joka and Opa Ela," he growls.

*Joka.* I tap my throat as he would, running my fingers down the length. "The Joka I know is tall and slim but strong. He has this…" The building creaks. Men shout. Footsteps louden and then soften. I picture Joka. Eyes dark and thoughtful, words always considered. "This kind intelligence about him. He has always been a good friend to me."

Setsu lets out a strange chuckle. "You know they don't allow soldiers to marry."

I gulp and shake my head vehemently. "I don't think of him that way." *Do I?* No. The Keeper doesn't think of anyone in a romantic way. "He was just one of the first Char to accept me. To treat me as an equal." Color rises in my cheeks. "He helped me."

Setsu rises, twisting his mustache with blunt oak fingers. "It's hard for a woman to be accepted by the Char army, I know."

Lies bulge on my tongue. "Right." I nod, relieved my story fit. "When I was having a difficult time, Joka would crack that bamboo neck of his and tell me to straighten up and prove myself."

Setsu's grin stretches rice-white as he points. "Ah, yes. Bamboo neck. *That's* my Joka."

He stomps and the walls seem to shake. "I need to find my son, Lye Li." He says my name in a very incisive way, and I wonder whether he suspects I am not who I say I am. He waves in my general direction. "Then you can see Fah."

# 35
## ASH KI

As light dies and a gray dusk falls over the field, painting everything shadowy silver, I sense water draining away. The problem: The thicker hose we've been following, that the idiot Sun cut, branches off in several directions to feed many farms. Meaning more than one Shen will be searching for the cause of the leak. I groan and slap Sun's back, sending thin, sharp ice flakes over his ribs. The first freeze of a pond at the start of winter.

"You get to the rear," I order and for once he listens.

At least in the dark, we can unfold our sore necks and backs and stand up straight. Heads sway back and forth, scanning for Shen farmers and the river. Luna hugs my side as we lead. The Carvresses in the middle and Sun and Ki Anah at the back. The chancellor is bumped and bustled in amongst the group of Carvresses. They're enjoying treating him roughly and every now and then I hear him grunt in protest as he's jostled.

It looks like someone took a dumpling cutter to the sky. The moon just an outline of light. The stars give us pinpoint illumination. But it's better this way. We can hide.

The rustle of wheat and the scrape of feet on hard, dry earth is the only sound. But whether it's just us, farmers, or creatures moving through the undergrowth is hard to discern.

"Quiet as you can," I whisper, searching for the river.

The Sand Otter Carvress extends a slender arm northwest. "Trees!" she exclaims with relief and an exhausted sigh. The Carvresses bolt forward desperately, making much more noise than they should.

Luna's hand brushes mine, without pain, and she says my name in a hushed warning, "Ash."

A long, high whistle, turning up at the end like the curve of a spoon. Everyone freezes. Ice not born of elemental power surges up my spine. Luna knocks my shoulder, soft hair tickling my arm like an ink brush. She's holding back her power, but I *feel* sudden fear. Not for herself but for her family.

"Something is close," she hisses between clenched teeth. "But I can't," she closes her eyes, reaching for a heartbeat. "I can't tell what it is." Her fingers curl into fists, a fight biding time within her palms.

A clean, long whistle pierces the night again and then a sound I haven't heard in a very long time. Almost like a yawn but it has an echo quality, like the owner of the jaws is as deep and hollow as an abyss. I curse. My own fingers spread wide, ice cracking. The Char in the group jump at the bellowing sound. The chancellor and I exchange grim, shaded looks. I expect triumph in his manner, but he's tense and panting like the others.

"Bearded dagger beaks," I say, ducking down like that would do any good.

Sun lets out a stifled snigger. Unsure. "That's just a bunch of words strung together."

We don't have time for lengthy explanations. "Think giant lizard with a beak as sharp as a chef's blade and a hunger for bone."

In the dark, the whites of Sun's eyes just got larger.

One of the Carvresses giggles nervously. "Well, we'll be fine won't we." She rolls her wooden shoulders.

"They're not the smartest creatures. They may tear you apart looking for bone even if you don't have any," I warn.

We sprint, tripping over barricades and blindly feeling for obstacles. The rush of scaly claws wriggling through the grass urges us forward. The yawning call of the lizards is coming short and fast. I look above the wheat, and it parts in straight lines as the animals crash through.

It's like we're being chased by a noisy ghost. "Luna!" I call.

She reaches out from her sides. A slight sheen on her forehead. The echoing bark stops for a moment, the rustle of wheat stilled. Her fingers pulse and flutter as she holds her breath. She strains and struggles. "I can't control them. The bond to their masters is too strong."

Three more whistles, this time short and piercing. An attack order from the farmers who control the lizards. Luna folds, grasping her chest, the effort too much. I wrap her arm around my neck and dash away from the din.

The scurrying of invisible creatures gets closer and closer. The snap of sharp beaks feels like it's right at our heels. We run without caring about the noise. Thinking only of escape, we breathe in sharp panicked bursts as they draw near.

Ki Anah lets out a small cry. Then we hear a nasty, crunching noise as Sun is pulled to the ground. The Carvresses scatter. The chancellor spins in a circle as the Carvresses veer off in different directions, leaving him undefended.

The blush-colored Carvress is the only one I see clearly. She stands straight, hands pinned to her side. Sun bashes at the head of the large lizard as it chews on his balsawood foot. I'm losing control of everything. Too many strings tied to my wrist, pulling in every direction. I need to round up the Carvresses before they get lost. I need to help Sun. My head swings back to the pale pink Carvress, spirit-like in the dark. The yellow beak of another lizard parts the wheat and stalks her.

*I need, I need, I need—Help.*

With Luna hanging from my shoulder, weakened, I lope toward Sun.

The blush-colored Carvress whimpers as the animal approaches.

Quickly, I bend down, placing a palm on the focused creature's head. I send icicles drilling into its brain. It convulses and releases Sun's foot. Ki Anah uses Sun's pole to hit it hard across the nose and it slithers away.

I turn my attention to the blush-colored Carvress, but she has bolted. The chancellor stands over a disoriented lizard clearly under elemental attack. His hair snakes down his forehead, eyes wild. He helped her. I don't know why but he did. *Has he started to feel compassion for the Char?* It was a simple plan. One that would expose him to them in an intense and dangerous situation and force him to work with us or not survive. A simple plan that has started to work. He wobbles a little, hands still bound and covered. He must have touched his face to the creature. As I stare harder, I notice little cuts from the creature's sharp scales on his cheeks. He risked his life for her.

I don't have time to dwell on this success. I help Sun to his feet, and we half carry, half drag Luna as we flee, Ki Anah close by.

We aim for the dark silhouette of trees, hoping that's where the Carvresses have headed.

Lizards thread toward us, carefully trained not to harm crops. They hiss and snap and breathe like an untuned accordion. The whistlers give orders we don't understand. But they sound harsh and unforgiving.

In the distance, rocks clink against rocks. Women talk in hushed, urgent whispers. Luna pulls away. "I'm all right now."

She thunders ahead. Running too fast. Too determined. She's not thinking.

There's no scream. I *feel* her terror for a mere second, then a splash and the even rush of the river. The Carvresses line up, their wooden faces tipped downward to a cavern of unknown depth. A cavern Luna has just fallen into. In one horrible moment, we've found the river and lost Luna.

The slimy hiss of the bearded dagger beaks is upon us. The farmers can't be far behind. I want to shout down to her. My heart pushes against my ribs, telling me to jump and find her. It beats out a frightening rhythm: A thousand pulses that are all my own, because I can't *feel* her any longer. There is nothing but dead space between us.

Ki Anah flies past me without thought, hurtling straight into darkness.

Sun grips my shoulder and curses. The Carvresses huddle on the edge. A creature lurches, claws scratching down the leg of the ebony Carvress. The two simultaneously shriek and are silent as the Ebony Carvress stumbles off the ledge, and the lizard pulls back, its front leg folded beneath it. I can't see how it's injured.

My hands spread wide and I apologize as I push the Carvresses like bottles from a ledge. "I'm sorry. Sorry." They tip off the edge. Small splashes sound one after another.

The Coalstone Carvress is last and she resists. "You must kill it. Leave no evidence," she says before gracefully leaping into the water.

"Find her, find Luna," I order after her, my tone brimming with panic.

Sun and I turn to the writhing creature, trying to use its tail to get up. I kneel down, frightened to touch it. Pulling my dagger from its sheath, I try to cut deep across its throat, so death is fast. The knife bounces. "What the…"

I touch its underside. Wooden. It's frilled, feathered beard should be as easy to puncture as a heartbird's breast but instead feels like chipped fingernails. In her terror, the Carvress turned the front of the creature to wood. It snaps at me with little energy. Running my hand over its back, I find a place where the wood turns back to scales. The sensation of its skin hardening to wood beneath my fingers is inexplicable. My mouth hangs open and my hand withdraws.

Sun finds a soft, flesh part, quickly plunging his knife into its belly.

It barely makes a sound.

We roll it over the edge, praying it doesn't hit someone.

It is evidence of the Carvresses' presence. Something we cannot afford.

The chancellor stands beside us, hands still bound. He holds them to me. "I won't survive if you don't cut my ties." In all this confusion, he could have run. Waiting makes little sense.

"Why didn't you flee?" I ask, too invested in his answer.

He thrusts his wrists in my face. "Those witless lizards can't tell a Shen from a Char. I am safer with you for the time being." That sounds more like the chancellor I know.

I cut them fast and shove him over, hoping I won't regret it.

We count five more yellow beaks, parting the grass like gold spears, attached to wet hissing faces.

Sun and I jump.

Air shreds past me. Time seeming to slow. The fall taking far too long. Men's voices disappear, sucked into the sky. My feet hit water like it's made of glass, pain shooting up my legs. Cold envelops me and the current pulls.

I kick and fight, other limbs tangled in mine. Water choking. Spluttering. An arm around my middle. Sharp rocks bite my face and I'm thrown onto the earth.

There are many exhausted, near-drowned breaths, each one indiscernible from the others. But I need to find one particular voice and I crawl over the dark shore, feeling hands out in front of me. Desperately needing an animal bite or scratch to fly up my arm. My smile is pale and eerie and my heart is frozen until I reach her.

# 36
## LYE LI

Setsu knows the pockets of Char rebellion like they're sewn onto his person. And he drags me over cobblestone streets, through broken buildings, to get to them. I almost expect his large feet to create cracks in the stones every time they pound the earth. He is a fearsome carved creature, bigger than a man in more ways than one. While he talks fast to other groups of Char, I keep quiet, so unsure of whether to reveal myself. I know every word I speak will dig a deeper pit of lies I will have to climb out of.

My ghost falls behind, showing his disappointment in me. His golden eyes are hooded and his head is bowed. His father needs to know the truth. Cowardly as it is, I just don't want to be the one to tell it. It pushes me to pick up speed. To find Joka and Fah. *This is their information to share,* I convince myself.

The soaring rock sails of the city are stunning and noisy. They carry the voices of men dying, fighting, triumphing as they stand sentinel over it all. They absorb the heat of the flames that bud and grow in a new place as soon as one is extinguished. Sunlight glosses them, black as tar and invulnerable.

My elemental energy is building to a spinning ball in my stomach as Setsu clasps my hand with his flesh one. Squeezing tight, propelling me. *I want, I want, I want.* To hurt him and to not hurt him. I search for an outlet before Setsu becomes my vessel.

I shouldn't be relieved when five Fire Shen thunder for us, swords out, hands ready to incinerate when they touch us.

Setsu throws me behind him, broad form filling the path. His Atmosphere is of predictable seasons. Leaves turning from bud to green to orange to brown and finally dropping to the earth. Always the same pattern. He has done this so many times, it's a familiar dance. A natural recipe.

"I can fight," I mention, stepping out to stand by his side.

He grunts, his focus on the Fire Shen who are burning inside and out with hatred. I look down at the Char uniform Setsu found for me. It hides my identity from these Shen for now, but my face may still spark recognition. I need to silence them.

I spin, sycamore arm providing cover from the Shen touch while my other hand finds skin and presses. I fight fire with a brighter, hotter, more devastating fire. Blue-white flames burn so hot, blood boils in an instant. My knife is a follow-up to cover my tracks, but they're already dead.

We stand in the center of five slain Shen. It was too easy. Setsu gives me a worn look, like all this death chips away at him. Like he knows it being *easy* is a very bad thing.

It should never feel easy to kill. It should never feel satisfying to harm.

I think of Luna. Grief splitting her fingers apart so they can harm others. The euphoric buzz of power I know so well that is both addictive and destructive. I should have counseled her better. *Helped* her. I glance at the darkening sky, cracking clouds bouncing off each other with malicious intentions. She wasn't ready to listen, not to me anyway. When her golden eyes cast rays over my face, they saw only the death of a brother.

Swallowing, I try to come back to Lye Li, push the Keeper behind me. The Keeper stands with Ben Ni; two figures who were not meant to be companions and always fight for attention. When one surfaces, the other fades.

We face more small groups of Shen. It is odd and not the way Shen are instructed to fight. Shen are highly trained, enacting formations and plans of attack. Organized in a way the Char are not, moving mathematically and with precision. Elemental fighting is intuitive, but Shen leave nothing to chance. Their hands are dipped in all types of warfare. The Char, on the other hand, are pure heart and instinct. But I know the Shen moves like a practiced dance. Feet bleeding and blistered from practicing them over and over. In truth, I designed many maneuvers.

*Their legs, striped with horizontal marks, show how much time they've been forced to stand here. Hands behind backs, eyes up, and back rod straight. My eyes slide to the boy closest to me. He has five marks, so he's been studying the scrolls of battle formations for five days. A cup of water and rice bowl lay untouched at his feet. His dark head is shaved high, leaving just a long black plait, lying like a slug over the center of his skull.*

*I wince when the shifu slides a long stem of bamboo dipped in black violet ink across the back of the boy's calf. It's a reminder of what it feels like to be powerless, robbing you of your element for hours to days. Pushing the importance of learning these formations to the forefront. It stings like nothing else but it works. I know those formations like they're written on the inside of my eyelids.*

*Gazing at the soft underside of my forearm, I poke it with my finger, shocking myself gently with a buzz of lightning. Would I like to know that feeling of powerlessness again? The question is pointless. I am the Keeper. My powers are needed and necessary. At all times.*

Setsu's flesh hand grabs my weak one. No power resides there, which is just as well. He flings me in front of him. The steepness at the apex of the city burning my calves and scraping my knees. The black sail rock scoops up to the sky and hoards clouds in its immense curve. Howls of wind mix with men bellowing. The acrid smell of gunpowder stings my nostrils.

We search for refuge and find Char black flags waving over a group of small buildings, chipped and square like an old man's teeth, nestling into the base of the black rock sails. A barricade has been hustled together by the Shen—coils of wire and broken furniture. It's a classic technique. Throw small kegs of gunpowder at the enemy and shift the entire barricade closer with each small attack.

We hunch behind a wall, watching as Shen toss their bomb at the sails. As it explodes, Water blue and Earth brown pick up the barricade and slide it closer. It begins to curl like a gruesome, barbed smile. I make contact with Setsu's wise eyes. Soon there will be nowhere for the Char to run. As it is some are climbing up into the sails. Backs to the black stone. Palms flat. Looking like they'll ride this wave to shore.

Setsu leans down and whispers in my ear. "We shall roll it down the hill." He points to the barricade.

I stare down the length of tangled wire and debris and shake my head. "It's too dangerous. We won't get within ten yards before they shoot us." *Or blow us to pieces.*

A familiar shout reaches us. "Don't waste your arrows until they're closer." General Fah's voice is pitted with fatigue.

Another pop of powder and smoke. Setsu springs from his hiding place. "Ten yards. Pfft!" Fearlessly, he runs through the smoke and I lose sight of him quickly. But I hear him roaring like a lion as metal scrapes against stone and Shen stumble in surprise.

I hesitate, knowing death is no longer a construct or flirtation. It is real and terrifying. He struggles, a hefty noise mixed with wire grating against rock. Death is also something I'm willing to face for the right reasons. I smile with delicious hybrid power. My sycamore arm will be very useful for this task. I stare down at its grotesque, scarred appearance. At least I won't worry about scratching it.

I run in from the side and assist Setsu, whose immense strength has already rolled the barricade over most of the surprised Shen. The smoke is clearing and Setsu's stoic face scrunches as he scrapes strength from the bottom of his broad chest and heaves. I put my arm to the roll of wire and push. Wiggling my foot from my shoe, I tap the Shen caught in the structure, skin to skin, with the flat of my foot, wiping his consciousness in an instant by filling his veins with silken mud.

"Keep pushing!" Setsu summons impossible magic to his hands, shifting a weight that should be immovable. Heart blitzing with fear, I throw my body into the barricade, feeling it move faster at the opposite end. Shen shout in confusion as it rolls over top of them, winding their arms and legs into the coils of wire and wood. Men trapped and tangled.

Setsu smashes the jaw of a Shen who won't surrender, then whistles long and loud.

"Take cover!" he screams. I jump behind a wall as arrows glide through smoky air. Landing in debris and flesh, the arrows wound and kill at random.

Char come to our aid, streaming from the sail, materializing like bats from a cave ceiling. Peeling away with wings open and fangs bared.

As they tumble down, taking care of what Shen are left, we run up the mountain side, ducking and weaving between Char and losing Shen.

The quiet is sudden and deathly.

For now, the enemy retreats.

A flurry of black. A bamboo neck glistening under a dying sun and firelight. Joka.

My chest ripples and seizes as he throws his arms around me and pulls me close. *Bite! Bite down on your powers.* My ear smashes against his chest and I can't control what comes: The call of a bird to its mate, red feather breast ruffled by sea breezes. "Lye. You're alive! I was so worried." His body tenses and relaxes as the feeling of warmth and belonging moves from me to him.

I push away from his embrace at the sudden feeling of wrongness. My heart thaws at his touch. It feels nice to have someone worry about me. To have someone care if I live or die without an ulterior motive. The feeling is as rare as the purple diamond sitting in the emperor's crown and can only be traced back to a handful of people. Joka entering that tiny circle is too much. I back away from him. I'm undeserving of such attention.

"Joka. I'm glad you are safe." I bow quickly.

"Glad," he repeats in a disappointed tone. "How did you find me?"

I scan the black for Setsu. He's easy to spot and I point to his hulking back. "Your father brought me to you."

There's a look of dawning dread and grief. A painful flash that destroys Joka's planed features and reminds me of my place in all this mess. Ben Ni tries to touch my shoulder and I shrug him off. I don't deserve comfort, real or imagined.

Joka stares into my eyes, asking a question without speaking and my gaze falls to my feet. "He doesn't know, I'm sorry. I didn't know how to tell him and I don't know if I should."

He pats my shoulder, warding off the ghost with his firm hand. He squeezes gently and my heart tries to flip in my chest, but it's constrained and can't complete the move. There are too many collapsed and crumbling walls leaning against it. I touch my sternum. Within my ribs is a warzone. I am torn apart and mirroring, quite accurately, the warzone outside.

"That's all right, Lye. It wasn't your news to tell." His eyes scrunch, holding back tears. I give them space, watching from a distance. Joka taps his father on the back, is swiftly lifted from his feet in a warm embrace. Then the world around them turns cold and dark.

The truth doing what no Shen could ever do to Setsu Yan: Bring him to his knees.

# 37
## ASH KI

It's as murky as the sea floor and we're the glowing creatures that sift through sand looking for dead things to pick at. I just hope none of us are the dead things.

My hands brush over river rock sharp as spearheads. I whisper Luna's name and am answered by every voice except hers. A scramble and a thud. "I have the chancellor," Sun shout-whispers, victoriously winning a slight scuffle. Yards above us, a dim yellow halo appears. The farmers with torches seem very high up and I don't think their light will reach down here. I close my eyes and open them again, trying to adjust to the lack of light. Wherever "down here" is.

Water rushes and I tense. She could have been carried downstream or she could have hit the rocks instead of the water. She could have drowned. Each possibility brings new terror. Dripping wet, I crawl away from the sound of the river. Shivering with cold and concern.

"Is everyone alive?" The Coalstone Carvress's husky voice asks.

We reply. One voice missing.

My hand touches a damp leg. When it doesn't react, I slide my hand upward, searching over a hip, climbing ribs to a collarbone, and then coasting to the middle. To hard ribs ringed with icy brass. "Luna," I whisper, hands shaking.

She doesn't respond.

Her skin is cool while wet clothes cling to her body. I feel no bite or sting. Nothing to tell me she's awake. I don't leave room for the possibility she's not alive. Leaning down, I part the top of her shirt. Lip between my teeth, eyes open but seeing nothing. I press my ear to her chest. Something I've never done before. Something I've both feared and wanted.

Luna's lungs expand, her heart beats, and I breathe again. The sound is like a practiced march. A thousand men stomping their feet into the earth. Perfectly in time. Painstakingly coordinated. The beat is beautiful. Unnatural. Wholly unique. *Just like my Luna.* I catch the timing of it. I listen like it's the only music I ever need to hear. The slide of the chambers as they fill and empty is like a child's magical puzzle box. Each lid opening to a new enticing mystery.

The fear I had about this moment washes away with the current. Her heart, her hickory heart, fills me with wonder.

Ki Anah breaks the spell. "Ai! Luna, *kamu di mana?* Where are you?"

I take a breath, ready to tell her I have Luna right here. That she's alive and she's beautiful and brave and burning with promise. But her finger coasts up my shoulder, brushes my cheek and presses against my lips. "Mama, I'm here." The finger stays pressed to my mouth. I am wrapped in fur, brushed by gentle paws. "I'm fine."

Luna's body shudders. My ear is still pressed to her chest and I don't want to move. I don't want to disconnect.

"It's too dark to travel. To even move. I don't want to risk someone falling into the river and being swept away. We're safe down here for now. Everyone just stay where you are, wring out your clothes, and try to get some sleep," I suggest as Luna's other hand moves to my back. She presses me against her. Chambers click. Breath comes in and out. My hand finds hers and we clasp together like a lock.

The darkness is so opaque, there can be no witness.

"I just want one good moment," she whispers heatedly, voice vibrating through her incredible chest and into my ear. "I *need* it."

*I need it too.*

Tomorrow she may curl back inside her turtle shell. The sounds of the others fade as I gather her warmth, her willingness to let me near her, and burrow it deep in my own chest. A memory to hold onto when she slips away from me again. I lift her fingers to my lips and kiss them, carefully, slowly. Each knuckle imprints on my skin. Leaves a permanent etch in my bones.

She strokes my back, creating ripples. Pleasure and pain in even strokes. Each feeling is like another stone thrown into a pond, stacking high and teetering. *Will they reach the surface?*

"Luna, you're killing me," I murmur.

"I know," she replies.

THE SUN doesn't reach the bottom of the canyon, cutting it into even light and dark halves. At least it's enough to see by. High above is a hopeful streak of blue sky.

My head aches, and my cheek is marked with stone dents. I send my hands to search for her, but of course she's gone. Not one particle of me wants to pretend last night didn't happen, even if that would be the wisest decision.

Sun kicks my leg. "Get up, sleepy head."

I flinch, needing to stay in my drowsy, dream-like state for a moment longer. *Ear to chest. Heartbeats counting down the scant time left.* Luna leans against the canyon wall and when I connect with her golden eyes, they shoot downwards, suddenly finding her clasped fingers intensely interesting. She feels some kind of embarrassment or coyness. She *feels* something. It draws a sleepy grin from my mouth. I want to ask her what last night meant exactly. *If our time together meant anything.* She pushes and pulls like I'm elastic and will always return. I work my jaw and the grin stretches thin. Elastic loses its ability to bounce back eventually. Then it frays and breaks.

Sun rolls his shoulders with a loud crack and the Carvresses crowd around, their eyes seem to retreat into their sockets. The wet and filthy chancellor looks less and less regal with every passing day, becoming one of us.

"What are *you* smiling about?" Ki Anah demands, tilting her head. She points up at the sky. "Can you not see how far we've fallen? How are we going to get out of this hole?"

I shrug as I stand, and my eyes land on a blob of red wax paper bobbing in the water, playing tag with the empty frame skeleton of a lantern, its panels long since dissolved. "We can't get out of it immediately. But it's not a hole, it's a canyon. And it will provide good cover until it leads us home."

Ki Anah groans. "Leads us to *your* home," she corrects.

"*Our* home, brother," the chancellor chirps and a cringe works its way between my shoulder blades. "Where the sky is wide and the—"

"Will you shut your Shen mouth," the pale pink Carvress snaps, reaching out to steady herself on a large river rock. "Everyone can tell you're just trying to get on his good side. Though to what awful end, I do not know."

Rage builds in dim lines across the chancellor's face but he keeps quiet.

The Carvresses gaze longingly upward, carved feet dragging over the pebbly beach.

My pack is soggy but will dry. I point at the river winding like a worm around numerous corners. "The only way out is through."

I wink at Luna, a reference to when we were stuck in the labyrinth on Crow's Nest Island. Sun rolls his eyes. "I bet Joka and your sister are having more fun than us right now. At least they get to fight."

Thinking of Lye makes me tense with worry for her safety and a newborn anger at her betrayal. I march forward, overhearing a yelp from Sun as Luna warns him to ease off his teasing.

Smiles are like seedlings. Feed them and they grow, sometimes too fast and wild to control.

She's giving me hope. I need to be careful how I take it.

We hike the base of the gray canyon; the walls are so straight they could be manmade. Knowing the emperor, they could be. Like a thirsty mouth, it swallows the cool air despite the earth-scorching heat above. It keeps those of us who are flesh and blood comfortable. The Carvresses however, wobble and grip the sides to support themselves seeming unwell.

I bend down to Ki Anah. "What's wrong with the Carvresses? They don't seem like their usual graceful selves."

Ki Anah's glance scales the cliffs. Her fine face chipping away with responsibility. "They're losing energy. They need to feed."

I halt, lost in watching the water—the way it erodes rock slowly, scratching down, down, down like a wound that won't heal. "We could try to catch some fish."

Hands on cherrywood hips, she huffs, frustrated at my Shen stupidity. "They can't eat fish. They need *energy*."

"Well, how do they get *energy* then?" I'm starting to get frustrated too.

Ki Anah stares straight ahead. "I'm not sure a Shen can understand."

I'm about to defend myself. Tell her I'm probably one of the most tolerant and understanding people she's ever going to meet, Shen or Char, when a disgusting smell wafts past my nose and I gag. Everyone holds their hands and arms up to their face or pinches their nose. Sun's exclamation is muffled but I catch the words, "*Apa?* What the? What is that stench?"

We press into a solid wall of stink and as we round the bend, the cause becomes obvious.

# 38
## LYE LI

Night brings an eerie peace. The clash of metal and sting of gunpowder has dissipated. If I know the Shen, they're re-grouping and referring to the next page in their memorized handbooks.

General Fah appears worn, skin dry and cracked like an over-washed chopstick with its lacquer peeling and wood splintering. We sit across from one another in one of the broken teeth huts at the base of the sails. "Were you successful in convincing the Shen of your loyalty?" he asks, doubtful.

Setsu leans back in his chair, narrow-as-toothpick eyes on my arm and then face. Mouth nailed closed.

I nod. "I was, General. I convinced him to send soldiers to validate my information by offering to go with them as insurance." Joka stiffens beside me. "But we were attacked by Char civilians." My chin falls, thinking of the Char with the wooden chest whose last act was to keep me afloat, saving my life. "I'm not sure what he will do now, without me. My gut tells me he'll send some soldiers, but not all, to check to see if my information is correct. I could return to him if that is your wish."

The general puts a palm up. "I don't think that will be necessary." Disappointed but not unimpressed.

Joka runs a hand over his neck and turns to me, chair legs squealing. "You offered your life as insurance? When they found out you were deceiving them, they would have killed you, Lye. Without question."

*I know. But it would have been an honorable death.* My hand reaches for him, stops short of actually touching. "I'm sorry. Giving myself up was always the plan. The general and I devised it on the journey to Black Sail."

His thin face slopes sorrowfully. "You never told me."

"I couldn't." It's a lie. I could have told him but didn't want to. It would have broken the delicate ties we'd established.

Setsu's oak hand has not unclenched since he learned of his son's death. It sits, foreboding, on the table like a rock. "Well, Keeper or Char Lye or whatever you are. Who really cares?" I am a *what* not a *who* in his eyes.

"Papa, you needn't be so harsh," Joka protests and receives a diamond-hard glare.

"Your plan was a failure. What do we do now? We still have so many of *your* Shen running through the streets like a disease." His words hurt. Even though I barely know him, Setsu Yan is someone from whom I crave approval. A quick survey of the room shows I'm not the only one.

Fah taps his friend's fist with trepidation. "Setsu. Friend. I know it seems strange to work with a Shen. It was difficult for me to accept at first. But Lye Li is trustworthy, I assure you. She has done much for the Char since her defection."

He shakes his head. "Shen don't defect. It's not possible."

Joka tries to catch his father's grieving eyes but they look everywhere except at the people facing him. "Things change, Papa. Ben Ni saw good in Lye. Luna also befriended her. She gave her—" I do touch Joka then, to stop him from talking.

Setsu stares down at our joined hands in judgement. I quickly withdraw. He tilts his head like he can't decide what to make of me. Dark eyes reaching for sea-colored ones. He wants to trust me, but years of war, of looking at Shen as enemies, make suspicion hard to shake. We're asking him to shed his armor before an enemy. How do I, as one Shen, compete with thousands who have hurt him or tried to kill him in the past? I stand behind decades of distrust, waiting in a very long line for my turn.

He stands angrily, chair flying into the wall. The green algae-cured eggs on the table rattle and roll and Joka fusses to collect them before they smash to the floor. Fah opens his mouth to speak and is silenced by an open oak hand, waving him off. "I need some air." He strides to the door and throws a disparaging glance at Joka, cutting like a star blade. It embeds in the heart and his son shrinks. "Not in a million salt moons did I think I'd see the day a Shen would have a seat at our table."

I see Setsu's youngest son in the shape of his mouth and the swing in his walk. My ghost leans to whisper on cold steam. Golden eyes blink true and sad. *Explain it to him. Make him understand. He deserves that much.*

And more.

SMOKE COILS white against black rock, twirling into unnatural shapes like it's a living, breathing thing. I halt, watching it rise behind the huts and fold into the shape of a dragon. Creeping daintily on curled claws across the sky and snuggling its belly down to an unseen bed. Stretching out its long underside and yawning its rectangular jaw. Incredible!

The memory of Joka's voice comes to me, raw and husked. Words spoken to a dying boy. Comfort in pain. *You can go home now, little brother. Mama's just put crystal buns in the warmer. Papa's readying his pipe. He'll do a dragon for you. Your favorite.* Ben Ni's presence wavers and his golden light turns to ash.

Anger, fear, and grief are so fiercely intertwined. The ones left behind don't have the end comfort but just the tangled cutting wires of not wanting to let go and the fear of what might happen if we do. *What happens if we do?*

Following the trail of smoke, I approach Setsu Yan, not as an intimidating Char war hero, but as a grieving father.

He squats on his haunches against the dark rock wall of the black sail, grunting when he sees me. The embodiment of his belief system is crumbling. It's a good fit, as I am crumbling inside anyway. Tapping his pipe of ashes, he relights it.

"Ah, I miss the sea. I know it's not far, but it is still too far, you know?" He strokes his chin. "I don't like smoking here. The air is too thick and humid. It smells like a thousand kitchen stoves burning a thousand garlic omelets." He snorts. "I like the salt stain, fish scale smell of home."

I sniff the air. In between the scents of war, it does smell like blackened saucepans and crackling oil. Garlic and ginger fried close to burning but made just right. I lick my lips. *I like it.* The palace, even the gardens, always smelled like the chemicals they used to scrub the rust-stained walls.

He puffs and blows a simple cloud of smoke into the air. "Tell me, Keeper, what do you want?"

My body freezes, swaying like a reed trying to hold its place against floodwaters. His Atmosphere is stark and gray, trees that have lost their leaves a season too early. *What do I want?*

No one asks me that question. The Keeper is asked, *How can she serve?* Lye is asked, *How can she help? How can she prove herself?* I swallow. Something of a squeak comes from my mouth and I flush pink with embarrassment. "I don't know. I suppose I want what everyone wants." Setsu's chuckle stops me short of saying the word *acceptance.*

"Child!" He groans impatiently. "I'm not asking for your hopes and dreams. I can create any manner of smoke animal. Snake? Fish? Scoop monkey?"

I laugh with the soft underside of my heart. The resigned part. "Oh." Eyes down. He feels and sounds like a father. But he's not my parent. *Will never be my parent.* I step forward but my heart leans away. "How about a jumble deer?" He's very quiet, mouth pursed, and I realize I've asked him to make a mainland animal he's probably never seen.

He clears his throat. Shifts on the rock and beckons me, patting the space beside him. "Describe," he orders.

I climb up and sit beside him, slotting my thin backside into the slate rock. Staring at the sky. "Jumble deer live in the marshlands. They have long, slender legs that swirl with a jumble of black and brown shapes, camouflaging the deer from predators." He nods, hands gesturing for me to continue. I sigh, half happy, half destroyed, as I recall chasing jumble deer from the marshes to protect sweet red rice shoots from being devoured before they had a chance to mature. I remember clapping my hands loudly with Ash at my side.

"Their heads are pointed and pinched at the nose. Big watermelon-seed shaped eyes framed by one black mark and one brown. Their ears are rabbit-like." I put my hands on top of my head to demonstrate, turning my palms back and forth. "Twisting toward danger."

He closes his eyes, concentrating, and puffs smoke into the air. A blob at first, it sprouts legs and a body. A pinched head and long rabbit ears. I gasp. My toes pressing into the rock with excitement. "Very close!" I grin.

"Humph!" Setsu turns to face me, tipping his chin up and down. "I thought the Keeper would be older." His eyes lift to where my hands are still playing bunny ears on my head and I lower them quickly. "And a man."

I twist uncomfortably under his gaze. "I'm surprised by your attitude, Setsu. Your daughter and wife are such strong, powerful women." His eyes darken and I clamp my mouth shut.

"Don't speak of my wife *or* daughter. You do not know them." He crosses his arms petulantly.

Using my weak hand, the powerless one, I pat his arm once, carefully. "You are right about your wife. I spent very little time with Ki Anah but I came to know Luna extremely well. I trained her and gifted her an Element." His eyebrows rise and he shakes his head like it's all too much. "She became my friend." Foreign words I'm trying to get used to.

"Yes, Joka told me of Luna, though I still can't quite believe it. I don't think it's something I can truly accept until I see her again." Setsu's arms loosen. Snakes of grief and missing work their way between his tightly held limbs to his strong beating heart.

I risk adding to his pain. "I also knew your son, Ben Ni, a little."

His chin falls to his chest like he's making sure his heart is still there. He breathes in long and deep so tears will not fall. Tradition will not allow it, but I sense his insides breaking apart like ice melting in arctic places. Cracks allowing room for seawater. Room for my memories of his son. His head lifts slightly and he rests the pipe beside him. "You knew youngest son?"

My bony knees knock against each other. My new clothes hang like ill-fitting tent flaps. They scrounged and scrapped to find me something to wear and I was too grateful to turn it down. Besides, it suits me. I am scrawny and slight. Small and pathetic. *How do I become worthy of Ben Ni's sacrifice?*

He closes his eyes slowly, golden dust on his lashes. *You are already worthy,* Ben Ni whispers.

*I want. I want. I want.* To believe him. I have to try. "Ben Ni saved my life—twice." He keeps saving it. Never stopped.

"*Apa?* What? My boy? My Ben Ni?" Words float like thin clouds about to disperse.

I explain what Ben Ni did for me, what he still does for me, as Setsu listens, solid and unmoving as a statue. "He was a unique soul, Setsu. I fear someone like him will never touch the earth again," I finish.

Perhaps these words live inside all Yans, passed between them like a sacred stick of incense. The smoke, sweet and pungent, heavy with purpose. One last scrutinizing look and Setsu speaks, "If Ben Ni saved you, then he must have believed you were worthy of saving." Resolve thickening across his chest like tightening armor. "Lye Li Koh." I nod solemnly. "You are the first Shen I've ever had a conversation with. It wasn't nearly as bad as I thought it would be." He coughs, clearing the smoke from his lungs and thumps his chest. "I just have one more question for you."

I grit my teeth. Stare out over the smoldering city. "Of course, anything."

He chuckles. A small, guarded sound. The rest is buried under sorrow. "What *do* you want?"

I run my hand over the roughness of my sycamore arm. "Oh. Um, maybe a snubnose dolphin?"

He slaps my back with his oak hand and I skid forward, my bony behind scraping along the ridged stone. "No, child. What is it you *truly* want?"

I twist back to answer, shouting words up the black sails. They whirl past Setsu's listening ears and echo. "I want to end this war."

# 39
# ASH KI

Bruised, browning vegetables, paper, animal bones, and all types of garbage tip dangerously close to the edge of the cliff above our heads. Small pieces flutter and spill, taking time to plunge into the water. Splashes and sploshes punctuate the Char gasps. The Yans stop short and gape at the pile, horrified. Even Luna has an expression of surprise on her usually blank face. Taking her plait in her hands and running it through her fingers like prayer beads, a nervous motion I haven't seen in a while. Heat makes the air over the garbage wobble and the smell so much worse. I pinch my nose, though it does little.

Ki Anah is the first to speak. "What is this?" Her slender arm points as something liquid slops down the pile with a chemical smell like acid. It singes our nostrils when it hits the water and spreads. The Yans jump back. The chancellor steps forward.

I open my arm to him. "Would you like to explain this, Chancellor?"

He smiles thinly. Dark teeth making his mouth look empty. "Why do you not call me by my name, Shek Ki Koh?" My shoulders pull up at the mention of our shared name, Ki Koh.

I glare. Anger swirling between betrayal but sympathy is spiked in there too. It catches between my teeth. He shares my name but was never truly acknowledged as a Koh. I move closer. "I've only had a short time to get used to the idea that my brother is alive. And that he's the chancellor, vile bringer of death and destruction. Perhaps you can allow me a grace period."

He snorts. "Grace will do you no good. The sooner you accept our fates are tied, the better off you will be." He says this through tight lips and then loudly talks to the others, attempting to gesture with his tied hands and failing. "This is a garbage depository. One of many around the country. Men collect the villagers' refuse and dump it into one designated area. It was the initiative of the great eleventh emperor." Some of the Carvresses huff and snort and I think I catch the word "typical." He ignores them and continues to talk. "It keeps the villages tidy and free of disease. It also provides employment."

Rats scurry like palace workers in and out of small openings. I take my breath in small bursts. Ki Anah shakes her head slowly, eyes squinting up at the seeping pile. "I don't understand your logic. What chemicals are leaking into the river? Will it not poison the water?"

The chancellor shrugs. "We've developed excellent fertilizers for our crops. They produce byproducts that must be disposed." He stops. Suddenly distrustful. Like the Char will steal Shen ideas. It's laughable. By the look on their faces, they would sooner jump into a cage full of piranha rabbits and be torn apart in a frenzy. "Besides, our land is vast. A few pieces of garbage and a few leaked chemicals are not enough to contaminate our immense water system."

The Char are aghast. "Perhaps not, but it will kill or damage some." Ki Anah presses into someone who is not easily dented.

He glances up at the heap, edging dangerously close, and rolls his eyes. "To succeed, you must be willing to do a little damage. We're talking about the greater good. A better way!"

I sense this discussion is creating further divide, like large hands separating brass from silver coins. Shen versus Char. Even Luna looks affected. She spreads her fingers out, making judging stars with her hands. Her lip pulls between her teeth, and I'm distracted by her beauty as she calls her power. Distracted and devastated. There's a cloud of new sadness about her as she taps her chest and whispers, "There's nothing but rats. The land is sick."

Sun approaches a small iceberg of trash that has washed ashore and kicks it with his wooden foot. Things topple and get caught in the current, starting to float away. "Of course it's sick. And so am I. This is disgusting." His nose screws up as he quickly gathers the garbage in his arms and dumps it away from the shore.

They stare at me like I'm part of it, adding bricks to a staggered wall that I've tried so hard to take down. Luna's expression is tired and disappointed. She asks, "Does this happen in the marshlands?"

My hands feel dirty though this isn't my fault. It's just the way we've always done things. Men take the garbage away. No one asks where it goes. I shake my head. I don't want to be singled out and judged in this manner. "No."

Luna sighs. She *feels* me. She knows I'm lying but she doesn't expose me.

The chancellor scrapes his long feet over river pebbles and scoffs. "And what do Char do with their waste, throw it in the ocean? How is that better?" It's strange to hear him sound defensive. Sun raises a finger ready to answer and the thin angry man turns his back to him. "Actually, I could care less what you do. Soon it won't matter."

I step to him threateningly at the same time as Sun, but our attention is drawn to the sound of a Carvress splashing through the river, water up to her waist, focused on a dangling rope. She makes it to the other side, tugs it to test, and then starts climbing up.

"What on earth is she doing?" I ask. She digs her toes into small divots in the rock, ascending desperately, like she *needs* to get to the top. Her face tilts, fixated on something specific.

The Coalstone Carvress shouts, "Come down now, sister, you could fall."

She turns and blinks, sets her mouth, and ignores her sister's pleas. The ebony Carvress clasps her hands together as she watches anxiously. "She's starved." She pats her stomach. It sounds like a drum. "We're all so very hungry."

Sun and I crash through the water to the rope that's twisting like a snake caught in a tree fork. Sun reaches out to follow her up the rope, but I grab his arm, quick flakes of ice shooting through my fingers. His cheeks flush with anger as he strains against me. "You can't," I explain. "We don't know what the rope is attached to. It may not be able to bear the weight of two people." We don't even know if it can take the weight of one Carvress.

He nods, conceding but irritated. We can do nothing but stare, necks craned as she flies up the canyon wall, swinging and shaking as she nears the top. No idea how long it will hold. *If* it will hold.

I don't understand why she's climbing, only that what she's doing is unsafe. I look to Luna who finally explains, pointing at the top where trees lean over the edge like daredevils. "She needs the trees."

My hands fist at my sides. "Can't she wait one day longer? The canyon will begin to lower very soon." If she'd said something, maybe we could have helped. Their lack of trust in me has become dangerous.

Close to the top, the Carvress's feet slip. The decomposing food, the chemicals, have coated the cliff in slime. Rubbish rains down, thwacking her head, splatting on the rocks at our feet. We part around the deluge, feeling helpless to stop it.

She swings out from the wall and we all hold our breath.

The Carvresses crush together in a huddle, mouths hanging open. The climbing Carvress hangs on. She's so close, only a yard or two.

"Her strength is waning," the ebony Carvress murmurs.

I reach for the rope. It's held her this far, maybe it can take the weight of two. I'm about to pull myself up when suddenly the rope becomes slack in my hand.

It has come loose from where it was attached and pours down on my head. Silently horrified, we watch the wooden woman fall. She doesn't scream or flail. Her heavy body just whistles downward like a log. I clench my teeth, thinking she'll be all right since she's wooden and will float to the top when she hits the water. Her sister's will chastise her, babble and bicker as they always do, and then we'll continue our journey.

I place my hands on the chilly canyon wall, bracing myself. Out of sight, I hear a crack and a cry. When I look up, the Carvress's wooden body is spinning further out from the wall like a tossed spool, hand still holding the severed rope. She hit a ledge on her way down and her head flops while her body twirls. Sun takes my shoulder and pulls me away just as she lands with a loud thwack on the water. The landing should be softer. The water should catch and cradle her. Instead, it feels like she's hit earth. Sun lunges at the floating body before it's swept away, lifting her into his arms as the other Carvresses begin to moan and cry. Clutching each other for support and kneeling as Sun places her gently on the shore.

I stand back as others race forward. The chancellor stays pressed against the wall with detached observation. The sunset colored Carvress sweeps her fingers over her sister's neck where she is… splintered. Frayed, spiked pieces of wood spray from the break. Her neck has snapped. Her eyes are open but lifeless.

The Carvresses hover over her, creating a cage I can't see through. Sun moves closer, peering over the crouched women. He makes a strange noise and stumbles backward over pebbles and water.

"What is it?" I ask, approaching. "Is she dead?" I know she is dead.

Sun's mouth hangs open. He pants the words, "No! I don't believe it. It can't be."

The Coalstone Carvress rises, showing me one slivered view of the fallen Carvress. "Our sister is dead." Her tears are thick, amber-colored sap. I lean, not wanting to move my feet, but needing to see more. The Carvress's dress is wet and lifted slightly to reveal her shins.

My breath catches in my throat and my thoughts are the same as Sun's. "It can't be."

I force myself forward, pushing aside the grieving Carvresses, to gaze upon her beautiful, cracked body. Instead, I see a tanned face with pink cheeks that quickly drain away to corpse gray. Soft freckled skin and a body made of flesh. My mouth drops open, because it's not the most surprising thing I see. *This is impossible.* Curling around her left eye is a small tattoo. A leaf that I've seen it hundreds of times. She is Earth. She is an Earth Shen.

Ki Anah's hands tremble, voice laced with fury and fear. She grabs Luna violently and drags her away. "We need to leave this place." She pins Luna to her hip, wincing as Luna hurts her, but she doesn't release her daughter. She points at me and the chancellor accusingly. "I don't know what you two Shen have done but this is darkest, darkest magic. It's not right. It's not right."

She splashes through the shallow water, Sun standing between us looking lost. Palms facing out like he's calling rain.

I'm too shocked to speak or move. Too confused.

*I don't understand.*

My eyes switch from face to face and find eight carved expressions that are full of grief and completely unsurprised.

I shout out. "Wait! K-ki Anah," I stammer. "This is not my doing. I don't even think this is the chancellor's doing." Shek Ki's eyes are like open windows to a cool breeze, taking it all in. Storing it for later in his book of dark and destructive memos.

The ebony Carvress separates from the group. Eyes lowered, she bows to Ki Anah who's frozen in the rushing water, daughter at her side, pieces of rubbish knocking against her legs. "Char Ki Anah, you are right to call this dark magic. But it is no one's doing but our own."

The Carvress of Cockle Fan Island is dead.

The Char have lost a leader. A priestess. And what is worse, they have lost their innocence.

# 40
## LYE LI

Joka and Setsu are more comfortable on the seashore. Their muscles relax and they breathe deeper. Like fish need water, they need the salt coat on their skin. All Char have been called to a makeshift headquarters, a large building whose sloping roof reminds me of hands clasped in prayer. And it should pray, for its bamboo and palm leaf constructed roof are dangerously vulnerable compared to the solid stone hideout of the Shen.

We sit at the back of a large hall, just beneath a colorfully decorated stage. Every beam of the grand ceiling is carved with wooden characters. Their bulging eyes and swirling mustaches are whimsical while their broad grins mock us. The way they pinch their thumb and forefinger together reminds me of something I can't quite place, perhaps a dance I've seen. Silks and bells that distracted the emperor from a small protest happening outside the palace walls. Farmers growing tired of sacrificing so much of their crops to exportation.

There are things that Shen and Char have in common. Ways in which we are the same. Some foods, words and traditions that cross over. Links in a chain that was once a whole piece. I wonder when the chain was damaged. When did it erode like cheap plated gold?

I refocus on the debate of how we can save a city turning to ash.

"Even if we fail, we will deplete the Shen army significantly. That, to me, is still a victory." Setsu's chest puffs with pride. Joka leans back. His eyes capture mine in soft intelligence. My heart beats a little faster and I swallow. These feathery, fluttering feelings are a distraction, and I look away. Setsu thumps his fist on the table and my feet vibrate. "We need to launch a final attack. All of us, together, and take out as many as we can."

Fah strokes his walnut jaw, slight annoyance building in his Atmosphere, like a wolf nipping the heels of prey it can't quite catch. "Setsu, your experience is appreciated." He tips a bow quickly. "But I am the general. I don't want to send men to die simply to deplete Shen forces." His eyes round with regret as he mutters, "I've done that once and I will not make that mistake again."

Setsu grumbles, shifting his large weight on a tiny protesting stool.

Fah calls a soldier to him with one long finger. "Captain Halong! How many barrels of gunpowder do we have left?"

The rigid soldier with a wooden elbow nods brusquely. "Seven, sir."

Fah grips the edge of the table, eyebrows arched high. "Only seven." He curses and the captain backs away.

"Seven is still enough to do some damage," Setsu offers. "Perhaps we could split into groups. Break the Shen apart and attack."

Fah considers this reluctantly, closing his eyes for a few breaths.

Joka has been quiet, hand on his neck while his mind ticks over a thought. He speaks calmly, voice like an alto flute. "Or we use all seven at once."

The rumble reply of the Char makes it hard to hear. Their voices rise in pitch and frequency like a wave. They shift anxiously around each other. The Char want action. Sitting here under this glorified parasol makes everyone nervous.

The men lean across the table like they're tired of holding up their heads. I sit upright. An idea starting to form, but I wait for the right moment to share. The mens' eyes blinking large and receptive.

"Second son, that would be a waste of explosives. And could destroy what's left of the city." Setsu frowns and pats his son's head.

Joka smooths his hair and gestures around the packed room, pointing out the large opening and the view of a city reduced to soot. "Papa, the city is already destroyed. What we need is one last, devastating attack. Then we flee like the women and children. We don't need to sacrifice what's left of our army. We saw Shen ships sail this morning. By my count, half have left on Lye's instruction. Their belief in her loyalty could be a great asset."

Fah crosses his legs. "This is true. And what is the Shen's true objective?"

He asks this to no one in particular, but I answer, "To make a Char-Shen hybrid." Resolve crystalizes like boiled sugar.

He nods slowly. "They are searching for a Carvress, but they also need a Keeper. From what you've explained, they need both for their plan to work, right?"

I nod, flexing my weak hand unimpressively. "They need me." The only way to get an effective hybrid is to gift elements after turning a part wooden. It doesn't work very well the other way around.

Joka stands excitedly. Finger pointing at the ceiling. "Then we use Lye as bait! We lure the remaining Shen to one location and"— he makes an explosion gesture with his hands—"boom!"

I shouldn't be shocked by this answer. Before I can stop myself, I mutter, "You needn't sound so excited about offering me up like a worm on a hook."

Collapsing back on his stool, he reaches for my arm, but withdraws under the sharp gaze of his father. "I am sorry, Lye, but it's a good idea."

Despite a twinge of hurt, I'm surprised at how we think alike. "I was going to suggest it. The Shen will come for me. If we place the barrels strategically, we could take them out in one explosion." I imagine standing in the center. After a flash of bright white heat, the briefest pain will hit me, and then only darkness. A night sky emptied of stars.

Fah and Joka nod, satisfied, and rise from the table to start organizing the men. My hand shakes and scrunches. Shakes and scrunches into a fist. I run a slow finger over the sycamore, tracing the black marks and recounting the memory behind each one. I shouldn't care that Joka so easily offered me as the lure.

Setsu pats my fingers awkwardly and reluctantly like a bird pecking at seed from an open palm, wanting to have faith but ready to flee. "I am impressed at your bravery, young Keeper."

I am not simply the Keeper. The labels they pin to my breast puncture and wound. "Setsu. I am not the Keeper. The Keeper hides in the palace while others fight her war. I am Char." I hold up my arm. "I am like your daughter, Luna. A Char with Shen powers. This is how I wish to be viewed. It is how I wish to be remembered." My arm falls to the table with a wooden thud.

Setsu bows low. "I wish I knew this version of my daughter, Char Lye Li." I bow too, mostly because I can't meet his eyes without showing my true feelings. That perhaps he is better off not knowing her.

"You will."

Setsu searches his pocket, pulls out a piece of oak, and presses it to his hand. The Call rings out. Other Calls join him. The sound is glorious and choral and almost lifts the roof from the flimsy walls. A tear bulges from the corner of my eye. My piece of sycamore probably floated out to sea so I cannot join them. Always, always separated. I sigh sadly. So tired of standing on my own.

His kind, dark eyes sweep over me and then suddenly, he disappears. Melting into a crowd of music and harmony that saws at my heart. Marking me in a way that can't be seen on the outside.

I close my eyes and listen. Let the music swirl around me and imagine I'm part of it. Light, golden and just beautiful.

Something taps my fingers. I open my eyes to Setsu standing proudly over me, eager as a child. "It's a hairpin." I turn the elaborately carved piece in my hand. "Char, I mean, our women use it to decorate their hair." He shifts self-consciously. "This is a theatre. I found it in the dressing rooms." His smile is quick but genuine as he flaps his hands at me. "Go on. Try it."

Confused, I lift the pin to my barely-there hair. His laugh is deep and bellowing like the sound of waves crashing in a cave. He swipes at my fingers and lays the pin across my wooden arm. My Call starts small and rises. Warm, petal-soft music lifting and mingling with the others.

*This. This. This.*

I glance up at the roof, afraid of how much emotion can be read on my face. Lines and lines of embarrassing script telling him how much it means to me to be part of this. It means... *everything.* My ghost, my conscience and my companion, nods his head. Like he knew this would happen all along.

Cold dread tries to poke at my shoulders, but I don't allow it. I only allow the feeling of belonging. It rests like a crown of wood atop my corn fluff hair.

# 41

## ASH KI

We risk a fire of trash. Our clothes are wet, and the deep sinking cold of the canyon is starting to nip our bones. The realizations brought forth by the Carvress's death linger over our group like a fog.

I stoke the coals with a wooden spoon I found floating in the river. The Carvresses sit back from the fire, separate from us. Warmth is unnecessary to them, and the fire is dangerous.

"Oh sister!" the pink-hued Carvress whispers, staring into the flames. "What an ending for you. After hundreds of years, to land back in the country of our birth only to die so pointlessly." Her head falls into her hands as she weeps.

The ebony Carvress pats her back, her eyes on the four of us as we watch these wooden gods with a new feeling of distrust. Particularly Ki Anah, who clutches Luna and Sun fiercely. Her whole world is dissolving, the belief system the Char is built around is crumbling. The ebony Carvress rises, dark limbs hanging sadly by her sides. Turning to her sisters, she says, "It's time." She mutters to her chest, "In truth, it is long overdue."

I feel like our known histories are about to be ripped from the page and thrown into the fire. Such is the gravity of this moment. We don't speak. We wait for the quake, the Call, the ruin.

Black hands wring together as she steps closer to us, talking over the fire, telling us a story, a fairy tale, that just happens to be true. It will change the world.

"The Char and Shen tribes live in blood and violence. But they were born from love." Her dreamy coal eyes flit to the sky. "Nine hundred and eighty years ago, the Shen royal family was large and happy. Nine princesses and one young prince ruled the mainland." I swallow a hard lump coated in sarcasm. Happiness doesn't live in the palace, it is taken away by it. "The youngest of the ten children, the prince was spoiled and doted upon by his nine sisters. The royal family were powerful elementals, and each sibling carried one element within them. Two Water, two Fire, two Air, two Earth, and two Blood." She taps her temple when she says Blood, and Luna shifts awkwardly in her seat, blinking quickly and with an eagerness I haven't seen for weeks. "The sisters loved the prince dearly and it saddened them to watch him grow from an innocent child with warm Fire in his heart to a charred and blackened young man with a need no one could fill. A need for absolute power." She clutches her ebony fist and shakes it as the other Carvresses nod their heads.

"The sisters could see greed spreading like a pronged tumor throughout his soul but they shook their heads and turned away from his disturbing behavior. They convinced themselves that somewhere inside him was good. That he suffered from a sickness. And if they loved him enough, maybe he would return to them."

The Coalstone Carvress sighs loudly. "Love should be enough. It usually is. But sometimes a person does not want to be saved. They embrace the darkness, revel in it. It feeds them."

The chancellor's eyes are hooded, hands in lap, legs out straight. If he sees me staring, he doesn't react. I know he's listening. A tale close to our own in many ways.

The ebony Carvress continues, "Where their brother struggled to even light a spark from his fingertips, the nine sisters were masters of their elements. They could summon floods and forest fires.

They could bring forth hurricanes and earthquakes. The two of Blood had control over every animal in the forest surrounding the stone palace. All of them, but the youngest, showed grace and poise, magic and ritual. No one could harm them." She squares her shoulder proudly.

My ears capture and wonder at this information. The Carvress speaks of a time when Shen could control elements outside of their body.

"When invaders came, the royal family faced them bravely. They fought on the frontline using their power to protect and led the Shen with strength. Caring for their families with gentleness and care, they didn't notice their brother's last shred of goodness wilting with envy." Despite ourselves, we lean in, faces ruddy and red from the fire.

Sorrow fills her chest and parts her lips. "The tumor of envy sank deep into his conscience. When he looked upon his fierce and beautiful sisters, he felt nothing but rage. He sought only one thing—to possess their elements. To become the strongest. To lead his country solely and stand above all others.

"He believed if he could be everything—Water, Fire, Earth, Air, and Blood—then he would have everything. And that swirl of doubt, that splinter of misgiving and mistrust, would disappear. He convinced himself that his sisters didn't love him, they pitied him. So, he was determined to show them he could lead." The ebony Carvress shouts to the stars, arms outstretched.

"His plan was wicked and dirty. And we, his sisters, never saw it coming.

"Ancient texts told him how to steal power from his siblings. The prince ran his fingers over ink the color of dried blood and smiled like a half moon shrouded in cloud. But he didn't interpret the consequence. He should have known old, dark scripts need to be studied for decades. Otherwise you only understand half the story. They make promises they can't keep."

Luna's hand finds mine, nestling into my fingers with the vibrations of an anxious spiker bird.

"Slipping down hallways with greed on his mind and light in his footsteps, the prince entered his sisters' rooms. He whispered shadowy chants in an ancient language and pressed his fingers to their Pulses. And while they slept, he drew all their power into himself." The ebony Carvress touches her chest with widespread fingers and gestures outward.

"It filled him, clung to his bones and flowed through his blood. All the elements inside him. He had *everything*, and the only ones who could have stopped him were now powerless to do so.

"His sisters' waking screams were a meal he was hungry for. *They are dying*, he thought, and he was glad of it." The ebony Carvress swipes at sap leaking eyes.

"They ran to each other as the prince stood in the hallway, aghast at the sight of them. Wooden eyes blinked, joints creaked, as the nine women gathered on the plush red carpets of the palace. They stared at their new bodies in awe and surprise. And then they turned to him. *What have you done, brother?* they asked. He didn't answer. He only stared at the monsters he had created." She gestures at the seven seated Carvresses, seven Shen princesses, who smile sadly.

"The sisters gazed upon him with love, though he couldn't recognize it. Power brewed and bubbled within him. They were supposed to die. Perhaps this was how he was supposed to end the ritual. Kill them with his stolen power.

"The prince rushed at eldest sister." She nods to the Coalstone Carvress. "He fired lightning at her. When nothing came, he grasped her arm, attempting to char her bones and boil her blood. He would see her wooden eyes roll back and she would cease to be."

The Coalstone Carvress rises and speaks with impossible earnestness and incredible sadness. "I felt nothing."

Sun, Ki Anah, Luna, and I try to absorb this information. This fairy tale history reworks pieces of what we thought we knew. Luna squeezes my hand tightly and I attempt to concentrate rather than revel at the closeness. At the fact that she chooses me for comfort.

"Nothing at all," the ebony Carvress exclaims. "She had become a shield no element could penetrate. The prince stared at his hands in disbelief. Something was wrong with his power. He didn't feel as strong as he thought he would. His hands flickered with all the elements, but not one was as powerful as when his sisters wielded them. Not one could radiate further than his fingers. The elements were now spread thinly. Possessing them all had made him weaker.

"The prince growled and spat at his sisters, who gazed at him with empathy. It only made him twist and writhe with fury. Hissing a warning as they circled him, wooden limbs knocking against each other, he viewed them as *inhuman.* He tried to harm them, but his touch didn't singe or flood or bite. *I am the emperor now!* he pronounced, chest expanding with foolish pride." Her hand shoots skyward as she imitates the prince's voice.

"*We know,* they said calmly as they restrained him and forced him to his room.

"*I still control the army, the peasants. You will have nowhere to hide,* he threatened, eyes black as death. They agreed as they bound him.

"*I will never stop hunting you,* he said, crazed with hatred and disappointment at how his plans had unfolded. For in taking his sister's power, he had changed the natural order of things. There is always a price, and his was hefty." She draws in a deep regretful breath. "They should have ended his life right then, but he was their brother. And despite his betrayal, they still loved him and had hope." Exhausted, the ebony Carvress implores her older sister to finish.

The Coalstone Carvress nods solemnly and spins her hands in an elegant, stationary dance. "There was little time to escape, so beneath a low moon and hovering mist, the sisters sailed from the mainland with their husbands, children, and some loyal servants. Dispersing themselves between the Char islands that were sprinkled like jewels across a crown." Her eyes find the Yans.

"The Char islanders were savage but welcoming. The sisters would not completely protect them from the Shen that would surely come. The curse of an everlasting life and a frozen body was one they alone should bear. But they could offer a gift. Share their power in small parts by bestowing wooden limbs that would make the Char stronger and shield against a Shen elemental touch.

"The prince's eldest sister had studied the texts. She knew something he did not. Stealing his sisters' power meant it was not his to own but he must share it. Now with the ability to awaken elemental powers in anyone of his choosing, despite not being the mighty elemental he had wished to be, he could create a formidable army." She dips her head in sorrow. "I knew he would come for us. He set a history in motion that could not be stopped. It was like the tide—endless, ebbing, and brutal.

"The prince became the first emperor and Keeper, and even after he had turned to dust and joined the stars, the legacy of his spell lived on."

My turn to squeeze Luna's hand. The reason for Lye, the way it all started, feels impossible and lonely. I miss my sister in this moment, and I wish she were here to listen to these words. We would be stronger together.

"A child was born to a Shen he had awakened, and they became the new spoke in the turning wheel. A new cycle of Keepers that never stopped turning." She draws circles in the air. Her voice turns icy.

"The sisters watched their husbands and children grow old and die. And they retreated further and further into the hearts of their islands with every death and every new loss. Until they were set deep in the caverns beneath the rising rocks." She sighs, deep and disembodied. A kind of sadness we mortals can't really understand about Gods who walk the earth.

Her tone changes and instead of looking at the sky, she gives us her eyes, her heart. "We can't pass over to the next life. We are trapped in our wooden bodies. Our only task, our reason for being, is to watch over and protect the Char. We must keep a promise made long ago that in return for shelter, we would provide a shield."

The tale finished, I can't quite find the words. I don't know what's more shocking, the Carvresses being Shen royalty or that they're a thousand years old.

Ki Anah stands, winding around the fire pit to stand in front of the Coalstone Carvress. She bows quickly and then does something I never thought she'd do. She wraps her arms around the Carvress in an embrace.

"Thank you, Carvress," she mumbles against a wooden shoulder. "For the truth and for your protection. This is hard information to swallow, but you've given us your heart." Then she laughs. These incredible Char. Ridiculously warm, forgiving, open people. "What a story I shall have to tell my husband when I see him."

What a story I have for Lye. It makes me wonder where she belongs in all this. Is her place with these women, these princesses? She is not their kin, though she is connected to them.

Sun stands and bows also. Then he turns to me. "Looks like we have some common relatives." He winks but I hear the wariness in his voice. This information is dangerous and life changing. In more ways than one.

The chancellor's eyes are narrowed to slits. A snake stalking prey.

MY WET shirt lies in a ball by my feet, jacket pulled tight across my bare chest. I wring it out and sling it over a stone to dry.

Ki Anah springs to her feet, wooden hips clicking and clacking as she ambles over the riverbank. She rips my shirt from the rock and throws it into the cave.

"Hey!"

She tuts as the others laugh in an airy, knowing way. "Ah, Shen. You don't have any sense in your head."

Fetching my shirt, I attempt to return it to its drying place, but Ki Anah wrenches it from my hands. I have half a mind to slap her hand with cold water or freeze them with numbing snow, but I hold back. "Stop it! You crazy woman."

"I'm *trying* to help you, silly Shen boy!" She takes the shirt inside again.

"I don't understand." Luna watches me with an almost forgotten heat. Coolness grips my skin. I approach the fire and open my palms, letting my jacket hang open to warm my torso. Her gaze slips to my stomach and I am very conscious of it coasting over my fire-lit skin. "Give me back my shirt, Ki Anah."

"Ahhh. No," she replies with a grim look. "Even though you are a Shen, I don't want to see your organs scattered over river rocks." Her nose scrunches in disgust.

I roll my eyes. "What are you talking about?"

"Hantu Pontianak, of course." The Char and Carvresses hum and nod in understanding.

"Hantu what?" I ask, eyes on my wet shirt, scrunched in Ki Anah's hands.

She squats, leaning back on her heels, eyes all serious. "Hantu Pontianak. She's a ghost. If you hang your clothes outside at night, she will come and suck your organs out of your eye sockets."

The chancellor snorts and I try very hard not to join him. "That's ludicrous."

Before I can stop her, Ki Anah throws my shirt into the flames in anger. I dart for it, retreating as my fingers are singed. "What the devil did you do that for?" Sun chuckles and I feel like I'm the butt of everyone's joke.

"Ai! You bring bad luck with your lack of faith." She glares defiantly. "Just because you Shen have no traditions or stories passed down from mother to child, it doesn't mean you can discount ours."

Anger pushes at my ribs, threatening to spew out. I throw my hands up in the air and storm out of the cave. I walk a good distance away, so I can calm down. Around a bend, I lean against the wall. I'm exhausted and I'm trying my hardest to keep these women safe, but they don't respect me. They treat me like an idiot. I run a frustrated hand through my hair and gaze up at the small slice of sky. A fissure of stars, a cut of the moon.

Pebbles rub against each other quietly.

"Don't worry, if the *hantu,* er, *ayam* takes my organs, I'll ask them politely to throw them in the river, so they don't offend your Char eyes in the morning," I joke bitterly to the figure approaching.

"The chicken ghost?" Luna's voice is amused.

I shrug. "Is that what I said?"

She closes the space between us like a slow door. "Yes, that is what you just said." Voice low. Soft.

I stop breathing. Too aware of how little space there is between my skin and hers. "Oh. Well it makes just as much sense as a laundry-sniffing woman who, against all natural laws, manages to pull whole organs through eye sockets."

"Mhm." Her hands dance through whispering air. Fingers spread wide. They land on my chest, drumming along to the staccato beat of my heart.

"Luna… what are you doing?"

Hands slide under my jacket and link at my back. Her touch is warm. Her blood is hot. She pulls me against her forcefully, standing on her tiptoes to brush her lips along my jaw.

Against my skin she whispers, "I'm doing what I want. Don't you want it too?" Her mouth closes over my neck, laying kisses down like a treasure map toward my collarbone.

I breathe lightly, small rises in my chest. Because of course I want it. I am no monk and the closer she gets, the more of my skin she grazes, the harder it will be to step away. I don't want to step away. I *want* to stay pressed close to her. I want to wrap my arms around her waist and lift her up. Kiss her. Touch her. Hold her.

But I *feel* you, Luna.

*Your touch is warm. Your blood is hot.*

With regret, I put my hands on her shoulders. Right now, her touch is solely physical need and my whole body burns with want. It's so difficult to not take what is offered. To look into her golden, glazed eyes and shake my head no, instead of rushing to yes. But I gently push her until her feet are flat on the ground.

*Your touch is warm. Your blood is hot. But your heart and head are cool.*

"Luna, I *feel* you," I murmur, lips burning with unfulfillment.

Anger flashes like sheet lightning, like a blanket of white light. "Then you know what I'm offering." I nod yes. She is shocked by the rejection "But you will not take it?"

My hands crunch into frustrated fists. How do I explain that she's not enough for me like this? Would she even care? "I can't, Luna. It will feel good in the moment and then it will hurt me more than a hundred arrows." I steal her move, patting my confused, pro-testing chest.

"I don't understand." She steps back, putting foot over foot between us.

As I approach, I hear her enter the water. "That's the problem. You can't understand because you're not all of Luna. And until you are, we can't do what you're offering."

My heart struts out a good, reassuring beat, but my body wants to punch itself.

"He's... I... I can't, Ash." Her voice cracks like drought-stricken earth. "I can't let it in. It will kill me."

I close my eyes, feeling her devastation just under the surface, eggshell thin and about to crack. A vulnerable creature scared to breathe the air and live in the world. She hurts me every day by degrees, small turns of the compass. By avoiding pain, she causes it.

"Oh Luna, don't you see? If you keep going like this, you may as well *be* dead."

She slips from me like a ghost called home.

Living but dead.

I'M NOT sure how long I've been sitting here. Back scratched and shuddering cold. Shifting and kicking stones like a sulky child. My mind repeatedly trawls over the minutes in which I chose not to have her. I let out a sigh that probably reached the top of the can-yon. Other men will hear it and shake their heads. My head collapses into my hands. Hands that *held* her body, *touched* her skin and then sent her away. But the *feel* of her burned with cold. The strike of ice on flesh blazing like a blue flame.

"You idiot." I throw a pebble into the river but don't hear a plop with the loud rush of water. "You stupid, proud idiot."

"You are no idiot, Ash Ki Koh." Ki Anah's voice is solid. It has its own shadow and weight. "Sorry for teasing you, young Shen. It's part of being in a Char tribe."

I shove those words in my pocket greedily. "If I'm part of the tribe, does that mean you'll start listening to me?"

She laughs softly, and it stretches into a sigh at the end. "Perhaps. Sounds like we have been part of the same tribe for quite some time now. A thousand years almost."

"Does that sadden you?" I find her form in the dark, long and thin and not very much like Luna, leaning against the canyon wall.

"It does not sadden me. It will not sadden the Char. Though it may confuse them for a time. We have based so much of who we are on our distrust of the Shen."

"You are not Shen though. You still stand on your own."

Her head bows slightly. "We are not Shen, but we have revered the Carvresses who are Shen royalty for a thousand years. We are born of Shen magic. We have let them change us into what we are now and are as linked to the Shen as can be."

She is right. They may have started as simple islanders, but the Carvresses, revealed as Shen, have changed their identity into something else. Shen magic lives in every single Char. They can't shake that off like a loose bangle. I frown. It's more like a tight cuff.

"Besides, you Shen are not all bad," she concedes, stepping out from the shadows. Her tight bun gleams glossy under the pale light. "Come back to the fire."

I tug my sleeves over my wrists. "She won't want to see me."

Ki Anah risks placing a hand on my shoulder. "You did the right thing. Turning her away."

Embarrassed and surprised. "She told you?"

Her fingers dig into my skin. "A mother knows." The water is powerful. One slip and you'd be sucked out to the sea. "Ash, I know you love her. Your actions have proven so."

At least she can't see the redness in my cheeks. The uncomfortable look on my face. "It doesn't really matter how I feel," I mumble.

She tsks. "Maybe not right now. But I have faith she will come back to us. And when she does"—she pauses, breathes in and out long—"you will have my blessing."

The words seem difficult for her to say and I do appreciate it, but I am honest with my reply. "Thank you, Ki Anah. I don't need your blessing, but thank you all the same."

She begins to turn, beckoning me to follow. I sense a smile as she says, "You may not need it, but Luna will." Her hips creak as they swing side to side, skirts flapping like bat wings. "When she is ready, that is."

*You mean if she is ever ready.* I don't share her optimism. Not after tonight. Hope is starting to feel like this laughable thing, like prayers burned or ashes blown into the air.

# 42
## LYE LI

The blackened sky seems appropriate, mirroring the scorched city. I turn in a small circle. The city is severely wounded. *After today, who knows what will be left.*

I did not get long before I was back in Keeper gray. Long, roomy sleeves of rough cloth cover my sycamore arm, my *Char* arm, with my hands clasped in front and my hood pulled back for them to see me clearly.

A knot grows in my stomach, guilt and death twisted together. The Shen must have killed the messenger Fah sent but they heeded his last words: That the Keeper had been captured and to come to the market square to fight for her release.

Rain buckets down. A thunderous full sound as it smashes over roofs and small shop verandas. The water drips down my robe, soaks my feet. I almost expect the rain itself to be black or at least a dark charcoal. I bite my lip to suppress a smile. The sky doesn't give; it takes.

My ghost hovers, golden behind my left shoulder. He is silent and still today, a witness to the world tearing open.

I know my friends are watching. I feel a slight tug on the ropes twisted around my ankles in the strange and extremely strong infinity-style knot. Loops and loops, forming a figure eight. A reminder that Joka has me. He's ready.

*With warm and gentle hands, he wraps the rope around my ankles as his eyes stay on his task and his lips pout in concentration. As his fingers brush my skin, I feel the course of small atoms colliding all the way up to my cheeks, which redden embarrassingly.*

"You are ready to offer me as sacrifice?"

*Joka pauses, clasping thin fingers around both my feet and squeezing. "You volunteered. Besides, it's a good idea. Probably our best chance of protecting the others." His touch makes me squirm. Not because it's unwanted but because it's so unfamiliar to be touched. I stare down at his hands, not wanting to meet his eyes.*

*"Lye," he whispers, one hand leaving my bindings and reaching for my face. His finger lands under my chin as he tries to lift my gaze. He gets a bee sting for his trouble. Withdrawing his hand, he shakes it and tries again. And I concentrate on not hurting him. "Would you have listened if I'd tried to stop you from acting as bait?"*

*His eyes are a dark, bottomless pool, like the side of the moon we wish upon. They swallow me with sincerity. "No. I would not have. It still might have been nice if someone had fought for me. I've tried so hard to earn my place with the Char, but no one cares. No one ever fights for me." I sound like a whiny child and his expression shows me he thinks so too. I cross my arms over my chest. "Duty is all I know. Perhaps it's all people see in me. I'm not a person but a thing to be used."*

*Joka's mouth rises to a strange smile. "That's not true at all and you know it. What about Ash? Luna? They care deeply for you. And you've somehow managed to convince my father of your worth. A man who has spent his life killing Shen."*

*I attempt to wiggle my legs. They're bound tight and feel like one solid limb. "He sees me as an asset. Nothing more."*

*"You are wrong. You convinced Setsu Yan that Shen are real people. Not monsters. Not by being the Keeper. Not even with this." He taps my sycamore arm. "You showed him by being Lye Li. The brave young woman who is nervous and vulnerable. Intelli-*

*gent and brave. A flawed person who doesn't run from her failings anymore. Someone who is trying to make amends."*

*His hand has traveled from my arm to my shoulder, and I was so caught up in his words, I didn't suppress my powers. But he doesn't withdraw. His hand coasts upward, over my collar bone, up my neck to my face. He tilts his head and smirks.*

*"What are you doing to me?" he asks. "It feels like, like..."*

*Unaware of what I've been projecting, I stumble to find the source. It's a nest. A burrow. A place where small creatures gather. Nuzzle and keep each other warm. "Like home?" I answer.*

*He nods with a smoother than a blade smile. His head inclines and his face moves closer. I'm restrained by rope but also by other things. Things I'm not ready to let go of. I freeze as he comes nearer.*

*His forehead presses to mine and his voice lowers. "Lye, you needn't look so terrified. I'm not going to kiss you."*

*I like his forehead touching mine and I very much enjoy the sound of his voice vibrating in my chest. "Y-you're not?" I stutter.*

*He shakes his head, still connected, so it grinds against my skin. His movements are awkward though he forces confidence into his words. "I'd like to, but I know it's not the time. I don't want our first kiss to feel like goodbye."*

*Gulping, I wish I could get free of the ropes and put distance between us.*

*He pulls back to sit in front of me and tugs on the rope. "That should hold you." He stands to leave.*

*"What? Wait! Aren't you going to untie this?" I lift my feet in the air.*

*Joka chuckles in a high-pitched way like he's swallowed a baby bird and turns around, kneeling at my feet. "Just joking, Lye."*

*Quiet spins out like air caught in a windmill as he swiftly unwraps my feet and leaves me with more questions than answers.*

This plan is foolhardy and dangerous. But with so few Char left to fight, it's our only chance.

I stare up at the sky again. *I know you do as you please, but could you just leave us be today? Open up. Let the sun pour through.*

Light touches my feet, teasing. I stand in the middle of a giant sun inlaid in the ground. The large representation of the Carvresses mark spreads over the biggest square in Black Sail City. At opposite ends of the spokes are the Shen and Char soldiers.

The Shen Captain Kinanh steps forward, pristine white hair tightly pinned. He's backed by an immense dark shadow of Shen that never stops moving. Halting out of arrow range, he shouts across the market square. "Return the Keeper and we will let you live." A repeated lie.

Fah steps forward also. Even though his Char uniform is a little smudged and dirty, he fills it with pride and elegance. He holds his sword out horizontally and I brace myself. *Take me. Take me. Take me,* I whisper to the sky. "You want the Keeper? Then you must fight for her!" he challenges.

This is excruciating but I hold still. I have to hold still. My feet wiggle in their bindings so it's not like I can run anyway.

Shen soldiers fill the space around us, moving closer and closer. There are very few Char behind me, just enough to appear to fill the streets beyond the square. The rest are softly sneaking down the cobblestones behind the Shen, ready to push them into the center of square. The ground shudders under the weight of so many soldiers. All eyes on me. Shen and Char.

The rope tautens. *Wait. A few more seconds.*

A colored barricade of bloodthirsty Shen approach. They view me as a prize or an idol to be collected and stored in the belly of a ship. Closing my eyes, my mind flips to a possible outcome of this plan: thrown at the emperor's feet, iron bars closing over my freedom. I'd rather die than go back there. My eyes snap open.

I am a slave no longer.

With care, I lie down on the ground. The Carvress's mark is my launchpad. A Shen grabs at my arms but misses as suddenly I'm flying. Up. Up. Up. Upside down. Shen colors cover the entire square like unmixed paint on a palette. Blobs of blue. Sections of orange. So much orange. The Atmosphere of the Shen is singular and nightmarish. It is eradication. A cleansing fire. A monstrous flood. They seek nothing but complete extinction of the Char.

I swing from my rope. Hopelessly, helplessly above it all. Some Char are caught in the square. Black dots surrounded by color.

Rain pours down my body, going up my nose, and my head begins to ache from blood rush. I grasp the rope and try to right myself. I feel like a spirit separated from its body. Watching the death below and counting who will join me.

There's too much color and not enough black. And at the same time there's too much black in the square when there shouldn't be any. Char should be bordering and barricading the Shen, but like dark flecks to an iris, some have been pulled into fights near the center. I should know by now, battles can be perfectly planned but never perfectly executed. I squint, trying to find Setsu and Fah, but it's just dark heads and fabric from here. The pulley I'm tied to creaks and I freeze. If I fall, it will all be for nothing.

The square is at capacity. The crowd hemmed in by closely packed buildings, Char plugging the gaps with no space between men fighting. The *ooffs* and outcries of bodies slamming into each other, in a space where they can barely swing a fist, is so loud I wonder if the clouds are shuddering. Faces flash upward, just pale shapes shining with water, watching me swing from side to side in the wind like I'm in a play, pretending to fly.

Suddenly, the tension goes out of the rope, and I drop. My breath stays in the sky while the rest of me plummets. The ground approaches. The end will be quick; my skull will shatter and then emptiness.

He's supposed to have me. *Joka, don't let go*, I beg.

My body seizes painfully, and I shriek as my fall abruptly ends. My ankles are raw. My spine feels like it's being yanked from my body. But I'm rising, fast to the long, wooden beam stretching out over the square. Using all my strength, I heave myself onto the beam. The rope goes slack a moment later and my heart feels like two halves of a stone cracking against each other. *He had me and now he's let go.*

Before I can think about what has happened to Joka on the other end of the rope, the explosives go off consecutively, each one taking a hammer to my head. Seven extreme bashes to my ears.

Debris whistles past my head. The beam shakes. I keep my eyes closed. Too scared to see what lies beneath me. A gaping hole. A star shaped wound in the earth. *A grave.*

Gripping the joist like a monkey to its mother, I can't look down. *I can't. I can't. I can't.*

The smell of burning and an ashy sting in my nostrils.

The smoke.

The silence.

# 43
## ASH KI

As grief strikes a match to the Carvresses heels, they increase their pace. The canyon begins to flatten and stretch, and a path opens. Winding up and out. Rocks crumble beneath our feet as I think about what we've just witnessed. We should be more careful, but these magical women, Shen devoted to the Char, race upward, slipping and skidding with hunger burning in their glossy eyes.

Afternoon sun slants across us in yellow streaks. "Wait!" I call quietly, not wanting to draw attention. "We don't know what's up there."

The women nod but bustle to trees that grip the canyon edge and seem to stretch their exposed roots toward us.

Sun shakes his head and spits, getting a slap on the back from his mother. "Ouch!"

"You show disrespect!" she mutters, shoving him.

Luna is behind me. Her voice small and unsure. "They have shown us disrespect, Mama, by not telling us the truth for so many years."

Sun's eyes are on the women as they anxiously scramble up the narrow path. "She is right, Mama. How do we move past this?

They are Shen, or were...” He curses and Ki Anah smacks him again. He rubs his arm where she struck him. “I don’t know what they are.”

“Shen or not, they’ve dedicated their life to protecting the Char. That’s got to count for something, doesn’t it?” I say, waiting for Ki Anah to hit me too.

She groans. “You children are missing the point.”

Heads swing in her direction. “And what’s the point?”

The grove of trees swishes and sways. Sighs in a human way. The Carvresses disappear, and I speed to catch them before they are seen. The others follow close behind.

“Never mind.” Ki Anah’s eyes slide to the chancellor. His eyes tight and his shrewd mouth gagged to avoid any screams for help as we climb away from the river. I think I know what she’s thinking, and just because she doesn’t say the words doesn’t mean my scheming brother isn’t thinking it anyway. This truth makes the Carvresses even more vulnerable and more capture worthy. Because if they are Shen royalty, they can overthrow the emperor. I climb over the edge, hands landing on soft moss crushed by eight pairs of wooden feet.

Sun grunts. Luna is silent.

Our position on this land feels more and more like a target.

Sun throws the chancellor against a tree, and we search for the Carvresses. We’re hidden in this small wood but the land slips away to a soft, grass hill on the other side of the cliff. I peer between trees to a Shen village at the base, daily peasant life going on below.

“Where in the stars are they?” Sun asks, head swiveling.

Ki Anah calmly watches the chancellor, hands on hips, blocking his view. His head twists around her body and she moves with him.

Stomping between trees, I place my hand on a trunk, scanning the area. Luna threads her smaller body between the close-knit woods, and I try not to lose focus as she nimbly moves between the plants. There’s a lightness to her feet as she avoids crushing bugs and beetles. I watch the way she pulls her hair into her fingers when she pauses to think, fingers spread as she closes her eyes, seeking the living. I bite my lip, fingernails scratching the tree bark. I *feel* her allowing herself to care about the creatures and the land. Her deep respect for the world around her reemerging. I also *feel* her pain of letting it in one small piece at a time. She is not as emotionless as she would like to think.

My lips spread into a smile. I could watch her wander the woods all day with ferns up to her waist and dwarfed by plants. Yet, somehow, she seems bigger than this place, filling the air, linked to all that wanders on or in the earth.

A flutter under my palm makes me jump. I lift my hand to reveal a pair of eyes blinking at me from within the tree, nature colliding with dark magic.

And then there is the sound.

Freezing us all to our places dotted around this small grove. It has the quality of the Call in its encompassing serenity. It's a choral mass, but a more natural sound. A stretching and creaking like the trees are growing several feet right in front of us.

Sun points and holds up his hand, showing four fingers. Luna holds up three. I hold up one. I guess we've found all eight Carvresses.

Ki Anah's hips snap and crack as she holds her position in front of my curious older brother. And she is right to block him. He has seen and heard too much as it is. I look at his slim, slimy countenance and shake my head. He shows only small signs of a conscience. Even if he can't be influenced to change for the better, he is my brother, I loved him once, and I don't think I can kill him. I gaze down at my hands as the noise, a flurry like a million leaves rustled by a sweet breeze, builds in volume around us. I don't think I could allow another to kill him either.

So, we are stuck.

The Carvresses have melded their bodies into the trees. Burrowing into the trunks as they consume the trees energy. The earth beneath me shifts and roots lift, pulsing like blood-filled veins. The Char expressions are full of wonder while mine shows impending danger. I lift my feet as roots try to trip me. I stare at the Carvress, her form barely visible, like the tree embraced and then engulfed her.

"Ki Anah, how long does this process," I gesture at Carvresses. "usually take?" I ask anxiously.

She shrugs. "As long as is needed."

Rolling my eyes, I don't feel wonder at the light bumps of the Carvress's chin, breasts, and toes in the tree. Feeling trapped instead of awe, I don't think I can pull her out, cut her out, or whatever one would do to pull a magical being from inside a trunk.

The chancellor squirms and tries to speak. I make my way over to him and carefully pull down his gag, pouring some water through his black teeth.

He coughs, gulping gratefully.

Ki Anah turns her back to us and keeps her eyes on the Carvresses.

As I lift the gag, he speaks, "Wait! *Brother.* Tell me, what do you hope to achieve with all this nonsense?" His clenched fists gesture to the watchful and alert Char. "You know you can't win this fight. I will get what I want eventually. I always do." It's a false claim that he clings to. There are wants I saw when we were joined that had nothing to do with power and greed. He aches for a mother's love that he didn't accept until it was too late.

I lean back on my haunches, tilting my head to take in the twisted form of a man who shares half my blood. "Why is it I can't *feel* you? How am I not connected to you the way I am to Luna after we joined powers?"

His tongue runs over his teeth, pink on black. Serpentine. "We are connected, brother." The way he says *brother* sounds like an iron prison gate slamming shut. "I feel you. I sense your conflict. Your loyalty to the Shen and your confusion about these people." He knocks his head toward the Char.

I shake my head. "I have no confusion about my loyalty." I reach for his Atmosphere, for anything, but I sense nothing. "It is you that's confused."

His silky eyes, a dying blue-green, slide over Luna, waist deep in a sea of plants. "She is attractive, I grant you. Though quite small and overly muscular, like an acrobat. But there are always attractive women to be had. If you came to court as my underling, you could have your pick of concubines." His smile is slick and dirty. "After myself, of course."

My nose screws up in disgust. He looks at Luna like a fine horse to be broken. "I suggest you look somewhere else, Shek Ki, before I smash those black teeth in."

His expression flips from enticement to anger in a snap. "You want to know why you don't *feel* me?" He slices the air with his words, while his voice rises in pitch and volume.

I'm searching for something worth saving. It's like trying to find a poppy seed in a sack of black rice.

"I know why," I reply. I shoved the insight down and ignored it until now, hoping maybe something would change. Now that he's spent more time with the Char, it has only opened his eyes to their value as a commodity. I think I knew he couldn't change but I held onto hope despite Lye's warnings. Of course, they're not the same, Luna and my... *brother*. They are worlds and hearts apart.

He leans back, hands resting in silk skirts. He is spoiled. Like food left too long in the sun. Black and shriveled and rotten. "Oh, you do, do you?"

I nod. "You seek to possess and control. We didn't *join* powers, you sapped mine—or at least tried to. Your greed seeps from every pore. I understand now why Lye sought to keep your identity a secret. She explained that you were born twisted. I didn't want to believe her at first, but I see nothing but darkness in you."

He blinks, unaffected, and simply smiles. And I hate that I see shades of *my* smile in the curl of his lips. While I use mine for defense, his is assault. "Darkness?" He snorts. "I am neither dark nor light. Your youth makes you naïve. I am doing what is necessary to preserve the Shen and extend our empire, nothing more."

I stand, shadowing him. He squints at me. "You are wrong, brother. If you have to tell yourself the horrible things you have done are for a 'cause' then that's your business, but do not pretend something dark and evil is not wrapped around your heart." I point accusingly.

He turns away. Perhaps there's shame or regret there. I'm not sure I care. I need to stop looking for redemption in him.

"So, what now? Am I to be executed since you've finally come to the rather obvious conclusion that I cannot be *saved*?"

My sister's words come back to me. *Slit his throat before he can utter one more poisonous word.* But I'm not my sister and I'm not a murderer. I run a hand through my hair, tying it. "You may still prove useful. Besides, I'm not the one who should have that honor."

I grasp the gag, ready to pull it up. He grimaces, unable to erase his ugly intentions. "I would kill you without a second thought, brother." A smile laced with acid. "Not even a first thought."

I pull the gag up, tightening it at the back. "I know," I say. "That is the difference between us."

I signal to Luna and Sun to follow me to the edge of the woods. We need to keep an eye on the village, and I need to put distance between myself and the chancellor before he makes a liar of me.

# 44

## LYE LI

Somewhere in the chaos, the rain stopped pouring and what had pooled on the ground was exchanged for blood. Limbs aching from holding on, my eyes refuse to open. My heart is broken and burning. My lungs are fighting for air over smoke. *There's so much smoke.*

I cough and gag.

*Open your eyes,* Ben Ni says. *Whatever you're picturing in your head is probably far worse than the truth.*

"You don't know what I'm picturing," I whisper, my lips pressed against the rough-cut oak. "Ben Ni didn't know me. He knew nothing of the horror I could imagine."

My ghost falters. The beam shakes.

*Open your eyes. Not for Ben Ni, not for anyone but yourself.* "Open your eyes," I demand a little louder as I shift my hands. My body wishes to straighten.

When I open them, I blink and my eyes water. My throat tightens like the chancellor has his hands around it once more. Squeezing until I'm just a breath away from suffocation.

A small cry could be as loud as a wailing eagle in this smoke-billowing silence.

Nothing but orange flame and gray soot fills the air, spreading like fast-paced lava.

The beam I hold is at least fifteen yards from the ground. The rope hangs slack. I picture Joka slain at the end of it and the image pierces between my ribs. I can't breathe. Another Yan dead. And I'm always at the center.

I must breathe.

I inhale and call down, my voice swallowed by grief and charcoal. "Is anyone down there?"

The beam wobbles. One end is aflame and it's going break at any second. The buildings bordering the square spew fire out open windows like hissing tongues. They are just a jump away.

My feet are so intricately bound, there is no time to untie them. I need Joka's hands. I need them not to be lying open and lifeless on the ground. The initial plan wedges in my throat like paper cuts. He was supposed to lower me when it was over.

The thought of giving up never enters my mind. I know this is a first. A first I will have to contemplate later.

No one's coming to save me. I huff. A strange giggle comes from my choking chest. I'm quite used to that. Hastily, I pull the rope up from the ground, through the pulley and into my hand. Trying not to think that I'm pulling it from Joka's cold hands, I tell myself that I must survive this. *I must live.*

I knot the rope so it sticks in the pulley. Then I wrap it around my sycamore arm and roll carefully from the beam. I use my wooden arm to feed the length slowly, so I don't plummet like a raindrop. Marveling at the sycamore, I feel the rope sliding over it, but it doesn't graze or hurt.

I descend into what was once the square and is now broken tiles and scorch marks. Forcing my eyes open, though I'm reluctant to see what lies at the end of the line.

Taking in the view like a fishing owl, my rope spins around in a circle. Black Sail City is burning out of control. There will be nothing left.

The creak and crack of timber being consumed by fire sounds like water flicked in hot oil. And the city is the wok. My ears strain for any small noises of survival. I reach for Atmospheres and find only one. It's the howl of a wolf searching for its pack. Lonesome and desperate.

The smoke is blinding. The square is crammed with the shadows of ghosts that aren't ready to leave. Knowing I can't be far from the ground, I start kicking my feet out, searching for a landing. The beam that I just left reaches out like a fiery arm, ready to strike, and I start to panic. As I release the rest of the rope, my bound feet flip upward and my body tumbles through the air. Landing with a soft thud, I roll out of the way just as the beam crashes onto bodies that are already charred.

My heart strains for that wolf. I've got little energy left. It doesn't feel like we won.

Although we knew the cost would be dear, I'm not sure we understood how dear.

I sit up, pulling my bound feet in, tucking my knees to my chest. I look around at what we have done. The lengths Shen and Char have stretched themselves to.

Tears streak my face.

I grieve my old people and my new.

My head falls onto my bony knees.

THE CRASH of waves on the shore is such an ironic sound in this desolate, cracked environment.

Gently, my ankles are pulled from the tight ball I've made with my body. The atmosphere of a howling wolf calms.

"I was beginning to regret my decision," a voice whispers as dry and devastated as my own.

I trace the shape of him in the smoke with my eyes. His fingers deftly untangle the tight knot around my ankles, and I release a sigh of pain and relief. "What decision?"

Joka's lanky and strong face appears, framed in ash. "Of not kissing you before the…" His eyes shoot to the side, doesn't finish. Standing, he offers a hand. "We need to get off the island."

I take his hand. Our touch is unelectric. There is too much pain for such things. "But Black Sail City will be destroyed. Shouldn't we try to save it?" Even as I say this, I know it is futile.

The vast form of Setsu Yan punches through the haze. "The city matters not as long as the Char endure."

"*Parut merah, merah,*" they both chant, thumping their chests. They look to me. Waiting.

Belonging brims and bubbles as I thump my chest and chant, "*Parut merah, merah.*"

I follow them to the boats.

Black Sail City is aflame. The Shen are defeated. Many dead, the rest have fled.

Char soldiers pack the small vessels. We are few but we survived. There will be more as the women and children return from hiding. My eyes bounce from face to face. Searching. Joka's hand goes to my arm, his fingers brushing over the scarred parts. Setsu's eyes fly downward, watching the water.

"He's not here, Lye," Joka says quietly as we push out from the dock. "General Fah is dead."

# 45

## ASH KI

L ying on our stomachs, heads in hands, we watch the village
until the sun drops to the base of the plains.

Sun lets out a long, bored sigh and jumps up. "This is dull.
I'm going to check on the Carvresses. See if they're done yet."

It's been an hour or so. I don't know how long it usually takes
but the soft recharging sound has not eased. I shrug, grass tickling
my chin. Luna is so close I feel her ribs expanding and her shoulder
is just a blade of grass away from mine. Her gaze is firmly planted
on the equally spaced huts laid out below. A toy village. *Toys for
the emperor to play with.*

"So this is what a Shen village looks like," she muses, finger
trailing from one end of the main street to the other.

A man pushes a cart of pink cabbages toward the store hall in
the center. Beyond the small huts are rows and rows of precisely
planted fields.

"It's very, uh, neat." Her lips are parted, body relaxed. Her attention focused on the details.

"You sound unimpressed." I knock her shoulder which makes her frown. She's right to call it neat. It's kind of a requirement. Homes are a specific size with exactly five rooms. All of them are a chunky L shape like the corner of a frame. The emperor's advisors plan every village, making sure each hut sits a certain distance apart and placing the store hall always in the center. I blow air through my lips in an annoyed way and Luna turns her head.

"Did I offend you?" Gold eyes glint like she half intended to offend me.

Shen peasants move between buildings. They stop and talk briefly, but they seem hurried and harried. Looking over their shoulders.

"No. You didn't offend me, Luna." Carefully, I shuffle closer. I *feel* Luna stretching past her wall and I don't want to chase her back behind it. "Tell me," I ask. "Apart from neat, what is it *you* see when you look at this Shen village?"

She taps her chin with a chipped fingernail. "I see people working hard. Children getting under parents' feet." She gestures to demonstrate the straight and angular way the village is organized. "I see that apart from the organized layout and the regrettable lack of ocean, the Shen live similarly to the Char."

Her mouth closes slowly. Scratching at the dirt while a blade of grass bends under the weight of six butterflies, she puts her head down. Every living thing wants to be close to her. *I know that feeling very well.* And despite the other night, I still want to be close. Placing my hand, damp with dirt, over hers, I trace the individual ridges of her thumb. I follow each line and joint. Her breath is held. Her heart does whatever it does. She might be holding her breath, but I've got her attention. She leans into me and lets me thread my fingers between hers without fang or claw.

A dark dot moves at the bottom of the hill. The tall grass hides it from view, a spray of sticks protruding from its back like a dead peacock's tail.

Luna withdraws from my grasp, pointing a dirty finger. "What's that?"

It moves steadily, gathering one piece of wood at a time, disappearing every time he bends down. The spray of sticks thickens. I think back to one of my jobs when I lived in the village. "It's just a child collecting firewood." A child interrupting one of the few good moments I've had with Luna and I'm reluctant to release it. The child zigzags up the hill. I grimace an unconvincing half smile. "They'll probably turn around before they reach the top. The basket looks almost full."

We track the child, arms grazing. And I want to believe it's not because she's distracted that we're so close. But I don't really know. "Luna, I need to tell you…"

Luna springs up and whatever stupid thing I was about to say is swallowed. Probably for the best. "She's heading right for us. We need to hide."

We return to what's left of the grove. The once corky bark, thick and textured like river ravines, has turned a salty ash color and is crumbling. The noise of the Carvresses has softened to a breathy whisper, but they're still "in" the trees. *I hope they stay there for now.* I brush my hand over a trunk. The bark disintegrates under my light touch as Luna pulls me toward a fallen log. A scampering hopper mouse flies through her legs and up my arm in panic.

Ki Anah, Sun, and the chancellor are further back, eyes hovering over a collection of boulders that looks like a tipped-over egg bowl. Luna's nails dig into my hand. She seems *different.* Eyes wide, golden edges burning bright and vibrant as fire. I let her hurt me. Push panicky, scratchy things under my skin. I let her because I don't know how long this small bridge of emotion will hold. It feels wobbly and poorly constructed.

Ki Anah signals for us to come to her and I shake my head. The child, a girl, is entering the forest.

We duck down as she rustles through finger ferns, curling five-point fronds that tickle you like hands. If she comes any closer, we'll have to disable her. My hand clutches my knife and water rises in my fingers, though I have no idea what I'll do. Luna's fingers spread, ready to call animals to our aid. We're ready to attack.

But then we hear her young, squeaky voice singing a song I remember from my childhood.

*The emperor stands upon our shoulders.*
*We bend, we don't break.*
*We are strong, we are bolder.*

It's supposed to inspire loyalty and to enforce the idea that peasants are the Shen foundation. That without us, the system breaks. The rest of the song is more patriotic nonsense. My ears prick waiting for the chorus of *We thank the emperor for his grace. Praise the emperor for guiding the Shen forward. We march to his song. Hail the emperor! Hail the emperor!* My stomach knots at the memory of it. Stomping feet. Palms slapping on desks. Shouting words we were forced to believe. Holding a man up to the sun, a man most of us would never meet in our lifetime.

My hand crunches tightly around Luna's, sending hot springs to boil over. Her face scrunches in pain and I recede. "Sorry," I whisper.

The girl sings the next verse.
*We mock the emperor for his ugly face.*
*We curse the emperor for his terrible stench.*
*We march to his song.*
*Take a bath, emperor! Take a bath, emperor!*
*Before your silk skirts stain*
*And you have to wear peasant clothes.*
*Oh, pity the thought! Pity the thought!*

Luna and I exchange glances. Her mouth twitches and mine stretches into a wide smile. Peeking above the log, I see a small girl, plaits looped over each ear like bag handles. She sings her alternative song while ducking down to collect kindling. Placing it in a basket on her back that's almost as large as herself. Her voice is sweet, innocent, and full of mischief.

She hums and comes up with more lyrics, all implying that the emperor is ugly, stinky, and spoiled. I tilt my head, wondering if she has met him. My grip relaxes on my dagger hilt.

Luna wiggles her hand, looking tense. "It's just a kid," I whisper.

She shakes her head. "I would never harm a child. But what do we do? She could still alert her village."

I place a hand over hers. "We stay quiet. She won't alert anyone if she doesn't know we're here."

The girl's song ends and the stretching, cracking noise of the trees takes over. Pausing, stick in hand, she spins in a slow circle as she tries to find the source. "Wa!" She swishes through the ferns, approaching a tree. Palm up like she's about to swat a bug. *It will be fine. She doesn't know what she's looking at.* The tree feathers and falls apart. The blush-colored, jittery Carvress steps out from the tree, ashen woodchips pouring from her body like sand. The Shen girl's lip quivers. The tree itself quivers and peels open like a banana. The girl stumbles back, stick dropping from her hand. She makes small, frightened sounds, gasping. She tries to turn and run.

The Carvress's pale pink hand shoots out with renewed energy, giving her whip-like reflexes. I jump from my hiding place and try to help the child. I only manage to take two steps before the Carvress of Pearl Shell Beach grabs the girl's shoulder and pinches her hard. The child cries out, just once. Tears sting her eyes, while her mouth opens in shock. She blinks and falls to the ground in a clattering, wooden heap. A discarded puppet.

We rush to the girl as the other Carvresses break from their trees. Sucked of all life, the forest begins to die. "Shei-Shei! What have you done?" the Coalstone Carvress snaps, flying over fallen logs and stones, floating like a ghost to fall to her knees at the poor girl's side.

I'm five feet away and scared to come any closer. I don't want to be party to this, this, *murder*. The Carvress killed a child. *How could she do this?*

Ki Anah, Luna, and Sun are stunned. Their heads bowed as the Carvress's name is spoken. These names are supposed to be sacred. No Char has heard them. But now the name streams from panicked sisters' mouths without thought.

The other Carvresses crowd around the girl. Their voices rising in fury at their sister. Other names are uttered. Sounding like music. Also sounding distinctly Shen. But this song is a furious one. Shei-Shei, the washed-out, sunset-colored Carvress of Pearl

Shell Beach retreats from the body, her chest rising and falling fast. "Sifah, I'm sorry. I reacted. I panicked."

Sifah, the Coalstone Carvress, stands over her sister, dark as a storm. "That is always your problem, sister! You're quick to panic. Always reacting without thinking. You have too much of our brother in you." Shei-Shei looks extremely offended and separates herself from the others, eyes downcast in shame.

The ebony Carvress puts her hands on her hips and shakes her head. "Well, this is a mess, is it not? What are we going to do with this child?"

Sifah frowns. "I don't know, Mi Asha. What a foolish, foolish mistake to make." She glares once more at Shei-Shei.

*Foolish mistake?* Anger builds. *How can they speak of a child's murder this way?* Like it's spilled tea on a rug. I break through the circle of Carvresses. Not caring whose shoulders I knock or what tradition I'm ignoring. "What in the stars is wrong with you? You just killed a child, an innocent child, and all you can think about is how inconvenient it is for you and your sisters?"

The women are silent, shuffling back to reveal the girl, curled in a bed of grass and ferns. The green contrasting to her rose-hued, knotholed skin. My breath catches and sticks in my throat like a pinecone. I search their faces for remorse. My fists thump my legs. "And what's worse, you turned the poor girl to wood. Her parents will not even give her a proper Shen burial, if they recognize her at all."

Luna speaks from behind the women. "This is wrong, Carvresses! It's wrong! You have crossed a line." As her eyes fill with water, her face becomes paler than a dead moon. She stands perfectly still and perfectly agonized, voice shaking with white hot fury. "You've crossed a line!" Something ripples through her. I *feel* it but only from a distance. It's too powerful, too personal to be shared. It rises like a towering wall of water, a tsunami. I live in that long moment when the wave seems at a standstill, giving the briefest feeling of hope before it crashes and destroys everything.

I bend down to touch the child, plaits now frozen in place around perfectly carved, wooden ears. "I'm so sorry." I brush her cheek with my fingertips, feeling the smoothness of the timber. A child once flesh is now as polished as the emperor's throne.

Shei-Shei bends at the hip, blinking her eyes down at the child with abject curiosity, like she's a carcass to be salvaged. I glare back at her. My fingers still resting on the girl's cheek.

"You stay back, Carvress! Your kind have done enough!" I warn. My teeth grind against each other, and I'm surprised at my own devastation. My rage is burning hot, but Luna's is bigger. Brighter. It swells beyond the grove. Beyond anything.

The girl with the hickory heart buckles and falls, eyes closed, a sound like a thousand birds having their wings ripped from their bodies pours from her mouth. Stronger than the earth could quake. Louder than a lion's roar.

All her pain in one true shattering sound.

Then the child moves.

# 46
## ASH KI

Creatures join Luna in her cry of pain. Birds screech and pitch to the earth. Livestock in the village squeal and moan like they know they're next to be slaughtered. Foxes bark from their dens. It's a warning. We need to leave.

"We must go. The villagers are probably already on their way." We cast our eyes to the child. She whimpers as she stares at her wooden hands.

Sun strides forward. "We must take the child with us." He points down the hill. "They'll never allow her to live. Ash, you must know that." His expression is strained, torn between the suffering girl and his suffering sister. Both staring at their hands for very different reasons. I nod to Sun, who scoops up the wooden child.

Skidding to my knees at Luna's feet, I try to find the words that will pierce her. "Luna, listen, you need to control yourself. You need to stop them." I point to the birds surging up to the sky and plunging to the earth. I take her wrists and shake. My eyes taking in all of her. Finally. All Of Her.

Luna is here.

Luna is breaking.

Her eyes burn. "They crossed a line, Ash." Words she can't seem to stop saying. "They crossed a line."

I press my forehead to hers. Squirrels run in disoriented circles. "I know, Luna, but she lives. Somehow, we'll find a way to make it right. We'll fix it." Promises I have no business making.

Her head loops slowly back and forth, full of sorrow. "It can't be fixed. It can't be made right. He's dead. He's dead and there's nothing we can do to change that." She thumps the dirt with open palms. Bowing like a prayer.

I start to say, "She's not," but then I understand. The dam has broken. Floods upon floods of pain are destroying everything in their path and she's going to drown.

Her eyes look to me with hope that shouldn't be there. "Yes, your brother is gone but you live. And if you want to stay alive, you must get up, Luna." I yank her up.

She swipes her nose with her sleeve and nods unconvincingly. I find it hard to breathe at the grief dripping off her body. And now we must run until our lungs scream for air.

THE CARVRESSES fly over the land with renewed energy, leaping gracefully from footing to footing. Sun clutches the frightened girl to his chest with a look of fierce protectiveness. Her limbs bounce around like the loose rungs of an old ladder. Ki Anah runs by his side, anxious eyes swinging from the Shen girl to Luna and back again.

Voices approach, but it's difficult to tell from where. We keep plowing through the woods.

My head swings back to the petrified section of the trees. A bleached spot on a dark tunic. The river rushes below and the marshlands shine like an oil patch in front.

We dig into energy reserves we didn't know existed. Running. Running. Running.

Endlessly kicking up dust, we try to keep our feet when all we want to do is rest. Luna folds over, coughing, and I shove her hard in the back. "We can't stop. Not yet."

We cover miles, not knowing if we're being pursued but needing to put as much distance between us and the village as possible.

In the lead, I head down a muddy slope.

We crash into paddies, sloughy water almost up to our waists, and duck for cover. The field is cold and full of slimy, hungry creatures. I shiver as we sink lower into the deep water paddy ideal for growing red rice, sighing deeply. We have reached the outskirts of the marshlands. *I am home.* Luna sweeps an arm around my waist. I freeze. The idea that the door opening inside her also leaves room for me seems too optimistic. My teeth chatter from cold and exhaustion.

Luna sends the tail of a snow fox to wrap around me, warm and fluffy, and I relax.

Until I notice one is missing.

Panic rose in our throats, clogged our brains, and stopped us from counting.

The chancellor is gone.

I turn to Ki Anah. "Where's the chancellor?" I whisper as a couple of villagers pull oxen led carts across the ridge above us. Their heads swing from side to side just like their thin beasts of burden. If they're looking for us, it is hard to tell. She shrugs, though not without fear.

The child squirms in Sun's arms and he coos to her in a calming tone, patting her birch head. "I'm not going to hurt you, I promise. You know that if they saw you like this, they would kill you." It's harsh but true. They'd throw her on a pyre before she could open her carved wooden mouth to explain. "Let me protect you, kid."

To her the credit, the child is quiet and still as the peasants pass, though whether it's because she believes Sun or is just terrified of him, I can't be sure.

"The chancellor, Shek Ki, where is he?" I whisper to the others.

"He must have slipped away while we were huddled around the girl," Sifah states, glaring at Shei-Shei, whose chin has not lifted from her chest since this began.

I start to rise, to find him, throttle him and drag him back. Luna pulls me down. "Let him go, Ash. He will be long gone by now." Her eyes are red, cheeks splotched with color. She's destroyed but she looks more like Luna than she has in weeks. Maybe now we can clear the rubble together and rebuild.

"I should have killed him when I had the chance." I splash at the water, which isn't very satisfying.

"You were never going to kill him," she whispers and then sighs hollowly. "He didn't deserve a brother like you."

"Ben Ni deserved you, Luna. You were a good sister to him." She planes her hand through the air as if to say *not now*. I feel her pain like a spinning blade, slicing through both our chests.

"Well, what do we do now?" Sun asks. "That rat will surely expose us. How long do you think we have before he reaches the emperor?"

I think we're safe for now. No doubt the chancellor will coerce villagers into taking him to the palace, which is at least a day and half's ride from here. He won't risk coming after us with just a handful of inexperienced farmers at his side. Soldiers will be collected first.

"I'd say we have about three days."

Sun kicks the water, the small girl still clasped tightly to his chest. With a shiver he makes the grim prediction: "Three days until we are all beheaded."

I smile. It creates a ripple of surprise through the group. "We only need one day."

# 47

## LYE LI

The last retreating Shen flee in shame from Black Sail City like a school of fish from a shark's widening jaws. From the boardwalk of Coalstone Village, we watch one ship cut through the heavy smoke. The others sit in the harbor, floating empty and full of ghosts.

The city we helped destroy is now a black scar.

Setsu's head falls. "The sea shall cradle you," he whispers, a clenched fist over his heart.

A spindly man comes to his side, fist also over his heart. "The sea shall carry you home."

I glance up, surprised by the wooden eye that rolls my way and then gazes at Black Sail Island. "Bullseye." Setsu claps the thin man on the back, and he braces himself, almost falling over the edge. "Tell me what you see." Setsu's voice is strained. He's bracing for a different kind of pain.

Bullseye cups a hand over one eye and purses his lips. "In the city, I see only charcoal and death, Setsu. I am sorry."

Setsu gazes at his feet and sighs a battle-aged sigh. "As I expected."

Char warriors trace the boardwalk, marching up and down, aimless. It's like they've been transported here mid battle, swords up, knees bent. And without their general to guide them, they're lost. The water shimmers in a middling fashion, awaiting streaks of sunset. I wander from the group toward the beckoning mangroves, hoping for a small pebble of peace.

I dip my toes in the water, creating ripples. *Should I shed tears for General Fah?* I also feel lost at the absence of the first man to listen to me, even if it was begrudgingly. He treated me as more than an instrument. I shake my head. Even if he tried to exploit me it was not against my will. Giving me choice over my own fate was a unique gift.

A foot nudges my hip and I look up into Joka's intelligent face. He tilts his head awkwardly. "May I sit?" he asks. I nod.

The salt and bitter smell of mangroves is alien but so very welcome. *New is promising.* I gesture to the gnarled branches and then to the huts hugging the side of the mountain. "Your home is-land is beautiful."

Joka sighs, pulling up his pant legs and letting his feet float on the small rise. "Black Sail City was beautiful too. You never got to see it in its full glory." Our eyes follow trails of smoke. Fires still rage over the mountain. Joka strokes his bamboo neck, a smudgy sound. "So many Char, so many homes and history, just… gone."

"You could rebuild," I suggest and receive a frown from the pensive man beside me.

"No, we cannot. Bodies fuse to the wreckage. Wood and wood. It must stay untouched. Besides, rebuilding is the least of our concerns. We have lost our general and several elders. The Carvresses are hidden. We are like seeds scattered on stone and can't find a place to take root."

"If there's one thing I've learned about the Char, it's that they always find a way. You'll find the cracks that lead to earth." Char don't stay down long. They're not designed to give in or give up.

Shoulder grazing mine, Joka turns. His young eyes have seen so much death and there is still suffering ahead. Yet hope lives in the perfect planes of his face. Love dares to twinkle in his dark eyes. He blinks and watches me, gaze warming as our faces lean in.

The boardwalk creaks under so many anxious soldiers' feet. Salt and smoke mix together. Life and destruction. Love and heat.

"Lye," Joka whispers with a look of fear and uncertainty. "I think I would like to kiss you now."

My cheeks blossom red and I close my eyes. His perfect nose collides with mine. I tilt my head one way and then another. Our lips bash together, slightly open, dry and unsure.

That moth in my stomach flutters and fades. My mouth opens and I laugh softly as these lips try to find a way to connect and simply cannot.

We pull back, both waiting for a reaction. Joka smiles and taps his neck. "That was not what I expected."

I wonder if I did it wrong. "I am sorry. It was my first kiss." I touch my lips. "I'm not well practiced at this sort of thing. I am not practiced at all!"

Joka shifts in his seat, putting comfortable distance between us. He grips the edge of the boardwalk with both hands and lets out an awkward giggle. "Me neither, and it was my first too."

I don't think I did it wrong. It wasn't perfect but it was still nice. I'm just not sure I want to do it again. Not right now anyway.

I put my hand on his. His friendship has meant the difference between sinking and swimming. Without his guidance, I would have floundered. I lean my head on his bony shoulder. He tenses for a moment and then relaxes. I don't want to lock the door on romance with Joka, but for now, it must be closed over. I sense he feels similarly. His Atmosphere: a turtle riding the current.

"I'm glad it was with you," I whisper.

He strokes my hair. It fills me with a peace I've never known. "I am glad also, Lye."

The sun has dashed away, barely a stroke of orange to announce its departure. We take this brief tranquility because we know it can't last.

Less than an hour passes before the first lanterns appear.

A spread of golden lights, rippling over the ocean like the tips of a wheat field catching the sun.

Joka and I stand, hands clasped. We are joined in a way that cannot yet be defined. Perhaps it doesn't need to be.

The refugees have arrived.

# 48
## ASH KI

Lye gave me something when she finally told me the chancellor was my brother. In releasing her guilt, she also released my memory. It has come to me in pieces. But a whole picture has formed now. It is the reason we are here.

Sun dances from foot to foot. "*Apa ini!* Why is this water so frigid? My balls are about to snap off and become a meal for the eels." Then he stands taller. "A very bountiful meal." Ki Anah slaps the back of his head and Luna snorts. The tiniest laugh puncturing her pain. I see Sun catch it, hold it with hope.

The girl blinks up at him and he remembers he's carrying a young child. "Nasi Merah. *Red rice*," she says with a small smile. She looks at Sun like he *is* the sun.

"Have you ever had red rice?" I ask. The Yans shake their heads. The Carvresses remain silent. I point to the mountain range behind the paddies. "The marshes are fed by a glacier. Red rice can only be grown in deep, near freezing water." I pull up a plant and shake it at them. Small red grains hit the water sounding like hail.

Ki Anah frowns. "We don't need a botany lesson. What is your point?"

Black mountains, sprinkled with snow at their peaks, stand severely behind the fields. "No Shen will cross the mountain."

Mi Asha nods knowingly. "Ah yes. The mountain lies on the border with the Dark West. Shen will not break that treaty."

The girl lifts her head. She can't be more than eight years old but her pale wooden face, seems wise for a child's. "The border cuts through the mountain. At this time of year, it is very hard to pass. And there's also the Dark West mountain tribe..." Her mouth purses and her fists scrunch closed fearfully. All Shen have heard the frightening tales of the Dark West tribe, ruthless, cannibalistic monsters who are twice the height of a normal men with teeth as sharp and powerful as a tiger wolf's fangs. Whether it's myth or truth, I don't want to take that chance.

My smile is a smashed plate glued back together. "You don't need to worry about them. We're not going through or even past the border, we're—" I narrow my eyes. "What's your name, girl?"

She frowns. Her ear resting against Sun's chest in an oddly comfortable manner. "Guen Ni."

Luna tenses, her control slipping as she shakes too many emotions from the tree. Things rain down. Some light as leaves—love and laughter. Others weighty as branches—guilt, anger, missing.

"Gu-en Ni," I pronounce slowly, trying to say it in a way that doesn't sound like Ben Ni. I'm not overly successful. "Can we call you Guen?" I ask and she tips her chin slightly. Poor child. She probably doesn't feel like she has much of a choice. "We're going under the mountain."

*"I can hold my breath longer than you, Lye!" I fill my lungs with air. They expand like a balloon about to pop, and I duck under the water.*

*Cold bites my bones as I kick slowly, trying to conserve my oxygen. I float just below the water line, legs crossed. I don't mind floating as long as one hand still grips edge. Not because I can't swim, I just don't like the darkness of the deeper water. Fingers pry my hand from the rock, and I panic, kicking my legs until they find the ground. I break the surface. Lye's laughing face is the first thing I see, followed by her slapping water at me.*

*"You're such a coward!" she teases. Perched on the edge, just her toes touching the pond.*

*I jump out, chasing her around the edge. She giggles, all skinny limbs and long brown hair. She's quicker and more agile than me, as she jumps from border rock to border rock, screaming hysterically.*

*Lunging, I grab her ankles, flipping her backward. She lands on the earth with a thump. I scramble up to her flattened body. "Sister, I'm sorry. Are you all right?"*

*Her eyes are closed, hands clasped over her chest like a body for burial.*

*I lean closer and she snaps her jaw. Chest exploding with laughter. It scares me so much I fly into the water, back hitting like it's solid. "Ash!" Lye shouts before I'm sucked under.*

*My eyes open. Sudden dread pulls at me like fingers sticky with coconut jam. Glimpsing a bright light, I swim toward it. I'm a good swimmer. My brother Shek Ki taught me well, and I kick my legs like a frog until I reach what I think is sunlight.*

*My head bursts through and it's not the sun. I'm in a cave covered in writings lit brightly by golden crystal worms.*

*Tree roots dangle and drip from the ceiling and carved steps lead away, fading to darkness. The Shen characters carved in the stone read that this is the safest way through the mountain but warn of the mysterious tribes of the Dark West Mountains.*

*I can't wait to tell Shek and Lye what I have found.*

I never got to tell my brother what I found. He was gone when we returned home, dripping wet and freezing cold. Mother became ill. When her heart broke, there was nothing left to fight the disease. And quite quickly, thanks to Lye's interference, memories of my brother faded to nothing. My mouth quirks. I always knew how to swim.

Memories become clearer with every step I take toward home, crystalizing like the worms hanging from that cave ceiling.

I pull the travelers from the glacial water, and we walk along the raised earth between each neat field. A checkerboard of sunken planting. Luna's steps are heavy with hurt. Everyone is exhausted. I guide them through the fields, an expert on this land, to a place far outside what is now the main village. The original village was abandoned when a sickness ran through like a bad wind. It became a place to send the sick and dying so as not to contaminate others. It's where I spent the snapped-stick remainder of my childhood before Lye and I were moved to the imperial compound.

My house.

IT LOOK LIKE a giant used it as a stool, but it still stands, *barely*. The timber is gray and fraying. Shingles like cracked teeth. A black circle painted on the door with a red strike through it. Guen points her jointed finger. Brass knuckles glinting. "Death door," she murmurs with a shiver, hand clattering to her hip. The mark of the infected was a way to quarantine. Whatever sickness dwelled in this place has long since passed, leaving the old village perfectly abandoned.

The others defer to me apprehensively. I smile with a quirk of the lip. A memory buried in the layers. "It's fine." I wave them off. "This is my home. And by the looks of it, no one's taken possession since we left."

I stride confidently to the door and swing it open. The bottom scrapes against built up dirt and gravel. My eyes land on my mother's broom leaning in the corner and I swallow as orphaned feelings long suppressed creep up my throat. *This is a shelter and it's safe. The memories that live here are just that. Memories.*

"We can sleep here tonight," I announce, trying to puff up my voice with surety.

Shoes at the door, the Carvresses shuffle in, claiming my parents' bedroom for themselves. Sun and I take the hearth. He gently deposits Guen on the floor, and she clacks her extraordinary feet over the stones. Lifting and staring at them with wonder and fear.

Ki Anah sweeps the girl into her arms, knocking her head at Luna who is slow to respond. "Don't worry, Guen, you'll get used to it." She smothers her tone in motherly warmth, sweet as honey. She pulls up her shirt slightly. "See, I have wooden hips. You're in good company."

Guen narrows her eyes for a moment but takes Ki Anah's hand. They disappear into Lye's old room. Luna follows, hand dragging across the spider web covered door frame.

# 49
## LUNA

The house breathes in a disjointed, dysfunctional way. Like it's sick, though Ash assures us there's no disease still lingering.

*Ash,* the boy who has stayed by my side even as I scratched, bit, and clawed at him. *Ash.* I mouth his name. Feel the way it coats my tongue with sugar and salt. How it pushes my lips to pout and warms my chest.

I have been at war. Grief marching forward flying a red flag. I didn't understand that love was painted on the other side of the flag. They exist in the same space. *Love* and *grief.* The two are unendingly and complicatedly intertwined.

I lie on the stone floor, dusty old blankets itching my legs. I sweep the place for creatures but since the woods, my Blood sense is off. There are too many other things within me vying for attention.

The girl, Guen, twists and rattles in the bed next to Mama. Wooden limbs clinking against each other, breath all sawdusty. After the initial excitement of our escape, reality crashed down upon her little head. Her hiccupping terror drilled holes right through us as she asked to see her parents and we had to tell her no. We held back the part where she can never see them again. She cried herself to sleep, only allowing Sun to stroke her hard, wooden head. She's a consequence of this war, perhaps the consequence of our own foolishness.

My heart talks to me in smooth slides and locks. It's the only thing that remains constant like constellations over an earth that's cracking apart. Everything else is disaster.

Sadness chokes me. I blink and see the knife plunge deep into Ben Ni's stomach. I breathe and his eyes dim to a cold brass. It turns my bones to ice thinking that I walked beside his murderer so easily. I tap my chest and remind myself this is what I'm meant to feel. All of it and all at once in a messy tangled heap.

I've trapped myself behind Blood and behind cold torture. Gruesome images flash through my mind. They hound me from sleep, and I shuffle out of the blanket, exiting the room. I leave mama to sleep soundly in her bed. She has travailed through her grief; her loss is a weight that she has learned to carry willingly. I shake my head as I pad down the hallway. Ben Ni deserved better from me.

His image strikes agonizing flames through me, and I brace against the wall. You deserved to be grieved as you were loved, fiercely and wholeheartedly. I was a fool not to see that.

*Ash* saw it. He sleeps like a pup by the hearth, curled into a question mark. *You deserve to be loved the same way.* My breath catches as he shifts and I question whether I can love him fiercely, wholeheartedly. Is it in me to do so?

Just as much as I need to grieve, I need the answer to be yes. Even if that yes exists on the other side of working through my grief.

Easing the door open, I step into unreasonable cold. Bare feet press into damp earth, hickory heart reaches for an easy way to sort through this basket of feelings. But of course, there is none. Life is not as simple as hickory. All of my feelings braid together like a thick rope. One I hope I can use to climb out of this hole I made.

"Luna." He touches my arm. My senses are confused, and I bounce from cubs nuzzling their mother to the threatened lash of a paw. I turn as he emerges from behind the death door, white moon-light painting his tensed jaw. His gaze cuts me into a thousand pieces, creases of pain showing how much it hurt to wait for me. *I made him wait.*

Sorrow sucks the air from my lungs as love fills them. I'm sinking and floating at the same time. "Is it too late?" I whisper, hands trembling. My voice sounds alien because it has hope.

He shuts the door carefully and steps closer. I hold still, though half of me wants to move away. "Too late for what?" He tilts his head and smiles. It's *my* smile. Saltwater and half-truths. He's right to hold back and protect himself.

I clasp my hands together and stare at the ground.

Smelling blood in the earth, I feel it in my fingers. My grief strangles me and yet nudges me forward with a shove in my back. Strong hands and golden eyes. *Be brave.* "Too late to tell you that I love you?"

Those words. Those words. Those words. Daggers and life-lines. Guilt and coming home. I shake my head to clear a fog that only thickens. It wraps around me like a blanket and a net. Can I be both breaking and healing at the same time? I take his hands and the answer is clearly yes. I always thought of love as happiness. And it can be, but the love I feel now is a buoy wrapped in sadness, keeping me afloat. I pull him across the path to the tree line, not allowing him to answer straight away. Moon shadows paint bars across the dirt.

"I *feel* you, Luna," he says, voice crackling with emotion, with that foolhardy thing I've kept at bay: hope. We're clutching it like it's a bird that wants to fly away. He runs his hands down my arms slowly. A sigh buried in deep pain and love. "It would never be too late."

I smile, sad and sweet. "Even if I sent piranha rabbits to chomp you to the bone?" The love I have for him is small and budding. The seed inside a dark, dark fruit, but it's there.

He mock winces and my body shivers in the most delicious and painful way. "Even then."

My voice is shy to admit the following words. It trembles, scared that what I offer is too little. "Even if my grief makes my love little?" I wring my hands. "At least to start."

Ash runs a hand through his hair, frowns, and kills me with his earnestness. "A little love from you is like a newborn sun. It will only grow in strength and warmth. Everything has its turn, Luna. Right now, even though the grief must be bigger, love will outgrow it in time."

Grief is a planet. Love is a newborn sun. It will warm the shadows slowly.

"I am so sorry." I bury my head in his chest, talking into his ribs. "I didn't understand. I didn't want to." I tilt my face up, staring up at the stars. "Forgive me, brother. I did wrong by our family and by you." Arms wrap around my waist and rest on my narrow hips.

"His death wasn't your fault." Ash says what everyone says, but I believe him this time.

I sniff, a mess of tears and torn apart emotion. "I know. That's not what I must seek forgiveness for." I talk to the stars and pray my Char ancestors can hear me from the Shen mainland. *Ben Ni, hear me.* "In not grieving you, brother, I put a hold on my love for you. I am so sorry for that. I should have done better. I will do better."

Love and grief. They cannot exist without each other. They cannot be separated.

Ash kisses the top of my head and it feels like a snowflake. It melts into my skin, becomes part of me. "You need to let him go."

"I wish I could just dig out the throbbing, slicing, painful part of myself and set it free," I mumble into his chest. "Let it fly away like an emerald moth from my hands."

"Yes, well, my love, it doesn't work like that." He strokes my cheek and leaves scalding steam behind.

"I know. It's more like a slow healing process. But I have to let it happen. I promise I'm going to try and let it happen," I claim sincerely. He smirks, then he laughs.

"This is funny to you," I ask, palms flat on his chest.

He shakes his head, hair falling over his high cheekbones, feather light. "No. I'm just…"

"You're just Ash. You smile at the worst times." He nods, leaning in so our noses touch.

"Am I dreaming?" he whispers, voice punctured with past agony. Pulsing with promise. "This feels like I must be dreaming."

I'm hastily constructing a bridge. Flimsy. Using string and bark. Twigs and feathers. It may break later, but for now, it holds. For now, it broaches this river of emotion. "Do you still *feel* me?" I ask. If he does, he will understand what I want.

He exhales fast, like the breath has been knocked from his lungs. His chin dips to add a yes. I touch my lips to his. It starts slow. A rediscovery of sorts. But I know this mouth. I know Ash, and it fast becomes a furiously passionate kiss. One that draws tears from my eyes and blooms heat everywhere else. It's grief digging its claws into love. Not to hurt it, to hold it up.

It is fierce. It is wholehearted.

HE SHIVERS in his shirtsleeves and pulls me against him for warmth. "We should go inside before we freeze." I rustle fur coats to heat him. Winter beasts that don't feel the ice. He laughs. I *feel* his elation and his fear. We risk much, tying ourselves to one another this way.

"I can keep us warm," I whisper in a shadowed, dusky tone.

"Even so." He embraces me tighter. "We still need to get some sleep."

Standing on my tiptoes, I kiss him gently. Watch as he sucks his lower lip in and shakes his head in a contented and disbelieving kind of way. "You go," I say. "I'll be right behind you. I just have something I want to say to Ben Ni. In private."

Reluctantly, he releases me. "Five minutes, then I'm dragging you in."

I allow a brief smile that feels like a promise. A quick invoice of what's to come.

The door closes.

I turn skyward, sorting out the stars and aligning them. Lines join to form warriors, lovers, the Yan family constellation. I open my mouth to speak, but a hand slams over my face and robs me of my words, a bitter taste like burnt garlic seeping into my tongue.

"*One* minute is all *I* need."

I manage one single shot of connection. A second split down the middle. And then my powers are dead. Unwillingly, I swallow the bitter material that was shoved into my open mouth.

*Ash, hear me.*

# 50

## ASH KI

I press my back against the rough boards of the door, tilting my chin to the ceiling. Everything is different. The landscape of my life has changed in an instant. I draw in breath and close my eyes, replaying the moment she said she *loved* me. *She loves...*

The sentence can't finish or the dream will break. I don't even get to exhale fully before Luna's single, silent scream punctures my center.

I *feel* her hate, terror, and confusion in one brief flash and then it's gone like a shadow to a bright light.

Throwing open the door, I sprint to the edge of the woods. Searching uselessly in the dark, I smash through bushes and trip on logs. Needing to scream her name, I tell myself I can't alert the new village. Stopping for a split second, I strain to catch that breath from five minutes earlier. How I wish I could spin back the minutes, roll them in like a fishing line.

Something flutters. A blue scrap of silk caught on a bramble.

I snatch it, squeezing so hard my fingers ache. He took her. *He* took her.

I return to the others, though my legs are desperate to chase. "He took her," I shout through the doorway. Sun emerges first, face drawn aghast, catching up easily. I charge at him, grasping his shirt. "You must guide the group now." Instead of looking terrified like me, he looks *murderous*.

He shakes his head in disbelief. "You expect me to let you chase that devil down alone? No. I'm coming with you. I will tear him limb from limb. I will rip out his throat."

Guen appears, light in a dark space, frightened and alone. Her thin birch arms hug her bird cage chest. The trust in her eyes is for Sun only. She darts to him, taking his hand in hers. Heaving a large sigh that shudders through his broad shoulders and makes his foundations crack, he knows he cannot leave her.

I quickly relay instructions on how to get to the entrance of the cave beneath the mountain. "Have you got it?" I ask, bouncing on my toes. *I need to leave. Now!*

Sun thumps his chest. "Got it. Now you go!" He nudges me towards her, a threat in his voice. "Find her, Ash." I nod sternly.

Ki Anah stumbles into the front yard after me, a cry bitten in half. I have no time to explain. "I'm sorry," I whisper turning my back to her and running. The rest of her cry of anguish and anger hammers into my back, driving me forward.

As I race along the river, memories flash: my brother and I paddling boats laden with red rice downstream; hands guiding my oar as I spin in circles; his shrewd face, impatient but trying, giving up quickly and slapping me away to take up the oars himself. Following this river is his best chance to get to the palace quickly, then he can deliver his hybrid to the emperor's feet.

A low branch that escaped pruning scrapes across my cheek, hot blood flowing down my face. I swipe at it, not slowing.

*I will kill him.*

*I should have killed him long ago.*

# 51
## LYE LI

All manner of Char cram the boardwalk, and they continue to arrive as the Shen boats that fled Black Sail zigzag their way through the other islands in search of the Carvresses. The line of refugees snakes around the mountain. People bite their lips and try to hold in screams of pain. The Char of Coalstone Village have lost so much and now they must scrape out more space to put all these refugees.

I push my way out from *my* refuge, the Yan house, the door catching on my feet. People stare with curiosity and a few with suspicion. Most know of my part in the last battle but I'm a new Char born as Shen. My sycamore arm stops them from killing me, and my sacrifice makes them respect me, but I do not think they trust me.

Threading through the crowd, I reach the meeting place where remaining Char soldiers gather to discuss next moves. There are no suggestions and little discussion. No arguments break out, but everyone seems stranded without a plan or direction. The surviving elders, only equipped to make decisions for their own villages, can't come to an answer. Their eyes twist from one to another, looking for someone to take the lead.

Setsu clears his throat, and everyone quietens. To me, it's obvious who should be appointed general. "The Shen have fled Black Sail, but I do not think they will stay away long once they've searched the neighboring islands and come up empty handed. They still seek a Carvress. They still seek our annihilation. The old pattern shall repeat itself if we do not act."

Joka nudges his father. "We have more immediate problems, Papa. Coalstone cannot support this many refugees."

My eyes lift to the silhouette of black sails in the distance, picturing the monastery behind. I push through to the front. "Does anyone know whether the monastery was destroyed?" I shout.

Mutters and murmurs carry through the village. A woman's withered arm shoots up from the crowd. They part to allow her through. She bows before me. "The monastery is untouched. The sails acted as a shield to the other side of the island."

Setsu pushes a crate at me with his foot and knocks his head in my direction. I step up, projecting my voice over dozens of war-torn faces. Every single one is smudged with soot. Unwanted war paint. "I suggest we relocate the refugees to the monastery. Our army will follow to protect them. It's on high ground and can be more easily defended."

People gasp and shake their heads, volume growing, even drowning out the sounds of the sea. I turn to the Yan men. "Did I say something wrong?" I ask, eyes wide.

Setsu rests a heavy hand on my shoulder, squeezing it. "No, Lye Li, but you're challenging their beliefs. Char don't usually return to the site of death by fire." His eyes count the Char. Since he understands them, he should make the decisions.

"I am sorry." I bow to Setsu and to the crowd. "But I'm not asking them to refuge there, only to travel through the city to the monastery. I'm only thinking of what's best for the Char. Some compromises between tradition and practicality must be made."

Some huff. Others listen. They're split down the middle. Wanting to change. Not knowing how. Several soldiers throw fists in the air. "We need a new general!" one shouts.

Setsu nods agreement, chest puffed up proudly. He will step forward since he's the most experienced and wise. They will listen to him.

A hand goes to my back, and I'm shoved from my crate. A circle breaks opens around me as I twirl, Char eyes watching. Setsu's voice is loud and strong. "I vouch for Lye Li Koh as general. She has the knowledge and the foresight to pull us into the future. As hard as it sounds, we must break from tradition if we are to survive."

My heart stammers and what was once a single tattered moth in my stomach becomes a flock. An excitement and purpose I've never felt before bottlenecking at my throat and threatening to pour out. This cannot be real. Can I do this? Can I lead the Char forward?

The crowd becomes silent as I shift and shuffle under their gaze. *Stand tall and let their belief hold you up.* It brings structure to my stature. "I, I..." I run a hand over my sycamore arm. In so short a time, this action has become a comfort. The black tally marks mean something new and different. They are the map that led me to this place, standing in front of chanting Char, convincing them of who I always knew I could be. I can be their general. I am the right woman for the job. This I'm sure of.

Joka smiles wide and brilliant to my right. Tipping his chin, he believes this to be the right thing and I *know* it to be. To my left, the boy who set me on this path opens his hand and he's telling me to take it. *Just take it.*

A once lost fierceness returns to residence in the center of my chest. I stare down at any Char who would oppose me. Not with anger or threat, but with surety. Holding up my arm, I shout, "Setsu Yan honors me greatly and I accept the position of general." I give the crowd my sternest expression. "I will do my best to live up to his faith in me."

A small chuckle from Joka. A strange sigh from Setsu.

The men shift and look behind me to the man who has warranted belief in my capabilities. Seconds pass as I let them decide for themselves to follow. Or not.

A stomp and a salute like a lock clicking into place. Solid and formidable. Unbreakable.

"General Koh!" they shout.

Setsu leans in. "General Koh, what are your orders?"

# 52
## LUNA

Hissing like a cornered snake, the chancellor sneers, "I have poisoned you with black violet, young Char-Shen. So you needn't bother wasting energy trying to summon a creature to harm me. It will not work. You have no Shen power to save you." His fingers worm their way over my shirt, flicking open a button and tracing my wooden sternum. Bile rises in my throat. "And your heart won't do you any good either." I surge backward, trying to get away from his touch, but he grips the back of my neck tightly, threatening to drown me with his Water power.

The gag cuts into the corners of my mouth and my wrists and ankles feel raw from being bound with thin cords. I shut my eyes tight, straining with gathered shreds of energy to find Blood nearby. But inside me is a numb nothing. The black violet has rendered me empty. Useless.

Boats clunk against each other in this vacant port. "Our *father* forced me to teach Ash to ferry rice across the river." He rolls his eyes, not even a grudging hint of affection. "He was a hopeless student and never really excelled at anything. His only accomplishment was being the brother of the Keeper." The chancellor spits and begins unhooking a boat from its mooring.

*You're wrong. You're wrong. You're wrong.* I want to scream, but it would be like throwing fruit at a stone wall and expecting it to topple. This lunatic won't listen since he doesn't understand that Ash is the heart of everything. "He does have a habit of associating with powerful women though." He snorts. "I mean, girls."

I reach for the flick of a fishtail or anything to give me hope I can survive this. My heart can do nothing for me. I need Blood.

Grasping my bound wrists, he throws me violently into the boat. My elbows and back are skinned as they hit the wood. His smile is a black hole. "I'm going to take you apart piece by piece. Splinter by splinter. Finally, I have proof a Char-Shen hybrid can be created. It will give the emperor great assurance and me great wealth."

I burn him with a hateful gaze, but he enjoys the look, touching his heart and exclaiming, "Oh don't try that with me. It's unconvincing at best. I heard you in the forest, talking about love and forgiveness." He shoves me hard in the chest, my back bashing into the lip of the boat, hollowness of all kinds sounding from within. "I think I preferred you as a torturer."

The chancellor rows into the middle of the river and the current grabs us. We travel fast. Much too fast.

He strokes lazily as the river does most of the work. "After I've finished dissecting you, I will find your family. Your mother is very attractive, irritating and very, very Char, but I'm sure I could beat that out of her." He strokes his chin. I feel sick at him thinking about Mama. Though I smile until it stings my mouth at the thought of Papa cutting the chancellor's seams until he splits apart like a dress pattern.

"All women can be broken, eventually." The chancellors foul black teeth show in a sly, disgusting smile.

Blood. Blood. Blood.

I stretch my fingers, reaching for an animal. But my power is buried under heavy rocks. I can't find it, see it or feel it.

Cutting the oars through the water, he observes at me like a specimen. "And the Carvresses... We only need one. What do you suggest we do to get one to comply? I think the quivery, quaking one might be the best target. What was her name?" Tap, tapping his chin like he's thinking about what he wants for breakfast, not how best to torture. "Shei-Shei?"

His revolting tongue wrapping around a Carvress's name is enough to make me gag.

My eyes slide to the river, wondering how deep it is. If I can't use my powers, perhaps I'll just have to use my body.

"You Char burn well, do you not? Quick like dry kindling." His expression is mad with greed and revenge. "I shall suggest we torch a Carvress a day until one complies."

The current strengthens and he puts more effort into steering. Water rushes rapidly over rocks. The ride is getting bumpier. "And the Shen peasant girl. She would make a good pet for the emperor. Or maybe target practice. A moving dummy. How novel!" He cackles, throwing his head skyward, the stars dismayed at this despicable man.

I seize my chance.

I throw my weight to one side as the boat squeezes between two large boulders. He reaches out to stop me, but the boat tips over and I'm flung into the water.

My hope was it would be shallow. Hope unfulfilled.

The rush of water over my ears is welcome relief from hearing each of the chancellor's horrible, horrible plans. But I'm sinking. Limbs bound, unable to kick to the surface, I simply buck and tumble. My oxygen is running out.

My brother welcomes me with loving arms. Though he is sad to see me.

*Ben Ni. Little brother.*

*Little Luna,* he says calmly, folding me into his arms. I nestle in but am ripped away by strong hands painfully pinching without care. Grasping at whatever part of me they can get. My hair is yanked. My face breaks the surface of the water. The gag is jerked from my mouth and I draw in desperate breath. *It is not your time.*

"No!" I scream.

The gag is pulled back over my mouth. "No?" the chancellor asks furiously. "You'd rather drown? I should throw you back in the water you pathetic, ungrateful little child."

## ASH KI

"No!" Luna screams, clear and long until suddenly cut off.

*She's alive.*

I paddle harder, every muscle burning and willing to break to find her.

# 53

## LYE LI

Brother, I wish you could see what I have accomplished. I wish you were by my side. You and I are not meant to be apart. But now my journey takes on an unselfish direction. I must follow a path lined with Char goals. If our maps don't converge, I'm afraid of never seeing you again. I mourn our simple life but this new life feels right. I'm no longer itching to get out of my skin.

Peace has come to me in the most unusual way.

Peace as a leader of war.

Setsu sits on a low stone shelf built into the wall of his home. Pillows and blankets shoved to the side. Hearth barely breathing warmth. I throw a log onto the fire. The coals redden and flames sink in their shredded fingers. I enjoy the smoky smell of this home. I revel in the knobby ginger roots resting on the windowsill and the knife shiny with onion juice lying in the sink.

Hands clasped in his lap, Setsu sighs wearily.

From my crouched position, I find his troubled eyes and ask the question burning in my chest, coals flaming to high heat. "Why did you do it?"

*I* know I'm the right one. But I want to know why Setsu believes it. He strokes his mustache slowly, winding thoughts around his finger. "Ah, I miss my wife." He musses the blankets. "And I miss my children. I'm tired of wondering if they live. Or if they are in the sky, waiting for me to join them."

I sit cross legged and poke at the pot of plum and pork stew just for something to do. Misshapen dumplings bob happily in the sauce. "It's hard being separated from one's family."

He grunts. "It's as if my heart is only half full."

I nod. I know of what he speaks. "Setsu…"

He stares with dark eyes that are testing change and finding it difficult but manageable. "I've been fighting my whole life. It never ends. There's never peace. Our leaders, though brave, have never tried an alternate way. They think like Char." He taps the side of his head. "Swords and limbs first. But you, you think like a Char *and* a Shen. You are our best chance of ending this war for good."

"You have too much faith in me." I lower my eyes.

He chuckles, gruff and sarcastic. "False modesty doesn't suit you, General Koh."

I smirk. "Very well. You are right to have faith in me. I do have one request though, Setsu Yan."

He places his hands on his trunk-like thighs. "Yes, General?"

"I will need your counsel and your support. Will you fight by my side?"

His reply is unsurprising. "Until my dying breath." This burden is heavy, lying across my chest like iron bars, warning me of what I have committed to. Of the lives now firmly in my hands.

I must not fail them.

This war must end.

# 54
## LUNA

Ripping the cords from my ankles, the black rag of a man wrenches me to standing. Poking the tip of a rice scythe to my back, he orders, "Walk!" When I don't abide, he presses the scythe into my side, cutting shallowly. It's papercut pain, quick and sharp, As blood slopes from between my ribs, over my hip and down my leg. A map of what's to come. *Splinter by splinter.*

I walk.

IT'S BEEN hours. Perhaps Ash didn't *feel* me. They may all be sleeping soundly in Ash's house, unaware their daughter, sister, friend marches at the tip of the chancellor's blade. I swallow. We share the blame for this ending. Lye was right to want to kill him, but I couldn't hear her then. I will listen now.

Death is his only cure.

Blood seeps slowly but steadily and I'm leaving a trail of red. "Eyes front!" I wish Lye were here. She wouldn't hesitate. Spinning like a crane, she'd strike, and he'd be dead in an instant. *Oh, little brother, why couldn't you leave well enough alone?*

She believed me powerful, stronger than most. Now, I am reduced and bleeding, traipsing to my death.

"Now that we have lost our boat, this will take at least twice as long," the chancellor mutters, irritated. Increasing his volume, he spews, "But since they're planning on dissecting you anyway, I doubt the emperor would object to me starting the process right now."

He slashes at my back. With that bright spark of pain, I clench my teeth together, a small moan finding its way around the gag.

A red droplet appears, small at first, like the first pump of a baby's heart in the womb but gaining strength and clarity. As blood seeps down my other leg, Blood sense returns. The poison is leaving my body faster than planned due to the chancellor's vindictive cuts and I just pray it doesn't leave so fast that I bleed to death.

I catch a flicker of scales. Large diamonds, tough as armor, thick as leather slither out of sight. A shy creature made of cobalt and green streams through water.

My pace slows, foot over foot, not wanting to lose connection but not ready to call them. I stop for a breath, folding over. "Don't you dare stop, Char-Shen slave. We have too much ground to cover." Oily voice from an oily man.

The scythe hovers at my temple. Taking a tentative step, I keep moving, but he slices at my ear all the same. A sharp, haughty laugh from his vile mouth. "You're a mess," he taunts. "How my brother could love someone as small and unremarkable as you is beyond me. You certainly don't fit with your family."

Blood snakes down my neck, warm at first but chilling as it soaks into my shirt and seeps across my hickory heart.

"They must be so ashamed of you." His blade continually nicks me like I'm a training post.

I want to scream and shout words at him in defense. He tears at every part of me with his insults. Perhaps because there's some truth to what he says. I don't know. He's skillful at harm and manipulation.

The pain of my wounds begins to take over. He may actually kill me before we reach the palace.

My family is not ashamed of me. I am Char. I am Blood. I am loved.

And the fiend will not speak another word.

Long yellow bellies scrape the riverbed. Sensitive snouts push at stones, unearthing terrified fish with no chance of escape. They like the peace of the riverbed, but I will need them to leave their comfort. I flick my hands, minute movements he can't see. I understand the danger of stretching my influence. I was warned already, and I feel the tautness of my powers in my blood. The pulse and flow becoming too hot and liquid to remain in my body. But there's no other option. Even if it kills me, he cannot be allowed to live.

Curved claws pull to the surface. Eyes emerge, black, slitted, and very, very keen. "He is your prey," I whisper, through my gag. It makes no sense to the chancellor, but it doesn't need to.

"What did you say?" he shrieks, incensed.

Diamond back crocodiles are fast when it suits them, capable of short bursts of incredible speed. The chancellor makes a liar of me as he shouts those last words, and then screams many unintelligible ones. The two fearsome, beautiful creatures snap at his legs on my command.

I don't enjoy the crunch or the breaking of bones. But I do feel relief. I know better than to watch and if I could cover my ears, I would.

There's no way to overpower them. His noise and scuffle is brief, just marbles clinking against each other in a box. Then silence, save bellies scraping the riverbank. He is dead long before they drag him under.

I imagine he makes a bitter meal. And I thank them.

I turn to the river. The only evidence is the two snaky paths through the sand and pebbles made by their bellies. It's like he never existed. These marks could be for many other reasons like overladen boats pushed into the water or children digging troughs.

My brain is fuzzy. I can't quite think of another reason. I collapse to the ground. Blood draining, chilling my clothes. Consciousness draining away as well.

I think of my family. And Ash and Lye. Of the sacrifices we have made and the pain I will cause them when they learn of my death. I wish I could tell them how I came back to them for such a brief moment only to be stolen away and flung to the stars.

# 55

## ASH KI

Rushing down the river in half-light, my head swivels as I search the bank for signs of life. I need to hear his shrill voice and her golden one.

Dawn will break but not soon enough. I stretch my heart to find her. *Feel* her, but I feel nothing. I'm terrified. I'm a fool. Anger closed my ears to Lye's warnings and now I've lost Luna.

Digging the oar into the water, I guide the boat between two boulders. The current sucks me through quickly and I travel faster than before. As I fly through the water, my oar snags on something. I pull in a sopping mess of cloth. The color is hard to tell, but it feels delicate, like *silk*. Throwing it in the bottom of the boat, I jam my oar, so I swing at right angles to the flow of the water. Scanning the bank, my heart swells to the point where it can't fit in my chest. Gray pebbles. Dark canyon walls. Fallen chunks of rock.

A curl of darkness against the lighter gray. Small. Little. Luna. *Luna.*

Jumping from the boat, I run to the shape of a girl on the riverbank. Spears pierce my chest. Teeth tearing at my flesh. She's bound and gagged. Soaked through. I search for any sign of the chancellor and find none. She looks so very vulnerable, knees to her chest, tied hands resting awkwardly on top. But I know her strength. I know she has reserves no one else has. *I know. I know. I know.*

Shakily, I untie the gag. "Luna."

The breath she takes sends a shot of light right through me like I've been punched by a fistful of stars. I lift her. Too hurried to untie her wrists, I loop them over my head. Tying us in a messy embrace. Her legs tuck into my lap, her face so close I hear every glorious breath. "I was coming to save you," I whisper, cheek against hers.

Luna whimpers as my hand touches her back. The sticky, warm feeling of blood is all too familiar. "I saved myself." She sighs, so strong even as she fades. Steel struts run through her.

She is remarkable.

Stroking her wet face, I whisper, "Of course you did."

Her face falls. "I'm sorry, Ash. But your brother, the chancellor, is dead. I killed him."

My brother, who never deserved the title, is dead. Instead of grief, I feel relief. Blood is strong, but it doesn't clear crimes from the board. In truth, he tried to break any bonds that we had at every opportunity. I feel a wave of gratitude to Lye for what she did for me as a child. Some memories are not worth keeping. Some grudges must be let go.

I want to pull Luna closer, but I'm scared I'll hurt her. I'm also terrified of these wounds that cause her to breathe like she's drowning and move like she's being drained. "No. Please don't say sorry. You did what you had to, Luna. There is no choice between the two of you. It's always, *always* you."

"I am losing—" She stops mid-sentence, her body swaying like a willow branch, her body as light as a breeze ripping through leaves.

I kiss her quickly, desperately. Utter words I hope she can hold onto. "I love you, Luna."

I unhook her from my neck and lay her on her side. Blood rushes out of her. I must work fast. Sunlight stretches to illuminate the slices on her back, neck, and ears. Ice to slow but not to freeze.

I concentrate with all my might. If the balance is off by just a fraction, I'll kill her.

She shivers, watching me with frightening detachment, slipping away. I remove my shirt, ripping it into long shreds, keeping my foot on her ribs so I can pass my Water element through her skin. Slow not freeze. Slow not freeze.

"Don't you dare kill me," she whispers. A tiny knife-glint smirk cracks the tip of her lip. Her words are just another tally mark to the growing number of reasons why I love her so much.

"Don't you dare die," I reply.

I will not let her die.

I bind her wounds as she moans softly and tries her best not to cry. Gathering her in my arms, I release my Water power. Warming her with my body heat.

She feels so cold.

*Let me save her*, I beg the sky that's lightening with pinks and fire orange. But I am not enough.

THE SOUND of the guard's chanting is loud and rhythmic. Colors of Shen paint the riverbank.

Luna's face is as white as an Air Shen's robe. Her body rattles with tremors while her blood gruesomely paints my bare chest. I have stemmed the flow but not enough to make a difference. She only has hours left.

I know this is a mistake, but it's a mistake that will save her life.

# 56
## LUNA

A straw mattress lies beneath me. Memories assail me of snap-ping teeth and bones shattering like my bamboo sword during training. Plaster dust sprinkling the courtyard. Fah's conde-scending stare. *Tomorrow, I'll do better. I'll prove to the general that I deserve a place in the Char army. My brothers and I will fight together.*

I shift on the bed. A raw, nerve-ending pain clambers up my ribs as fast as a lava lion scaling a cliff. I touch my sides. Sliced open like gills.

The past feels safe. I squeeze my eyes shut. In the past, Ben Ni lives. Sun and Joka are still learning. We were together and not scattered like star blossom petals carried by a bitter wind. Crushed in the dirt, sinking through water. My chest tightens like I'm a spool to winding thread.

*I don't know how we will survive this.*

The scrape of chains against a hard, stone floor grates my ears. So familiar and so disheartening. "Luna," he whispers. "Don't give up."

I reach for my ear. The throbbing, blood-filled wound screams as I touch it. I am maimed like a stray dog that got into too many fights. I open my eyes to an iron-barred vent the size of a goodbye letter punched high in wet stone walls the color of dried blood. I could almost laugh for how circular this feels. Only now, we are in far more danger.

"Are we where I think we are?" The worst place. The heart of Shen evil.

Ash's voice is iron heavy. "Yes. We're in the palace."

"What did you do?" I speak to the wall.

With the sound of dragging iron, I hear desperation in his voice. "I did what I had to. If I didn't tell them what you were you would have bled to death. I couldn't let you die. Please, Luna, turn around."

"You told them I was a hybrid?" Perhaps he saved my life in that moment, but now I will die slowly, taken apart splinter by splinter, as the chancellor said.

"I had no other choice." Ash is regret and defense.

"Do they know I killed the chancellor?" I ask and get my answer in the bow of his head.

"Your Char-Shen power outweighs even that crime."

I shake my head. Perhaps, but it will make them hate me more. Add layers to my imminent torture.

Candlelight attracts a giant carpet moth, its velvet wings flapping against the bars of this dungeon. A soft persistent sound like batting dust from a rug.

*Mama. Sun.* I turn over carefully. His outstretched hand strains for me through thick iron. My wooden heart cannot skip a beat and it cannot slow. But my soul aches at the sight of him and whatever anger I felt flies from this place on soft, butter brown wings. I shuffle forward, edging from the bed. I want to rush but I'm scared my skin will open. Grabbing at his hands through the bars greedily, I pull myself into them like they're a vine to climb. A lifeline.

"Oh Ash! What have they done to you?"

Rods press into our chests as we scramble to get closer and fail. He whispers into my matted hair, "It doesn't matter. I am alive. You are alive. Now we must work out how to remain that way."

I pull back to find his sea green eyes. "What about the others?" I keep my voice as low as possible. The shadow of a guard wobbles in flickering candlelight around the corner.

"They're safe, at least for now since they know where to hide." He laughs, short and bruised. "It's why I'm still alive. Because I know where they are." He glances around. I press too hard on his arms, and he winces. "Can you, you know, summon something to get us out of here, or are you too drained from…?"

*Killing your brother?* "I was. Do you remember when the Carvress said I needed to find balance? It feels like now that I've let my grief in and allowed my heart to function the way it was supposed to, Blood and hickory have found that balance. It's almost like a new kind of power." I flex my hands, reach for creatures. Not even cockroaches or the occasional mouse are present. "There's just not much living down here."

Ash grimaces. "The emperor does keep a very clean, pest free environment." He points to a bottle on the table. "See that, it's pesticide. They spray the walls and floors with it."

I sigh, desolate. "That explains it."

"At least they don't spray it in our cells." He swipes the floor with his finger. "It's pretty smelly stuff."

I frown. "That is not much consolation."

Light moves as another moth dives from the small window, flaps against the bars and follows it around the corner. Ash's voice rises with panic. "Could you send a message to Lye to come for us? There's so much she needs to know. The Carvresses being of royal blood changes everything. There may be a way to use that to our advantage."

My forehead hits the bars, cold and biting. "Ash, stop! Don't you understand? There's no escape." A tear forms in the corner of my eye. "We will not live much longer." And if this is true, I want to be in his arms as long as I can. I press myself to the prison bars.

There are no birds. No paper to write on. There's no way to get word to Lye.

"I love you," I whisper, voice halfway breaking.

He shakes his head, shackles grazing the floor. "No, don't say it like that. Don't say it like goodbye. Like it's the end."

I see only torture and eventually death in our future. The chancellor may not be the one to carry it out, but the promise of taking me apart piece by piece has already begun.

My hickory heart snapping in two shall be the first pieces.

A SHEN woman wearing gloves kneels at my bed, dressing my wounds. "Why treat me when I am to be dissected?" I ask. The woman doesn't answer. Merely shrugs and continues her work.

Another carpet moth flies at her candle, drawn to the light. She bats at it, and it lands in the shallow bowl of water she's using to clean me. There's a needle pinned through her apron for stitching me together. Helping it seems a pointless task. The large, hapless insect tries to flap its soaked wings, each one as large as my hand. The woman picks it up, flinging it to the floor with a splat. It flutters in the dust with wings that can fly no longer.

Holding up the needle, she orders me to face the wall. As she stitches my skin together, my attention is on the moth. Desperately clinging to life when it's futile. Large wings spread flat on the ground. Plain brown. Unremarkable but persistent and stubborn. A little like myself.

A snip and the woman prods my shoulder roughly. I could send snakes slithering through her skin but what would be the point. I'm locked up tight. Blood can't bend iron bars.

I can't take my eyes off the moth. *Why doesn't it just give up?*

"You look like someone cut your wings," Ash says with forced, empty lightness.

*Wings.*

Turning swiftly, pain splits me every way, like my skin is barely able to stay on my body. The woman scowls at Ash. He grins, distracting her long enough for me to grab the needle sitting in the now pink bowl of water. I press it under my hip and wait for the woman to leave.

Ash watches me curiously, always trusting.

Hope springs from the strangest places.

Once we're alone, I squat down in the dirt, scooping up the dying insect. I stroke its soft wings, thick as the name suggests. Its legs patter slowly in my palm, tapping out its last message. One I will never forget.

The needle is sharp. It will do nicely.

I look to Ash and smile. A true smile of dark, fragrant wood and Blood magic.

This is going to take all night.

# 57
## LYE LI

Swatting my face, I wince at the horrible sensation of knowing an insect is on my cheek. I fly from the bed with a moan.

The mosquito net hanging from the open window billows inward with force like a ghost pushing its way into the room. With the breeze, I feel tickles up my arms and a flapping at my ear. There's a sawdust tinge to the air. Striking a match to my candle, I gasp loud enough to match a scream.

The room swirls with giant carpet moths. Wings spread wide on the walls. Furry feet tapping. Bodies heaving. A noise like a thousand sheets being shaken out at the same time. *I should scream. I should...*

I clutch the bedclothes to my neck. Not knowing what to do.

They're everywhere. Huddled wing to wing, over my bedspread. Antennae twitching. Abdomens pulsing. Beauty and terror strung together, but for what reason? My brain flurries with blinding snow. *It is magical. It is powerful. It is Luna.*

I finally open my mouth and shout for Joka.

Bursting into the room, his whole body seizes when he takes in the view. "What on land and sea!" His sudden movement sends them flapping upward. One flutters in front of me, wings opening and closing, a foot from my eyes. Light from Joka's lantern shines through its dark brown wings. I squint, neck craning. It's a pattern. *No, a character.*

My hand shoots up. "Shut the door! Don't let them escape!" My heart buzzes and bounds.

Eyes wide and stunned, Joka does as I ask, back pressed against the wood, staying as far away as possible from the huge moths who fly up and settle with every small disturbance. My eyes go to the window as one catches in the mosquito net, trying to exit. I jump up and slam it shut.

"Lye, what are you doing?" Joka asks, bewildered. "Why would you keep these insects in? Don't you want them out of your room?" His shoulders pull in and he shudders.

Grasping at one of the moths too roughly, I tear its delicate wings. Cursing, I am more gentle next time, pinching it ever so slightly, and spreading the wings open over my lap. They're punctured with dozens of tiny holes forming the character for "royalty" on one wing and a number on the other. It's a message, written by way of Blood.

Looking more closely at the wallpaper of moths, I find each wing reveals a character punched out in pinpricks. Numbers and words. Numbers and words. But they make no sense on their own. It's a code. I shake my head in admiration and fear. Because it is brilliant, but also implies desperation. Danger.

Joka is still pinned to the door, hand in front of his face, terrified as moths flap close. "Luna and Ash are in danger." His hand drops to his side.

IT HAS TAKEN hours and hours. The sun has risen and bakes a breakfast warmth on the cracking floorboards. The moths, now dead, are laid over the floor in lines, all numbering one through to twelve. One missing.

Joka and I kneel over the grisly display and read the characters together.

Luna Ash Palace Prisoners Others Hidden Carvresses ... Shen Royalty Claim Throne. My brother and Luna have been captured. It is my worst and most terrible fear. I pause to inhale. Trying to breathe when there's something wedged in my throat. Joka touches my arm and I jerk away. "I can't find eight." My eyes are unblinking. If I close them, I will picture the things they'll do to them and I simply won't survive it. My hands scramble over the floor. "We need to look again. Look again!"

Joka helps me sort through every one again. Putting a finger up, he gives a grim smile and peers under the bed. "Found one! Here," he says, holding a barely flapping moth out to me, disgusted. "Take it!" He looks like he might be sick.

It's number eight and it reads "equal." I place it in sequence. "*Equal.* Carvresses *Are* Shen Royalty," I read aloud.

Hands on hips, Joka says, "Not possible. You've ordered it incorrectly." He reaches out but doesn't touch. I slap his hand away with a seal flipper.

Shoulder to shoulder, I tap the dusty wings, counting the numbers. There's no mistake.

"Then it must be a lie." His voice wavers. Disbelief twisting to a truth he doesn't want to acknowledge.

"Why would they send such a message? Why would they go to such lengths if it were not true?" I demand, firm in my belief of my brother and Luna. My mind already packing for the journey to the mainland. My body not far behind. "What do you know of how the Carvresses came to be? How did they get their powers? Did they appear on the islands, were they born on islands?"

Joka's blank stare is answer enough. He has no idea. Frowning, his fine brows pointing down to an impossible future. One that boggles the mind. "Well, suppose it's true—do you understand what that would mean?"

*It means everything could change.*

"It means my brother got them to the cave safely. It means Luna and Ash require rescue. It also means our world is about change forever and for the better."

The way forward becomes a sharp, crystal-like thing. The plan marked in dotted lines like the maps plastering Joka's bedroom walls.

Change can be small, chips and chisels shaping the world incrementally, gradually. But sometimes it comes crashing down like a hammer. A sound ringing out long and loud and definite. Violent and overpowering.

*The emperor can be overthrown.*

# 58
## LUNA

My eyes dredge through thick tiredness. Fingers ache from the painstaking work of puncturing close to one hundred carpet moths with a message for the Char. One we're not even sure will reach them. I released them one by one, attaching a wish to every soft-edged wing: Reach the Coalstones. Reach it by morning. A morning I missed, and now the strong light of a midday sun screams in my eyes like an angry vanity bat.

Blood seeps through my bandages, pushes at my skin from the strain of calling so many creatures one by one to my window. Crusted blood plugs my ears. Ash's muffled voice barely scrapes through and I scratch at one ear to clear it. Hands gather stray straw as I roll to face him. Ash. Shen boy who keeps pace with my wooden heart.

I smile and he clutches his heart in a joking way. "Oh, that smile," he says, this beautiful, blooming feeling swarming my chest and stretching my ribs. Expanding past what I thought I was capable of. This love is boundless. So dangerous. But worth every injury. Every cut. Every bruise.

"Do you think they made it?" I ask.

*They must. They must. They must.*

He grabs my hand, squeezing it so hard the bones of my fingers crush together. A pain I would happily repeat over and over. "They are fast and know how to catch the wind."

"What if all the characters don't make it? The message won't make sense. I know we did several of each, but still, a bird could take one. Or they could die before they reach the Coalstones." I try to focus on his thumb brushing over the back of my hand. This feeling opening inside me like a moon blossom with delicate, gray-veined petals but so easily damaged.

"They'll get it. I promise." He's so sure. Or just trying to make me feel better.

"You cannot make such promises."

Shen guards approach noisily, stomping down the dark corridor. The gate to Ash's cell slides open. He grips my hand tighter. My heart wants to close over, to retreat from this growing pain. A rift that feels like an axe slices the space between us. The guard clamps down on Ash's shoulder. Even then, his ocean eyes do not leave mine. They burn a perfect blue-green and stay with me as he's dragged from his cell. With his hair falling over his cheeks, his jaw tenses in defiance. I stretch through the bars. "No!" I shout. "Please. Take me." I can take it. I can bear torture. I *was* torture, for so long.

He's pulled to his feet. Hands yanked violently behind his back and bound. He begs me to be silent. "Please, Luna. It will be all right." A quick nod of the head. Flattening of the lips. Small messages only I can read. He's bracing himself and trying to reassure me.

But nothing, *nothing* eases this moment. No hickory heart can help me. I feel pain tall as a wave.

Hopelessness: A stone tied to my neck.

Hope: A hand reaching, reaching.

I must close the distance. I cannot sink. I must reach back. "Don't you dare die!" I warn, lips quivering.

Impossibly, he smiles. And it's bigger, brighter, than any one before it. It's my saltwater smile. Half hope, half a lie. "I won't," he promises. "Cross my heart."

Turn the page for an excerpt from the
next novel in the series:

# THE GIRL WITH THE SYCAMORE SCARS

Hickory Heart, Book 3

Available now, wherever books are sold!

# 1

## LUNA

## BRIDGES OF BLOOD
## AND SALTWATER

I *feel* Ash.

I *feel* him clutch to his promise to live like a handful of still hot coals. Dropping them on the cold, acid-cleansed floor as they drag him further away from me.

*Don't die this time—when they tie a rope tight around your wrists and ankles and cut you with their torturous blades. When they kick, punch, and sneer become an impenetrable block of ice.*

I *feel* the coarse fibers of seagrass rope chafing his skin as they begin. "Don't die. Don't die," I whisper to the blood-red walls of this palace prison. I graze the stone with my fingers, expecting them to stain. Grains of sand trickle down but my skin remains the same. Whatever colored these walls is old and seeping and comes from somewhere deep. I sniff. The scent of iron, blood, and straw.

My Blood sense finds insects, moving desperately, stupidly, between cracks in the floor. It finds death and dying everywhere as bugs reach the air and are poisoned. Nothing can survive here. Every night the woman comes with her pungent mop and brushes acid over the floors and walls, killing every animal as she disinfects and drenching my hope.

I shake as I spread my call to the night while the guard kicks his feet up on a chair, his shadow becoming still. Ash's torturers are working slow today, giving me a moment to summon a white ghost butterfly. It flutters through the narrow bars high above my head, long silky threads hanging from almost transparent wings. As delicate as the thinnest rice paper, she looks as melancholy as I feel. I let her alight on my finger.

"Don't touch the filthy, poisoned floor, beautiful one. You are too good for this place."

A shock of jagged pain passes slowly through my body. I gasp, "Ash." It pulls my limbs against my chest as it radiates from my shoulder to my fingers. The ghost butterfly lifts into the air, hovering just in front of my eyes. I scrunch them closed against the agony, only but only succeed at pulling it closer against my bones. I'm being whittled, grated, until I am nothing but screaming nerve endings.

My lips forms an empty O, knowing it must be even worse for him.

I *feel* every second of his torture. Clenching my fists, I tell myself he is strong. He is the strongest. He can survive this. He promised.

A chair squeaks across the floor. The halo of candlelight widens like the sun rising above mountains. *Oh, how I wish I were home!*

"Ai ya! Gi Shi, come look at this." I open my eyes to two guards staring through the bars, their mouths like tree hollows. Eyes wide and disbelieving. One in Earth brown robes and one in Air white. The candle holder quivers as the guard rolls his gaze over my body. Wobbling, I rise to my feet. Pain cracks through me again and I stumble. I'm terrified, but I need to remember I am also a terror. A dress of white ghost butterflies covers my filthy clothes. A Blood sense wedding dress. I flick my finger and they flutter out like a full skirt. Blood fills and supports me.

The guard holds up the key. Lifts it to the lock and pauses.

My stomach suddenly pulls in as Ash is punched in the gut. I cry out and double over. The butterflies leave my body as I fall to the ground. Swarming through the bars at the guards in a gust.

They have no sting. They are not dangerous. They are beautiful and gentle, and the guards stomp their gossamer bodies into the ground. Spraying them with a chemical from a blue perfume bottle on their table. The puff on the end makes a soft, almost soothing sound that contradicts its danger.

They die quickly, wings dissolving into the earth. At the same time, my sense of Ash fades like he's also dissolving, disappearing. My throat dries like a dammed stream.

Gi Shi turns to the other guard and says, "Ah, Wen, maybe we should move her, you know, further down." He points at the ground with a pudgy finger. His tightly bound plait swings like a monkey's tail.

Wen shrugs his narrow shoulders. "We can't do anything without talking to the doctor." The way he says that word sounds more like *monster*.

Doctor. The idea that they care about my well-being seems as far-fetched as a gravel goose flying west instead of south. I'm guessing the doctor is not the healing kind.

I agonizingly pull myself up to the bed. Every ounce of my skin feels sharp hurt but shows no injury. Perhaps this is my penance. I am deserving of mountains of pain after the horrors I performed on Shen soldiers. But Ash deserves none of it.

I lie on my back and stare at the damp, water marked ceiling, feeling every punch, every cut and twisted limb. I have borne it for weeks and I will continue to. In a way, I'm glad to feel it. It means he has told them nothing of the mountain tunnels where the Carvresses, Sun, Guen, and my mother are hiding.

It also means he's still alive.

THE SHADOW of a boy and two guards grows over the corridor walls. His head hangs as he is dragged back to his cell. His knees scrape the stone. He mutters something and gets kicked. I shake my head for the boy who will never learn.

But he lives.

Ignoring my own injuries, I rush to the front of my cell, hands stretching for Ash. My hickory heart cracks like ice when he lifts his face to meet mine. Hope dies like so many crushed butterflies. "Oh, Ash!"

He tries to smile, blood cracking and flaking from his cheek. "I'm all right, Luna," he lies.

The guards scoff as they throw him into his cell. His body makes a sound like spoiled vegetables thrown to the pigs as it lands on straw and stone.

"You're not all right. You're anything but all right." I press to the bars, fingers grasping at his clothes and then his skin. I push comfort into him: baby birds in their nest, warm and safe beneath their mother's feathers. He sighs hard, coughs, and blood spills from his mouth. And in that moment, I wish he had left me to die by the river.

Thoughts of Ben Ni pass through my chest and layer my ribs with both pain and a soft kind of sweetness. If Ash had left me, I would be in the stars with youngest brother and Ash would be safe. I shake my head. It does little good to think of what could have been.

"I kept my promise, didn't I?" He manages a quick smirk, and it kills me. He says this every time he returns. The words are both relieving and cursed because they're getting thinner. Less likely to be repeated.

I cup his face in my hands and it's enough to pull me back from that wish. Because he's here. I am here. Some sort of hard-as-rock, strong-as-sea love links us together. "You did." *This time.* I lay soft kisses on both his bruised cheeks and then his forehead as he shivers and struggles to keep himself upright.

"I should get tortured more often." Ash winks a swollen eye.

I smile, but it's tense and terse. "I love that you can do that." The guards watch us closely. Voyeurs to a painful romance that is not quite blossoming, more like a tight bud wary of opening to frost.

"Do what?" He brings my fist to his bruised lips and brushes them over my knuckles. Filling my wooden heart with bright sparks that might burn me to ash.

"Find light in the darkest place." He found it in me.

*The straw should be growing pea shoots for how many tears I have rained upon it. Weeks of weeping water. But then little grows from salt water. And yet he holds me still.*

*"Luna," Ash whispers, lifting hair that has stuck to my cheek. "You may flood this cell with your grief. As long as you feel it. Hold it."*

*"Holding it hurts," I blubber. Tasting the salt on my lips. Feeling that sting of too many tears. My heart wants to close over this aching wound.*

*Ash nods. He knows grief. He has lost a father, a mother, and possibly a sister. "Yes. Until it hurts less and less."*

*I swipe at my snotty nose and grip his grimy sleeve. "But when will it stop?" The pressure of his loss compresses me to the size of a coriander seed, easily crushed to powder.*

*Ash shakes his head and I already know what he's going to say. "Your grief for Ben Ni will always be a part of you. It will never stop, exactly. But as time goes on, the shape of it will change and smooth out until you grow around it."*

*I touch my heart. "Right now, it feels like a throwing star in my chest."*

*He smiles sadly. A crease in the face of a boy who has been through so much. With me, but also on his own. "Yes."*

*"I'd like it to become a piece of ocean-polished glass... like the ones Ben Ni used to collect." I manage between the sharp, dagger breaths of someone who is not done crying.*

These weeks have changed the shape of my grief. Not yet polished smooth, but not the spinning blade it once was.

Our eyes connect. Bridges of blood and saltwater that are creaking and in need of repair. He looks close to death. I tap my heart and he asks, "What's the shape?"

"Blunted blade."

"Improvement." He touches his forehead to mine and whispers, "We will find a way out of here, I promise. I'm watching and waiting. I saw someone different today. He seemed important." He shrugs his shoulders, a twitch in his cheek. "Maybe I'm moving up in the world." The cheerful words don't match the darkness of his tone.

I shake my head. *Stop making promises*, I want to say. They feel like flesh-wounding arrows, shot to maim. My back stings with the weight of them, but I can't rip away what little hope he has left. "Who did you see?" I ask.

Ash lowers his gaze. Mutters barely audible words in a voice as frightened as a terror mouse facing a cobra's open jaws: "The doctor." He leans against the bars, forehead creased with worry. "He asked so many questions. So many."

My eyes widen with worry, but he's already shaking his head. "I didn't tell him anything, but it made me play those last minutes before we separated from the Carvresses and your family over and over in my head." He taps his temple, a strange seriousness crossing his features like he knows something is wrong but he's not sure what.

I take his blood-crusted hand and squeeze, feeling his anxiety cross into my own chest. "What? What is it?"

The guards strike the bars hard with their batons, patience thinning. We spring apart. "Get back from each other," Wen growls.

Ash retreats to his bed and stares at his hands. There's a scene playing behind his eyes. "I just feel like—like something is missing." He picks at the tattered gold thread of his borrowed uniform. "You know that feeling? When you can't shake the sense that you left something behind?"

I pull my dry lip between my teeth. We did leave something behind: eight Carvresses, a wooden Shen girl, my mother and brother. But that's not what he means and it's starting to scare me. "Try and remember," I urge.

Gi Shi bashes the bars again, his eyes like darts. "Be quiet! Or they'll send the boy up for another session."

We close our mouths, but they can't stop us from *feeling* each other, and they certainly can't stop us from bridging the gap with our eyes. Caramel and saltwater. In that gaze is a ripple over the ocean. Something strong and steady, waiting to rise.

If you have enjoyed reading

# THE BOY WITH THE SALTWATER SMILE

please consider leaving a review.
It helps readers like you connect
with  books they'll enjoy!

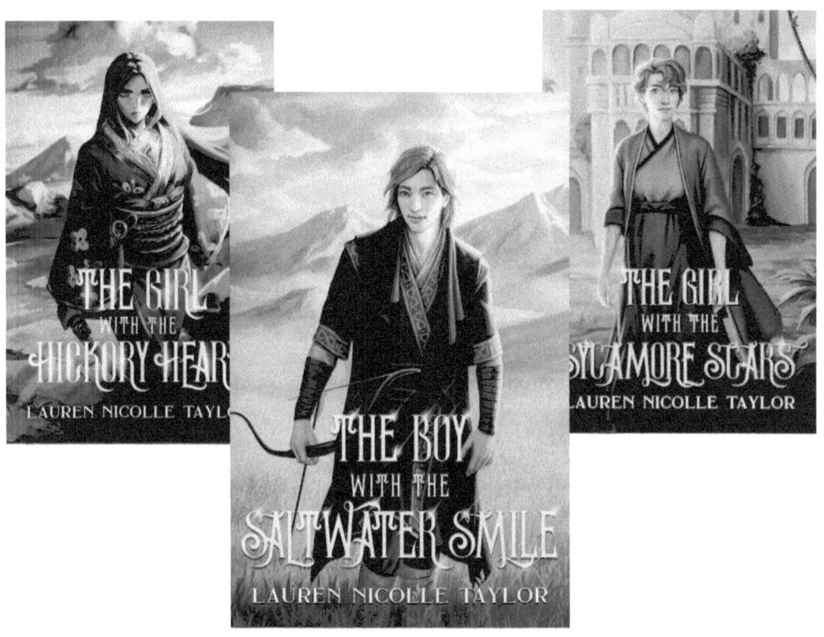

# ACKNOWLEDGEMENTS

The Boy with the Saltwater Smile was written during a year that tested me and my family to its limits. Our eldest child suffered a traumatic brain injury during a soccer match of all things. What followed was six months of missed school, rehab and the need for constant supervision and care. It shoved writing to the side while I dedicated all my time to looking after my thirteen-year-old child who, for a time, couldn't walk, couldn't go to school, couldn't even watch TV.

Here was a child who loved to read, devouring two novels a week, now not able to read more than a couple of sentences before intense headaches and vomiting would begin. Suffice to say, audiobooks saved us! There were many other challenges, and it was heartbreakingly, hard work but we never gave up. We inched our way forward through recovery millimetre by millimetre.

It was a very long road but when we got out the other side my mind was itching to write, desperate to pour my creativity into something other than how to get my child down the hallway without breaking my back (desk chair on wheels worked well!). This book came so easily my fingers could barely keep up with my brain while typing. It's how I knew, no matter how long a break I took, my story-telling ability wouldn't leave me. It wouldn't dry up or decay. It would live in my odd head forever.

So, this was my longwinded way of acknowledging 2018, the year of a traumatic brain injury, of persistence, and faith in myself and my incredible child. We got there and we have so much to show for it!

Don't miss these other titles by
# LAUREN NICOLLE TAYLOR

**"Lyrically written, this powerful and at times painful read captures the reader and does not let go."**
**—Booklist, starred review**

In 1953's post-WW II Japanese internment camp era, two teenagers facing extraordinary hardship collide at a time when they need each other most. Their stories, a collection of events, are each on their own harmless. But together, one after the other, they change the world.

Nora's struggles are just beginning, and she must now become Kite—a stronger, more independent version of herself. Kettle must accept that he is also Hiro: a Japanese American with every right to happiness and freedom. They must rely on each other, otherwise it's their future in jeopardy, along with the fates of the street kids in their care.

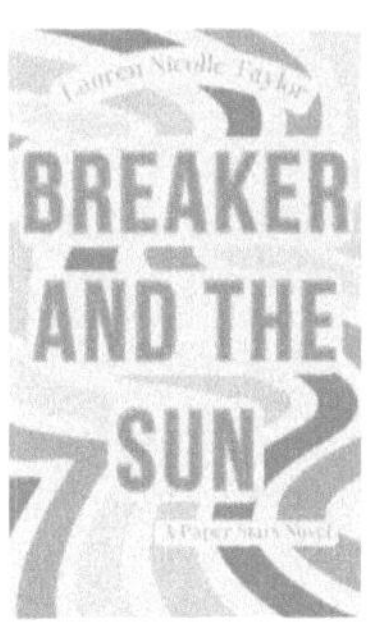

A recently returned Vietnam vet struggling with PTSD and a high-achieving Chinese-French immigrant find solace in the Catskills at the Ugly Tree, where they find themselves lulled toward an enchanted, peaceful sleep.

**LAUREN NICOLLE TAYLOR** is the bestselling author of The Woodlands series and the award-winning YA novel *Nora & Kettle* (Gold Medal Winner for Multicultural fiction, Independent Publishers Book Awards), which is the first book in the acclaimed Paper Stars series.

She has a Health Science degree and an honors degree in Obstetrics and Gynecology. A full time writer and artist, Lauren recently moved from Australia to Canada with her husband and three children for a new adventure. She is a proud hapa and draws on her multicultural background in all of her novels.

Lauren is represented by Golden Wheat Literary.

Find Lauren at http://www.laurennicolletaylor.com.

**#HickoryHeart**
**#TheGirlwiththeHickoryHeart**

facebook.com/TheWoodlandSeries
twitter.com/LaurenNicolleT
instagram.com/laurennicolletaylor